THE SUN AND THE MOON

by Willa M. Scantlebury

For my mom, Louise.
You're embedded throughout.
Wish you could have read it.

For my dad, Arthur.
So much of the story is because of
what you've taught me in life.

For my husband, Tony.
Without your support and encouragement,
this wouldn't exist.

Preface

I'm dyslexic. Self-diagnosed as an adult; but man, it explains why I couldn't do math in school, play a piano, or enjoy reading. Yet, I joined a book club... So, I could drink wine and kibitz with my summer friends.

I struggled through a few books, read only a fraction of what they decided on. Most books just made me mad, like, "Why did I waste so much time on that?" Focusing was a chore. The last pick—that I forced myself through—was pathetic and predictable. My sister suggested we do what her book club was doing:

A woman had moved into her neighborhood (a playwright of sorts.) She joined their book club. She wrote a fictional starting chapter, and each member added to the story with another. "Brilliant!" I thought. I decided to do the same. So, when it was my turn to pick the next book for *my* book club, I presented this idea. Out of fifteen, I had about nine takers. Fun, right? I wrote what is now the prologue.

After the initial excitement and about five chapters in, like my sister's book club, the idea faded and the story died. But I didn't want to stop writing, and my graphic design business was slow, so what the heck? I continued to write. I had a few friends who coaxed me, "Your writing's great! Keep going." The coincidences that happened as I wrote practically possessed me. Still, it took time. Thank God for spell check!

In two years, I had 36 chapters; a complete story. However, it took over six years to publish. I spent a lot of time editing, tweaking, sending out, and hoping it'd fall into the right hands. Now it's in yours. I hope you enjoy the story. It helped me through one of the most difficult times in my life. My mom was not well and this was my escape.

Prologue

Robin emerged from the tent into thick, diffused gray light with absolutely no idea of the time. It had to be somewhere around 6:00 a.m., but instead of morning's first warm glow, their camp was blanketed by low-lying clouds. The quietude that surrounded her was nothing shy of eerie. No birds, no wind, complete stillness.

Afraid to make any noise herself, she delicately removed her backpack from the foot of the tent. Digging to the bottom of it, she pulled out a small orange box, a canister of butane, and a small pot. A few feet from the tent by the split log bench, she cleared a level area and set up the ultra-light stove she had bought on a whim during her last year in college. *I knew one day this thing would come in handy,* she thought. The foggy chill in the air brought her thinking back to the first time she met Bryce:

It was a rainy afternoon in May when she thumped onto the huge log-beamed porch of the High Peaks Information Center, dripping from head to toe. Stomping the mud from her boots, she took off her rain jacket and gave it a good shake so it wouldn't drip all over the floor inside. *There should be enough time to unstuff my backpack and dig out something warm and dry to wear before the class begins,* she thought. Her morning hike had been much colder than anticipated.

Robin wasn't quite sure what to expect from this session, it was a survival class that focused on the weather and how quickly it can change in the Adirondacks. Previously she'd been to classes on mushroom identification, "Understanding What You Can and Can't Eat," and on animal tracking, patterns, and behavior, "Hunt or be Hunted."

The High Peaks Information Center was rustic and spacious. Built by mountaineers in the late 1800s, it had been used as a bunkhouse and shelter during the summer months when workers cleared and developed over 150 trails throughout the Adirondacks. The HPIC's huge timber beams evoked both hardship and community. One could just imagine the stories told and the stalwart characters that once occupied the great space.

Robin pushed the creaky screen door open and entered into the main room, feeling a blast of heat from the massive stone fireplace. The sweet smoky smell that permeated the air reminded Robin of her grandfather, and the scotch he would sip. With a sweeping glance across the room, she realized she was the first to arrive. Heading past all the chairs to the back of the room, she systematically hung her pack, rain gear, and her hiking poles on a peg on the back wall. Having finished the morning hike up Mount Jo, she was looking forward to a seat, a snack, and completing this last class, which would finish up the requirements to earn her mountain stewardship.

Suddenly, from the corner of her eye, she spotted movement. A man came out from behind a counter near the souvenir and supply section of the building. He gestured toward a table in the front of the room displaying: pump thermos containers, a basket of Clif Bars, brochures, and a pile of papers with information on the next lineup of classes.

"Coffee? Hot chocolate?" he offered.

"Oh thanks, that'd be great," Robin answered.

He then approached her with an extended hand, which she thought was awkwardly forward. She obliged and offered hers back.

"I'm Bryce," he said.

"Oh hey, I'm Robin. Are you leading the class today?"

"No, not at all!" Amused, he continued, "I'm covering a shift for a friend who works here. He got banged up on a hike yesterday; one *I* recommended for a first date, so I feel pretty guilty."

"Ouch, which mountain?" she asked sympathetically.

"Cascade. It's a great place to catch the sunrise. About a two hour hike up. Have you been?"

"No, I haven't."

"How about Mount Marcy? It's the highest peak and one of the longest hikes." He looked for her interest and continued. "Some people camp from a quarter way in, to anywhere below 3500 feet. Here's some info…" he gestured again towards the table.

Robin didn't want to share with him just how much she knew about the high peaks. Feeling a little coy herself, since realizing he was flirting, she inquired, "What happened to your friend?"

"Oh, he slipped and gashed his leg open; needed nine stitches."

Music suddenly erupted from his pocket. *Da na na na na.* It was the famous riff from George Thorogood's "Bad to the Bone." *Da na na na na.*

He fumbled for his phone.

"Ah, it's him!"

And as if in slow motion, he looked deep into Robin's eyes and gently touched her shoulder softly saying, "Please excuse me."

Spinning on one foot, turning back towards the supply area, he scurried away. Resuming his position behind the counter, he glanced over at Robin and smiled in a way that made her wishful.

She felt a rush of heat steam up from under her collar. Standing somewhat dazed at the table, she mindlessly pumped

3

herself a cup of hot chocolate, grabbed a Clif Bar, and made her way to the back of the room. She thought, *I don't need any brochures, I have a year's worth of mountains outlined in my head. The last thing I need is literature to weigh me down; my research material already does that.* But then rethinking things, she returned to the table. *I'll just grab some anyway so he doesn't think I wasn't listening.*

She could feel his eyes on her as she made her way around the table and then back to her seat.

Just then, the door creaked open and a few hikers walked in. A fog seemed to roll in with them. Now she could smell the cold, wet air.

Settling into her seat and wrapping her hands around her cup, she peered through its steam over towards the counter. *He's pretty hot; he's got awesome hair,* she thought. *Long, sun-streaked, kind of wild... Jeez, I hope he's not one of those man-bun types.* With curiosity, she continued to daydream, slowly slurping her hot chocolate as a steady flow of hikers came in.

One particular group shuffled across the room in a cluster, making their way to the table up front. Like uncivilized buffoons, they made a mess of things with sugar packs ripped open and drink stirrers flung about. *I bet they're stoned,* she thought. *There go the Clif Bars!* Then it dawned on her. There was a full moon bonfire later that night, famous for bringing out the stoners. She remembered seeing posters throughout town and at the guide house when she first pulled in.

Quietly sitting in the back of the room, she recalled being at one of those bonfires—about a year ago—with her BFF Tommy and his college friends. They smoked, she drank, and they spent the night in a lean-to about a mile into the woods. She remembered the chaos of hiking drunk and vowed to never do it again. They all had donned headlamps, and even though the moon was full, it was hard to see the trail through the thick of the pines. Stumbling on an occasional rock and bitten by far too many bugs, she was eager to bury her head in her sleeping bag and be done with the night. But Pauly, one of Tommy's friends, thought it would be nice to squeeze into the sleeping bag with her. Taking complete liberty, he slid himself right in. Seconds later, he had his hands up her shirt and his lips all over her. Suddenly, being both drunk *and* disgusted, she lurched up and puked all over him.

By now, the stoned and obnoxious buffoons had made their way through the chairs and halfway down the room. When Robin glanced up, she couldn't believe her eyes. There, just three rows ahead, someone stumbled. "Oh my God, freaking *Pauly*," she muttered to herself in anguish. Slipping and sliding in his own wet drippings, a chair caught him by the ass and stopped his fall, determining where he and his group were going to sit. *Thank God he didn't see me,* she thought. She pulled up her fleecy hood, slid down into her chair, and made sure to avoid eye contact.

Sadly, this now meant no raising her hand after the presentation, no questions, no nothing. As studious as she was, she'd rather have unanswered questions than to have to deal with Pauly. Sinking lower and lower, she could almost taste the puke in her mouth all over again.

The slap of the projection screen as it raveled back up brought Robin to her senses, just as the lights of the High Peaks Information Center flashed back on.

Wow! she thought. *I've never dozed like that.* She wiped at the side of her face. *Shit, did I drool?* Rubbing her eyes, she looked toward the counter for Bryce, but he was no longer there.

The monotone voice of the park ranger who led the class must have lulled her to sleep, or was it sheer boredom from knowing most of the class's content? Maybe with all the research she was conducting and with graduation only a few weeks away, she truly was exhausted, and a mere darkened room was enough to send her drifting off.

* * *

Robin struck a match and lit the mini stove. Emptying her water bottle into the pot, she thought, *Voilà, now I can make hot chocolate.*

Just as the water began to boil, she heard a zip. Slowly, he rose from the tent, running his hands through that awesome hair. She felt her heart thump, and butterflies fluttered in her stomach, remembering how intimate last night was. He had pleasured her for what seemed like hours. She thought, *I can't wait to tell Tommy.*

Bryce stretched as he walked toward her. "I promise you I usually don't sleep with someone so early in a relationship," he said.

She zeroed in on the word *relationship*. She was excited he felt that way and felt herself blush.

"You call that sleep?" she asked. "How are we supposed to hike with so few hours of actual sleep?"

"Hike?" he questioned back. "We can't go anywhere yet."

With an extended arm, he fanned the area and pointed toward the trail. The campsite should have offered a sweeping view through the trees and to the valley and brook below, but the fog obscured everything. "If this weather doesn't clear, we'd be wise to sleep in."

With that, he stepped up so close to her she could feel the heat from his newly awakened skin. He gently cupped her chin and tilted her head to the side. She felt him breathe her in as he kissed her neck. Speaking softly, he continued, "I'm serious... If it doesn't clear up, I know what we can do for breakfast."

1

School Daze

Robin met Tommy in sixth grade when he moved from the North Shore of Long Island to her North Jersey neighborhood. *This kid has the same exact freckles across his nose as I do,* she thought. Realizing this, they bonded instantly.

During Tommy's first few weeks of school, Robin heard a nasty rumor that his family moved because a priest supposedly had molested him, and before the story made it to the papers the priest had left the church and gone into hiding. Asking a few random questions here and there, Robin never believed the rumor. The school's *other* new kid was the one spreading it; the one who didn't bond with anyone and was quickly becoming the school bully. The truth she had come to understand was simply that Tommy's family decided to relocate after they had sold their tire store.

Tommy and Robin went through sixth, seventh, and eighth grade together experiencing the same teachers and same issues. Both were very smart but not very popular, and both thought their freckles had something to do with it.

Come spring, every day after school they'd walk home together deciding whether to play video games at Robin's or at Tommy's, and at whose house to have dinner.

Robin's house was small and orderly, it always felt warm and inviting. Her mom, June, was divorced, overworked, and underpaid. She was a regional manager of five Talbots stores. Her husband had left her when Robin was twelve.

Robin would never forget the day her father went away.

She went off to middle school wearing her first bra. Tommy was the first to notice as he snapped it against her back, asking sarcastically, "What's this?"

Robin's father had picked her up from school because she had been suffering sickening cramps. On the way home, she bled all over his front seat. She was mortified. Not only by the leak from her period, but by his screaming, the screaming that continued through the night between her mom and dad.

The next morning before Robin left for school, she noticed that the suitcases had been pulled from the hall closet. Later that afternoon, she came home to her mom sitting alone at the kitchen table, sobbing. Oddly enough, Robin had never felt closer to her than at that time. Her mother explained to Robin how it would be easier not having her father around, and that she had been feeling completely detached from him.

"I've felt like this for quite some time too, Mom. There were so many times when I'd go to Dad for help on my homework or whatever. He wouldn't even look at me, he'd just shush me away!" Robin had said.

Robin knelt and laid her head on her mom's lap. June stroked her hair as the two of them lightly wept.

"You and I?" June sniffed, controlling her sobs, "We can do this. But honey, I don't want you to feel hurt or betrayed. You are the most important thing in my life. I'm sure your father is just going through something. I need you to understand that I will always be here for you, and I love you more than you can imagine."

Abruptly, Robin stood. Pulling her mom up and hugging her with sudden confidence, "Oh, I have an idea of what Dad is going through, and it's better for both of us that he won't be here."

Once the apple of her dad's eye, Robin was their only child.

Though neither of them dared to mention, they knew his secretary now outshone that apple.

Robin continued, "You and I can do this; we can handle anything Mom, you watch! It will be easy, just the two of us."

June had wiped her eyes with the paper towel Robin handed her, "Don't you mean the three of us?" she asked. "Isn't Tommy here tonight for dinner?"

* * *

Tommy was also an only child. His mother, Margo, was a stay-at-home mom, but rarely was she actually at home. Most days she had tennis lessons, a yoga class, a mani-pedi, or a dye job at the salon which took five hours and six colors to happen. About once a month though, she'd prepare a fancy gourmet dinner. Robin and Tommy would set the table and then run upstairs to play games on his hi-tech video console. Margo would sashay in the kitchen, stirring sauces, drinking wine, and talking on the phone. The smells that wafted up the stairs would be incredible. And like clockwork, Tommy's dad would pull into the driveway just as Margo rang the dinner bell.

Before they even sat down to dinner, Margo would demand, "After dinner, you two are going outside to play and get some fresh air!"

Robin loved the outdoors, but if Tommy wanted to stay inside, inside is where they stayed.

* * *

Throughout high school, Robin and Tommy had nearly all the same classes, but completely different schedules. Their lunch periods never seemed to line up. Hanging out and catching-up couldn't happen until after school. They'd meet outside by the flagpole and walk home together. By now, they were BFFs and completely inseparable.

Senior year, Tommy drove to and from school and always gave Robin a ride home. He had a BMW and she had nothing. In fact, Robin didn't even bother to take her driving test. She figured it would be at least two more years before she could afford a car and since she lived within walking distance to school, her mom didn't acknowledge any of her pleadings.

"What on earth do you need a car for?" June would ask. "Besides once you're in college…Well, they don't even allow students to have cars until sophomore year!"

On the mornings before school, too anxious to wait for a ride from Tommy, Robin would take the ten-minute walk, making sure she'd get to school early enough for last-minute studying. The walk did her mind good. She called it "airing-out:" Ten minutes to collect her thoughts while listening to the birdsong of daybreak.

Tommy, on the other hand, barely made it to school by the first bell. Suddenly he cared more about his appearance than his grades. He had grown about four inches since junior year, slimmed down, and buffed up. Handsome had become him. The BMW didn't hurt either.

Most afternoons, Tommy and Robin were solid though. They'd drive into town for an "After School Delight," something they had named and thought themselves so clever. At school, they'd purposely speak loudly while mentioning it, hoping others would overhear and conjure up a rumor of romance or a story to dish about.

On cold days, they were all about cookies and hot chocolate, choosing from a number of coffee and sandwich shops, or the dingy luncheonette that should have closed in the 60s. The warmer days were mostly spent at the frozen yogurt shop. Often Robin wished it were more than just an afternoon snack. The older she got, the more she yearned for something more than what Tommy— literally—brought to the table.

Spring became lonely for Robin. Tommy was in the school play, (ironically) *Tommy*. For weeks, he had to stay after school to rehearse. Previous years he had tried out for other productions but never landed the role he wanted. This was finally *it* for him. Often, Robin would stay after school too, but she'd be in the library or down at the high school track, airing-out and pretending to watch.

Regardless, Robin and Tommy were inseparable. They never developed close friendships with others. They did go to parties, and as the years progressed, so did their popularity. But Robin always felt protective of Tommy. Maybe it was because she wanted him all to herself, or maybe it was because it seemed other boys were jealous of him. Robin wondered if the jealousy was because they wanted her, or because he was so damn good looking.

By now, Robin herself had fully blossomed. Her slim frame never registered the snacking afternoons with Tommy.

What the hell is wrong with him? she thought, catching a glimpse of her willowy reflection in a window, heading into the frozen yogurt shop.

Sometimes Robin was just plain mad at Tommy, so it was no big deal when she had to cut their "After School Delights" short. She needed to be home earlier to start dinners. Her mom had taken on a few more stores and wasn't able to get home until much later. The routine had changed and as soon as dinner was done, Robin needed to hit the books. The need to maintain her GPA and class rank, had become her excuse to Tommy for the recent cold shoulder. But it was the truth too. Academically, Robin had been hoping for a big, fat scholarship, so every second that wasn't spent with Tommy was dedicated to just that.

Every letter that came from colleges did, in fact, give Robin the highest awards they offered. Each and every trip to the mailbox was exciting for Robin and June. Because of her outstanding academic status, when Robin decided on a state school, it turned into a full academic scholarship. From here on out, she absolutely needed to maintain her GPA and everything else the university expected of her. Come fall, Robin would be heading to SUNY New Paltz to study Ecosystem Conservation & Management, and Environmental Sustainability. Tommy's college plans had him heading to Tisch School of the Arts at NYU to study drama and acting.

The end of the school year snuck up on them, and so did the prom. Ever since middle school, Tommy and Robin promised each other if they weren't dating someone, they'd go to the prom together. There was no question this would ever change. Even as mad as she was at him lately, she knew it was exclusively because of the way *she* felt. They'd been so close for so long, how could she expect him to feel the same way? She was like a sister to him. But there were a few times she'd blush in embarrassment letting her thoughts go there. Deep down, she still had a faint glimmer of hope.

They shopped for her dress together. He was a perfect gentleman, oohing and aahing at everything she tried on. Except for the dark green one. He said, "No way, you look flat in that one!"

OMG, he noticed I have boobs! she thought.

She decided on a light pink strapless gown with rhinestones embedded in the thick layers of pink tulle that draped from her waist to the floor. Emerging from the dressing room with a twirl, she swore she saw Tommy catch his breath. He choked as he tried to whistle, fumbling with the straw, slurping the last of his frozen latte. *Yup, this is totally the dress*, she thought.

The following day, they pranced in and out of tuxedo shops. The one at the mall had a velvet jacket that smoldered with dark purples and magenta, circling in a paisley pattern. It was a striking complement to the pink in Robin's dress. Onlookers practically gasped when Tommy came out of the dressing room.

"Look at those heads turn!" Robin said sarcastically, all while imagining the two of them making an entrance like a royal couple. She continued to daydream while he made the purchase at the counter. *Maybe he'll kiss me on the dance floor... After the night is over? Just somehow, somewhere...* Feeling herself flush, she quickly changed her thoughts, *What about shoes?*

On prom night, Tommy and Robin appeared to float in as they entered the ballroom, and just as she imagined, everyone watched in awe. With cupped hands over ears the crowd seemed to whisper secrets. "Hot damn!" they overheard, coming from a line-up of watchful teachers no less. Whoever said that proms were magical was right! Robin and Tommy held hands as they sauntered around the room, only stepping onto the dance floor when they heard a song that was worthy. At one point, Tommy spun Robin inward and whispered into her ear.

"Whadd'ya think, prom king and queen?"

"No way, that is so rigged. Don't get your hopes up!" she declared.

They hovered back to their table where Robin's phone lit up. She grabbed it and rushed towards a corner of the room where she'd be able to hear. Tommy watched her and the look of concern grow on her face. Her jaw dropped, and her eyes widened, she seemed to freeze in place. Unable to make out any of her conversation it was obvious something was wrong.

Frantically, she rushed back to the table. "My mom's been in a car accident, can you get me to the hospital?"

"*Shit*! Of course!"

He grabbed her purse from the back of the chair along with her shimmery pink shawl. They fled. Halfway out of the building, Robin shrieked.

"Shit, my shhh-" She didn't even get the words out. Tommy was back and under the table feeling for her shoes.

* * *

They stood at the foot of June's bed in the emergency room. A pile of bandages was thrown on her lap as a nurse continued ripping them open while inspecting each cut.

"I hit a deer. And OH MY GOD! I ruined your prom! I'm fine! Go back!"

Robin and Tommy simultaneously looked at the doctor that was looming over Robin's mom.

"She is fine. And she is lucky. The windshield crashed down on her as the deer continued up and over the top of the car."

"The poor deer was not so lucky," June interrupted.

"I'd like to keep her here for a few hours for observation. There is no head trauma and all her vitals seem fine but to calm her, I gave her a sedative. Again, just to keep our eyes on her. Let's say two hours." The doctor finished his diagnosis saying, "And you two look fabulous!"

June stared at the two of them and then she began to tear up. "I'm so sorry, please, please, go back, I beg you."

"Mom, don't be ridiculous. We ate, we danced, there's nothing more we need to do. I'm just *so* relieved you're ok. We're fine just hanging here, really."

Tommy broke in to say, "'Skuse me, I'm going to find the

16

men's room."

Ten minutes later, Tommy came back and resumed his post at Robin's side. With a drug-induced slur—but with a genuine and adoring look—June turned to Robin.

"How on Earth did my little girl turn out so beautiful? And your handsome date is a sight to behold!"

Again, getting choked up in the moment, when June was able to regain composure she added, "If you must stay, go to the cafeteria or someplace where people can see you. You two look fantastic! Go grab a bite or go sit and relax. Or..."

"Mom, Mom, we're fine!" Robin firmly grabbed Tommy's hand and looked earnestly at her mom. "We'll just go outside and chill on the park benches out back. It's a nice night and there's a full moon."

Then June answered in a songful tone, "Oh how my Robin loves the outdoors."

Robin whispered as she backed away from the bed, "Yup, she's a little woozy."

They turned away, but Tommy glanced back to give June an assuring wink.

"Oh and Tommy," she sang, "Thank you for *everything!*"

The back entrance of the emergency room didn't see a lot of action. For a full moon, it was a quiet night. A few nurses were outside on the sidewalk smoking, while two quieted ambulances pulled into the empty overnight lot. Tommy rushed Robin past the bench where she thought they'd sit.

"Follow me," he said.

Halfway through the parking lot he stopped in his tracks. He stood still and grabbed Robin's hands. Suddenly from three corners of the lot, ambulance lights flickered on. No noise, just rotating red and blue lights. Scratchy speaker music transmitted from one of them—an old tune Robin recognized from her mom's Saturday morning vacuuming routine. "Is that Frank Sinatra?" she questioned.

"Yup, I downloaded it and handed my phone to the driver. I guess ambulances aren't equipped with great speaker systems." Tommy chuckled.

Tommy then grabbed Robin's arms one at a time and placed them around his neck. There they stood in the middle of the parking lot. They began to sway. Robin couldn't even look at him. The endearment she felt for him right then was so deep. She didn't want to chance altering the perfect moment with something as profound as kissing him, so she simply laid her head on his chest. She was nervous, she was elated, and her heart was in her throat. She wrapped her arms tightly around him and began to weep.

"Tommy, what the hell am I going to do without you?"

He broke from her hug, looked her straight in the eye and said, "What the hell am I going to do without you?"

Until now, Robin and Tommy never thought about the fact that they would be completely separated come fall.

Amidst all the clapping coming from the small crowd that had gathered at the back entrance, they walked back into the building,

"Where's the cafeteria? Tommy asked. "We need some hot chocolate."

* * *

When graduation night arrived, Tommy wanted nothing to do with the huge party that most of the graduating class was going to. It was at Matt—the football hero—Brown's house. The last time Matt Brown paid any attention to Tommy was in March when he was making fun of him in the lunchroom. He couldn't resist poking fun at him for playing the lead role. "Tommy wants to be Tommy," he'd say as he flopped his hands out front and swung them from side to side. "Deaf, dumb and blind fag!" he teased. Robin only heard about it after school when Tommy met up with her, with his split open lip. Matt apparently looked even worse and both he and Tommy spent the remainder of the day in the principal's office.

The following three days, during their suspension, Matt and Tommy spent hours cleaning under the bleachers, cleaning the locker rooms and painting over the graffiti that covered "Senior Rock": the huge rock that was down near the track. When Robin heard they had to repaint the rock together, she freaked out.

"What? Why the hell did they have you paint over the rock? What did Matt say?" She questioned Tommy.

"Chill!" he replied. "Someone painted a big dick on it. I told the principal I'd paint the school's logo on it if he promised to have Matt do something *else* during the final day of suspension. Something that didn't involve me!"

"Since when did you become an artist?" Robin snapped.

"Since I can't stand spending one more minute with that asshole! And what the fuck is wrong with you?" he snapped back. "Since when do you give a shit about Matt?"

The end of senior year and the reality of it being over was both bittersweet and exciting. Tommy and Robin came to grips with their angst during the final week of school. Summer was going to be chaos. Tommy was working with his dad full time and Robin took a summer job at Starbucks. She really needed to save for a car. Both their jobs started the day after graduation. Hello, worst summer ever.

But in that last week of school, after school every day

for an hour and a half, just as they'd done for most of the school year… They could be found at one of their spots, huddled and laughing at a table in a corner, with what seemed to be not a care in the world.

2

Here's Pauly

Receiving the Presidential Scholarship at SUNY was a tremendous help financially, but it only covered tuition, not room and board. Robin's mom was able to manage half of the mortgage and half of the high taxes, but any big-ticket item above and beyond that was very difficult. The deal with Robin's father was he would pay the other halves until the house was paid off in five years. June would then flat out own the house. Until then it was going to be tough making ends meet.

Robin decided she could help out by becoming a Resident Assistant in Training. This offered a discount on both room and board. All RATs had to remain on campus during holidays, breaks, and weekends. Only if the campus population dropped to less than 50 percent would Robin have an opportunity to trade off with other RATs and be able to leave campus. Being a RAT also came with a literal serving of banter as students were known to tape cheese on doors and make squeaking noises in their company.

Tommy drove out with June and Robin to help set up her dorm. The drive was over two hours and taking a train was not an option so the prospect of Robin coming home often was simply out of the question. Regardless of her new RAT status, the fact was she still didn't have a car. Tommy had promised her he'd drive out to visit the minute she figured out when it was possible.

With Robin's dorm room half done—with respect to her side—now fluffy and complete, June and Tommy alternated embraces as they began their goodbyes. Suddenly the dorm door flung open. Large boxes with legs walked in. Behind them were three people: a very tall man wearing jeans and a tie-dyed Grateful Dead shirt, a girl—about Robin's age—with a matching shirt, and then a younger boy. The man dropped the heaviest box and immediately extended his hand to June.

"Afternoon!" he announced, then he glanced back over his shoulder. "This is Daisy, my daughter and your roommate."

Robin never saw her mom blush—*ever*! June placed her hand in his and gestured toward Robin, who was just breaking out of another hug from Tommy. "Don't be silly, I'm Robin's mom, June."

With a loud slap, Daisy dropped *her* box on the vinyl covered mattress over on the side of the room that had not been invaded with puffy turquoise pillows, collages, and posters (which Robin had meticulously hung). She walked right up to Robin and hugged her.

"Helloooo Roomy!"

Robin was befuddled and offered Daisy a delicate hug back. She tried to drum up some enthusiasm but responded with a plain old, "Hey!"

Noticing the little boy teetering with a heavy box, Robin instantly pulled away and asked, "Can I help you with any boxes?"

The awkward moment seemed to linger so Tommy reached for June's hand. "I think this is our exit."

Robin followed them out the door, but Tommy turned around. "Just go back in and help," he said. "I hate goodbyes and I'm only a text away. Text me tonight."

June hugged Robin one final, air-constricting time, and fought back tears. "I'm only one text away too, but please give me a call. I need to hear your voice."

Three days later, Tommy started at NYU. From his house it took just over an hour to get into Manhattan, plus he had plenty of train options, so he left his car at home after the initial move-in day. His building, Alumni Hall, was one of the few undergraduate dorms that offered single rooms. It even had single bathrooms. This kind of dorm was cheaper than a garage for a car so that was the deal Tommy made with his parents. Single room. No car.

Tommy didn't always come from money, but now his father owned a chain of BMW dealerships in New York and New Jersey. Of all the concerns his parents have had, money was no longer one of them.

* * *

At first, college was rough for Robin. She missed home, she missed her mom, and of course, she missed Tommy. Due to her academic track record, she was in the honors dorms, which was a relief because she knew there would be way fewer shenanigans. As a RAT, it'd be much easier to manage. Having to spend time with a watchful eye over the dorms also gave her more time to study, thus keeping up her grades.

Daisy was turning out to be pretty cool. With long brown hair, green eyes, and freckles (like the ones Robin couldn't wait to outgrow), she was cute, smart, and her carefree attitude allowed everything to just roll off her back. She had positive effects on Robin.

On the first day they had off from classes, a Thursday in late September for the Yom Kippur holiday, Daisy suggested, "Let's take in some local color. Literally!"

Robin loaded up a daypack for herself. Daisy, a photo technology major, loaded up a camera bag instead. They hit the trails of the nearby Shawangunk Mountains.

The brilliant fall colors had just begun to appear and the late morning light cast a warm glow that spread throughout the entire valley. From road and trail alike, the mountain ridge—known for welcoming hikers and climbers to the area—rose majestically from many angles.

They hiked to Sam's Point Summit, the highest elevation in the Shawangunks, or 'The Gunks' as they learned from a passer-by on the first wrong turn trying to find a trailhead.

Settling on a rock cliff that overlooked the valley, they found a perfect spot for lunch.

"So, tell me about Tommy," Daisy mumbled through her PB&J sandwich.

"Oh he's just my BFF, I've known him since, like sixth grade."

"Well he's pretty frigging hot. Have you done him?"

Robin almost spit out a mouth full of trail mix. "Hell no! He's like my brother." She continued, "So what about you? You have a little brother and your dad seems funny."

"Awe, Rob and Robbie II, they're buddies. Robbie's just seven. My mom died when he was four. Breast Cancer."

"Shit, I'm so sorry."

Daisy leaned into and bumped up against Robin's shoulder and almost in an apologetic manner she said, "I just feel so bad for Robbie. I mean like I was a freshman in high school when she died so of course it sucked, but it's hard to see a little kid without his mom. I got real busy caring for Robbie and going to school while my dad silently struggled. But this last year dad got a grip. He got a new job and he's a lot more positive. He manages a big construction company from home, so he's there one hundred percent for Robbie. They are each other's rock. He made me come here for school. I didn't want to leave them. But it's weird... now that I'm here away from them, I kind of think a lot more about my mom."

They hurried off the mountain when they realized how much time had flown. Robin had to be back by 6:00 p.m. for a new job she was about to start.

On the nights her RAT duties were not in effect, the campus shuttle would drop her just fifty feet from The Gravity Café. It was a place where college hipsters and hippies alike came to hang out. They came for coffee, for food, and most weekends, they came for the music. Robin waited on tables and did whatever else was needed. Poetry readings were on Thursday nights. Daisy *loved* the place...She went there almost every Thursday.

On a cold and dreary Columbus Day, Tommy surprised Robin at the café. He showed up with his friend from school, Pauly. Bored with their own studies, they decided earlier that day that they would make the drive up. Pauly lived in the city and had a car at his disposal, his parents' car but nevertheless, his disposal. To Pauly, hearing that Tommy's best friend and her roommate were both pretty hot was reason enough for a road trip.

Robin, who'd been working for just a few weeks, was still nervous about doing everything right. Tommy caught her totally off guard. He walked in and snuck up behind her.

"Guess who?" he asked with his hands over her eyes.

"OMG Tommy!" She spun around and gave him a huge hug.

"How in the hell did you know it was me?"

Robin didn't want to admit it, but she could identify him by scent. Even more so since prom night when he doused a little extra cologne on himself. It was a scent she'd never forget. It reminded her of a pine forest and made her desirous if she stopped to think.

Scrambling for words she said, "I saw your reflection in

the window just as you came up behind me." (Tommy looked but didn't see the window.)

Robin's boss noticed what was happening and he signaled her over. "Robin, we're dead. Go out and get a good dinner with your friends."

She hugged her boss, hung up her apron, and in thirty seconds they were out the door. Before Pauly could even get a word in, Robin was texting Daisy.

"Meet us at the Otter. OMG Tommy is here!!!!!"

They waited outside near the front entrance of The Gilded Otter restaurant. Daisy turned the corner on a bicycle and pulled up to the bike rack where they all stood. Introductions were made as they walked toward and into the building through a glass door entrance.

Inside, blasted by the smell of burgers, practically panting, Daisy said, "I'm starving!"

They sat at the bar. Only Pauly ordered a beer; he was twenty-one and the others were not. Daisy immediately started chatting up Pauly. Tommy caught Pauly raise a brow and flash a huge smile, indicating his interest.

Feeling secure with the way things were progressing, Robin spun on the bar stool to face just Tommy. Looking at each other they both nodded their heads, shrugged their shoulders, and laughed.

"Works for me," Robin said. She clinked her pint of diet soda against Tommy's iced tea.

"But I tell ya," Tommy began, "The next time we sneak in a visit up here, we're staying! That ride was hell. Pauly talked my freaking ear off! Do you think next time Daisy'd allow us to crash on your floor?"

"Probably not a problem, but let's see how this goes." Robin pointed with her eyes and nodded toward the others, laughing and carrying on.

Thanksgiving of that first year, Robin wasn't able to swap-out her RAT duties, Tommy said he couldn't get up for a visit, and Daisy went home for "Turkey-Day." But all was not lost. Robin's mom booked a cheap hotel in town and they spent the Friday night after Thanksgiving at a charming restaurant tucked alongside an old canal that once ran through the area.

The Canal House was in an old stone mill renowned for local "farm to table" food. Robin thought, *Jeez, what mom is spending on dinner could have easily paid for a much nicer hotel.*

Sitting at a white linen-covered table in front of a fireplace, Robin confessed, "Mom, thank you for this, and for coming all the way here. I really, really, miss you... And home... But school is great. I have so much to be thankful for, especially now."

Robin spent the night in the hotel with June. It *was* cheap... And wonderful!

* * *

That same Friday night, unbeknownst to all, Pauly showed up at the Gravity Café. It was an open mic night: a showcase for stand-up comics. It coincided with what Pauly was going to school for. Robin heard about Pauly's bit from her boss when she went in the next day. She video chatted Tommy, "Did you know he was coming up?"

"No idea."

"Do you know if he saw Daisy?"

"No idea again. He's taking a course on comedy in performance. He mentioned an extra credit thing. I didn't take him seriously though—he's been doing a lot of partying and I think his grades are slipping."

"Hummm," Robin said, "I'll ask Daisy if she knew, I'm not sure how much they talk. Do you?"

"Again, no idea!"

Enthusiastically Robin piped in with, "So what's the Christmas break plan? Can you come up at all? I'll try and get a few days covered. Maybe we can do something?"

* * *

The first semester was complete, and Robin was officially a Residents Assistant. Besides more savings, the occasional "squeak" from fellow students was now a thing of the past.

On Christmas Eve, June came up and stayed in the cheap hotel again. And on Christmas day, she spent the entire day with Robin watching her scurried between floors and rooms checking on the few students that remained on campus.

"Honey, do you think you'll be able to get covered so maybe you can actually come home at some point...Soon?"

"The second or third week in January, one of the other RAs promised to cover for me and I should be able to come home for a few days, basically at the end of winter break. Tommy said he'd come and get me. He's got a decent stretch of time off."

Tommy did in fact, come up. It was during a snowstorm so instead of two hours, it took seven. His BMW was not the best in snow.

"Seven fucking hours!"

He was drained and having Pauly tag along, the conversation was per-usual, non-stop. Robin, annoyed, was looking forward to some alone time with Tommy. She said nothing in fear it would make matters worse. They crashed in Robin's dorm. Pauly dove into Daisy's bed (who'd been home with her family all of winter break). Tommy set up on the floor with the fold and flop chair pulled out from under Robin's bed.

"I'll be fine," he whispered.

It was barely daylight when Tommy woke scrambling around looking for coffee. He made his way to Robin's bed and lightly kissed her forehead.

"Rise and shine," he whispered.

They left a note for Pauly: *"Back in a few with breakfast."*

A foot of snow was piled up on either side of the freshly shoveled sidewalks. They walked two blocks off campus to the donut shop.

"One coffee, two hot chocolates and six glazed cinnamon swirls, please," Tommy said, kicking the snow from his boots at the register.

Robin elbowed him out of the way. "Make that four cinnamon swirls and one egg white, whole wheat, flatbread sandwich, please... Seriously?" she said, rolling her eyes at Tommy.

Tommy twisted away from the register and looked behind at Robin's butt. "You are looking pretty fine I might add."

Again, she elbowed him hard, almost knocking him over. *What am I supposed to make of that?*

By 9:00 a.m. they were all in the car, pulling out of campus, and heading south. Robin was excited to finally get back home. Two hours and twenty-five minutes later, Tommy pulled into her driveway and helped her unload.

"I have to run," he said. "Say hi to your mom. I'm dumping Pauly at the train station and I'll be back to pick you up later. Text me the plan."

It was a crisp, clear, and sunny winter morning. Not as much snow there as back at school but it was enough to blanket the neighborhood. The snow clung to every surface and the tiny branches of the Dogwood tree in the front yard twinkled in the bright morning light.

Robin was relieved to be home. Once through the front door she walked down the hall, sniffing the air. "Baking? Do I smell something baking?" (Her mom was *not* a baker.)

Dropping her bags at the base of the stairs, she entered the kitchen and jumped into her mom's arms. Sensing something weird, she took one-step backward just as June said,

"You remember Daisy's father, Robert?" Robin hadn't noticed him sitting at the table when she entered the room.

"Oh my God, of course I do!"
June continued, "I ran into him at one of my stores. He's the contractor we've hired to change-out all of the stores. We're rebranding."

Upstairs as Robin unpacked, she texted Tommy. *"Holy shit! My mom has a boyfriend and if you can believe this... It's Daisy's dad!!!!!!!!!!!!!!!!!!!!!"* Her phone was low on juice otherwise she would have typed a hundred more exclamation points. She plugged it in and called Daisy next.

After a miraculous homemade pot pie lunch with June and Robert, Robin and Tommy went to the mall, caught a movie, and per plan, ended the night with a late bite in their old dingy luncheonette. As luck would have it, they had recently added dinner hours because of the winter festival happening in town.

Music filled the streets, vendors peddled their wares, and the aroma from the cider donut machine wafted through the air. Chilly revelers packed their little old luncheonette. Thankfully, they were able to sit in their regular corner spot.

From underneath the table, Tommy produced a shiny gold wrapped gift. He leaned toward Robin and handed it off.

She sneered at him saying, "We have a no gifts deal!"

"But I saw this, and I immediately thought of you. Consider it not a gift, but a necessity!" She hesitated, but the gold wrapping alone made her excited. Ripping the paper off, exposing a hinged white velvet box, it practically sprung open itself. Delicately, she pulled on a silver chain until a sun charm (about the size of a dime), dangled and twirled, collecting all of the light from the corner of the room. Mesmerized, she watched it. Dropping the box on the table, out flew a note. She unfolded it, peering at Tommy with a face full of question.

You are my sun, I am your moon.

With the light of each day, the sun is always there for me.

You won't always see the moon.

But you must know, I am forever there for you.

Robin's bottom lip was quivering, and she could hardly breathe. The waitress paused at their table and Robin choked out, "Can we get a couple of hot chocolates please?"

Tommy pulled down the collar of his sweater revealing a silvery moon dangling from a chain around his own neck.

* * *

Tommy was called into work with his dad the next day. June and Robert had planned to get Robin and Daisy back up to school together, (another small surprise of sorts).

Pulling into the driveway, a beep from Robert's car sent Robin dashing out the door. On the road, the girls thought they would burst with excitement. Daisy had been home for the whole winter break, so she and Robin had a ton of catching up to do. They couldn't really talk–out loud–about their parents' little crush, so they texted each other back and forth the whole ride up. Their snickering and laughter was hard to contain, especially when Robert reached over and grabbed June's hand! Robbie, in the back seat, was happy and silent playing on a new game device.

Instead of turning into campus, Robert pulled into the Otter. "Let's finish up your winter break with a nice family dinner," he said.

With complete excitement, Daisy grabbed Robin's hand and the two of them skipped into the restaurant like little kids. Robin opened the door for Daisy. "After you sis!"

* * *

And just like the proverb says, "Spring came in like a lion and out like a lamb." The warmer days were here to stay; the end of freshman year was in sight.

By the end of April, Robin had saved up enough to buy a car. Her boss's mother no longer drove, so the cute little red car was actually "Driven by a little old lady." 60,000 miles, garage kept, fifteen years old, and for only $1500... Robin found her perfect first set of wheels. Since students weren't allowed to have cars on campus until sophomore year, her boss allowed her to park it behind the café.

Tommy was her first destination so the next weekend she worked a deal with a fellow RA. She drove home and spent the morning with her mom. From there, not quite savvy enough to drive into the city, she took the train. It was her turn to surprise him.

She knew on Saturdays he'd go to Washington Square Park and watch impromptu performances. There were a-cappella groups, ad-lib comedians, and now that it was warmer, all sorts of musicians came out as well.

How the hell did he get that piano here? she thought, making her way through the park. There was so much activity. *I'll never find him if he even is here… I'll just send a text.*

"Hey moon, what're ya doing?"

"Hungover, text me later."

Perfect! she thought. *Well not really, but I can just show up at his door.*

She announced her arrival with an authoritatively loud knock.

"Who is it?" she heard him say in a voice she could hardly recognize.

Wow, he's in bad shape, she thought. She knew he would peer out the peephole and suddenly the door flew open.

"What the—Robin!" he said, sounding relieved. He flung his arms around her. She stepped back and peeled his arms off her.

"You stink!" she laughed. "Get your ass up, get in the shower and show me around. The sun is shining today!"

"But the moon likes to hide," he grumbled. Under his breath, she heard him complain, "Fucking Pauly."

"Get going!" She pushed him into the bathroom shutting the door behind him.

They spent the weekend exploring the Village, finding perfect places to sit and relax, and just enjoy each other's college anecdotes. It was reminiscent of their "After School Delights."

"I think this place might be my favorite," Robin said sliding into a seat. "I know we just got here, but I already like the way it feels."

The Four Faced Liar is an old Irish bar known for its twenty-ounce pints, decent music, friendly bartenders, and games. The walls aren't covered with all the typical Irish ornaments, mostly just old photos. It has high tin ceilings and warm dark colors. A long oak bar with sturdy wooden bar stools welcome you as soon as you walk through the doors. Cozy leather booths surrounded by chunky wooden molding offer private spots to comfortably sit. *Definitely a neighborhood bar*, Robin thought.

Oddly enough, it was right next-door to the Pink Pussy Cat, probably the most famous adult erotic boutique around.

"Two hot chocolates... And two shots of 43 to start please," Tommy said, bellying up to the bar. "And can you see if Jenga is available?"

3

Breathe

Summer flew by. Tommy again worked at one of his dad's dealer-ships. It was decent money *and* he was able to arrange his schedule around appointments and casting calls. His portfolio and a P-Vid (personal video), which he made in his Professional Representation class, was making its way through a few ad agencies, so quite often he auditioned for TV spots and commercials. He got a few call-backs, but it wasn't until late July that he finally got camera time with a national eyewear franchise.

The day it first aired everyone gathered at Tommy's house: his mom and dad; June and Robert; Robin, Daisy, and little Robbie.

Tommy explained how the commercial was supposed to show him in four different pairs of eyeglasses.

"OMG! Can I have your autograph?" Robin teased.

"Shut up, it's a start," he demanded.

A whopping three seconds of his face showed off a chunky pair of horn-rims.

"Fucking editors!" he snarled, clicking off the TV.

Tommy's mom warned, "Watch your mouth!" pointing towards little Robbie, who's face was buried in a bowl of ice cream and hadn't heard a word.

Throughout the summer, Robin kept her waitress job at the Gravity Café. She remained living on campus, not in her dorm, but in split housing for students that volunteered to help with summer classes and tours (two more things she did to add to her credit).

Driving home on any given weekend happened often enough but it seemed every time she made the trip, Tommy was busy with his "calls."

June was now regular with Robert which Robin was thrilled about. And now since Robin had more nights (than she preferred) available, she would watch little Robbie so the two of them could go out on a date night.

Daisy landed a job at Rock-N-Bowl, a concert hall, bowling alley, and restaurant—in Brooklyn, of all places! The commute was hell, the hours were worse, but it gave her the opportunity to photograph the different bands that played there.

"People are starting to request my photos," she boasted.

When Robin saw some of her photographs, she was astonished. "Wow! You really do have an eye for this stuff!"

"Right?" Daisy urged. "People think it's my camera. I hate when they ask, 'What kind of camera? It takes nice pictures.' Grrr-rrrrr, makes me so mad. I take the damned photos, not the camera!"

* * *

In the fall of her sophomore year, Robin's dad came from out of left field and decided to help finance Robin's education.

"Mom, did Dad break up with that woman?" Robin asked.

"Honey, I have no idea, but if he wants to be more involved with your life, and if that means helping to pay for college, then make a little more time for him. An occasional lunch could prove to be beneficial. He's really not such a bad guy. Maybe that woman dumped *him*!"

Robin and her dad's relationship over the past few years had consisted of Christmas-time fancy dinners, and during summers he'd rent a shore house for a few weeks and allow Robin to bring a friend with her. One year in particular, Tommy fell asleep on the beach. Using sun-block lotion, Robin squirted a big smiley face right in the middle of his chest. Now she laughed every time she thought about it. That smiley face was noticeable for days.

Since room and board at school were no longer financial burdens, Robin quit her duties as an RA, moved up one floor in the honors dorms (with Daisy in tow), and cut back her hours at the café. Excited that she now had more time to explore the outdoors, she bought a real pair of hiking boots and a set of hiking poles.

With almost every weekend off, Robin found herself with spare time. This was a pure novelty and the more time she spent on the trails, the more she became interested in the local flora and fauna. Alone in the woods, she established a new sense of independence; a personal sanctuary, she concluded. Hiking in the area was a pilgrimage of discovery for her. "Nature on crack," she often stated, trying to convince Tommy many times to join her.

The surrounding parks, the Mohonk Preserve, and all the trails throughout the area amazed her. Turning over wet, decaying bark, she'd expose little orange salamanders–Eastern Newts, she learned. She also learned to identify animals by their tracks and even began studying their scat. She grew familiar with the certain types of fungi the damp October woods had to offer. There was always something to look up on the Internet when she came back.

"Mushroom Identification," she typed. Up popped a class offered in the Adirondacks at an information center. *Road trip,* she thought immediately. *I wonder if I can convince Tommy or Daisy to come with me.*

Robin now spent most of her spare time on the trails. Daisy worried, but Robin convinced her she was fine. Never was there a day that she didn't pass *someone* during a hike. The area beaconed outdoorsy people of all types. Robin was never alone in the woods.

Maybe I'll meet someone.... Someone who likes this kind of stuff, she thought. She was definitely independent, but she was lonely too.

Autumn in the Mohonk Mountain Range (the same vicinity of her university) was extraordinary, and Robin was now the one dragging Daisy out on hikes. "Just come out and shoot some of this stuff. The colors are amazing!"

* * *

With the holidays closing in, Tommy's schedule opened up, and Robin was finally able to spend a few days with him. They planned to go see the tree in Rockefeller Center, catch the Christmas Show at Radio City Music Hall, and hang out to do some serious catching up. They were way overdue.

By train, Robin got into the city on Saturday evening. Tommy met her at Penn Station. Immediately hailing a cab at the street, he whisked her away to a Christmas party. As they walked into the front door of a lavish five-story brownstone in Gramercy Park he said, "A friend from school lives here."

He smiled, watching Robin standing in the foyer looking up the stairs and around the room in complete awe.

"Wow this place is beaut-" she began, but he cut her off.

"Here put this on."

He handed her a green mini dress with striped leggings and a fuzzy green Santa hat. "You must have noticed on the ride here, it's SantaCon. Anyone who is dressed up like Santa or an elf gets free beer! A shitload of bars participate; it's a fucking jolly ass time! Here," he continued, directing her down a small hallway.

"Really? Jolly?" She looked down at the green pile as he closed a door between them.

Minutes later, she emerged from the guest bathroom questioning her elfin attire, but realizing it wasn't so bad as she watched

Tommy struggle with an oversized pair of red Santa pants.

"See, you look adorable!" he said. "And I hope those shoes are comfortable. This party is our first stop and the official start of a really fun weekend!"

After hours of bar hopping and beer drinking, the two of them made their way through Washington Square Park in a drunken stupor, and then five bewildering blocks beyond. Zigzagging by some of their favorite hot chocolate spots, they finally made it to Tommy's dorm on 3rd Avenue.

Out of nowhere, it dawned on Robin. "Shit! My clothes!"

"Don't problem, tomorrow we go Grammmmercy," he slurred.

The walk seemed to sober up Robin, but Tommy was a staggering mess.

Throughout the night, Daisy had texted Robin a few times. In Robin's final text back, she tapped:

"Heading back to Tommy's dorm now TTYT."

Tommy couldn't even focus on the doorknob let alone get the key into its hole. They fell into the room after Robin got the door open.

Robin laid Tommy right down and went into the bathroom to get a plastic garbage pail to leave by his bedside. Sitting next to him and watching him settle into a subconscious state, she stroked his hair and thought about all the times in the past that she wanted to kiss him. So many times at the luncheonette or yogurt shop; junior year in high school, when he was so upset about not getting the lead in the summer production of Grease; and after each dress she tried on for the prom. There were too many times to remember. Sadly, Robin had decided long ago that she would not be the one to cross that line. If it were ever going to happen, it had to come from him.

Suddenly, he rolled over taking her arm with him, forcing her to lie down on her side. He spooned her. Just by the way he took his breaths, she could sense the ease and comfort he felt with Robin next to him. She acquiesced silently, snuggled into him, and drifted off to sleep herself.

A few hours later, her arm had fallen asleep. She tried to wriggle away, but he woke. In a whisper she asked, "Hey, where are your extra pillows and blankets?"

He pointed to his closet. "Top shelf."

Robin darted into the cold and quickly made her way back to bed with an armload. He moved over to give her ample room.

He pat the opened spot and said, "My sun needs to set."

She told him to get under the covers and instead of crawling underneath with him she laid on top and covered herself with the extra blanket. He threw his arm over her and pulled her in close. He nuzzled his nose into her hair. She could feel his warm breath; in and out, in and out. He was inhaling her. Robin's mind was going a million miles an hour. Nervously, she lay as perfectly still as she could. He began to kiss the nape of her neck. Slowly, kissing, breathing.... She lay there in shock, remaining completely still, not knowing what to do. Suddenly she felt a drip.... A tear? It rolled down her back. Tommy buried his face in behind her, and softly he began to weep. She spun around so she could look at him. There was barely any light in the room; only what came from the street through the high dorm windows. She could see his cheeks were wet. The light caught his face with a soft silver glow yet suddenly all she saw was anguish. Robin's heart was now pounding with concern. "Oh my gosh Tommy what's wrong?"

It was hard for him to hold back tears; it was hard to speak. His breathing was broken and labored. He sat up, cradling his knees. Struggling for words, struggling for air.

"I want... I need to... I have to tell you what happened... What happened to me back in fifth grade."

4

Now That's Funny

Daisy had spoken to Pauly a few times over the past year and had decided to go and visit him in the city during winter break. She didn't want to tell Robin, who would tell Tommy. She knew they would make a big deal of it and put together a series of double dates. She was *not* interested in that. Daisy had only one night to spare, and she was interested in just one thing. This happened to fall on the same night that Robin was going in to visit Tommy. Daisy planned to text Robin all night to keep tabs on her exact whereabouts, but Robin texted Daisy first, *"Just got into the city. There are Santas everywhere. Tommy calls it SantaCon!"*

On Daisy's train ride in, she texted Robin back, *"LOL, are you drinking already?"* Daisy figured out she was on the train just behind Robin's. There was a huge group of Santas a few rows in front of her (though she dare not mention). Instead, she sat back and relaxed, ironing out the evenings plan in her head. She needed to define things with Pauly.

Pauly lived at home with his parents in a beautiful luxury apartment on Bond Street in the Village, about five blocks from Washington Square Park. Once the doorman found Daisy's name on the list, he held the immense glass door open for her. She took the elevator to the eleventh floor and then ventured down a narrow corridor finally spotting the correct door. *"Look for a huge brass door knocker. I like big knockers,"* Pauly had previously texted.

With a loud bang, the heavy brass pineapple shape slipped out of Daisy's hand. Promptly, as if she was right there behind it, a woman opened the door.

"Pauly, your friend is here!" she immediately yelled down a hallway over her right shoulder. Her hands were busy with a dust rag in one and polishing spray in the other.

Daisy stepped inside. "I'm Daisy," she said, wiggling out of her backpack placing it on the floor. "I'm sorry I didn't realize that door knocker was so heavy!"

"No worries, any lighter and no one would hear it." Turning her head, again the woman screamed down the hall. "Pauly, your friend is here! Honestly, like this is the Taj Mahal or something." She turned to walk away but suddenly stopped herself. "Oh, please call me Rose." And then with a tilt of her head, gesturing down the hallway, "His mom."

"Hey!" Pauly shouted as he slid out of an opened door at the far end of the hall. Then, with a few giant steps, he ran and slid right up to Daisy. Standing there in beaming white socks, he said, "Just polished floor!"

The apartment was a spacious open floor plan with high ceilings and dark Austrian-style wood flooring. Most of the walls were white with gilded framed paintings centered on each. The street-side windows stretched from floor to ceiling, and light flooded the whole apartment. It was like a museum. Every room had either a fireplace or a terrace.

Pauly grabbed Daisy's backpack and threw it on the bed in the first guest room just down the hall on the left. "Follow me!" He then began to slide down the remainder of the hallway, making his way to his room.

Pauly's room was in transition from kid to college student.

"Don't mind the mess, we just had the room painted."
Two of the walls were royal blue, one was beige, and the fourth

was all windows.

"I like the blue," Daisy said, catching the smell of fresh paint.

One side of his room was set up like any regular bedroom: a queen-size bed, matching end tables, and two dressers. A giant yellow Pikachu pillow sat half buried in his unmade bed, peeking out like a spy. The room was huge. The other side of it was set up like an office. A high-tech glass desk was pushed up to a wall, and two blue leather chairs sat on either side.

"Check this out," Pauly said. He slid up to the desk and pushed a button underneath it. The edge of the desk lit up like the inside of a limo. It changed from neon blue to purple then to green. He clicked it off. "I can make it any color I want, and sync it to music. Cool huh?"

"Really cool!" Daisy agreed, and she wandered toward the wall of windows. Placed at a curious angle in front of the windows, sat a beautiful red velvet chaise lounge. Scattered on it was a pile of framed photos, waiting to be hung. Daisy picked up the top one from the pile.

"Shit, you met Jerry Seinfeld?" she asked.

"Yup, a few months ago he was working on a fundraiser with my dad. He came here for drinks. I was awestruck *and stoned,*" he whispered, leaning into her. "I barely remember our encounter. That photo is the two of us standing right here." Pauly threw open the terrace door and jumped outside. A rush of cold air came in.

"But that was this past summer and it was much nicer out!" He jumped back in and slammed the door shut. "Brrrr!" he said, shaking in his big white socks.

"All these windows? How do you..." Daisy began, but

45

Pauly jumped to the corner of the room where he pushed another button, and the mini blinds embedded between the panes of glass began to slowly cascade down.

"I've never seen you so animated. Are you stoned now?" she asked.

"Maybe," he said. And he moved closer and closer to her as the room grew dark.

Daisy threw up her hands. "Wait, what's the plan? You are supposed to wine and dine me," she demanded.

"Relax!" he said, sliding two steps back. "I made reservations at Carbone. A killer Italian place, about seven blocks from here. Rez is at 7:00."

"Nice!" she said, now making her way towards the hall. "That should be enough time." Looking down at her watch. "I'm wearing a pretty dress. I hope you'll put on something smart?"

"Of course, milady," he said in a borrowed accent as he bowed to her.

Oh my God..., she thought, walking down the hall to her guest room. *He's so stoned!*

It was only a four to five block walk to most of Pauly's classes at NYU from his apartment. He pointed that out as they walked by one of his buildings on their way to Carbone. "Does anything come difficult to you?" Daisy asked.

"Whatd'ya mean?" he challenged her.

"Well I don't know.... It just seems like everything in your world is perfect. You live in the best city in the world. Your folks are *freaking* loaded. You seem to have everything you want...." She paused. "Yeah, I know it's not fair for me to say, I don't know you that well, but shit! And you want to be a comedian?"

"Pretty funny right?" he answered back. "I'll say this: it's no walk in the park!" (He hoped she'd notice the sign for Washington Square Park directly in front of them and think him funny, but she didn't.) He continued, "Trying to be a comedian, a stand-up, a funny guy? Well, people always expect you to lift them up and make them laugh. And I'm not talking about when I'm just in front of a microphone either. Ya know how hard that is?"

"Actually no. I guess I don't," she said. "You were pretty darn good at the Gravity Café last year!"

"Thanks, but I'm taking business classes too. Comedy…? I think luck has a lot to do with it. I try to pull material from everyday life, and my perfect little life.... Well, let's just say that I'm always stirring things up for the sake of material."

Daisy felt a bit guilty for calling him out and thinking he's a spoiled brat. They continued silently past a few more NYU buildings. "I'm just gonna text my dad, to let him know I got in alright." She pulled out her phone and texted Robin instead, *"What are you wearing?"*

Robin texted back, *"I'm a green elf, Tommy is St. Nick! I'll send a photo."*
Daisy was now on the lookout, she flipped up her coat collar and pulled the fur ears of her bomber hat down.

"That's attractive!" Pauly quipped.

"Shut up," she said, giving him a shove. "It's cold!" She glanced at the photo on her phone and quickly tucked it back in her coat pocket, not taking a chance that Pauly might see that Tommy and Robin were in the same vicinity. *Tonight, he's all mine*, she thought.

Daisy pulled her hat off as they entered the restaurant. It was warm and inviting. Individual candles flickered at every possible seat. A plate of something sizzling and garlicky was carried past them, and the aroma was tantalizing. The maître d' ushered them to a table in the back against a crumbly brick wall. The next table over was set up for an about to be flambéed dessert. As Pauly helped Daisy out of her coat, he nodded toward the table and said. "Now that's my kind of calorie! If you dare, I believe we need to order that ahead of time. Shall I?" Then after handing her coat to the maître 'd, he stood motionless, staring at her while she fluffed at her hem.

Looking up she said, "Let's do it!" Taken by the way he stared at her, she continued, "Dessert I mean."

He cut her off. "You look beautiful."

Much to her surprise, he was a perfect gentleman through-out the entire evening. He ordered a ridiculously expensive bottle of wine, they split a "Fruits de la Mer" appetizer, and he even ordered a specific dinner entree for her.

"Trust me, you've never had a lasagna like this!" he said.

Daisy was delighted.

On the walk back home, he lit up a half joint and handed it off to Daisy.

"I'm OK," she said, waving her hand in front of her.

"My folks are having a little party back home. We'll just brush through the crowd and make our way back to my room."

Chilled to the bone, they hurried through the front door of the apartment. Daisy waved at the crowd in the living room. Catch-ing Rose's attention, she mouthed "good night." Then she ducked into the guest room.

Pauly made his way down the hall and into his room, think-ing, *Ah she's going to slip into something more comfortable.* He snickered to himself.

He set his desk to red and synced it to his jazz playlist. He pushed the other button by the windows and watched the lights of the city extinguish. He made his bed and put Pikachu in the closet. He ditched his dinner jacket and pants, and changed from his shirt and tie into a t-shirt and shorts. He thought, *No, it'll be sexier if I wear something half unbuttoned.* He put his pants and dress shirt back on. He lay down on the bed with his half-unbuttoned shirt.

After lying there a while he wondered, *What is taking her?* He buttoned back up and tiptoed down the hall. Looking over his shoulder to make sure no one took notice, he tapped lightly on her door. Hearing rustling on the other side, with his lips pressed into the door frame, he whispered, "I'm ready when you are, come on down."

Hurrying back, he wished he had his white socks on so he could have slid his way down the hall. Closing the door behind him, he jumped on his bed and lay flat on his back. He halfway unbuttoned his shirt again, pressing it partially open to expose as much of his chest as possible. He unbuttoned and unzipped his pants. *Nah, I'll let her do that,* he thought. He zipped back up. He lay there waiting, and waiting…

He fell asleep.

* * *

The next day, Daisy was gone before anyone else was up. She had slipped a note under Pauly's bedroom door. Out in front of the apartment building she hailed a cab. "Rockefeller Center, please."

All along, she had planned—that next day—to go and photograph the tree and the ice-skaters.

The day was cold and windy, but it was also clear and bright. By the time she got there, it wasn't crowded just yet; making it perfect to shoot. She had planned to make greeting cards with some of her images, having already made a few Thanksgiving cards with the foliage and nature shots she took hiking with Robin. They sold like hotcakes at the college art fairs.

It was just over a year since the infamous Friday night after Thanksgiving of their freshman year, shortly after Daisy and Pauly first met. That night Pauly had come up for an open mic night at the Gravity Café, and Daisy had agreed to go and watch.

After his routine, they had hit a diner for a late bite. Pauly had left his wallet in his car parked at the café, so besides their meal, he couldn't buy anything at the liquor store afterward either.

"Let's get tequila!" he said.

"No way. I hate that shit. It's beer or nothing," Daisy demanded, placing two six-packs and her fake ID on the counter.

Earlier at the diner, Pauly had convinced Daisy to let him spend the night. "It's such a long drive, Robin won't mind. Pleeeeeasse!" Pauly looked like a lost puppy.

"Fine."

Back at the dorm, one six-pack later, Daisy had a good buzz on and she slipped up by saying, "Robin's at some cheesy hotel with her mom."

That's all Pauly needed to hear. He cracked another can and made a deal with her: "If I put on the TV and it's a car commercial, you have to guzzle this whole can." He handed her a can. "If it's a beer commercial, then I have to!"

"And if it's neither?"

"We just moderately drink and wait for the next commercial."

It was a car commercial and she guzzled it in record time, (though she spilled a third of it on herself). With their backs up against the bed, there they sat, on the floor laughing hysterically. Pauly had insisted she change her beer-soaked shirt. He helped her

50

to stand up and in doing so he helped her right out of her shirt too. Next, he unhooked her bra and his lips were all over her.

Feeling pretty reckless herself, Daisy thought, *Oh what the hell.*

He pushed her on the bed, peeled off her pants and had his way with her.

The next morning, he was gone. Daisy rolled over and saw nothing but empty beer cans on the floor. No note, no nothing. Just cans.

"Shit," she whispered, with no one to hear.

That rat bastard texted her a few weeks later, *"Wazzz up?"* She texted back, *"Who's this?"* Then he tried to make contact a few more times. Daisy would blow him off every attempt.

"I think Pauly has another gig at the Café," Robin would mention.

Daisy made sure she wasn't available, "Mid-terms, no way!"

Daisy had never told Robin what happened. She knew Tommy was buds with Pauly. It was just a sticky situation. She kind of blamed herself for letting him take advantage of her. *One day, I'll figure out a way to tell Robin,* she thought.

5

Confession

"Fifth grade?" Robin questioned.

Tommy flung his legs over the side of the bed and pressed both hands up against his eyes, wiping outward away from his face. Drawing both hands slowly down under his chin almost in a prayer position, he looked up in despair and became solemn.

At that precise moment, Robin was so overwhelmed with concern for Tommy, she couldn't breathe. She lay there motionless.

He gazed at Robin intensely. Offering her his hand he pulled her up right next to him. The seriousness of the situation obliterated any lingering drunkenness.

Apprehensively, Robin rose from the bed, and with a long cleansing breath, she paused in front of Tommy. She released his hand from hers and said softly, "Let me just put on your desk lamp; I can't see shit."

Abruptly, Tommy got up and lunged toward his mini fridge. Flinging the door open, he grabbed two bottled waters. He handed one to Robin and cracked open his own as he plopped back down on the bed. Now with a determined look on his face, he took his own cleansing breath and began.

"I was an altar boy working toward my Confirmation. Every Sunday after mass, it was my responsibility to collect and replace all the candles."

Robin already had a bunch of questions, but she dared not break into the story about to unfold. She gulped some water and propped a pillow behind her back. She was completely ready to absorb his words, knowing—even without asking—that this night was going to answer all the questions she's had all along.

"There were a lot of candles. Gigantic ceremonial candles.... Candles just for lighting the incense.... Prayer candles and long thin pillar candles that lined the altar. If they became shorter than three inches, they had to be pulled—they wouldn't last through another mass. We had a box back in the kitchen where I put the candle ends, and every few months when the box was full, they would be melted down and made into new candles."

Tommy stood up and slowly paced back and forth across his room. He continued. "I was planning to make my Confirmation by the end of May, and I had missed a few of the necessary classes, so anything extra I could do, I would. Monsignor Stoyer offered me candle duty, accepting it in place of any of my missed classes. I remember being excited about the opportunity. It seemed like an easy way to meet the requirements. I can almost hear him...

'Son, during this time, if you behave well and prove to me you have sufficient knowledge, enabling yourself to understand the love of Christ, then in faith and with devotion, I will acknowledge and accept your Sacrament of Confirmation by May's end.'

Tommy paused in front of his bookcase, rhythmically tapping the top shelf, trying to collect his thoughts; recalling in detail that tainted moment of time.

"One Sunday, Monsignor Stoyer asked me if I'd like to learn how to make the candles. He'd be making them that evening and suggested I come over to the rectory after dinner.... So I did."

* * *

Around the back corner of the rectory, there was a garden and a small patio off a kitchen porch. Surrounded by a waist-high white picket fence, it was a private and peaceful spot. The house itself was an old white painted colonial with weathered black shutters. It was just steps from the church's large parking lot amidst a cemetery that ribboned throughout the back property. Out front, a sidewalk lined the street, conveniently connecting everything together.

Tommy opened the gate and stepped through. "Monsignor?" he called out, announcing his arrival.

"Hello, son," the Monsignor greeted back, startling Tommy who hadn't noticed him. He sat on the porch swing off to the right where he had been patiently waiting. He rose and gestured for Tommy to follow. Tommy went through the back kitchen door as the Monsignor held it open.

In the far corner of the kitchen sat a huge old potbelly stove. On top of that sat a large copper pot containing the remnants of many candles already beginning to melt. To the left, on an old gray Formica countertop stood a series of antique candle molds. They were lined up like revolutionary soldiers ready to move. The back row had two tall molds with built-in handles that could produce a dozen candles each. They stood firm in their old wooden frames. The middle row contained shorter and wider tin molds while the front line was composed of four chunky molds made from timber, for votives. A fat spool of waxed twine, a pair of scissors, and a pile of long thin wooden dowels lay on old newspapers next to the army. All seemed to be in order.

The Monsignor held a set of long narrow metal tongs. Handing them off to Tommy he ordered, "Remove the old wicks as they appear. One by one they will eventually float up to the top of the melted wax."

Tommy stood there doing what he was told, plucking out old wicks, and placing them on the newspaper. He could hear the Monsignor in the background, banging around a few bottles and adding ice to a glass. He poured himself a drink and offered Tommy a soda, placing a bottle of orange fizz on the kitchen table directly behind him.

"When you are here, in my home, you don't have to be so formal. I'm OK with you calling me M.S."

"For Monsignor Stoyer?" Tommy questioned.

"Precisely."

Once all the wicks were removed and the wax mostly melted, MS opened up a door to the right of the stove revealing a bedroom.

Still standing at the stove, Tommy peered in. It was dark, and he was barely able to make out a bed against a back wall across the room. Framed photos sat upon a dimly lit dresser against another wall on the left just past a window. His eyes adjusted. The window shade was drawn, leaving only an inch of light. The sun was setting and through that inch, a bright yellow beam cast across the floor. In it, newly disturbed dust particles swirled about.

M.S. walked into the dark room and disappeared to the right. Tommy heard another door open, and a light turned on. "Tommy, come and look at this," he beckoned.

The closet was huge. A long wooden rod on the left-hand side ran the length of the closet. It held all kinds of liturgical garments and clerical clothing. There were golden vestments and embroidered cassocks. One section held everything black, but there on the end wall—as if on display—hung a silken white Ferraiolo. It gleamed in the minimal light that the single exposed ceiling bulb offered. Tommy wanted to ask about it (having never seen M.S. wear it), but taking notice or wandering any further into the closet didn't seem proper. The closet had a stagnant smell: musty and smoky, reminding him of the hippy shop at the mall.

M.S. stepped deeper into the closet, creating room for Tommy. With a wave of his hands, he presented a series of higher shelves. There, out of Tommy's reach, was a copious array of small ornate bottles. Some of the bottles looked so old he assumed it must be some kind of antique collection. M.S. reached for a few bottles, pausing and thinking as he pulled each one down, one by one. Cupping them in his hands and holding them against his chest, he hurried past Tommy. Delicately, he placed them all on an end table next to the bed. Clicking on a lamp, he intently looked at each bottle, eventually choosing just three. He brought them into the kitchen. Tommy diligently followed. He twisted off the cap of the first bottle and held it up to Tommy's face.

"This is Cedarwood; smell it." As Tommy inhaled, M.S. continued, "I've collected essential oils from all over the world. Every scent takes me to a special place." He grabbed the next bottle. "This is lavender."

Tommy took a sniff, and M.S. seemed pleased when he saw the look of interest on Tommy's face.

Finally, he opened the third, a dark amber bottle. Tommy couldn't see how much, or if any, oil was even left in it. "This one is Egyptian musk oil." He didn't offer this one to Tommy, he just faced the pot of wax and unscrewed the cap. With the attached dropper, his hand hovered over the hot wax. Suddenly stopping, he stepped back and said, "Here you do it."

He placed the amber bottle in Tommy's left hand and placed the dropper cap in his right.

"There's about a gallon of wax in there, count twenty drops."

Tommy counted while M.S. explained about having beautiful aromas in the air; how it helped people free their minds of trouble, which was necessary if they were coming to worship the Lord.

"When the candles burn, they emit a mild scent. I choose different oils depending on the time of year, and sometimes depending on the mood of the congregation." He laughed. "Last Sunday, the crowd seemed irritated, so I chose to burn some of the lavender candles. It was quite settling."

"Twenty!" Tommy announced.

M.S. took the bottle from Tommy and placed it on the kitchen table next to the orange soda and what looked like a glass of whiskey. By now, whatever ice was in that glass was almost gone. M.S. stirred the wax mixture with the long tongs and waved his hand upward to inhale the aroma.

"Heavenly," he exclaimed. "Another twenty minutes and we'll be ready to pour."

He asked Tommy to hand the bottle back to him, and when he did, he told Tommy to set the cap aside. "Now, hold out your hands."

Tommy did.

MS poured some oil into his hands. He told Tommy to rub his hands together and feel the warmth. "Let the aroma relax your nerves."

Tommy tried.

Now gazing at Tommy, M.S. stepped slowly backward into the bedroom, gesturing for him to follow.

He did.

Backing up towards the bed, MS unzipped his pants. "Please, if you would, with the warmth of your hands, help my mind to ease. Rub the musk oil on my penis. You shall be saved."

Robin gasped.

Tommy banged his fist on the desk. "I mean what the fuck was I supposed to do? My mom was really pissed I missed getting confirmed the year before. I was desperate... I thought this was my only way to make up the classes. If I didn't make Confirmation that year, I wasn't going to be able to go on the summer church trip."

"Oh my God Tommy, I don't know what to say."

Robin reached for Tommy, but he turned his back to her. He hung his head low and whispered, "I'm so ashamed."

It was now starting to get light out. The street lamps that offered the faint glow were off and the morning's warmer light began to soften the room. Robin sat back down on the bed. Speechless, she knew there was absolutely nothing she could say.

Tommy began slowly pacing again, pausing with every turn, reviewing each and every thought before he could continue. He stopped directly in front of Robin, and with almost an apologetic tone he said, "I couldn't tell my parents. M.S. made me promise that I would keep it our little secret. He assured me I'd make Confirmation and he reminded me of *all* the fun things the kids do on the summer trip, which was only a few weeks away."

Chugging the rest of his water, he opened the mini fridge and grabbed another bottle. Looking over his shoulder at Robin, she shook her head and uttered, "No thanks."

Now pacing faster, even his breathing picked up speed. Louder, he continued, "About a month later—just after my fucking Confirmation—M.S. asked another kid to," he held up his hands to make air quotes, "'*help make candles.*' I think that kid spilled the beans. I think that M.S. did more to that kid than to me. I think he *fucked* him up the ass!" With the word '*ass*', he stopped in his tracks. He glanced at Robin with a frightened look. "Word got out, and my parents asked me if anything like that happened to me. But it really didn't... I mean he didn't..." Tommy hung his head, abashed. "He didn't do anything like that to me. I knew M.S. was in big trouble, and I thought by keeping quiet, I got off easy."

"You mean he got off easy!" Robin added angrily.

The tension of the whole conversation suddenly broke. Tommy looked at the floor, shaking his head. He finally sat down next to Robin, and she threw her arm around him.

"At the time, I was unsure that what he did with me was so wrong. I mean... for God's sake, I was only a kid." Then he simply laid his head against Robin. He was spent.

Realizing that the whole conversation started because he had been kissing the back of Robin's neck, he pulled away and looked at her.

"Shit, I'm sorry. Like hours ago, I was making moves on you."

Robin felt herself blush. "Oh, yeah. Ummmmm... Well..." She looked down and laughed at herself. She still had on the green striped leggings and one of Tommy's t-shirts. "How about we to go back to Gramercy. We can get our clothes, find a nice breakfast place, and we can talk—*Really* talk. I have like a zillion questions, and I know you could use a big fat breakfast."

* * *

They had a taxi drop them off at the Waverly Restaurant. It was a busy and blustery winter morning. People hustled about with their faces buried in scarves and turned up collars. St. Joseph's church bell rang a few doors down. Tommy rolled his eyes.

They were lucky enough to get seated right away, so into

a booth they slid. Robin unwrapped her scarf, took off her hat and gloves, and systematically placed them all inside the sleeve of her coat. She then folded her coat and put it next to her in the booth. Tommy drummed his fingers on the table, watching her.

"You're so anal."

"Speaking of anal," Robin couldn't resist... but the look of disgust on Tommy's face made her quickly regret it. "OK, so some other kid let the cat out of the bag. What the heck happened to M.S.?"

Tommy blew into his cupped hands, trying to warm them. The waitress stepped up to the table, and before she even got a word out, Tommy barked, "Two hot chocolates, a western omelet with cheddar, dry whole wheat toast, and instead of home-fries, can I get some of your famous potato pancakes?"

She nodded and then looked down to Robin.

"One of those hot chocolates I assume is for me," Robin said, throwing Tommy a bewildered look. "And can I get a bowl of oatmeal with granola and fresh berries.... *Please?*" She emphasized 'please' to indicate Tommy's rudeness.

"You most certainly can." And away the waitress went.

They leaned in close to make sure no one could hear.

"I'm not sure what happened to M.S., but in keeping my cool, I pretended to not pay attention to what was being said," Tommy explained. "I heard that the police went to the rectory, and all his shit was gone so they couldn't press charges or even question him. *Poof!* He disappeared! They closed the church for two weeks, for a 'renovation.' He used air quotes once again. "I think it was for a big ass investigation. It was so fucking weird. The whole town knew about it, but nobody was talking about it. I mean, I only got what my folks talked about, and half the time it was because

61

I pretended to be upstairs, but in reality, I'd be around the corner eavesdropping. They'd be all like: *'How can we be sure he didn't do anything to Tommy?'* I remember my dad pounding his fists on the kitchen table. *'If that mother fucker laid one finger on my son-!'*

Two steaming hot chocolates were placed in front of them. Tommy wrapped his cold hands around the cup and sat back to gather his thoughts. Then, leaning back in towards Robin again, he continued, "It was crazy, I was scared. Scared my dad would flip out. I had myself pretty convinced that what *did* happen was nothing. I didn't want them to know I cheated to make Confirmation, 'cause that's what it felt like. M.S. was gone, and we were planning to move. Then the story hit the papers. Dad said it was definitely a good time to sell the tire store; he had an interested buyer and he was planning to invest in a dealership. He just chose one in Jersey, instead of Long Island."

Robin then continued with more questions. "OK, so M.S. vanished, and your family relocated. What about you? What he did was not right, and you were so young. Oh my God Tommy—all those years back, you know what he did was wrong, right?"

"Yeah, well now I do.... Of course, I do! But I really buried it. I mean, we didn't even go to church once we moved. Hell, I was happy about that, but I thought, what the fuck did I do all that Confirmation shit for?"

"Well, you *do* think about it though. Like how 'bout last night? That was insane. I never saw so many emotions pour out of you in since, like, *ever!*"

"I know. I do realize I buried it, but sometimes it rears. Wait before you have a field day with that word... I mean... Sometimes it just materializes in my mind. See, I know it messes with me. I don't know what to think. I don't understand some of the emotions that rush in when I do stop to think about it. I'm *afraid* of what I think! Shit Robin, I don't know, it's just fucked up. I do know that anytime I try to get close to someone—like last night—it fucks with me."

"You mean with other girls too, not just me?" Robin inquired.

"Well, yeah, that. But sometimes I think of guys...."

Their breakfast plates were spun in front of them. "Two more cocoas?" the waitress asked.

"That'd be great," Robin answered anxiously.

Tommy sat back again, and this time he put his hands behind his head, filled his cheeks full of air, and slowly exhaled. "Robin, there haven't been any other girls."

"Excuse me?"

"I mean it." He hunkered down low, moving in closer than before. "Robin, I've never been with a girl. I'm a virgin!"

"Get the fuck outta here." Robin looked side-to-side to make sure no one heard her say that.

"I know, I know. It's not normal. Shit, maybe I am fucked up! I just... I don't know... I guess I... Sometimes I wonder if I'm even straight." He took a deep breath and hesitated. "I'm afraid of what I think when I get close to someone, so I just never did!"

"Oh, Tommy, I'm surprised. And I'm a little sad."

"Whoa, don't feel sorry for me!"

"No, no I won't, I mean... Well shit, Tommy, all the fricking years—you never made a move on me? That makes me sad. I know we are and always have been best buds, but shit! I wanted to kiss you like a zillion times!"

Tommy sat back and retreated. "Shit, maybe you should have; maybe that's all it would have taken."

Robin looked down at her bowl of oatmeal. "Crap, our food is getting cold. I think we need to act on this."

"Act on this? What do ya mean?"

Robin hesitated. She didn't look up at Tommy. Instead she busied herself taking a big spoonful of oatmeal. With a full mouth, she began, "Tonight after the show, let's kiss and see what happens."

Now Tommy became engrossed in his omelet. Shoveling in cheesy bites, he giggled and some egg fell from his mouth. "Kiss, kiss? Or Kissssssss." He sang, holding his fork up waving it like a maestro at a crescendo.

"Well, we'll see." Robin said decisively.

The rest of their conversations reverted back to their winter break and the fun it promised. They discussed going to Times Square to take in the sites and getting show tickets from the TKTS booth under the red stairs in Duffy Square. Their plan was to go to Radio City Music Hall and catch the Christmas Spectacular, and then get a nice dinner.

They finished up breakfast, got the check, paid, and hurried away from the table, refreshed and ready to start their day—now in a different kind of light. They were giddy and content, almost like a first date.

He held the door open against a strong chilling wind. Robin walked out of the restaurant howling, "Brrrrrr! I can't wait for summer!"

Tommy had to push hard on the door, forcing it to close behind them. He shrugged up underneath the bulk of his jacket and hooked onto Robin's arm. Proceeding along the sidewalk he said, "I never did get to go on the fucking summer church trip either!"

6

Rum and Done

They got a great deal on show tickets, but they ended up in the very last row, up in the nosebleed section, where they were able lean their heads against the back wall of the building. Bad seats didn't matter; they loved the show, especially the end scene with the live nativity. Robin started to tear up. Looking over at Tommy she said, "I don't know why I'm emotional. This stuff doesn't really matter to me."

"Awe." Tommy grabbed her hand and gave it a squeeze. "It's tradition and it's what Christmas is all about."

"I'm such a softie these days."

"Are you fricking kidding me? You are the strongest, most independent girl I know. I should have gotten you a *rock* charm for your necklace!"

Robin felt through her sweater for her sun charm, confirming it was there. A constant reminder of their endearment, always having it around her neck, made her feel secure.

They decided to head back down toward the Village and grab a bite there. The wind had died down, but it was a bitter cold night. The taxi dropped them on West 4th and Perry Street. As soon as they jumped out of the cab, the restaurant directly in front of them was called Extra Virgin.

"Well, well, well," Robin sarcastically said. "What have we here?"

"Shut up!" Tommy said, tugging on her arm and pulling her in through the front door out of the cold.

With just a twenty-minute wait for dinner, they sat at the bar and in typical fashion, Robin tucked her scarf, hat, and gloves into her sleeve. Tommy cupped and blew on his hands.

"Remind me to buy you a nice pair of gloves," Robin muttered.

Noticing the drink specials, Tommy asked the bartender, "What's a Hot Buttered Rum?"

Batting his eyes, he responded, "Hot apple cider, spiced rum with pat of butter floating on top, rimmed with a cinnamon sugar concoction. It's dreamy!"

"Sounds delish," Then putting up two fingers, Tommy indicated his order.

Robin leaned into him and whispered, "I think, he thinks, you're dreamy."

"Oh my God, stop!" Tommy urged. He grabbed her shoulders and shook her. Then he looked poignantly at her and said, "I'm so relieved I told you. And I'm so sorry for all those years I made you sad."

"Tommy, remember our parking lot prom?" Robin asked.

"Of course, I do. Why?"

"I said it then and I'll say it again now: I don't know what I'm going to do without you, but in here," she tapped on her chest, "I know I'll always have you."

Then from the top of her sweater, she fished out her necklace and dangled the sun charm for him to see. He did the same, unbuttoning the top of his shirt, pulling the collar back, exposing his moon charm.

A waiter sat them at a dining table up against the front window. They watched people scurry past in the frigid air. Across the street, plumes of steam billowed up from the subway grates. The night was still young, the menu looked awesome, and it had just started to snow.

Very full bellies and a bottle of wine later, they decided to walk briskly back to Tommy's dorm. They paused at The Four Faced Liar and popped in.

"Only one," Robin demanded.

"A shot of what?" Tommy said leaning up against the bar.

"How about rum? We should stick with rum."

Moments later, out the door, arm and arm, they met the frosty street again. Tommy backed up a few steps and nodded toward the business next door.

"Seriously? The Pink Pussy Cat?" Robin asked.

"Come on; it'll be fun, Let's just look."

They could hardly contain themselves passing the blow-up doll in the front window, and they snickered when they walked into the heart of the store. Glaring at one another in amazement, they wondered, *What the heck is some of this stuff?*

Circling back past an assortment of dildos towards the front door, Robin stopped at the counter. "I'll take one of those." She pointed to the shelf behind the over-pierced, and over-tattooed cashier.

With bag in hand, Robin laughed looking back at Tommy as he followed her outside. Tommy practically slammed the door shut saying, "A penis candle? Is that supposed to be some sort of joke?"

Robin's face dropped. "Shit I didn't... I wasn't thinking... Look!" She jammed her hand into the bag and pulled it out. She waved it in front of him shouting, "This, is funny as shit!" (The giggling couple that walked past them thought so too.) "I *so* didn't think of it, the way you are... or wherever you went with it. Don't take it so personally! SHIT! Just 'cause I know... I'm sorry." She stopped and faced him. "Tommy lighten up! I can't stop from being plain old silly, now can I? I honestly meant nothing by it."

"You're right."

He grabbed the penis candle from Robin's hand and delicately placed it back in the bag, pushing it back at her.

"Have I always been this sensitive?" he asked.

"Yes, as a matter of fact, you have. And that's what I love about you!"

Still facing him, Robin pulled both of his hands out of his coat pockets, holding them and looking deeply into his eyes. "Please know I will never speak a word of this to anyone—I promise. If it's your secret, it's my secret. I'm sorry."

"No, I'm sorry," he said, letting go of just one of her hands and they continued down the sidewalk.

"No, I'm sorry," she laughed.

Just two blocks from his dorm, it was only 9:00 at night. They were exhausted from the arduous night before, but this was Robin's last night in town and they weren't about to let it fade. They stopped at a liquor store.

Hand in hand, Tommy swung Robin's like two kids in a candy shop. "What should we get?"

"How about rum, we should still stick with rum," she chuckled.

* * *

The lime fell out of the bag that was tucked under Tommy's arm, as he fumbled with his keys. "Don't drop the bottle!" Robin urged, setting down the six-pack of Diet Coke to offer a hand. "You have ice, right?"

Robin hung up her coat and tucked everything neatly into

her sleeve while Tommy answered back with a clang of ice cubes and the fizz of a just cracked soda can.

"I only have these huge tumblers; they're gonna be big ass drinks."

"Extra lime in mine then, please."

She kicked off her shoes as he handed her the tumbler. She plopped herself down and spun around in his desk chair. "You really need a nice comfy chair or something fluffy in here."

"Fluffy?"

"Yes, fluffy," she joked.

Sipping her drink, she continued to spin herself around and around with one foot.

Tommy caught the edge of the chair and stopped her mid-spin. He looked down at her and pulled the drink away from her lips, placing it on the small end table by the bed. He held out his hand inviting her to stand. She did.

On the top shelf of his desk, he tapped a small round device, and music came from the speakers on either side of his room.

"Classical? You listen to classical?"

"When I study, I do. I was cramming last week. I forgot what was queued-up."

He leaned over to change it and Robin pushed his arm away.

"Leave it."

For endless seconds, they stood there in the middle of the room, facing each other from inches apart. Tommy held both his hands up, like a mime in a box. Without touching, Robin mimicked him. He slowly waved his left hand down in a circle. She followed. He waved his right the same. She followed again.

Excited and nervous, Robin thought he would hear her

heart pounding out of her chest. Tommy gripped the bottom hem of her sweater on both sides. He gazed at Robin like he was sending a message. As if in a trance, she slowly raised both arms up towards the ceiling. He pulled her sweater up and over her head, tossing it to the side.

"Wait," he said, stepping back. "Stay there."

Over by the door, she heard the rustling of a bag. Then Tommy walked back next to Robin where she had remained motionless. He reached behind her as he clicked off the desk lamp. The room was suddenly black. With a flick of a match, there on the end table was the penis candle. As he held a match above it, he couldn't help but laugh and Robin joined in. "That's gotta hurt," she said.

The wick caught the flame, and now the room gained a flickering hint of light.

Tommy stepped right back to his position and gazed upon Robin again, willing her with his mind. One by one, Robin delicately unbuttoned his shirt, eventually pulling it off from around his broad shoulders, allowing it to fall to the floor. She pursed her lips and blew out a restless breath.

Tommy gently set both his hands on Robin's hips. He tucked his fingers in around the edge of her jeans. Sliding in, he unbuttoned them, unzipped them, and pulled her jeans to the floor, holding each pant leg firmly, so she could step out one at a time.

He stood and Robin again mimicked him. Unbuttoning, unzipping and holding each pant leg so he too could step out.

There they stood with only a whisper of light. Nervous. Anxious. Breathless.

"Wait," Tommy said again. "Open the drawer behind you. There are some condoms there."

"I'm good. I'm on the pill."

"Really?"

"Really. Since like 7th grade. It regulates my period and—"

"That's good, I don't need to know any... I mean, I'm good," he said as he cut her off.

"Where were we?"

Robin reached behind her and snapped her bra off. It fell to the pile on the floor. She took one of Tommy's hands, kissed the inside of his palm and then placed it on her breast. She followed suit with his other hand. With his thumbs, he softly rubbed Robin's nipples. They hardened and she arched her back pushing into his touch. He dropped to his knees and he began kissing her navel, slowly working his way up, licking and kissing her, pausing at each breast and then moving up to her neck. Robin groaned.

With his arms behind her, he slid them down her thighs and he lifted her up. She wrapped her legs around him. She clung to him as he stepped forward, gently placing her on his desk. He kissed her deeply now. Robin's hands were all over him. Settling on his hips, she slid her hands down, working his underwear off... Squirming and groaning.

At the side of the desk there was a thud. They broke away from one another, realizing they knocked Tommy's laptop to the floor.

Tommy lifted Robin again. He spun around and carried her across the room. With one arm, he ripped back the bed covers and gently laid her down.

"I'll be right back," he said, stepping out of his half-off underwear, making his way to the bathroom.

Robin pulled the sheet up over her head and lay there ecstatic and aroused, thinking to herself, *"Holy shit I can't believe this is about to happen!"*

Before he shut the light off behind him, she could see his erection as he came out of the bathroom. She thought she would explode right there.

Approaching the bed, he hesitated at its side for just a moment.... Then he pulled the sheet back away from her. With the rush of cold air, she let out a playful squeal. Grabbing her underwear at both sides, he slid them down and around her ankles as she squirmed. He climbed on top of her, keeping pressure on his knees like he was afraid he'd squish her. She lifted her legs, inviting him in as he passionately kissed her. He kissed her neck... He licked behind her ears.... He was about to push into her, but suddenly he withdrew.

A flicker of the candle had illuminated her sun charm as it lay still on her moist skin. He pulled back and kneeled on all fours, hovering over her.

"Robin," he softly spoke. "I don't know if I can do this."

"Like hell you can't!" she roared.

Throwing her arms down at her sides she then questioned, "What's wrong?"

"Robin, you're my best friend. I can't ruin that."

Now withdrawing herself, she sat up and asked, "You've heard of friends with benefits, right?"

"Well yes, but this is different."

"How so?"

"Seriously Robin," he said. "You know what we have isn't normal. Nobody has a friendship like ours. I can't take a chance and lose you. You know: you are my sun and I am your moon.... That! Nobody has that. That's all us!"

Robin sat at the edge of the bed next to Tommy, their thighs touching—still lustfully warm. She ran her fingers through her hair and tucked it behind her ears. She abruptly stood up.

"I got this."

Tommy remained sitting on the bed. She leaned over him unhooking his necklace from behind his neck, allowing her breasts to rub across his lips as she fumbled with the latch. She slid her leg up in between his legs, pushing up against him. She then reached around behind her neck and unhooked her necklace. She placed the two of them out of sight on a coat hook.

"OK, so you're an actor," she began. "Who should I be?" She handed him his drink and she stood there, naked in front him, sipping from hers.

"What?" he questioned.

"You don't want to do this cause I'm Robin, so make me somebody else!"

She walked over to her coat and pulled her scarf out from her sleeve. She walked back in front of Tommy and took the drink from his hand, placing it on the table. Then she wrapped her scarf around Tommy's eyes.

"You are crazy!" he said.

Robin pushed Tommy down.

"Lay on the bed and think of anything, but just don't think of Robin. I'm on a mission here. Remember at breakfast I said I think we need to act on this?"

"Yeah?"

"Well, consider this *Act One*. Besides, how else are you ever going to know what it's like?"

"So, you want me to pretend you're not Robin? Aren't you a little insulted?" he asked.

"Que Sera Sera," she said. "But I actually do understand,

and appreciate it. Hell, the last thing *I* want to do, is screw up our friendship too. Consider this a favor. Besides, you already got me all worked up and really, I don't mind…." She tightened the scarf. He had inched his way back up, "Just mentally detach and let's have some fun with it." She pushed him down again

Classical music filled the room and the candle had burned low enough that it no longer looked like a penis. Robin was a little relieved.

Tommy lay there quietly, blindfolded and baffled while Robin topped off their drinks. She allowed him to sit up so he could take a few sips.

Watching him sip, she realized that she, too, had to detach. What she once wanted with Tommy so long ago—and even recently—was not in the cards. She wasn't sad though; she knew she'd always have Tommy as her dearest friend.

Not allowing herself to get caught up in her own thoughts, she pushed him flat, climbed on top, and began kissing him. It was entertaining watching him squirm while he had the scarf on. It was fun now. She straddled him and rocked gently back and forth, kissing his chest and his neck, pausing to take a sip of her drink.

"Now you can't move at all with what I'm about to do," she said.

"Umm, OK?"

She sipped her drink, sucked out an ice cube, and placed it in the middle of his chest.

"Aah, that's cold."

"It'll melt fast," she said, "Now you can't let it slide off your chest. You have to remain perfectly still until it melts. Got it?"

"Got it."

She sucked out another ice cube and slowly peeled herself

off him, making sure the cube on his chest didn't move. Delicately, she slid to the foot of the bed. She stroked him with a firm grip and then took him into her mouth. With her tongue, she spun the ice cube around his penis. He moaned. And from under his breath he whispered, "How is this even fair?"

Saying nothing, Robin continued. This seemed to liven things up, but not a minute later the ice cube was gone. The initial sensation and then the complete warmth of her mouth made him completely hard. He moaned more.

She straddled him again and pushed him inside her. Throwing her head back, she got caught up in the moment and began to grind hard on him. As a small puddle ran down his side, she stopped briefly, bent down, and sucked up what little was left of the ice on his chest. Full of fervor, she then thrust her hips forward and paused to let herself get lost in her orgasm. Squirming in the whirlwind of it all, she adjusted her position, picked up speed, and grinded on him even harder. In a final rapturous moan, he pushed hard up into her and came.

Like hot molten lava, she smoldered down on him and slowly rolled off to the side.

Bleary and satisfied, the first minute passed. But in the silence of the next minute, Robin's mind reactivated and her thoughts raced. *My God, will this affect our friendship? Did I just kill what we do have? Could this make him straight if he is gay? Can I... Do I even want to win him over?*

Caught between the physical desire for Tommy and her sudden mental anguish, she realized if she succumbed to her thoughts, she'd certainly exhume her old feelings: the feelings she buried on prom night when she thought she'd lose her best friend by kissing him.

We're BFFs, like soul mates. It's not worth the price of our friendship. No one has that.

She needed to clear her mind, let it go…. Again. After all, it was just a favor, for a friend.

Abruptly, she leaned up on her elbow and snickered. "You can take that scarf off if you want now."

He slid it up and over his head. Toying with her, he laughed, "Who are you?" Then he wrapped his arms around her and pulled the covers up around them.

7

The Door Opened

Morning came rushing in with the sound of sleet hitting the high dorm windows. Tommy glanced at the clock. It was almost not morning.

"It sounds miserable out," Tommy whispered. Looking at Robin, he realized she was still sound asleep. With silent precision, he gently inched out of the bed.

About a half-hour later, Robin woke. Tommy had just come out of the shower.

He stood in front of the sink with a towel wrapped around his waist. She watched him shave through the partially opened door, which allowed his clean fresh scent to escape with the damp air. She breathed it in. Many times, she'd seen him half clothed or in a bathing suit, but it never felt like this. She yearned for more of him. She wanted to beckon him back into the warm bed. She wanted to melt all over him, again.

She put the pillow over her head and willed herself to stop thinking about him.

"Hey, you're up," he said, noticing the twitching under the covers. He pushed the door all the way open with his foot.

She couldn't resist.... She spun to her side and leaned up on one arm, slowly pulling the covers off her shoulder to expose one breast.

"Act two?"

"Are you crazy? I'm good... I mean I'm great.... Last night was great. I mean I'm phenomenal!" He grasped his towel to make sure it wouldn't fall off and scurried over to her. He sat on the bed, covered her back up, and kissed her forehead.

"So, who was I?" she asked, looking up at him. "I promise I won't be offended. Like I said last night, I get it. We're BFF's and you don't want to screw with that. But who?"

"Honestly, no one, I thought of absolutely no one. Per your request, I just emptied my mind. Having never done that, I didn't know what to expect and... Well... You're good at that!"

"I am!" she concluded, grabbing for his towel, trying to undo his grip.

He jumped off the bed and ran into the bathroom. She watched his bare ass fly through the room. He shut the door as she lay laughing with the towel dangling from her hand.

"Are you sure?" she yelled.

He cracked the door back open and peered out. "I'm perfect."

She dropped the towel, threw the pillow back over her head, and thought, *Yes, yes you are.*

* * *

The final plan for their time together was to get to Rockefeller Center to see the tree. Robin had to catch a 5:30 train back to Jersey later that evening.

"I promised mom I'd be home for dinner," she said.

They bundled up. This time Tommy remembered to wear gloves—holes and all.

"They're all I could find!" he said feebly.

Robin rolled her eyes, pulling his knit hat down over his ears like a mother would. "You're pathetic," she said.

The sleet had turned to snow by the time they arrived at Rockefeller Center. The sidewalks were slick underfoot. They clutched each other as they gingerly walked among the iconic trumpeting angels towards the famous tree.

Tommy nudged Robin. "It's not going to be weird for us, after last night, right?"

"I won't let it," she said, nudging him back.

"I'm glad we did it. You really put my mind at ease."

"No, Tommy, you put your own mind at ease. I know you still have some figuring out to do, but I think you'll be alright."

"Have you *been* with a lot of guys?" he asked.

She blushed and then peered at him. "Two," she said.

"Including me?"

"Nope."

He nudged her again. "How have you never told me any of this? We talk about everything!"

"Well one was more recent and one was a while ago.... You weren't really around."

"When have I not been around?"

"Oh, please! Back in high school, you were all busy with the plays you were in. And now? Come on, you know we have NOT been able to hang out that much."

"OK, OK, but it's not like we are within walking distance anymore."

They turned the corner and they could see down onto the skating rink. It was mobbed. Dodging tourists taking selfies, weaving their way through the crowd and continued toward the tree.

"Who was your first?" Tommy asked.

"Trust me, you don't want to know."

"Why not? You know my first!" he boasted.

"Ha ha." She snapped sarcastically.

He nudged her again. Losing her step this time, she

knocked into a passerby. Now she was a little irritated.

"*Fine*! I'll tell you, but just promise me you will wait a whole minute after I say, before you comment." She dropped his arm, sidestepped for balance, and pushed up her sleeve to expose her watch.

"Ummmmm, wow. OK?" Tommy said with concern.

She faced him, looked down at her watch, and then back up at him making sure he could see her watch too. When the minute hand hit twelve, she announced, "Matt Brown."

Tommy pressed his lips together filling his cheeks with air. His eyes widened as he threw his hands up in the air then landing them back down on his head. If he were playing charades anyone would guess: "OMG!" Or the act of astonishment.

He spun in a circle and stomped his feet. Another passerby looked at him like he was nuts! He paced away and then marched back up to Robin and started loudly tapping his foot watching the seconds tick away. By now, witnessing his little dance, Robin wasn't so worried… It was just too funny to watch.

The minute hand hit twelve and Tommy gasped out, "What the fuck?"

Robin grabbed for his hands, but he pulled away.

"You know I hate that guy, don't you?"

"Of course, I do! Tommy, listen... All those afternoons when you stayed after for the play? Well, Matt was making a play for me. I would go and watch track practice and come on, he was so cute. We flirted all spring! He said he'd always been interested in me, and he pretty much admitted he was jealous of you! When I told him that you and I were just close friends, well that was it. After track practice, we'd hang out and make out. The day I was going to tell you about him was the day you two got into that brawl. He was still jealous of you even though I was with him. But when you both got suspended, that ended it for us too."

"Hummm.... But you hooked up with him... Where? How?"

"Senior rock. Track ended early one day and we had the place to ourselves. I kinda like that rock. He was such a hottie!"

"Ooooooohhh," Tommy howled. "So that's why you freaked out when he and I were sentenced to repaint it!"

"Jeez, I don't know how you remember some of this shit, Tommy."

They relocked their arms and carefully continued around the rink.

"Yup, he was my first," Robin bragged. "Now you tell me, you at least had a first kiss, right? Who was that?

"Scott Baxter."

"*What*?!" She broke away from him, throwing her hands out, astounded. "Ho-lee-crap Tommy! How? Where? When...? Didn't you have an inkling then?"

"Chill!" he demanded. "It was, if you can believe, at an after-school rehearsal. The two of us were behind the curtain in the back of a set. He came right up to me and just laid one on me! I was shocked, but I also didn't push him off. We basically couldn't look at each other the rest of the year. But I did think about him... A lot. It was still confusing though."

Robin reached for Tommy's hand as they stepped up close to the base of the famous tree. Simultaneously, they looked up. They stood quietly for a moment, taking in all its sparkling glory.

"Tommy? Do you think you're one hundred percent gay?"

"Robin, I think maybe I am." Then he turned to look at her and he said, "Is that going to be a problem?"

"God no, Tommy," she paused. "But last night.... What

should we make of that?"

"Listen, Robin, that, was fucking awesome. Literally! No regrets from me, ever! You told me to think of nothing and you allowed me to experience sex—great sex!"

He took both her hands and placed them around his neck, like they did on their prom night. Looking at her very matter-of-factly, he said, "Robin I love you, but I don't think I could ever be *in love* with you. Something deep inside just won't let me go there." He paused in deep thought for a moment, "I hope that doesn't hurt you to hear. You will always be in here." He tapped on his chest.

Robin laid her head on his chest where he tapped and she hugged him. "Damn-it, Tommy, I love you too."

The snow stopped and the crowd thickened.

"I'm starving!" Robin said, pushing away from Tommy.

Tommy grabbed her hand. "Let's hit the burger place on 51st."

Scurrying to cross the street, in his best French accent he said, "We have to come back for hot chocolate at *La Maison Du Chocolat*! Zee best place in all of Manhattan for our favorite libation."

"Oh la, la, mon frère!" she said back. "Sounds like you are learning more than just acting, in school. French?"

"Oui. I have an accent class—if you can believe."

* * *

Coming back through Rockefeller Center, passing by the ice-skating rink, Robin said, "Next time, let's skate!"

"Deal!" Tommy replied.

They stopped at the edge of the rink to watch

"And why, a Greek statue as a focal point I wonder?" Robin asked.

"Apparently the Rockefellers liked Greek Gods. This one is Prometheus, bringing fire to mankind. Atlas is around here somewhere too," he answered in a clever tone.

"Oh, look at you? Since when do you like Greek statues?"

"What's not to like? Maybe I'm partial to muscular statuesque men!"

"You are so gay!" Robin sang slapping his shoulder. He clutched her arm and scooted her away towards the street. Throwing a hand up to hail a cab, he looked sideways at Robin and admitted, "I always thought Matt Brown was a hottie too!"

The cab dropped them outside at Penn Station where Robin spotted a street vendor with a table full of winter garments. Tommy tried to rush by, but Robin stopped. She padded through a few piles, finally grabbing a pair of Nordic-looking gloves and a matching scarf. The sign said all items $10. She eyed the vendor.

"I'll give you $15 for two," she said.

The vendor obliged and stuffed them into a bag, while Tommy tugged at her.

"You don't want to miss the train!"

They walked quickly through the station and dropped down a level to New Jersey Transit. Pointing up at the train schedule Robin said, "Look we have like five minutes!"

They walked half way down the platform and Robin forced another stop by a garbage bin. She pulled the gloves from the bag and handed them to Tommy, motioning him to toss out the ones he was wearing. He rolled his eyes but did. Pulling the scarf out of the bag next, standing in front of him, she wrapped it delicately around his neck and gently folded it, so it lay neatly against his jacket. She pet the scarf and looked up into his eyes.

"You know, Tommy, you really are very handsome," she said. "Are you sure you're not straight?"

"Robin, I'm not sure of anything."

The train rumbled up, screeching to a stop. She reached up for him and kissed him knowing that *that* would be the last time she would ever kiss him like that again.

When their bodies separated, he looked down sympathetically at her. Lightly shaking his head, he whispered, "I'm sorry."

"Don't be," she said, shrugging her shoulders. "People would kill for what we do have! But ya can't blame a girl for trying."

She flung her hair and spun on her foot, turning towards the train. Stepping sideways in through the doors, she threw Tommy a nefarious look and shouted, "Remember *my* scarf!" She held it up and waved at him with it.

"I'll call ya tomorrow!" he shouted back.

She disappeared into the crowd of the Jersey-bound train.

8

Take Note

The last few weeks of winter break were different. Robin had spent Christmas with her dad and his *new* girlfriend. He had moved to a Jersey Shore house; so it was a weird scene for Robin to be there... When it wasn't summer.

* * *

"Honey, I'll be fine with Robert and Little Robbie," June explained. "You need to spend some time with your father."

"Whatever, Mom, I'll make it work." Robin replied.

Daisy was excited and busy with a holiday job shooting Christmas portraits at the mall. "Overtime!" she boasted.

The girls hadn't any spare time to spend together. "It's insane! Here we are on break and I see more of you at school."

"I know right?"

* * *

For New Year's Eve, Robin and Daisy decided to stick close to home. June and Robert were planning a lobster feast and it sounded too good to pass up.

"Little Robbie is sleeping at a friend's, and honestly, we'd love to have you girls join us," June offered with excitement.

"Can we drink?" Daisy asked, peering over at her dad leaning on the kitchen counter.

"It's up to June," Robert said shrugging his shoulders, throwing the decision right in June's lap.

"Well, I'm not going to pretend and be stupid, I was a college kid once too." Firing a dirty look at Robert she continued,

"Promise me that neither of you girls will leave this house after the first beer is cracked."

"Promise!" Robin and Daisy both shouted.

On New Year's Eve, they took turns in the kitchen, each coming out with their own concoction or version of a party snack.

Pizza bagels in hand, Daisy announced excitedly, "It's kind of fun drinking and hanging with you guys!"

"Of course it is—you're drinking all our stuff!" Robert laughed. The noise from Times Square was blaring on the television in the background so no one noticed the sound of Robin popping the third bottle of champagne. "I'm still surprised, though.... No boys? No Parties?"

Robin sighed, "Tommy has some BIG party in the city. And I'm *so* not in the mood for the city again."

"Same," Daisy said, holding her glass up to signal Robin, who promptly crossed the room to fill it.

Overfilling the glass, Robin quickly slurped at it trying to catch the overflow. Daisy laughed and snorted so loud that all four of them now howled out in laughter.

Suddenly, at the corner of his eye, Robert caught a glimpse of something. "Crap!" he said and dashed into the kitchen. "A lobster got lose. He's trying to escape from the sink. Stay there... I'll cook them up now. We can feast in about ten minutes."

"I don't even want to think about what's going on in there." Robin said, frowning.

Daisy walked over to Robin. "There, there," she said. And she poured more champagne into *her* glass. They both burst out in laughter again.

"Need help in there, honey?" June called out, rolling her eyes. "These girls really need some food!"

They decided to not bother setting the dining room table. They sat around the living room and stood in the kitchen—snacking, drinking, laughing, and finally devouring lobster. It suited them all just fine.

"We don't need to be *fancy*!" June quipped, swirling her glass. She swirled it so hard that half of her champagne sloshed out and up against Robert's face. Now June—hysterically laughing—began to lick his face.

"Oh gross! Mom, get a room!" Robin chuckled.

"Which reminds me," June began, pulling Robert in even closer. "Robert?"

He placed his arm around June as he announced, "Girls, I'm moving in!"

June grabbed the bottle of bubbly and topped off both his and her glass. Robert glanced to Daisy for approval, but she was distracted in a wrestling match with a lobster claw.

"What?" She said, setting down the set of crackers and licking butter from her fingers. "No seriously, what did you say?"

Robert hesitated and threw a concerned look at June. "Um, June thought it would be a good idea if I move in here this spring."

No response came from Daisy. (Robin, having had such a notion, stood on the sidelines and remained silent.)

Robert continued, "Little Robbie will transfer to this school system. He's quite excited about it...."

Still, nothing came from Daisy. Emotionless, she walked up to the fridge and slowly opened its door, keeping her back to the others.

Robert cautiously continued. "Robbie will take over the guest room, and I plan to expand Robin's room upstairs. I'll add a bathroom and make a suite for the two of you to share." He glanced over to Robin asking. "If that's OK…?"

Robin nodded her head, but widened her eyes in concern for Daisy's lack of enthusiasm.

Daisy had kept her back turned the whole time Robert explained the plan. Almost hiding within the fridge with its open door. Without anyone able to notice, she slowly rocked a bottle of champagne from top to bottom, top to bottom.

Robin grew even more concerned and pushed away from the kitchen table to approach Daisy, but suddenly Daisy spun on her foot, simultaneously popping the cork spraying everyone with champagne.

"Are you kidding me?" she shouted. "That is the best news I've heard in like *forever!"*

June squealed and the four of them stood there in the kitchen, hugging, toasting, laughing, all dripping wet with Champagne.

"I think we missed the ball drop," Robert said, wiping his face with a dish towel.

"Works for me. Best New Year's ever!" June added.

Robin clinked everyone's glass and made a play for the bottle, hoping to be able to douse Daisy, who needed to be equally soaked.

It was after 2:00 in the morning by the time they cleaned up and took turns showering. Robin fell into her big, fluffy queen-size bed, where Daisy had already buried herself.

"Move over rover!" Robin ordered. "Let's talk about our new soon to be suite room!"

"Screw that! Tell me about your weekend with Tommy." But then Daisy stopped herself and anxiously shouted, "Wait!" Rolling her eyes, she continued. "Before you bore me with another story about why you didn't just jump his bones, I should tell you

88

about my weekend, with Pauly!"

"What?" Robin shouted, pushing Daisy right out of bed with her feet. "When the hell did this come about?"

Daisy climbed up from the floor, laughing, and slid back under the covers. "Well, it's kind of a long story. Maybe you should go first."

"Oh no you don't," Robin demanded. "I need to know right now! My Tommy story is a *very* long one, so you first! But let's go downstairs and make some hot chocolate. This sounds like it's gonna take a while."

Already halfway through a bag of marshmallows, they sat at the kitchen table, stirring their hot chocolates and trying to keep their conversation quiet. It was nearly impossible with all the shocking facts and the occasional outbursts of, "OMG!", and of course, loads of laughter.

"You little slut." Robin exclaimed laughing with her nose buried into her mug. She splashed cocoa all over the table.

Thankfully, June and Robert were in June's bedroom on the other side of the house and heard nothing.

Daisy finished up her story, "So that night with him in the city, after dinner, when we got back to the apartment, Pauly lightly knocked on my door. I ignored it and instead constructed a note:

You look for some sex as you tap on my door
Remember last year when you actually did score?
The phone only rang if you needed my floor.
Once was enough, there will be no more!

"I thought about finishing with, *'and I'm not your whore!'* but that was just too brutal. I mean… it's not like it was *all* his doing." Daisy lowered her head looking a bit ashamed.

"That note is brilliant!" Robin said. "I can't believe he did

89

that to you last Thanksgiving! What a dickhead! *And* I can't believe after all this time you never told me!"

"I know, I know, but I thought I would hear from him after the fact. And the more that time passed, the more embarrassed I got."

With her elbows on the table, balancing her head in her hands, Daisy shook her head. "He's a total dickhead when he's drunk or stoned, but that night at dinner," she paused and looked up in thought, "he really was a perfect gentleman, a perfect date in fact. I had a great time with him! The sad thing is: that dude definitely has some issues."

Daisy looked at Robin earnestly and said, "I'm sorry for not telling you. I just didn't want to come between you and Tommy."

"Oh Daisy, I get it, I really do." Robin pushed away from the table. "Speaking of Tommy…." she stood up, walked to the fridge, and pulled out a loaf of bread. "Peanut butter and jelly? This is going to be long."

It was pushing 5:00 a.m. by the time she finished telling Daisy *her* story.

"But you hooked up with him! Holy shit! Are you sure? Like totally sure he's gay?

Robin continued, "In his words… 'I'm not sure of anything.' But then I gave him a final kiss, and the spark was gone. *Poof*! So, I jumped on the train."

They cleaned up the kitchen and silently padded upstairs.

"I think for my New Year's resolution, I'm going to find out who *I* am." Robin said enthusiastically, and she plopped her head into her fluffed up pillow.

In a half-asleep response, Daisy grumbled, "I hate resolutions."

9

Love Bugs

Robin began the second semester of her sophomore year with vigor, deciding to completely immerse herself in her studies and determine exactly what she wants—and what she expects—from a career in Environmental Sustainability. It wasn't so different from high school; she was used to burying her head in her books. She regularly video chatted or texted Tommy, but with him truly off the table and no interest in any one else, she focused on herself and developed a mantra of sorts. Over and over she thought, *Do what I'm passionate about and become a product of that.* The more time she spent buried in her books the more her future seemed to unfurl. Regardless of her classwork, with great interest she began studying alpine plant biodiversity.

"Daisy, did you know that there is a whole host of endangered alpine plants that can help in the treatment of various diseases?"

"Robin, do you know that you are boring the shit out of me?"

Daisy tugged at Robin's shirt. "We need some sun and fresh air. Aren't you supposed to spend time in the woods studying some of this crap?" she asked. "Let's go hike and get a burger at the Otter afterward."

Daisy herself needed to unwind. Most of her spare time had been spent printing photos and making more greeting cards. The sales from the art shows at school, the few shops in town that now carried them, kept her busier than she ever intended.

At the Otter, they sat at a table in the middle of the dining room, surrounded by familiar faces as most of the crowd was

SUNY students.

"Robin, seriously, no one is attracted to a bookworm or a shutterbug. We need to get out more. We're almost half way through college, and we're sitting here dateless on a Saturday night!"

No sooner had Daisy spoken than a waitress approached their table and placed two large draft beers in front of them. "Compliments of the two guys sitting at the corner of the bar."

Robin and Daisy both turned to look. "Do you know them?" Daisy asked.

"I think they're in my Entomology class," Robin said, lifting her glass and giving a slight head nod. Daisy, on the other hand, waved them over.

"Really?" Robin questioned. "You want them to join us?"

"Did I not just remind you it's Saturday, we're dateless and halfway through college?"

As they came up tableside, one of them spun a chair around, straddled it, and immediately sat while the other pulled out a chair and waited for a proper invite.

With a dubious eye roll and another head nod, Robin gestured for him to take a seat. As he sat, he held out his hand, taking Robin's first.

"Hi, I'm Peter."

Another hand shot over the table straight to Daisy. "And I'm Aron, minus one A."

"Minus one A? Do you always introduce yourself like that?" Daisy questioned, returning handshakes.

"I do! It's the Norwegian version of the name, it has no biblical meaning, *AND* it's an icebreaker," he sang, all matter-of-factly.

"Don't people confuse it and call you A-Ron?" Daisy asked.

"If I have this conversation with them first, they never do! In fact..."

He tried to continue, but Robin cut him off by announcing her and Daisy's name, then probing to get Peter in the conversation, she looked directly at him and asked loudly, "So what are we drinking?"

"It's called, 'Rail Trail Pale Ale,' Peter said, smiling at Robin. "I don't know if you two even like beer, but it's really good with lemon. If you'd like..." With wide eyes and a look of astonishment, he added, "... I can get a few wedges?" But Daisy had already lowered the emptied glass from her lips.

"Nah, this good!" Daisy chirped, wiping her lips with the back of her hand. "Norwegian huh?" she asked, now shifting her gaze to Aron.

It then became quite obvious to who had whose eyes on whom.

They eventually all ordered food and the night slipped away. "Last call," reverberated from the bar.

Aron and Daisy exchanged numbers as they all walked back to campus together. Stopping at the sidewalk intersection where their paths split apart, Daisy assured them, "Ok, we'll meet up with you two at the party this Thursday night for sure!"

Now, they walked in the opposite direction from the boys, "How Ironic." Daisy said to Robin.

"Ironic? What do you mean ironic?" Robin asked.

"We got picked up by Entomologists! You're a bookworm and I'm a shutterbug!

* * *

Sophomore year wrapped up in a blink. Daisy and Aron had become an item. Peter was a great guy—a really great guy—but there was no chemistry between him and Robin. They both recognized that early on and by default became good friends. Frequently, Daisy would spend the night at Peter and Aron's dorm, sending Peter off to study or watch movies with Robin in hers. Peter would *always* fall asleep.

"What are you doing?" Peter asked, having been just woken by the sound of a smartphone camera.

"There was a fly on your forehead! I'm sending Tommy a photo."

"What kind of fly?" he asked. Then laughed and rolled over, knowing Robin could actually answer that question.

* * *

Junior year, Robin and Daisy lived off-campus in an apartment on North Oakwood Terrace. It was only a few blocks away. Aron and Peter helped them move in.

"He's my Viking slave," Daisy would joke. They were completely smitten with each other at this point.

The apartment itself was the top half of an old stone house that had a separate entrance by means of an old fire escape. Its busy street was convenient to everything and the yard was all but a tiny fenced-in patch of grass around back.

"What more could we possibly need?" Daisy positively proclaimed. She was the one who discovered the apartment in the student-housing bulletin.

The owners lived in the bottom half of the house. They chain locked the main second floor entrance each night when they went to bed. Apparently, the apartment stairs creaked too loudly and their bedroom was just a thin wall away. The separate entrance was a clunky old metal fire escape that sucked in winter because the wind would whip around the house and blow right up the stairs. By early December they already had had two big snowstorms.

Thankfully, the snow fell through the iron treads and never needed shoveling.

"I'll shovel the front walkway if you make me dinner," Aron would negotiate with Daisy. He'd become a regular evening fixture.

Robin really enjoyed winter. She still had her job at the Gravity Café, which now took her all of four minutes to walk to. Sometimes she'd take the back way just to lengthen her stroll and air-out. Now with most of her spare time, she'd head up to the Adirondack Mountains where she would spend time in the North-woods studying alpine ecosystems and their sustainability in harsh conditions. By providing a full report, her environmental classes granted her credit and class time via these trips.

"I can climb mountains instead of sitting in a classroom! How great is that?" Robin would boast to Daisy.

And every time Robin packed up her backpack Daisy would say, "Just make sure you have cell service if you don't have someone with you."

"This weekend there's an Animal Tracks Identification class at the High Peaks Information Center. There'll be plenty of people prancing around... You should come!" she offered Daisy.

"Way too much snow for me!"

"Oh come on, those tracks might lead to something you can shoot. With your camera of course," she laughed.

"Nei takk," Daisy answered. "What about Tommy or Peter?"

"Peter? Nah, he's cramming on a project. I'll give Tommy a try, but lately he's in a self-discovery mode. I'm afraid to even ask what he's been up to! And what the hell is nei takk?"

"Norwegian for no thanks."

"OMG!" Robin rolled her eyes. "You better learn to like

winter if you going to be a Viking!"

It felt like years since Robin had seen Tommy. She sat at her computer and video called him. His face appeared.

"Please, please!" Robin began to beg. "Say you can come up this weekend and go to a tracks class with me.... Please?"

"Shit!!" Tommy blurted out. "I guess you haven't heard."

"Heard what?"

"That's why I thought you were calling." Tommy drew a huge breath. "Matt Brown died yesterday."

"Oh my God, NO!" Robin shouted.

Stunned, she withdrew and bowed her head, hand over her mouth. In silence she pushed away from the computer screen and began to tear up.

Tommy had only seen Robin cry one time: the night of their parking lot prom, having realized college would separate the two of them. Looking at her now, he wished he could be there to comfort her.

Robin covered her face with her hands and she started to openly weep. His heart sank.

"He was in a playoff game for the national championship. He got tackled and never got up. They still don't know exactly what happened....Whether it was a really bad hit or a previous heart condition. They carted him off the field on a stretcher as he gave a thumbs-up... And... *Fuck!*" Tommy pushed back away from his computer, slamming into the back of his chair. "He died in the fucking ambulance."

Tommy drove all the way up to get Robin from school. The ride back down was both pensive and thought provoking.

"How sad and awful this must be for his family. You know he wasn't my favorite person," Tommy huffed. "It was *you* that we fought over! But the poor guy didn't deserve this."

"I thought you got in a fist fight 'cause he called you gay?" Robin snarled.

"He called me a fag, it's different. He was jealous of me being so close to you! And shit!... It's not like I knew about the two of you at the time."

Robin angrily reminisced, "He was smart, good looking, athletic... The whole damn package. It's so not fair!"

"So not fair," Tommy agreed. "*And...* I didn't know I was gay then, so he certainly didn't either."

"Maybe he did. Just saying!" Robin said, throwing Tommy a sarcastic look.

* * *

The line at the funeral home went out the door, circled around the back of the building, and all the way to the end of the parking lot. Tommy and Robin joined the somber crowd. For a mid-December day, they were pleased it was mild out.

"I'm impressed you're actually wearing the gloves and scarf I got you," Robin said.

"Are you kidding me? I love these!" He said, taking Robin into his arms hugging her, pensively stepping ahead. She became weepy.

It was amazing once they got inside. Collegiate banners, giant red R's, flags and pennants of every size and shape draped over every surface and hung on every wall. Almost every possible square inch was covered in red.

Following the crowd, Tommy and Robin slowly made their way down a long hallway.

Up against the walls on both sides were narrow shelves and tables full of trophies and framed photos; every school year portrait and every team photo. It hurt to look. Robin's eyes met Matt's in his senior photo. *Damn it! It shouldn't have to be a memory. He should be here so everyone can look into those beautiful blue eyes,* she thought.

Tommy shuffled along in front of Robin as she kept her forehead down against the back of his coat, maintaining a tight grip of his hand. She fished a tissue out from his coat pocket.

They turned the corner into a giant room and there at the far end stood the whole football team in complete football uniform. Their heads were bowed, and their helmets were in their hands. Matt was laid out in a white casket in front of his teammates. Across the length of the casket was a red banner with the word "Champion." His family sat in high-backed chairs—like guardians—placed in a small row off to the right side of him.

"I can't go up there," Robin whispered. "Pull off to the left about halfway up."
The two of them side-stepped to the end of a long row, and dropped into a set of green velvet chairs.

"You OK?" Tommy asked.

Robin tilted her head up to prevent the tears from running down her face. Holding up her finger she mouthed, "One minute." Breathing slow and shallow she silently concluded she'd never lost someone of significance.

Five minutes later she finally spoke. "I'm having a tough time with this."

"I know," Tommy said. He grabbed her hand, "Not to make you sadder, but look around, many others are too."

Robin took a deep breath, lowered her gaze and scanned the crowd.

Many tear-stained familiar faces were from high school;

teachers and coaches with handkerchiefs crumpled in their grasp. At one of the high-backed chairs, Matt's little sister knelt at their mother's feet with her head in her lap. Matt's dad stoically stood behind them with his hand on her shoulder. The mom looked numb. Robin took a deep breath and tilted her head back up towards the ceiling again.

Tommy leaned into her and whispered, "The flowers are crazy."

She lowered her head and peeked. Besides the gigantic arrangements in vases and urns placed on every table, standing on wire easels at the foot of the casket was a giant football made out of carnations and a tremendously beautiful white rose wreath that said "Beloved Son and Brother." Just below and in front of those stood a deep scarlet heart made from dwarf petunias. It was velvety and delicate. In gold script lettering on a white sash, it said "My Love."

Suddenly Robin was scanning the crowd to figure out whom this might be from.

* * *

Matt's family booked the entire restaurant for the after-wake gathering. The valet parkers were running around like mad men. Robin and Tommy arrived with the first wave of people. "I had to get outta there!" Robin said, slightly relieved when she flumped onto a bar stool.

A steady flow of people ensued. The football team marched in like a parade and began hanging up all the banners and flags.

"I didn't see them before?" Tommy indicated, pointing to a crowd of cheerleaders gathering in the foyer. "And wow! Take a look at the girl dressed in gray that they're surrounding."

"Awe," Robin sadly sang. "That must be his girlfriend.

Wow is right! She's beautiful!"

"Don't you see it?" Tommy asked.

"See what?"

"Robin... she looks like *you*."

"Bartender!" Robin demanded with a wave. "Can we get a few drinks here?"

The tone at the restaurant was much less dismal, but Robin still couldn't bring herself to confront any family member to offer her condolences. She held up her Cosmo. "Here's to Matt...." She paused, wanting to continue, but she felt herself well up. Instead, she just clinked Tommy's beer and once again looked skyward.

"Let's just have this one and head out. I'm emotionally done."

"That's fine," Tommy said. He seemed preoccupied. "Skuse me one minute, would you?" He darted off without an acknowledgement from Robin. She watched him disappear into the crowd.

He came back all smiles. Curiously Robin asked, "What the heck was that?"

"Scott Baxter! I can't believe it—Scott Baxter! I *thought* that was him! We swapped numbers. We *so* need to finish that first kiss."

"OK, maybe one more drink." Robin said, again waving the bartender over. "I'm *so* not used to this gay stuff from you!"

After a dinner visit with his folks, Tommy decided to spend the night at Robin's to help fend off her sorrow. June was used to him spending nights there, though usually it was in the blanket forts they made as kids. Robert and even Robbie had come to understand their friendship: everlasting, but nothing beyond that.

He stretched out on Robin's huge new bed with his arms behind his head. "Robert did an awesome job on this suite of a room for you guys."

Robin tugged at the covers, crawled underneath them, and through a huge yawn she offered, "You can sleep right here with me or take Daisy's bed."

"As long as you don't try anything funny, I'm good here," he joked.

"Don't you wish," she joked back.

Robin clicked off the light and rolled over to face Tommy. "Promise me you'll come hike in the Adirondacks with me at least one time before I graduate."

"I promise," Tommy assured her. "Can I bring Scott?" he kidded again, but Robin had drifted off.

10

And Away We Go

Daisy felt terrible for Robin. "Listen if that animal tracks class runs again, I'll go with you," she offered.

So in February, after the class at the High Peaks Information Center, out at the trail-head, Daisy double checked her camera equipment while Robin unloaded the gear from her car.

"Snowshoes! Really?" Daisy questioned.

"We won't be able to track and find anything if we can't move in the snow." Robin said, handing her a set. "Trust me, these aren't as difficult as they look."

* * *

At the Spring SUNY Student Art Show, a juried exhibition featuring over 300 pieces submitted by SUNY's sixty-four campuses, Daisy's photo of an Ermine won First Place. She had submitted three photos from her series titled "Christmas Critters."

"Robin, I totally owe you! If I hadn't gone to that tracks class with you, I would have never, and I mean *never*, gone out in the snow to photograph that little guy."

"Does this mean you like snow now?" Robin inquired.

"Nope! Daisy is a summer flower." She emphasized this by wrapping her arms around herself, mimicking the chills. "But tonight, we celebrate! I'm buying dinner for the four of us!"

"Really? Otter?" Robin asked.

"I was thinking maybe something different, something special! Listen, we're all about to finish our junior year. These two"— she bopped both Peter and Aron on top of their heads as they sat on the floor playing video games—"well, they'll be off to Norway for the start of their senior year *and*"—she snapped the check in front of Robin—"I've got this big fat check for winning the show!"

The four of them deliberated about what place would be special. Aron grabbed his laptop and typed in: *Special, Dining, Award Winning, New Paltz.*

"Well you won an *award,* so that's what it has to be, right?"

They peered over his shoulder as he continued to click around.

"Where the heck is this?" Daisy asked, pointing to a photo that popped up in a local top ten list. "The Mohonk Mountain House? Looks awesome. Let's do it!"

She immediately tapped the number into her cell phone and made a reservation.

* * *

Once they cleared the gatehouse, they continued through the private woodland of The Mohonk Mountain House. With Peter behind the wheel, they navigated their way up a long and winding driveway noticing trails off to one side and then past a golf course on the other.

Suddenly, as if it were rising out of its own vast and magnificent gardens, the mountain house itself slowly appeared in front of them.

"This place is freaking insane!" Aron exclaimed.

A Victorian castle that dates back to the 1800s, its grand structure was unlike anything they'd seen. It was an evolution of architecture: part castle; part estate house, with an acropolis of towers and jagged rooflines. The building's mid-section was like an Adirondack Great Camp set out over a crystal-clear mountain lake. Its huge porch was lined with rocking chairs beckoning an afternoon tea.

"Oh my God!" Filled with wonder Robin sang out, "It's like something out of a fairytale!"

"How the *Hell,* have we never been here before?" Peter asked incredulously, "It's like only fifteen minutes from school!"

Aron agreed with a very lively head nod.

They made their way around to the back side of the castle and parked in the no valet area over by the tennis courts, past horse stables. Upon walking towards the main entrance, Daisy stopped and twirled like in a scene from *The Sound of Music.* "This place is simply enchanting!" she cried out.

Aron laughed, grabbed her hand, and led her through an elaborate stone arched opening, which then led to and through a series of grand wooden welcoming rooms.

With a little time to spare, they ambled around the building and grounds in complete awe of the mountain resort. Robin thought to herself, *I've got to get back up here and check out all these trails.* (Of which they discovered were many and that it was essentially a resort for outdoor enthusiasts.)

Upon inspection of the clientele and luxurious surroundings, Daisy thought to herself, *Jeesch, after dinner I hope I have enough money left over to buy the new lens I want.*

At the dinner table, Daisy sat erect in her chair and raised her glass high. "Here's to special friends, at a special time in my life, and at a special place." She clinked glasses with everyone.

"Special friends indeed!" Robin agreed.

"Thank you for this night Daisy!" Peter clamored.

Aron threw an adoring smile at Daisy and then simply said, "I'm starving."

* * *

Daisy was offered full paid tuition for her senior year by accepting the position of SUNY New Paltz's, stock photographer.

"What kind of position is that?" her dad asked.

"Starting this July, I'll remain at school and shoot whatever they need for all their promotional material. You know, brochures, web, and ad campaigns. They're rebranding and updating all their stuff!"

"Congrats darling! You're officially a professional," Robert proudly announced.

Summer was already off to a great start.

* * *

Robin asked Daisy, "I know it's a long shot, but I'm meeting Tommy and some friends at the High Peaks Information Center for a full moon hike and bonfire, the second to last week in June. Any interest in coming?"

"Will Pauly be there?"

"Not sure. Tommy said he's bringing a few college friends. I'll find out though."

Daisy shook her head at Robin. "Eh, don't bother. Aron will be leaving soon for his semester abroad, and I want to spend as much time with him as I can."

"You're going to be a basket case when he leaves, aren't you?"

"Well at least I'll have other things to focus on...*literally*!" she laughed. But she knew it was going to be hard to have him so far away.

* * *

During the hike, the full moon was the brightest Robin had noticed in a long time.

"That's because your head is buried in your books," Tommy argued.

"Shut up!" Robin said as she pushed Tommy, knocking him off the path. "It's important stuff, just you wait and see!"

"Well I'm glad you're busy with that stuff, at least," Tommy said with an apologetic tone.

"What's that supposed to mean?" Robin glared at him.

"Aren't you the least bit interested in any guys around here?" he questioned.

Robin pushed Tommy again. "Shut up!" Then she muttered, "Interested in guys... Of course, I am! I just haven't found the right one. Waddabout you?"

"Well, I'm still testing the waters. Zig is pretty hot though," he said, referring to the guy up in front leading the way down the trail with Pauly.

"Daisy would just shit if she joined us," Robin whispered. "Did Pauly tell you about their little rendezvous?"

"NO! What the...? Tell me!"

"Shhhhh."

They proceeded along the trail as Robin explicated a short rendition of the infamous night. Tommy summed up the conversation with, "That Pauly is such a horn ball."

"Why the heck do you even hang with him?" Robin asked.

"Are you kidding? He's a fricking riot. All we do is laugh!" Tommy enthusiastically continued. "I always wonder why he hangs with *me*! I think he works on his"—he made air quotes— "*gay material* when he's with me and my friends. There's always off-color dialog between us that is so freaking hysterical, people would pay for it! You should see his stand-up routine now. He's really fucking good!"

"I'll wait until he's famous," Robin huffed.

Finally making their way to the bonfire, they could feel the heat from the flames twenty yards away. Tommy grabbed Robin's arm and said, "Let's find a good spot to sit. I want to snuggle up to Zig and see if the fire makes him even hotter!" He chuckled. "Come on…." He moved towards a bench made from a huge split log. "Pauly's got some weed and some booze. Let's chill out and have some fun."

"Hey what happened to Scott Baxter anyway? Robin asked.

"Oh, he's still in the picture!"

"You little slut!" she snickered.

Just then, Zig slid sideways across the log, clearing a spot for both Robin and Tommy to sit. Pauly slid up next to the other side of Robin and handed her a large Bota Bag.

"What's this?" she asked.

"Fire-Ball!" he coughed out, lowering a joint from his lips.

* * *

"And then I puked all over him!" Robin howled, telling the full moon hike story to Daisy.

Daisy concurred, "He is *such* a dickhead!"

They were making their way to Peter and Aron's dorm. There was a problem with the travel visas and Aron and Peter had to leave the U.S. earlier than they planned. As students, they needed two consecutive 3-month visas to fulfill the length of a semester. Out of nowhere they had to leave for Norway that day.

Aron stood on the sidewalk with Daisy's head in his big hands as if to keep her steady. Wiping her tears with his thumbs and staring into her eyes he desperately spoke. "I swear, before you know it Christmas will be here and I'll be back."

Robin and Peter stood off to the side just watching. "I'm starting to tear up," Peter joked sarcastically.

"Awe, it's sad, shut up!" Robin said, elbowing him in

the side. "I'm gonna miss you too you jerk." She threw her arms around him and kissed his cheek.

Robin comforted Daisy as they stood and watched the car pull away.

"Fucking Meligethes Norvegicus!" Daisy complained.

"What the hell is that?" Robin questioned.

"It's a pollen beetle exclusive to Norway. They're going to study them... and moths and flies."

"That's pretty cool! Maybe they can export them, bring them here to the U.S., and help with our bee situation. You know, if our bee population continues to decline, we'll be in deep shit!"

"Yeah, yeah... I know."

They continued slowly across campus. Once they hit Main Street, Daisy suggested, "Let's hit the Otter. I need to drown my sorrows. Six months without Aron is going to feel like an eternity."

Robin put her arm around her. "You know Daisy, I've never had a best friend since Tommy. Until now, that is."

Daisy looked up at Robin and began to cry... again.

Their apartment seemed so quiet without the boys around. Daisy kept herself busy for the remainder of the summer doing her regular photography work and photo shoots for the school. Robin continued working a few evenings per week at the Gravity Café; they were like family now but she longed to be up in the North-woods. She began developing an exploration list where she could monitor and map out specific alpine vegetation areas. She was driven to say the least.

"Did you know the extraordinarily fragile alpine ecosystem is exclusively located above the tree line? You wanna go to the Adirondacks with me this weekend?"

"Shit girl, you need to get laid! Not hike! You're obsessed!

Let's go to the Otter."

"Laid?" Robin questioned. "I haven't found anything out there that interests me besides alpine vegetation. Don't worry about me, I know what I want. Maybe I'll find someone in the mountains."

"B-o-r-i-n g," Daisy sang. "And that just sounds scary… finding someone in the mountains. Besides, didn't we promise our folks a visit this weekend?"

"Shit, I forgot!"

"It's Robbie's tenth Birthday and end of summer pool party. A bunch of little kids. Maybe you'll meet someone there," she joked.

"Shut up!" Robin scoffed.

* * *

In September of their senior year, a pharmaceutical company hired Robin on the spot. The company had been there to give a symposium on alpine ecosystem conservation, specifically for the use of, and research on, drugs and dietary supplements derived from the fragile alpine plants.

With a 4.0 GPA and advanced knowledge of alpine ecosystems, Robin was the perfect candidate for a position with the company. They assured her, upon graduation, she would have a job as an alpine plant management specialist and mountain steward. It was a co-op with the company and the Adirondack Council. She was permitted to collect samples and data, and begin efforts on the re-vegetation of endangered alpine plants.

"Robin! That is freaking fantastic!" Daisy said with complete admiration.

"Right? I have to fulfill a few mountain steward certification classes, and of course finish the coursework to graduate, but I still get to spend time in the mountains collecting data. If they use my data now for their research, I'll get a paycheck and complete my courses at the same time. A paid internship with a classroom in the sky! I'm so excited Daisy. This has become my dream."

11

Going Out with a Bang

Robin had become completely preoccupied, anticipating her career and submerging deep into her coursework. But halfway through the first semester of her senior year, she was suddenly caught off guard, realizing she had the hots for her Ecosystem Conservation & Management professor, Professor Gaine.

Is it because he has in-depth knowledge of all the things I am fascinated by? She pondered. *Or quite possibly, it's because he seems to behold the maturity and refined intelligence that I haven't yet come across.*

"Or maybe it's the plain fact that he is tall, dark and have-some," Robin confessed to Daisy while clutching at her heart.

"Are you serious?" Daisy said in shock. "A professor?"

"I know! I don't understand it! I sit there in class staring at him, and I can't even hear, let alone retain, what he is saying. He's so hot! I think he's only about twenty-six, twenty-seven. He positively entrances me. It's crazy Daisy! And how have I never said that to you before?" she laughed.

Robin was completely giddy; she was blabbering. "When I pass his desk every afternoon, I feel a lump in my throat."

"But you really want to feel the lump in his pants!" Daisy joked.

"Oh my God! Stop!" Robin shrieked. She tilted her head sideways, daydreaming. "But could you imagine?"

"Well good thing you know all the material he's teaching or shit, you'd be failing the course!"

"I know, right? But oh, what I'd have to Gaine!"

"Oh, that was just bad," Daisy droned, closing her book and turning off her bedside lamp.

* * *

One evening, Robin stayed late after class to work with Professor Gaine on study techniques for the upcoming ECM mid-term.

The classroom was like a typical lecture hall except for the hi-tech greenhouse that made up the entire back wall. The professor's desk sat at the base of the room at the lowest level with large display tables on either side. All the mini terrariums and specimen containers that housed a great variety of plant species were crammed together on one table, giving him and Robin ample room to spread out all the study material on the other.

With the turn of every page, he spoke passionately about conservation, cause, and effect. Everything Robin was interested in. They sat close, side-by-side, as they leafed through the material. Robin caught herself staring at him and thinking of what it would be like to kiss him.

"You OK?" he questioned.

"Oh, sorry, I'm fine, just a little stressed."

He hesitated, but he lifted his hand and felt her forehead. "You look flushed."

"Fine really." She pulled at her top, bellowing it from her chest. "Just a little hot."

"That you are," he gingerly muttered.

He lowered his hand from her forehead, intently observing her. He tucked a loose strand of her hair behind her ear. "Yeah, you're definitely hot."

With a lump in her throat, Robin stared at him. Then, like something possessed her, she leaned in and kissed him. He responded back with fervor, pulling her chair between his legs. With his hands, he delicately cradled her head as he passionately continued.

I can't believe this, she thought. *I can't believe I'm sitting here, kissing him and he's kissing me back! I can't stop... I have to stop... what if someone sees?*

They finally broke apart. Robin slid her chair back, drew a huge breath and straightened out her shirt.

In an abrupt swoop, he stood, taking her hand and helping her to her feet. "You should call me Evan," he said.

* * *

"Are you serious?" Daisy screamed when Robin finished explaining. "So now what? He's a professor for God's sake. I don't think that's legal?"

"Legal?" Robin laughed. "Well it's certainly not illegal. I don't know what's next but I'm certainly going to have some fun with this!"

Her Ecosystem Conservation & Management class was on Fridays from 6 p.m. to 9 p.m. Robin had been angry at the beginning of the semester when she realized, *Crap, that's my best tip night at the Café.* But now she thought, *I am so going to have fun with this!*

The following Friday, she made sure she was the first to walk into his class. He was standing at his desk stacking papers.

"Evening Professor Gaine," she announced enthusiastically.

He looked towards the door to see that no one else had followed in behind her. "Evening!" he enthusiastically stated back, with a huge grin.

Robin took a seat in the back of the room higher up than usual. One by one, students promptly filtered in and quietly sat. It was a test day and Professor Gaine distributed a test to each student, placing it face down on his or her tabletop. He then stated, "In precisely ten seconds, you can flip the test over and begin. Please wait for my call." He took his seat behind his desk and announced, "Begin."

Robin flipped her test over revealing a sticky note.

"Stay late," it said.

She did.

The classroom emptied, and she straggled behind. She made her way to the door, but suddenly all her books fell from her arms. "Clumsy me!" she said.

He rushed to help her pick up the papers that were now strewn across the classroom floor. Low to the ground, almost on his hands and knees, he crept to and peered just outside the classroom door. Looking to the left then to the right, he crept back in and shut the door. Robin, who was crouched low on her knees, had inched right up behind him. Once the door was shut, she essentially dove on him.

* * *

"You are killing me!" Daisy laughed.

"Yup, we were rolling all over my papers!" She held up a torn diagram and laughed. "I'll never be able to look at a Taraxacum the same way."

"Taraxacum, what the heck is that? And *tell* me you didn't do him, did you?" Daisy prodded.

"A Dandelion, and no!" Robin laughed. "I might need to get... as you said, *'Get laid,'* but I think that was hardly the right time or the right place. We actually went over to the Café later. He had a coffee; I had my chocolaty usual."

The next week when Professor Gaine handed the tests back,

Robin's was graced with an 'A' and another sticky note. This time it said:

Vinifera or Humulus lupulus. Immediately following class?

Again, Robin made sure she was the last to leave the classroom, returning the sticky note as she passed in front of his desk. She added to it:

Wine or beer, sound great! 124 N Oakwood Terrace - 2nd floor.

She stuck the note on his stapler.

It was ideal. Daisy was heading home for the weekend so Robin had the apartment to herself. She stopped and picked up a six-pack of 'Make My Day' IPA, and a bottle of Cabaret Cabernet. The bottle said, "This wine will sing for you." Robin knew nothing about wine, but was a sucker for a catchy label.

About 9:30 p.m., she heard the owner's TV through the thin stairwell wall and was relieved knowing the front entrance would still be unlocked. Sending Evan up the old fire escape around back just made the whole thing seem shady.

Enthusiastically, she opened the door to his knock. He followed her up the staircase. They entered the tiny kitchen and he placed a large eco bag on the small table, pulling out a six-pack, two bottles of wine, and a quart of Chinese food. "I didn't know if you liked red or white, and I hope you like fried rice."

Robin stepped right up to him, grabbed his collar, and pulled him into her. "Hi Evan!" she playfully announced. She planted a big warm welcoming kiss on him and slowly pushed him backwards into her room. Except to refill their wine glasses, they didn't make it back out of her room until the next day.

That morning, Robin refried up the fried rice with eggs, and they laughed and toyed with each other.

"So, what are we to make of this?" he asked. "We can't prance around campus together. It's not exactly ethical."

"Sadly, I concur," Robin said. Getting up from the table, she walked over to Evan, hiked up her oversized shirt and straddled him. "Who says we have to be seen together? I'm pretty happy meeting like this...." She playfully fed him with chopsticks.

* * *

"Where the hell did we get all this wine and beer?" Daisy asked, opening the fridge.

"I had a *great* weekend!" Robin cheered.

"Oh boy! I bet I can guess with whom!"

* * *

Winter break was closing in. There wasn't much of the semester left. Evan was off to study climate change in the Andes for the spring semester, working toward his Ph.D. in Climate Change and Adaptation.

"I know, it sucks! He's really nice and we're having a great time but life goes on," Robin sorely complained to Daisy.

With only a few Friday classes left, Robin would sit up high in the very back of his classroom. Flirting with him... holding up notes... admiring him.

One time, he choked on a mouthful of coffee when she'd flash a boob at him.

An early snow canceled one of his classes, and the next Friday, Robin was heading home for the weekend, having promised Robert and June that she and Daisy would take Little Robbie Christmas shopping. Robin also hoped to catch up with Tommy in the city. She couldn't wait to boast about her secret meetings with a professor. But as usual, he had no time.

"I'll make it up to you I swear! Between finals, the theater production, and the short films I'm in, I don't even have time to think... I miss you too!" Tommy expressed apologetically.

It was the last Friday of the semester, the last day of ECM class and quite possibly the last time Robin would see Evan before graduation. He was leaving the very next day.

In typical fashion, making sure to be the last one to leave the classroom, Robin sauntered towards the door and just before she exited, she flipped up the back of her skirt revealing her panty-less bottom.

"Excuse me Robin?" he said with authority, ordering her back into the classroom. Evan peered out the door and looked side to side down the hallway. He retreated, silently shutting the door, he locked them in, and turned off the lights. Now only the heating lamps at the far end of the greenhouse remained. They cast long shadows of its framework across the floor and up through the rows of stadium-like chairs.

He turned around, picked her up, marched to his desk, and plopped her down. Sitting there on the edge of his desk he looked at her sternly.

"We both know this is hardly the place and would be completely inappropriate"—he took a deep breath— "I'm both sad *and* relieved that this is the last day of class. I think you have a pretty good idea of what you do... I mean how you make me feel. If we ever got caught... Well I hate to think of the consequences." Without hesitation and barely a breath between sentences, he intensely continued, "I want you to know that I'm delighted you approved of me and I'm grateful to have spent this absurdly small amount of time with you. You are an extremely bright and beautiful woman."

During his long-winded speech as he hovered over her,

Robin slithered up to her feet. She became squeezed between his body and the desk, and she could feel he was hard through his pants. She rubbed him, virtually cutting off his babble.

"I enjoyed your class Professor Gaine," she began. "I probably won't see you again until the commencement ceremonies. You've been a great sport with my antics. You've given me knowledge and confidence in *so* much more than this class. There's a whole sustainable world out there to explore... Certainty it is in my hands."

And with the most voracious look she gave him a long hard stroke. She unzipped his pants and spun around. She flipped up her skirt and leaned on the desk grasping at its edges. The faint glow from the heat lamps beamed on her bare ass as she slowly swayed. Looking over her shoulder she invited him in, "One for the road, Evan?"

* * *

"Are you kidding me?" Daisy roared. "There in the classroom? I tell ya, I'm impressed by how bold you've become!"

"Well, I wanted to give him a nice send-off!" Robin explained. "It's such a shame he's leaving. He's so handsome and fun. Maybe when he gets back…"

Daisy cut Robin off. "Speaking of getting back... Aron comes in tomorrow! I'm so excited! Do you want to come to the airport with me? I'm picking the three of them up."

"Three?"

"Oh shit, didn't I tell you? Peter fell madly in love with some chick over there. Her name is Astri and she's coming back to spend the holidays with him. I think it's a big deal."

"Wow! Good for Peter!"

Daisy hesitated and peered at Robin. Timidly she asked,

"Would it be alright if Aron stays here with us. Just over the break?"

"Fine," Robin agreed. "And I'll make sure I'm NOT around tomorrow night. I'm heading home, and you two love birds can have the place to yourself."

"I love you Robin!" Daisy ran off clapping and skipping. "I'm so excited! I can't wait to see him... can't wait to see him."

During the drive home, Robin realized that when she was with Evan, her mind seemed clear and more focused. No stress, no worries. *Could sex have that much of a calming effect on me?* She laughed to herself, realizing this was a new level of empowerment. *Daisy was right all along; I just needed to get laid!*

Robin was always determined and in control. But this was a zealous new feeling. She thought about how she couldn't graduate fast enough now. She was *so* ready to get out and give the real world a spin.

During winter break, Daisy was inseparable from Aron. They spent Christmas at home with her family, which was a treat for Little Robbie who couldn't get enough of him, then over to his folks in Ithaca to finish out the holidays.

"Jeeze he eats a lot!" June cited.

"Is it serious?" Robert asked, nodding toward Robin for a *real* answer.

"A little serious," Robin confessed.

"How about you honey?" June questioned Robin.

"Nothing serious for me, Mom. Evan is spending the next semester in the Andes."

"*Evan? Andes?* Honey, you should have done a semester abroad."

June pat the spot beside her on the couch beckoning Robin to sit and tell, but Robin quipped. "Mom, I'm hardly ever *in* a classroom these days, travel is my future."

"Fine. But for now, sit!" June demanded, "Tell me about Evan!"

* * *

Peter was crazy in love with Astri from Norway, but she was actually from Galschjodt, Minnesota where *they* drove to spend the holidays.

"Now that's serious!" Aron exclaimed. "Who the F goes to Minnesota?"

* * *

Robin met up with her dad and his fiancée for a few days after Christmas. It had become a holiday routine now, and she was beginning to like "Amanda."

On New Year's Eve, Tommy convinced Robin to head into Manhattan.

"Come and spend New Year's with me. I promise we'll have fun. I want you to check out the scene," he insisted.

She took the train in, and they met up at the Four Faced Liar. She beat him there and grabbed a favorite corner spot. She ordered two hot chocolates and two snifters of 43.

Tommy walked in just as the waiter placed the drinks on the table. Robin was elated to see him. Her heart filled as he approached the table. *Shit, he's still so damn good looking.* She stood up and threw her arms around him. "My God, I didn't think I could miss you this much! How's my moon?"

Tommy lifted Robin off her feet with a big bear hug. "How's my sun?" Placing her back down, he looked around while taking off his coat. "It seems like a whole year since we've been here."

"More like two!" Robin admitted.

"I love what they've done to the place," he joked. (Nothing had changed.)

Robin laughed and hunched towards him as they sat huddled facing each other.

"OK, update me!"

"You first!"

Robin spared Tommy just a few minor details as she told him all about Evan.

"Well then," Tommy declared. "That explains why you seem a little more laid back!" He stressed the words a second time. "*Laid* back. Get it?"

"Really?" Robin admitted sarcastically. "That's just what Daisy said."

"And in the classroom no less?" Tommy laughed.

Matter-of-factly, Robin continued. "Well nowadays I pretty much just go after what I want! The opportunity presented itself, so I jumped on it!"

"You did more than jump on it!" Tommy said, giving Robin a look of admiration. "Nowadays? Bull shit," he snickered. "You ALWAYS go after what you want. But the Andes?... That sucks. I'm sorry he left town."

"Meeee toooooo!" she sang. "Now how about you? Have you figured out who Tommy is?"

Tommy pounded what was left in his snifter and waved the waiter over. "Can we get two Absolute Mules, please?"

He tried to keep it light. Robin could tell he was in a funk. He admitted to her he still didn't know what he wanted. He told her how he had recently slept with another girl to "test the waters."

"Shit Robin, that was difficult... thanks to you," he said,

peering at her. "Look at who I have to compare her to!"

Robin blushed and turned away, silently recalling how steamy that night was. Playing dumb, Robin asked sarcastically, "I don't know who you are talking about?"

Then in a moment of awkward silence (something they never have), Robin could sense Tommy's aggravation.

"What about Scott or Zig?" she prodded.

"Well, without giving you too many details..." he began.

Robin quickly interrupted him with, "Thank you for that."

"Zig pretty much had his way with me and then off he went. Made me feel like a piece of meat."

"Is that so bad?" Robin questioned, "I know that sounds so naïve but...."

"Bad? I don't know. Probably not. I don't know how I'm supposed to feel."

Tommy hung his head low and sucked from his cocktail straw. Robin reached across the table, taking Tommy's hands.

"And what about Scott Baxter?"

"Oh, he's still in the wings. I think he's more confused than I am."

"I'm sorry Tommy."

Tommy looked sternly at Robin, snatching his hands back.

"Do not feel sorry for me!"

"Whoa," Robin snapped back, "I don't feel sorry for you. I'm just sorry you're confused, damn it! Take it easy!"

Tommy reached back for Robin's hands and politely said, "Shit, no. I'm sorry."

"You should talk to someone. I don't know; a professional? I certainly can't advise you. But if you feel disconcerted..."

"Well I wouldn't call it disconcerted, just confused. Listen, it's not that bad, I'm having fun too ya know."

He sat back and retreated. He waived at the waiter for the check.

"And I haven't even told you the great news!"

"What?!"

"I got the lead in the spring production of Macbeth! So tonight, we celebrate more than the upcoming New Year!"

* * *

Tommy needed to ease Robin into the gay scene; expose her to just a little bit of what his world had become. By now, he was well versed and deep in the throes of it. He kept all his stories to Robin rather vague.

That night, New Year's Eve, he was anxious for her company, desperately wanting to think of absolutely nothing but having a great time with an old friend.

After a nice dinner at the Mermaid Oyster Bar in the Village, he brought Robin to the Stonewall Inn. It was a historic gay bar on Christopher Street where every walk of life entered, and many a gay person publicly kissed.

By midnight, the place was standing room only. When everyone began counting backward from ten, Robin thought her ears would explode.

"Happy New Year!" Everyone shouted simultaneously, and Tommy gave Robin a big hard kiss.

"Thank you for being here with me Robin; means a lot to me."

If there was ever a time to get used to that scene, midnight on New Year's Eve was definitely it. Tommy was right, everywhere Robin looked, women were kissing women and men were kissing men. And the Stonewall Inn was definitely the place.

"I'm happy to be with you here, now, and always Tommy.

You know that."

They walked into the New Year hand in hand, making their way to Tommy's dorm.

"Tommy? If I went for you," she hesitated, "you know... made a move on you, way back when... like in middle school or something. Would you be straight? Can it even work like that?" She interrupted her own line of questions with, "Again, I'm sorry, I'm so naïve to this stuff. I just want to make sure to keep our conversations open and honest."

"Why are you going to try some funny stuff on me tonight?" he questioned laughing as he keyed open his door.

"Shit no, I promise!"

He smirked at her and continued, "Oh, Robin, I wish I knew what made me think and feel the way I do. But it comes from deep inside. Whether I fight it or go with it, it has nothing to do with you."

He hung up their coats and grabbed the extra blanket and pillow from the shelf.

"I would love to love you Robin. You know, more than just friends. It would be so easy if I could."

Yawning, he peeled off his clothes and threw on a t-shirt and handed one to Robin. He sneered at her again. "No funny stuff."

"Stop!" she sang as she shoved him. He accepted the shove and fell into bed, immediately burying himself.

He was asleep by the time she changed and climbed into bed. He threw his arm over her and pulled her in with a snort.

Robin quietly lay there, thinking, *I really am over him, but shit, now I am kind of worried about him.*

* * *

Snow melted, alpine plants bloomed, and data was collected (in addition to Robin's first paycheck).

Anticipating graduation, in conjunction with the Adirondack Council and the pharmaceutical company, Robin outlined where she would hike all summer. She had one more class to attend to meet the Mountain Steward criteria. It was a survival class offered at the High Peaks Information Center where she had taken the two other classes. This one was on weather and how it can go from one extreme to another in the high peak region. Proper certification was necessary to continue as a full-time employee. It turned out to be one of the rainiest days in May to hike and take the class, but graduation was only two weeks away; she had no other choice.

* * *

"Daisy?" Robin began. "There was this really, *really,* hot guy at the High Peaks Info Center today. He came right up to me and introduced himself. His name was Bryce. Shit, even his name is hot." Robin seemed miffed describing the scene to Daisy.

"You know me; I'm usually pretty forward...."

Daisy interrupted, stating sarcastically, "Ya think?"

"But I just kind of smiled at him. It was weird, like I was actually tongue-tied!"
Robin poured two big glasses of wine and handed one off to Daisy. She threw herself down onto the chair at the small kitchen table and audibly sighed.

"I should have flirted and got his number or something. *What* is wrong with me?" she questioned, lightly banging her head against the wall.

In disbelief, Daisy tilted her head sideways at Robin. "Wow, you *are* beside yourself!" She handed the glass of wine *back* to Robin. "Since when in the hell do I drink wine?"

Daisy laughed, opening the fridge to grab a bottle of beer. "That was dumb for someone who always has her shit together and goes after what she wants!" She continued by shaking her head at Robin. "What the heck happened?"

"I don't know? Like a silencing fog rolled in...." Robin then emptied Daisy's wine into her own glass. "I'll tell you this," she said sternly, "If I ever see him again, you can bet your sweet bippy I'll do or say something!"

Daisy laughed. "What the fuck is a bippy?"

12

Pomp It Up

Graduation was upon them. Robin caught a glimpse of Evan one room over from the dean's office, where she went to collect her honors sash and Summa Cum Laude medal. There had been a convocation ceremony where students formally received their awards, but Robin had to meet with the Adirondack Council that same evening to accept her official Mountain Steward Certification.

After meeting with the dean, Robin walked slowly back out of his office. She threw her sash up over one shoulder catching Evan's eye. He could only offer her a ponderous look as his eyes followed her. She acknowledged him with a slight nod, but unable to contain herself, she projected a beaming grin and hurried off.

Man, I had a lot of fun with him! she thought.

Graduation time in New Paltz was simply jubilant, like the carnival had just rolled into town! Main Street was bustling with students and their families. Every restaurant was packed, and the sidewalks that ran through town and to campus became almost impassable. The whole town was fused in festivity.

Robin had previously reserved a table at The Otter: the very table where they all first met. They went on the last night of classes, and before graduation.

Robin, Daisy, Aron, and Peter celebrated hard, clinking their glasses to their friendship, their grades, and their accolades. They almost broke their glasses when they toasted their futures.

"And who knew we'd all become such good friends!" Daisy proclaimed, with a swooshing clink, soaking the table.

Subsequent to graduation, Daisy would continue shooting for SUNY which had become her first real client. And after her brief presentation, the Mohonk Mountain house had hired her to photograph their gardens in summer. With her eye—and the way she captured nature in the lens—there was no doubt the Mohonk Mountain House would turn into a very big, second client. On top of that, the greeting cards she had been producing had developed into a publishing deal with the local printer, and they now planned to make calendars with her images.

"So much beauty *and* opportunity in this area. I cannot, not stay here," Daisy insisted. She and Aron planned to stay local and move in together, full time. "Aron, we need to make a decision on a rental A.S.A.P.!"

But Robin cut Daisy off. "Don't even bother looking. While it's not immediate, I will eventually need to move north. The Adirondacks are calling, and that commute would fry me. Besides, who are you kidding?" she joked, looking sternly at the two of them. "Like when was the last time Aron slept in the dorm with Peter anyway?"

"Skål!" Aron shouted, clinking Robin's glass. "I kind of thought you didn't notice."

Peter added to the ruckus, holding his Rail Trail Pale Ale up high overhead. "Astri will be here tomorrow with my folks for our commencement ceremony. Then next week we head out to Minnesota to watch *her* graduate. Then in summer, it's helloooooooo Norway! Skål!" he shouted, clinking everyone's glass, again.

The table was now completely soaked from their enthusiastic celebration.

"What's the final plan for when the two of you get to Norway?" Aron asked Peter enviously.

"If you can believe this," Peter cheered on, "we both have an interview for the same position at the University of Tromsø in the Entomology Department. So, one of us will work there, and one of us will have to figure something else out. It should be quite interesting."

Daisy rubbed Aron's shoulders and said, "Don't worry honey bee, we'll get there to visit. If that organic farming company hires you, maybe you can eventually conduct a coleoptera pollination study with Peter and establish a European collaboration."

Silence fell over the table. Shortly followed up with an uproar of laughter.

No one knew Daisy could make such a serious statement. While a study like that was totally feasible, other than photography, Daisy usually didn't let on that she understood the slightest thing about entomology.

"Shut up!" she scoffed.

Aron, meanwhile, had been interviewing with Lily Fields in New Paltz: a diversified farming operation that produced eggs, culinary herbs, and edible flowers.

Robin slid in her chair away from the table and stood with her glass in hand. "Tomorrow is a big day for all of us, and if I drink anymore," she said, swaying in place, "I'm going to get all sentimental on you." Clearing her throat and trying to compose herself, she continued. "Seriously, our degrees all have a common thread, an environmental thread, if you will! Let's call it a cellulose fiber…" (She was blabbering.) "I have no doubt that our lives, slash careers, will somehow overlap." Snickering and snorting, she finished with, "Maybe someday we can all start a pot farm together!"

With a final wet clink, they called it a night.

* * *

On a crystal-clear day, mid-May, Robin and about 1700 other students sat contently listening to SUNY's president, a handful of guest speakers, and a variety of deans, including some from the honors program, who seemed to address Robin directly:

"Students who engage in deep learning practices and conduct scholarly research are the cornerstones of our foundation here at SUNY New Paltz…"

Robin spotted Daisy who was sniffling into a tissue a few rows ahead, but she wasn't able to spot Peter or Aron.

The vast sea of blue caps and gowns was a sight she'd like to emboss into her memory forever. It was at that very moment that Robin felt immensely proud. Proud of herself and all she's accomplished. She thought her chest could burst. *How is it possible that time has passed so quickly, and here I sit?* An elbow to her side made her come to, realizing that her wave in the sea of blue was about to flood the podium to collect their diplomas.

And one-by-one they did.

Retrieving her cap from the ground after the traditional air toss, she stood up and noticed the parade of her family striding towards her. June and Robert approached with little Robbie bounding alongside. Her dad and Amanda, hand in hand, hurried right along with the pack. Then, finally, with a tilt of her head, she caught sight of Tommy now in a full sprint running towards her.

If there was ever a single moment that could encapsulate sheer joy; an intense sentiment of elation, honor, and pride—all at once—it was that exact moment.

She did burst. All the tears she held in exploded with one single hug from Tommy.

* * *

Tommy's graduation was quite a production.

NYU had two ceremonies for Tisch students: NYU's All-University Commencement and the Tisch "Salute" ceremony. Both are held at Radio City Music Hall just a few days apart. It featured special speakers, performances, and an elaborate send-off by the faculty and staff.

Tommy eagerly advised Robin, "Plan for the Salute only. It will be an exciting night for everyone, *and* Martin Scorsese is the guest speaker."

The timing of this worked out just right for Robin, otherwise she'd have missed the drunken beer fest at The Otter on *her* final night of school.

The crowded scene outside Radio City Music Hall was reminiscent of the time she went to the Christmas Spectacular with Tommy. The weather was certainly not as cold, but the crowd sure was. *Pushy too!* Robin thought. *Parents and relatives of a bunch of entitled brats.* Then, she questioned her own angry disposition. *Ok that's not fair, I guess I'm just out of sorts. I haven't really spent any quality time with Tommy, lately.*

Finally, she pushed through the front doors, tired, hungry, and impatient. Robin buried her looming concern for Tommy within her own angst—which was becoming a regular thing for her. Not being able to spend time with him always got her in a funk. She had all but convinced herself that. *He's got all new friends and just no time for me.* It was easy for her to think this, since she had no idea what he was up to. It was just easier to be mad.

Tommy's folks, Margo and Frank, had been staying in the city for all the graduation events. The only plan Robin knew was that she was to sit with them, and they'd all go to a restaurant after-

133

ward. She grabbed her ticket from the Will Call and made her way through the lobby. The ticket said, orchestra 4, row LL, Seat 11. *At least we have good seats,* she reasoned.

With the stage now in sight, she made her way to her seat.

Frank's, big, open, welcoming arms, and his genuine bear hug, instantly snuffed out Robin's sour mood. And Margo was like a second mom to her. Growing up with Tommy, Margo spoke to the two of them like brother and sister. Robin always felt relaxed at their house, especially the kitchen table. Not two minutes in her seat, Margo began planning a day when Robin and Tommy would come over for dinner. "Just like old times," she indicated.

A feeling of comfort surged inside Robin. She sank into the cushy chair.

Then a thought about the previous winter popped into her head: the night when she and Tommy sat there, in the same venue. She laughed to herself thinking, *Little did I know how hot and steamy our night together would turn out.*

Yet suddenly her hidden despair reared. Anguish washed over her knowing Tommy would never, ever be hers. She sank even lower into her seat.

This particular night seemed to be a culmination of everything Robin and Tommy had been through together. It felt as if an emotional roller coaster had grabbed her from the street outside and taken her for a ride.

Sitting there with Margo and Frank, about to witness an epic event for Tommy, she started to tear up, now feeling solemn and quite sorry for herself.

But the music began to waft up from the orchestra pit. She felt the bass drums throb on her insides. She straightened herself up, tall in her seat. *I need to get over myself. Poor Tommy is the one with issues.* She turned her thoughts around. *That was a fun night with him; the show, the shots, the Pink Pussy Cat, everything.* Adjusting her position again, she settled in, now selfishly thinking, *This show better be good.*

The lights dimmed. Margo grabbed Robin's hand and gave it a squeeze indicating her excitement. Robin could hear hundreds of feet shuffling behind the enormous red velvet curtain.

To Robin's complete surprise, Tommy had a lead part in the ragtime medley that he and about forty other graduates were performing.

Margo leaned into Robin. "He said he's a little nervous, but as soon as he sings it's gone."

"Sing? I didn't know he could sing!" Robin exclaimed, but one of the irate parents from outside, tapped Robin's shoulder from behind.

"Shhhhhhhhhhhhhh!"

But HOLY SHIT could he sing!

* * *

A talent scout had seen the dress rehearsal for the "Salute" and pounced on Tommy immediately afterward. He asked him to come and do a reading for a role in *Significant Other*, a new off-Broadway show just in production at the Roundabout Theatre Company. So, later that evening, between fussing for a window table and ordering appetizers, Tommy was uproariously telling them all about it.

Margo and Frank weren't surprised by any of this. Robin, on the other hand, felt a little left out.

A preoccupied Margo and Frank were in a competition of who could name the most Scorsese films. She asked the waiter for a piece of paper as she fished two pens out from her purse.

"Honestly Tommy, since when can you sing?" Robin asked

eagerly.

"Well if you came to see more of my plays, you would know!" he sarcastically snapped back.

Robin whacked him on the head with an extra-long bread-stick. "Cut me a break, Tommy! You know how far SUNY is and how crazy my work and work-study program is."

"You mean was."

Yikes... the real world. It was still a new thought process for both of them. Robin had her plans all laid out, and this reading for Tommy could turn into something great for him.

Aware of the thickening air, a slightly tipsy but extremely cheery Margo held up her pink champagne.

"To your futures!" she toasted, breaking the tension... and almost her glass.

* * *

No matter what, Robin was still worried about Tommy. She couldn't put her finger on it, and she couldn't just get mad and hide her concerns anymore. She knew she would be seeing less and less of him.

The next few chapters—in both their lives—was putting even more distance between them. And there was nothing Robin could do except go to the mountains.

They were calling.

13

Walking on Clouds

Per her thesis on Alpine Plant Biodiversity and the prevailing job requirements, Robin was to hike six high peaks over the next four months. She would collect samples and designate off-limits areas where she would continue with follow-up studies. Each high peak has existing Mountain Stewards that would help monitor and guard the newly designated areas. It is extremely important that the areas are well protected and remain completely untouched.

Having completed the program and becoming a Certified Mountain Steward was Robin's first step in building a trusting relationship with all the other stewards. In addition to the skill set they all currently possessed, it was now crucial to educate them on which plants are endangered species and which are not—requirements they never needed before.

Robin's official job title was an Alpine Plant Management Specialist. Exclusively because of her studies and the content of her thesis, she was the first person ever appointed to the position. It was as if she had invented her own future.

Through the Adirondack Council and the pharmaceutical company she had been working with all senior year, they recognized the potential of such studies for both medicinal and ecological applications. Robin was the only person in the Adirondack's Forty-six high peaks permitted to collect these endangered samples. Hence the trust she now needed to develop with fellow Mountain Stewards. Thus, she began the necessary efforts for the determination, categorization and the possible re-vegetation of endangered alpine plants. If Robin was not on a mountain, she was in a lab with botanists, ecologists, and pharmacologists. Every sample and all the data collected was vital information because each year was different. Year to year, the climate was never the same. The whole project Robin was working on was to discover the optimal environment where alpine plants could thrive every year.

* * *

Hikers were continually stomping in and out of the High Peaks Information Center. Of course, it was busy; the weather was perfect for hiking. Like a scene from an old western movie, there was a dusty bustle of activity in the parking lots *and* at the trailheads.

The smoky, scotchy smell, and how it reminded Robin of her grandfather, never got old. It was a pleasure to be in the HPIC on such a warm spring day for a change. It was only her fifth time there, but it somehow felt like home.

The screen door slapped behind her when she entered. There were a few hikers inquiring at the information counter, so she stepped back outside to patiently wait there for her chance to speak to the guide. The sun hit her face. Closing her eyes, she tilted her head back to soak in the warmth. She took in a deep cleansing breath. *This is my kind of stuff,* she thought. *This is where I begin.* In a trance of positive energy, she anticipated the first steps of her new career, her new life... until she was almost knocked over by someone that hurried past her.

"I'm sorry!" trailed a voice that whipped past and into the building behind the screen door.

Robin collected herself and decided to go back inside to wait. Except for the just-added hurried person, the line for the guide had diminished. She stepped up next in line, almost eavesdropping on Mr. Hasty's conversation with the guide behind the counter.

"Yeah, the last time I hiked Cascade I gashed my leg open... nine stitches. It was a first date too!"

Robin took a step back, thinking, *Oh my God, this is Bryce's friend, the one that he covered for. I have to say something, but what?*

Mr. Hasty, now fumbling, dialing his cell phone while folding up a trail map, backed away from the counter knocking into Robin, again.

"Really?" she quipped. "You almost took me out the first time!"

"Jeeze, I'm such a klutz." Without any eye contact, he apologized, "Again I'm sorry."   His call must have gone through. He scurried for the door, shouldering it open. He lifted the phone to his ear and ducked back outside.

Suddenly Robin heard it from the back of the room: the ringtone that made her heart skip a beat.

Da na na na na. Then a pause. *Da na na na na.*

She spotted him quietly sitting in the back of the room. Lifting the phone to *his* ear, he answered softly, "I know you're late. I'm here at the trail-head waiting."

He then stood up. Tucking his phone in his pocket, he kept his eyes locked on Robin. Slowly, he moved towards her.

She felt breathless. She could feel her heart thumping in the whole cavity of her chest. He approached calmly and held out his hand.

Gazing at him completely flustered and speechless, she took his hand in hers.

"Your name is Robin if I remember correctly?" he said.

Stunned, she only nodded. Quickly becoming concerned

he might notice how flushed she was, she bowed her head and scuffed her feet, desperately searching for words. She didn't let go of his hand. Finally, she mustered up the courage to speak, "Bryce, right?"

He ushered her toward the giant fireplace away from a new parade of hikers making their way to the information counter, her hand still awkwardly in his. She gently pulled it away shrugging her shoulders in embarrassment. They sat down simultaneously on the oversized hearth.

* * *

Oh my God! He did ask me about my hike that first day right... after the survival class? Did I ask him about his friend and his leg? Oh my God, did I ask him what he would tell his friend who would be expecting him at the trailhead? I know I told him I just gradu-ated. Did I even have the sense to ask him what he does or where he goes? Holy crap! I never even spoke to the guide at the counter. I'll just have to ask the steward his or her name. I think it's Dylan. Robin's thoughts were scrambled. With every step she took as she ventured up the trail, she tried to recall every word that he spoke, and she tried to remember everything that she blabbed. *Oh my God, I'm such an idiot! Oh my God, what is wrong with me? Why can't I even think straight?*

She stopped dead in her tracks. Looking around, she real-ized she was already a quarter-way up Algonquin. *Holy crap my head is in the freaking clouds,* she thought.

Pulling out a PB&J from her backpack, she moved off the trail to a sunny rock where she could gather her thoughts.

From the small front zip pocket of her pack, she pulled the piece of paper where he wrote his name and number.

Bryce R Hamilton - 518-867-5309

Underneath that it said, "Call me." And it was underlined three times!

Just thinking about it, her heart began to pound. She finished up her sandwich, guzzled some water, and dug out a pen. She pulled out her notepad and wrote his number on that. She tapped it into her cell phone and then on her voice recorder she left a message, stating the number on that. *No way am I going to lose his number,* she thought. Then considered, *What if I lose my pack?* She wrote his number on her leg.

Continuing on, she thought her feet wouldn't hit the ground for the rest of the day. *Man, this hike is going to be interesting!*

Following along a series of rock cairns and finally cresting the peak slab of Algonquin, she spotted the Mountain Steward standing right at the survey mark. She stopped to catch her breath and from her last class at the HPIC she recalled,

Survey markers, also called benchmarks, are used in geo-detic and land *surveying. The markers were necessary to develop accurate maps and elevation data. Not every high peak has one. Some folks search for the markers, but some have long since been stolen or buried.*

Studious thinking always relaxed Robin.

She introduced herself and immediately inquired about the wind, which seemed to be extra strong for the first week of June.

"Nope, it's normal. And hey, I'm Miller," he said, extending a gloved fist, offering Robin a fist bump.

Robin obliged and thought, *Don't know why the hell I thought his name was Dylan.*

"Let me show you the predominant area of vegetation," he said as they ambled about forty yards away and around a series of giant boulders. "It's protected by these bad boys," he added, patting one of them.

Directly behind the boulders, an expansive field of Alpine tundra was suddenly at her feet.

"This patch is low enough on the south side that the wind doesn't seem to interfere too much."

"Nice!" Robin said, dropping her pack. "I'll be here for about an hour. Once I set up the boundary lines, I'll come back to review with you."

"Perf!" he chimed, and then Miller strolled away.

* * *

It always seems longer coming down a mountain than going up. Robin turned her thoughts to Tommy...

I wonder if he'd like Miller; he was boyish yet rugged. I don't know what Tommy likes... I need to call him.... But I'm so calling Bryce first.

14

Bert

Tommy stood on the corner of 39th and 7th waiting to cross. He was on his way to Bryant Park after his reading. He planned to enjoy the spring day, contemplate life, people watch, and grab a bite at the park's grill. There was a skip to his step.

He knew he did well. *I'm pretty sure I looked the part,* he thought. *My life isn't so far from the actual role... maybe that vibe will resonate with them and I'll get the part.* And with a sudden rush of confidence, he thought, *Yeah, I nailed it!*

As he sank his teeth into a fancy tuna melt sandwich, a slab of avocado plopped out onto his lap—just as an extremely good-looking guy walked by. One that Tommy had previously spotted halfway across the park earlier.

Keeping his cool, he stuffed the avocado back in and adjusted the foil-wrap so it wouldn't happen again.

"Napkin?" he heard from behind. An arm reached out past him, dangling one. At the other end of the arm was that same, really hot guy.

"Why thank you!" Tommy said taking the napkin, careening around to get a full view.

Looking down at Tommy, he teased, "If that happens again and it hits the ground, someone could slip."

"No, I think you have that confused with a peanut butter and banana sandwich," Tommy joked back.

"But isn't your sandwich called, The California Slider?"

As soon as Tommy realized the name, he burst out laughing, questioning, "Is that why they call it that?"

"I don't think so, but it's one hell of an icebreaker."

And with that, the hot guy sat down opposite Tommy. "Mind?"

"Please," Tommy murmured with a full mouth and a gesturing swoop of his hand.

"They don't really have a peanut-butter and banana sandwich up there." He nodded his head toward the garden grill. "Now do they?" he asked.

"Not that I'm aware of," Tommy said, shaking open the napkin. "I just... Well you know... Bananas and the reference to slipping on them? It was a good comeback, right?"

"It was a great comeback!"

"I'm Bert," he said as he reached across the table offering his hand.

"Tommy," he replied with a firm shake.

Bert was tall, dark, handsome, and built; not unlike Tommy. In fact, when they walked through the backside of the park towards the New York Public Library, a couple of giggling girls stopped directly in front of them asking, "Are you guys twins?"

Tommy and Bert stopped dead in their tracks. Enlightened, they turned and looked directly at each other. Bert held out his arms, shrugged his shoulders, and said, "I knew there was some reason I liked you."

It was uncanny. They totally could pass for twins, or brothers at least. Meandering from one side of the park to the other, the flirting continued.

"Bert? What's that short for?" Tommy asked. "Robert? Albert?"

"I'll just cut to the chase—it's embarrassing—I usually just say it's short for Robert, but the truth is... It's short for Engelbert!"

"Embarrassing?" Tommy questioned.

"Yeah, well how many Engelberts do you know?"

Tommy fell silent. A few steps later he claimed, "Well, I'd say it's unique."

"Awe, you're a nice guy," Bert said. "See my grandmother was a huge fan of Engelbert Humperdink and I was born just a few days before she died. When my mom told her the news of my birth, she wanted to make her smile so she fibbed and told her my name was Engelbert. Weeks later my mom felt guilty for making up the story so my folks went back and had it officially changed to that. They refuse to tell me what I *was* named for the first few weeks, so I convince myself it was something even worse like Adolf. One day I'll find out for real."

"Well Bert works just fine!" Tommy insisted.

"Damn right it does. I tried in grade school to work with Engel, but I got teased." And in a sing-songy voice he said, "He's not a straight angle and he's certainly not right!"

"That's awful. Kids can be so mean," Tommy consoled.

"No worries, I'm considering revisiting Engel again."

Their meandering paused now finding themselves at the edge of the park on 40th Street. Bert disclosed, "Well, now that I'm out, and I'm totally fine with my sexuality, I'm considering it." And without a breath, he glossed right over the subject by promptly asking, "So where to now?"

Not wanting the flirty afternoon to end, Tommy suggested the library since they were right next to it. "Public Library?"

Bert moved around to stand directly in front of Tommy as excitement grew in his eyes. "How about the Morgan instead?"

"Morgan?"

"Yeah, the JP Morgan Library and Museum. It's like five blocks from here and the collection of art, artifacts, and of course books, is pretty impressive."

"Lead the way!" Tommy replied enthusiastically.

Other than apartment hunting, Tommy had no plans for the rest of the day. He had two weeks to find a place and move from his dorm or it was back home until he could. But opportunity was knocking, and it was knocking loud.

This was a completely new experience for Tommy. He was elated. He felt like he wanted to grab Bert's hand and scamper down the sidewalk. He thought about Scott Baxter and the 'thing' they had. He thought about Zig and the 'thing' he wanted Tommy to be. But this actually felt like a good thing.

Pausing at a few store windows to comment or ogle, Tommy speculated to himself, *This, is what it's supposed to be like... I think.* They made their way down 5th Avenue.

He collected his thoughts just before stepping into the museum. *This is like a real date!* Allowing it to finally register, he had a hard time keeping himself from instinctively grabbing Bert's hand.

Inside the museum, time flew by. It was dark by the time they stepped back outside. Bert suggested coming back to the museum for another visit at one point.

"I hear they are going to display the original manuscript of *A Christmas Carol* from the vault collection. "That!" he demanded, "We need to come back for!"

Tommy felt very enthusiastic now. That statement alluded to a future date.

Realizing things were going smoothly, a sense of certainty and confidence settled nicely inside him.

"So, this is going to sound aggressive," Bert stated, cutting Tommy's stride short on the sidewalk out front. "I'm a great cook, I live two blocks from here, I'm starving, and I don't have work for another twenty-four hours. Can I interest you in dinner at my place?"

Tommy really didn't know what to make of it. That's a lie... he did know what to make of it. He just wasn't used to being swept off his feet.

"Lead the way!" Tommy once again enthusiastically said.

They entered through a side door. The apartment building took up a large portion of the block.

"There is a main entrance, but we'd have to walk around the corner. This is like a short cut," Bert said, fumbling with a set of keys.

Up three flights of stairs, and two more locks to open, Bert held the door for Tommy to walk in first.

Tommy felt the heat of the apartment blast him.

Hanging the keys on the wall just behind the door, Bert explained, "The people downstairs crank the heat until it's practically July, so it's always really hot in here. Oh, and don't mind the mess." He kicked what looked like a cat toy and sock out of view.

Standing in the narrow entrance hall, Tommy leaned back against the wall to allow Bert to pass. Bert paused in front of him and said, "Jacket?"

Tommy obliged and struggled trying to get his arms out in the tight space between him and Bert. Bert laughed, taking the jacket from him. "Shirt?"

Tommy paused and looked into Bert's eyes trying to understand if he was serious or not. Bert laughed and then kissed Tommy's cheek. "I'll get that later."

Bert stepped back allowing Tommy enough clearance to pass into the open space of the studio apartment.

It was definitely hot now!

* * *

Facedown with his broad torso and his bare ass peeking out from the white sheets, Tommy woke to the sounds of a noisy kitchen. He heard running water, pots clanking, silverware being stacked. Glancing over, he could see Bert standing in front of the kitchen sink. Naked.

Bert tilted his head and glanced out over to Tommy. Saying nothing, he threw a dish towel over his shoulder and came through the room. Sitting down on the bed next to Tommy, he put his hand lightly on Tommy's ass, still saying nothing.

Tommy rolled up onto his elbow and asked, "Where'd you learn to cook like that?"

Bert got up and while making his way back to the kitchen he answered, "My first job was in a restaurant. I started waiting tables, then behind the bar, but many times they were short in the kitchen so I was like a sous chef."

"And what may I ask, do you do now?" Tommy questioned.

"It's kind of the same deal but at a club."

Bert then looked at Tommy and continued matter-of-factly, "So you're an actor, you come from the burbs of New Jersey, your dad owns a chain of BMW dealerships, your mom loves tennis, and you are an only child... I couldn't get you to stop talking last night!"

"Yeah, I was nervous."

"Are you now?"

"Nope."

"How much longer can you stay?"

"A while."

"Any questions for me?"

"A ton!"

Bert threw the dish towel on the counter and made his way back to the bed. He piled up a bunch of pillows, leaned back into the pile and slipped just under the white layers next to Tommy. "Go!"

"OK. First question." Tommy pointed to an old VCR machine underneath the huge TV about ten feet from the foot of the bed. The gigantic flat-screen took up almost the entire wall. There was an old VCR tape half popped out of the slot. "What'cha watching?"

"Breakfast at Tiffany's."

Tommy was a bit relieved. Not completely sure about last night's escapade, he awkwardly thought it could be a porn tape; *Like who even watches those old clunky VCR things?*

"Wow that's really old. A classic right?" Tommy asked. Then he looked over at Bert, who suddenly seemed a little sad.

"Definitely a classic," Bert solemnly answered.

"Why the sad face?"

"It was my parent's favorite movie *ever*." With a deep sigh, Bert continued, "My dad died my sophomore year in med school..."

Now taking a deep breath, he held up his hand to stop Tommy who was about to inquire more.

"Prostate cancer... Med school at Columbia... Mom moved to Vermont and took up snowboarding with a tree hugger, and my sister is here in Manhattan. Real estate."

Now looking to drastically change the subject, Bert finished with, "Ya know, I can give you her number. She can probably find you a decent place." He reached over to the side table for his phone.

Just then, Tommy's phone rang. Bert grabbed Tommy's jeans from the floor and tossed them at him. Tommy retrieved the phone from his pocket.

Bert—wanting to give Tommy a bit of privacy—got up and disappeared into the bathroom.

He came back out a few minutes later to a huge grin on Tommy's face. Tommy announced, "I got the part!"

Bert collected glasses from the end table. "Let's celebrate!" he cheered, glancing past Tommy at the clock on the wall. "OMG, It's almost noon! That gives me just about…" he had a devious look in his eye, "eight more hours with you!"

Tommy buried his face in the pillow and screamed and kicked his feet like an excited little kid.

Bert sat back down on the edge of the bed and put his warm hand on Tommy's bare ass, again.

15

How Sweet It Is

Coming off Algonquin, now much more composed than the way up, Robin decided to call Bryce. He answered on the second ring. "Are you still on the mountain?"

"No, I'm in the HPIC parking lot, why?" Robin answered, surprised and amused.

"Well, I'm still in the area and thought if you have time, maybe we could meet up for a drink. Or if you're hungry, how about dinner?"

In the few available seconds before a longer pause might make it awkward, visions flashed in her head: *What clothing is in my pack...? Or maybe my car... that doesn't smell, looks clean, and could be considered date wear?* Realizing nothing would suffice, it was that last second she realized it would be far worse to miss out on seeing him. She hastily replied, "If you don't mind being seen with someone who looks disheveled and smells like the woods, I'd be happy to meet you for dinner."

"Then how 'bout the diner in Keene Valley? And... I like disheveled and I love the smell of the woods!" he declared.

On the drive out to the main road and down into town, Robin felt a twinge in her gut and pondered her composure. *Oh my God I'm getting all nervous and jerky again. Why does he have this effect on me?*

Looking to calm herself, she decided to call Tommy.

No answer, she left a message.

"Tommy! Damn, where are you? I'm on my way to have

dinner with a guy I met like three weeks ago. I'm really nervous and I need you to calm me down. If you get this in the next ten minutes, PLEASE CALL ME!" Not wanting to worry him she trailed off saying, "But I'm so excited!"

Pulling into the parking lot she spotted Bryce four cars down, casually leaning against his car, looking down, and tapping away at his phone. She thought she'd take a minute to clean herself up but he spotted her and marched right over.

He came directly up to her car door and opened it for her. Like something blasted him, he fell back and waved his hand in front of his face. "Wow you *really* smell like the woods!"

Robin silently sat there, pondering her stench.

To help her up and out of the car, he held out his hand. Seeing a shamed look on her face he was compelled to apologize. "I'm kidding, I'm kidding, I'm sorry. I swear you smell fine!"

She accepted his hand and rolled her eyes at him. Stumbling on the rise up and out of her car, she fell right into him. He caught her with both arms and actually inhaled her.

"I'm serious, you *do* smell good. Did I mention I love the smell of the woods?" he teased.

Robin got her footing and backed away. Bewildered and embarrassed, and suddenly realizing she had butterflies the size of bats in her stomach, she grew flush. Desperate for a clever comeback, all she could mutter, "I'll wash up inside."

She did just that and then joined him in a booth that overlooked the parking lot of the Noon Mark Diner. She slid in the bench seat across from him.

Looking displeased, he grumbled, "Now you just smell like Dial soap."

Robin smirked and opened up her menu, peering over the

top, directly at him.

"I hope it's OK, I ordered two hot chocolates," he mentioned, as the waitress appeared placing two steaming mugs in front of them.

"Thanks, that's fine." Robin answered, feeling a bit guilty. After all, it was almost exclusively what she and Tommy drank when they were together—it had become their tradition. But now was *not* the time to explain. Instead, she took comfort in the steam and held the mug up close to her nose, analyzing him over the rim of her mug.

"What's good here? I'm quite famished!" she lied, attempting to relax and trying to convince herself that the butterflies were just hunger pangs. Then in a silent mantra, she repeated to herself: *Just breathe... just breathe.* She took in the steam from the hot chocolate, slowly sipping. *But my God he makes me weak in the knees.*

"Everything! Pretty much everything here is good. People travel far and wide for their pies," he said, placing his menu on the table.

Without words, a waitress appeared with a pen and pad hovering over them. Looking to Robin for her response first, she ordered.

"I'll have the chopped spinach salad with grilled chicken, balsamic dressing on the side, please."

Still wordless, the waitress now nodded to Bryce.

"The Cajun chicken wrap," he said.

"Fries?" she asked.

"Sure, thanks."

The waitress spun on her heels and left.

Slightly more at ease, Robin began with a series of questions. "How was your hike? Was your friend able to find you?"

"Yeah, my friend Stewart." He chuckled and began to play with his fork. "I caught up to him a few minutes after you headed out. We hiked Mount Joe. Stu isn't the best hiker; he gets anxious and concerned about anything over a three-hours, so we stick to quick hikes or lower elevations."

"Didn't he hurt himself on Cascade a few weeks back?"

"Yeah, it was that hike with a girl he's keen on. About half-way up is when he fell and gashed his leg open. But luckily, she's a nurse's aide and she cleaned him up before bringing him to an urgent care place for stitches." Bryce shook his head and chuckled again. "See Stu is…" gesturing air quotes, "on the spectrum."

"You mean autistic?"

"Yeah, but nothing debilitating, mind you. I've been working with him on and off for a few years and…well, we've bonded a bit. He works at the camp with me, and at a senior center here in Keene Valley, and of course as you know, the High Peaks Info Center supply counter. He even has a blog on the stereotypes of autism. It can be challenging though, because he takes *everything* literally.

"What d'ya mean?"

"Once when he was becoming impatient with me, I said, 'Hold your horses.' He got so confused because he never had horses and didn't understand why I would say such a thing. But there's a bonus to taking everything so literally too. And by that, I mean, it's remarkable how well he writes for his blog. He's a different person with written words. Brilliant in fact."

"Wow that's amazing!" Robin chimed.

"Now, tell me about *your* hike," he asked. "Did you meet the Mountain Steward and accomplish what you needed to?"

"I did! His name is Miller. And there is a ton of rare alpine vegetation up there!"

Now excited (and sidetracked) talking about her work, Robin finally began to truly relax.

The waitress reappeared placing a loaded plate in front of Bryce first. She cautioned him, "Careful it's really hot." Then she placed a wooden bowl, heaping with green, in front of Robin asking, "More cocoa?"

Bryce looked at Robin to answer.

"Actually, can I just get a big glass of water, please?"

"Two!" he called out. The waitress was quick to move.

Robin reached over to touch his plate. "I'm always compelled to touch the plate when they say that. Like their hands are made of asbestos or something!" she laughed.

Bryce grabbed Robin's hand before she had time to pull it back.

"I thought I might never see you again," he blurted out.

"Really?" she said. *Shit, here are the butterflies again.*

He stroked her hand with his thumb as he continued. "But it seems you will be spending a lot more time in the mountains! Right?"

"Is that a good thing?" she asked.

"That's a great thing," he responded.

He let her hand slip away, and she fumbled for her fork. With her heart skipping beats, she asked, "Where do you live?"

"Fish Creek Ponds, just west of Upper Saranac Lake."

"All those Saranac lakes confuse me," Robin admitted. "I'm not all that familiar with the area."

"It's the furthest one from here," he began. He described the chain of lakes in the area trying to create a visual for her, but

Robin felt herself getting lost in her thoughts just looking at him. Then he asked, "How about you? Where do you live?"

Snapping back to reality, she answered, "Oh, I have an apartment in New Paltz with my best friend from college. But I'm looking for something up here."

"You mean you have to commute back there tonight?"

"Oh, no! I go home on weekends, but I usually stay at the hostel when I'm here."

"You mean the one right here, like across the street?"

"That's the place!" she answered.

With an awkward tilt of his head, he looked sideways at her. He wanted to somehow offer some help.

"It's nice, actually," she said, sensing his concern. "During the week, there are hardly ever others there, and it's a perfect location for my work."

With a mouth full of chicken wrap he muffled out, "If you say so."

Robin laughed at Bryce with his full mouth and she stuffed a huge fork load of salad into her own. She couldn't bring herself to speak until she swallowed.

"Honestly, it's fine," she claimed. "Besides, this area is where I'll be looking for a place... Really, it's fine!"

Bryce continued to smirk at her, keeping his comments to himself with the help of his wrap, but she could tell from his eyes he was still baffled.

"Stop!" she said laughing. "OK, when we're done here, I'll show you."

The waitress cleared their plates. "Y'all don't think you can leave without a slice of pie, right?"

Robin peered across the table at Bryce. "Your call," she said.

Bryce looked up at the waitress, "She'll have the carrot cake pie and I'll do a slice of the triple berry, please. To go!"

The waitress clicked off the open sign as soon as the door shut behind them.

Bryce stopped and stood at the passenger side door of Robin's car holding two tins. Puzzled, Robin looked over at him.

"You drive us there," he explained. "I'll protect our pie on the ride over and I'll walk back for my car later. Really, I'll be fine walking back later. No need to worry about me."

"Get in," she laughed.

On a couch in the common room, they sat side by side with their backs to the only other person in the room: someone who must have *just* come in off of a trail. He seemed flustered, studying a large map spread out on a big wooden table with his headlamp still on his head.

On the coffee table in front of them, Bryce spun each tin, opening them up. Robin ripped open the plastic-wrapped napkin and utensil sets the waitress had included. Bryce handed her a tin. She handed him a fork. She kicked off her shoes and pulled her legs up underneath one another. One bite in, she began her questions. "So what do you do? We never even touched on that. And oh my God this *is* good pie!"

Bryce put his tin down and unlaced his hiking boots. Kicking off just one boot, he lifted his leg up, tucking it underneath the other. He rotated to face Robin. "Well, I guess you could say I'm a caretaker. I live in a cabin just off-site, at a Great Camp that I help take care of."

"Is that the camp where you work with Stu?"

"It is. It's a private Great Camp. It's pretty exclusive. People come from all over the world to stay there. The cabin I live in was my grandfather's. He was a mink trader from way back when. Everyone knew of him. The resort company wanted to purchase the cabin and the parcel of land it sits on, so they drew up a new deed. It's sort of homage to my grandfather. The deed protects the cabin and me. And because of my credentials, I get to work for the company."

"Credentials?"

"I have a degree in Urban Studies, which kind of falls into place for what they needed. We worked out a deal: I got a re-vamped cabin and a job, and they were able to extend their proper-ty and hire me as a professional."

"That's a crazy story. Did you know your grandfather?"

"Sadly no, he died when I was about three, but he willed the cabin to me. It was in pretty bad shape. Back then, it was a ratty little hunting cabin. He always wanted a legacy mink trader in the family." Bryce laughed. "I understand he was *not all there* when he died. But through my dad and my uncles, I've heard many cool stories of the ol' mink days."

"Urban Studies?" she questioned next.

"I know, weird major, right? It's everything from public health, economics, land use, public interest, and even landscape design. You wrap that up in a package with"—he put his pie down and flexed his arms like a gorilla—"an able body, and boom! Per-fect caretaker."

Robin rolled her eyes. "I think I've heard, *and seen* enough," she howled. Then she put her tin down and took his. She began to delicately hack away at his pie.

"Oh, I see how you are," he toyed, trying to get it back.

"Wow, this pie is yummy too," she teased.

Had it not been for the frustrated hiker and a concern for

noise, a pie battle would have surely developed. (It was 10:00 p.m. and considered "Quiet Time" in the hostel.)

Robin showed Bryce the bunkroom, the fire-pit, the kitchen, the bathrooms, and the washer and dryer.

"Thirty bucks a night. You can't beat that!" she said enthusiastically. Then she walked him out on the front porch to say good night.

They descended the few front steps and stopped where the stone walk began. Bryce pulled Robin in close so they faced each other. With one hand on each of her shoulders, he looked at her and said sincerely, "OK, it is a decent place. I won't worry about you being here."

"And I won't worry about you walking back in the dark," she answered sarcastically. Careening her neck around him, she added, "I can see your car from here."

When she looked back up at him, wham! The butterflies were instantly back. He tucked a loose strand of her hair behind her ear. "Can I see you again...? Soon?" he asked.

"Maybe we can meet up somewhere between Fish Creek Pond and here?" she suggested. "Or I can come closer to you."

"Can you?"

He pulled her in even closer and kissed her. Softly.... Sweetly.... Pie had *nothing* on him.

16

All is Well

Heading back inside the common room, Robin didn't see the frustrated hiker. She cracked the bunkroom door and heard deep sleep breathing. *Oh God, I hope he chose a bed on the opposite side of the room,* she willed.

She went outside and retrieved her backpack and duffel bag from the car. Noticing the plastic sample bags containing her collection of plant material made her realize what a successful day it was, all around. Several different species were tossed onto the back seat when she had hastily ripped through her pack looking for a clean shirt. Then she thought, *Shit, someone might mistake these for bags of weed. That's all I need!* She filed them side by side into a box and put them in the trunk.

Stopping to sit on the front stairs, she took a minute to reflect on their kiss. *So soft,* she thought. Bam! they were back. *Stupid butterflies.... Why in the hell does he have this effect on me?* With a huge breath, she tried to compose herself and her fluttering stomach. If it wasn't for the heavy weight of her backpack, she thought she might just float away. Hoisting it up and over her shoulder, she continued imagining. *Mmmmm his lips were so sweet.*

Her phone suddenly rang. Ambling it up to her ear before she could even speak, an excited voice announced, "There's my sun! Are you alone?"

"I am! How the hell are you, my moon?"

Having made her way up the front porch stairs, she thought, *I'll stay right here. The last thing I want is to wake the angry hiker with my elated phone conversation.* She dropped her gear and delicately took a seat in a weather-beaten wicker rocker.

"God Robin, I miss you!" Tommy roared. He began to tell her about Bert. "Robin, he's so hot. I'm literally tongue-tied!

"Ew, don't even tell me if that's some gay thing."

"Stop!" Tommy screeched. "Don't try to be funny; I'm being completely serious. Bert makes me feel…." It took him a few seconds to find the right words. "Well, he makes me feel the way I *think* I'm supposed to feel!"

Tommy was on a roll now, spewing bits and pieces of information.

"We met at the park…. He likes museums…. He studied Pre-Med…. He has a killer apartment…. He's an executive manager at a club…. And oh my God, Robin, he can cook!"

"Wait, executive manager? That sounds inflated," she responded.

"Well, I don't know the real title, but he runs the place. Oh, and wait… The best news of all. Remember when I had the reading just after graduation?"

"Yeah?"

"I got the part! It's an off-Broadway show called *Significant Other*. Ironically, it's about a gay guy that spends most of his time with his high school girlfriends. So, besides my dashing good looks and diverse skill set, as you can imagine, I'm perfect for the part."

"Oh, Tommy that is freaking fabulous!"

Robin was truly thrilled for him. In the recent past she only witnessed a sad, lost, and confused Tommy.

"I'm *soooo* happy for you, my moon! Let's plan a day to celebrate."

"Let's!" he agreed. "Let me know the next time you are home. Maybe we can hit our old luncheonette for some hot chocolate."

Suddenly Robin felt guilty about her hot chocolate cheat. Visions of Bryce swirling in her head: *Through the steam he was even hotter*. She cut her mental lapse short. "OK, now my turn."

"Of course!" he replied.

Robin began to tell Tommy about how she had met Bryce the first time, and how she felt the stars had aligned so they were able to meet again.

"You're gushing! I can sense it. Aren't you?" Tommy asked.

"Shush! We're supposed to meet up again in another day or two. Tommy, I haven't felt this giddy about a guy since... well... you and me at our prom."

"Shit Robin, that makes me sad."

"Please don't be; that was so long ago. It's fine, and I'm really excited to be where I am now. And work is pretty great too!"

Tommy and Robin continued to reminisce. Old times. New times. They admitted to feeling relieved by just being able to confide in each other, finally, again.

Robin looked at her watch. "Shit it's freaking 2:00 a.m. I've got to get my samples to Albany tomorrow. Promise me you won't be so hard to get in touch with?"

"I promise."

"Oh, one more thing," she added abruptly. "If you can believe, freaking Pauly was in the class that I took for my final certification. The one when I first met Bryce at the High Peaks Info

Center. He didn't see me, thank God! He was a complete stoned ass!"

"Seriously? That's crazy!" Tommy admitted. "But you gotta cut him some slack Robin. He fucked up his last year at NYU and his folks stopped paying, so he dropped out. He's going nuts trying to figure out his next move."

"OK, fine. I wish nothing but the best for him," she snickered.

* * *

Her alarm went off at 6:30 a.m., and the bunkroom was empty. Looking out of the only window in the room, Robin saw the sun's first direct hit. The mountain peak behind the hostel seemed to be wearing a golden cap. It made her feel like a little kid, eagerly anticipating game day.

Her plan was to re-write her field notes and then make her way to the Albany office to drop off the samples. Two hours there and two hours back allowed time for lunch at the Gourmet Café just down the street from the hostel. She planned to grab a bite there and peruse the real estate magazines and rent sections of the local papers. But a phone conversation with Daisy—halfway to Albany—convinced Robin to continue south.

"Like when was the last time we spent any time together?" Daisy demanded. "For Pete's sake, I haven't seen you since graduation!"

"Fine, fine! I'll come. And speaking of Pete: how is Peter?"

"He left for Norway with Astri yesterday. Aron is pretty bummed... he's still waiting to hear about the job at the farm. But I'm keeping my assistant busy."

"Assistant?"

"He's quite helpful, actually. I'm shooting a bunch of interiors for SUNY and lugging around the lighting equipment is brutal, so for now, I really need him."

"That's cool. What about Mom and Dad?" Robin chuckled. She always laughed when she said that. She certainly could refer to them as June and Robert, or my mom and your dad, but the simple irony of the whole situation made it too easy not to.

"They're completely nauseating! They keep kissing in public and it weirds me out. And Robbie is all sweet on an older girl. An 8th grader!" Daisy howled.

"K, enough of this chatter. I'll be in New Paltz around noon. Save some stories for me then."

"Drive safe sis!"

Robin considered calling Bryce to let him know it could be a day or three before she made it back up to the Northwoods. Since she was visiting Daisy, she thought, *I should at least visit Mom for one day, too. If I spend one night at the apartment with Daisy, and then one night at home with Mom, I'll be able to get back up to Keene by Sunday afternoon.* She grabbed her phone. First call.

"Hey Mom!"

"Hey sweetie!"

"I'm going to the apartment tonight and can be to you for dinner tomorrow. Got any plans?"

"Oh no, sweetie! We're going to a matinee," June said sorrowfully.

"Ma! Don't be sad; this was a last-minute plan, and I thought I'd just pop in if you were around."

"You sure? I can try to get back in time to make a nice dinner."

"Don't be crazy! I'll give you fair warning next time I have an open weekend, and we can make a real plan. I'll see if Tommy is around."

Then Robin thought, *Screw that!* Instead, she pushed the voice command button and said, "Call Bryce."

He answered in what seemed to be a rather serious tone, only saying, "Robin."

It dawned on her how deep his voice was. It caught her off guard.

"Robin?" he said again.

"Sorry I'm here... I'm... just driving.

After another moment of awkward silence, (Or was it a bad location? Actually, a nervous lull), she finally spit out, "Are you around Saturday night?"

"I am! Whatcha thinking?"

"How far is Fish Creek Ponds?

"Too far. How about Saranac or Placid?"

"Placid."

"Any preference? Food? Drinks? Pie?" he laughed.

"All of the above," she answered.

"OK, call me Saturday just before you pull into downtown Lake Placid, I'll figure out a good spot. 7:00ish? Is that good?"

"That's good!"

"Until then…. And drive safe."

"Bye!"

Her heart was in her throat. She forced herself back into business mode so she was able to cut off the butterflies before they really took flight. Looking around, she realized she had pulled into one of the furthest parking spots away from the office building's entrance. Then she deduced how Bryce always seemed concerned for her welfare. A little mystified and a little elated, she decided the longer walk to the building would do her good. She grabbed the sample box from her trunk and made her way across the lot.

* * *

All was well in the apartment. Daisy and Aron were like two pigs in a blanket.

"No really! You guys live like pigs!" Robin said, as she shook her head, noticing the pile of dishes in the kitchen.

"But your room is totally untouched and clean," Daisy muttered apologetically.

"It'd better be!" Robin laughed as she entered her room with a packing box. "It won't be much longer before you two can mess up this room too. I'm hot on finding a place in Keene."

"So, tell us now, what else you are hot on?" Daisy sarcastically inquired.

"What? How? Who…? I just got here!"

"Oh, please! There is a glow about you. I saw it when you were doing that professor, and I can see it now!"

Robin threw the empty box at Daisy. "Shut up! Really?"

"Really."

Daisy flattened the box and padded the seat next to her on the couch.

"Spill!" Daisy demanded.

Robin's glow had turned to a full-on blush.

17

The Butterfly Effect

"Call Bryce."

As she made her way into the town of Lake Placid, he explained, "Go all the way through town, and when Main Street curves left, stay straight and park in the first open spot you see. The Cottage comes up on your right and it overlooks Mirror Lake. You can't miss it. There's a big outdoor deck. I'll be there."

Damn it! she thought. *These butterflies have got to stop!*

Robin parked just past the curve he mentioned. She had walked past the deck by the time she realized it was even there. The main entrance to The Cottage was only a few feet further down the sidewalk.

Once inside, she made her way through the crowded bar and to the far side of the restaurant where a wall of windows and a door led to the deck outside. She paused before heading out to try and spot him. Then she did.

Across the deck in the furthest corner, she spied him sitting comfortably near a modified potbelly stove. (Dusk was upon them and the June evenings in the Northwoods still get pretty damn cold.) Smoke from the potbelly hampered her view, so out the door she went. She zigzagged through the full tables and seating area. *Popular spot,* she thought.

Bryce spotted her coming toward him. The glow from the potbelly's fire illuminated his smile.

And there they are again, Robin thought. *Freaking butter-flies.*

He stood as she neared, and when she stepped up in front of him, he slid his hand around her waist and pulled her in close. He kissed her cheek and whispered softly in her ear, "There you are." Inhaling deep, he drew in her scent.

She sat adjacent to him in a cozy corner bench with large pillows and woolen blankets. He insisted she face the lake.

"The moon should come up right about there." He pointed, but she couldn't take her eyes off him.

'Dreamy' was never a word she would normally think of, to describe a man. But that was what immediately came to mind.

The evening had a chill. The warmth of the potbelly soothed her, and the clamor of the crowd drowned out the nervousness she anticipated. The night was young and now sheer excitement charged Robin.

A waiter came over yielding a chalkboard and a wine list. They decided to order the first four appetizers on the list and two glasses of the Bobsled Red.

"Please, if you could bring the apps one at a time, that would be great," Bryce requested. He leaned over to Robin. "No reason to rush the night, right?"

"Right."

The half-wall surrounding the entire deck was a chunky wooden frame structure, with huge panes of glass. The planters— placed at every post—were beginning to swell with vivid spring colors. The sun was setting in the great distance behind the Adirondack's majestic peaks. Twinkling white lights began to emerge from the surrounding neighborhood, while a rising moon ushered in the brisk night air.

Bryce squished a pillow against the back of the bench on the far side of Robin and slid even closer to her. He leaned his arm up on the ledge, anchoring his chin on his fist and stared at her.

Good God, this is just downright romantic! she thought.

"So, tell me more about what you do," he queried, interrupting her flash fantasy.

"Really? It's boring to most..." she trailed off.

"Bore me!" he demanded.

"Well, I originally planned to major in Business and Environmental Sustainability. You sure about this?"

"Go."

"But I focused on Plant Biodiversity. In my case, specifically, alpine plants."

"Which means?" he questioned.

"Plant life balances ecosystems, protects watersheds, mitigates erosion, moderates climate, and provides shelter for many animal species. The number and variety of *plants*, animals, and organisms that exist is known as *biodiversity. Got it?"*

"Got it."

"Biodiversity is the essential component of nature ensuring our survival by providing food, fuel, shelter, medicines, and other resources."

"OK, makes sense... go on."

Wow, he's really listening, she thought.

The waiter brought over two large glasses of red wine.

"To resources!" Robin said, leaning her glass against his.

"To you!" Bryce insisted.

"OK, but the minute the first app comes out, we're done with this particular kind of conversation!"

"If you say so."

Robin finished up the lecture by telling him about current conservation and protection efforts for the alpine plant communities.

"There are almost ninety acres of an extraordinarily fragile alpine ecosystem in these ADKs. It's constantly changing due to climate. Because of its adaptation to extreme changes and how these plants continue to thrive in harsh environments, pharmacologists, microbiologists, botanists, and chemists, study, use, and continue to search for such vegetation, ultimately for use in drugs and dietary supplements derived from these plants. Which has increased tremendously in recent years, I might add."

Robin spotted the waiter moving in on them with a tray held up high. She nodded toward him, indicating his approach.

"On a closing note," she sped up, stating, "twenty five percent of modern drugs used in the U.S. have been derived from plants. Done!"

"This crock is really hot," the waiter warned, placing it on a small metal table off to the side. Sliding the whole table right in front of them, he warned them again, "Really hot!"

Robin went to touch the crock and Bryce grabbed her hand. Surprised he was trying to stop her she looked at him and said, "You know I have to!"

"Well, it's an excuse to hold your hand then."

Robin retreated and leaned back against the pillow. She collected his other hand and retreated even more with a moan of contentment. With an alluring gaze from him, suddenly everything around her seemed to dissipate. Time came to a halt and the crowd fell silent. He gently leaned into her—now just inches away—she looked breathlessly at him. She could see the potbelly's flame reflecting in his eyes. He kissed her. Her mind raced and desire roared through her veins.

The sound of a breaking glass broke them apart.

"So sorry," the waiter said. He had bumped into their table

and Robin's wine glass took a nosedive. He threw a dish towel over it. "I'll be back with a new glass of red, so sorry."

"No problem," Bryce conceded, noticing the reason for the bump in the first place: a couple was squeezing into a table and chair combo, right next to them.

"Sorry to hone in on your space. This place is really packed," the woman of the couple said.

"It's a beautiful night, can't blame anyone," Bryce said. Then with an affectionate glance at Robin, he continued, "I can't think of a better place to be."

Kill me now! Robin thought.

One by one, the waiter brought out each appetizer they'd ordered. They talked a little more about Robin's degree, and she explained how it transitioned into the perfect career for her. Then Bryce explained to her a little more about how his grandfather really wanted him to become a mink trader.

"He was 104 when he died. I don't think he realized that fur wasn't such a good business anymore. He had been extremely successful with it."

"Excuse me?" questioned the man of the couple seated right next to them. "If you don't mind me asking, how long have you two been together?"

Robin raised her eyebrows in surprise while taking a sip of her wine—she nearly choked.

Bryce chuckled. "Actually, this is just our second date. Why?"

"Well, we've been married a few years, and well... you two look so comfortable together. We were trying to guess."

The look of embarrassment on the woman's face was so profound it compelled Robin to respond. "I'll take that as a good sign!" Then Robin poured some of her wine into Bryce's—almost empty—glass, and sat tall in her seat. Hoisting her glass towards the couple, she added, "And cheers to exactly that!"

She swayed her head back to Bryce. "I'd love to order more wine, but I've got a bit of a ride back and I know how you worry," she teased.

They decided to get two hot chocolates. It was the perfect segue to: "I must tell you about my friend Tommy...."

Robin revealed quite a bit. She mentioned how concerned she'd been for Tommy over the past few years, but also how she felt that he may have finally figured things out.

"He really is my oldest and dearest friend. It can't be easy admitting you're gay, no matter how much easier it is now that so many people accept it. Often, I think about how he must have struggled with it during his life. So now, to finally find happiness with it... well, I'm just so happy for him."

"You sound like a great friend, Robin."

"Thanks, but I'm not so sure that I always have been." Robin simmered in thought for a minute.

Bryce changed the subject. "Let's talk about our third date." They considered hiking Mount Marcy.

"You've done the second highest peak, so now we should do the highest together," he suggested. "Weekdays are easier for me, and since they are a workday for you, you can show me what you do. Right? I mean I'm sure Marcy has the kind of alpine plant life you're looking for, right?"

"*Fernald's Bluegrass*!" Robin reported in delight. "I thought I'd save Marcy for an end of summer hike, but having had a warm and rainy spring, it could prove to be a bountiful time."

Robin tapped on her chin, conjuring up a plan. "*Fernald's

174

Bluegrass is in extreme peril. It's globally rare and it's at the risk of extinction. I've done extensive research on it. It's been spotted near the summit, but it's so close to the trail that it gets trampled. If we find it or seek out another patch... Well, it could change every-thing!"

Bryce could see the fire in *her* eyes, and it wasn't from the potbelly stove.

18

Where Will This Lead

The longest days of the year were here, which meant enough daylight to get up and down Mount Marcy. Late June didn't always
mean warm weather. At those elevations, snow flurries were not
out of the question.

Robin and Bryce met early Thursday morning at the HPIC.
She texted him, *I'm parked in the lot closest to the trail entrance.*
Robin had just hit send when he pulled up right next to her.

Looking through his car window at Robin through hers, he
flashed a pure smile. Anticipation in the form of butterflies once
again consumed Robin as she smiled back.

Though time was on their side, Robin knew she would have
to spend a decent amount of it on the summit collecting samples
and reviewing information with the Mountain Steward. Jumping
out of her car, she wanted to run into Bryce's arms and give him a
big welcoming kiss, but instead she decided she needed to be professional (and reserved). She composed herself by slowly rounding
the car and stopping to open up her trunk. With a squeak from its
hinges, she contained her excitement and pulled out her backpack
asking, "Are you sure you're OK doing a work thing with me?"

Stepping up closer to her, he ardently answered, "Absolutely."

She felt goosebumps run up her spine and she willed
herself not to blush. "Let's make sure we both have a proper day's
supply, shall we?" she instructed.

"Yes ma'am!" Bryce saluted her and dropped his pack at
her feet.

Reviewing their packs, Robin made sure she had everything she needed to collect samples and data. Bryce made sure he had all the proper items for every possible outcome.

"A tent?" Robin questioned, noticing one strapped to the underside of his pack.

"It's June, it's the Adirondacks, and it only weighs four pounds," he answered defiantly.

With a smirk of approval, Robin simply nodded her head.

Bryce then grabbed her pack and held it high behind her so she could slide her arms right in. Then in a curious tone, he asked, "Don't you think a tent is a good idea? You're certified, you know... all that safety and survival course stuff?"

"I am!" she declared. Turning back around to look at him, she snapped the clasp of her pack's waist belt and tilted her head matter-of-factly. "My tent only weighs three pounds!"

Bryce captured her hands at her waist belt and held them firmly in place. "Is..."—he kissed her cheek—"that..."—he kissed her neck—"right?" He hovered over her.

She drew him in and he gently kissed her lips.

"Get a room!" someone mocked.

They broke apart giggling, noticing a group of hikers who scurried into the woods just ahead of them.

About one hour in, they made it to a popular spot called Marcy Dam.

"I used to come here when I was little," Bryce shared as he grabbed Robin's hand and pulled her from the main trail onto an older one.

The view completely opened up and they stopped at a large clearing where they could see the structure of the dam.

"In 2011," he began, "Hurricane Irene damaged the whole

area, and instead of rebuilding, they decided to let nature have its way." He pointed north. "This was once a huge pond not a stream. Sadly, one day, trees will take over and eclipse this beautiful view."

Robin dropped her pack and fished through it. Pulling out her phone, she said, "Then we need to document it!"

In selfie mode, she framed herself and Bryce off to the left, with the W-shaped horizon line of the mountains and a portion of the stream, over to the right.

"There!" she stated. "If the lighting is better on the way back, let's do a real photo shoot."

Bryce tugged at her hand and they headed towards the footbridge where they would cross the stream and continue on the main trail, all the way to the summit.

Now back in route, she said eagerly, "Did I ever tell you about my friend Daisy?

Bryce stepped to the side allowing Robin to pass. "No! But now seems like a perfect time," he said, waving her through.

* * *

The warmth of the morning seemed to be evaporating. After another hour in, the trail became steeper and narrower. Nothing they couldn't handle, but a mist was now creeping in. Slipping on a rock just ahead of Bryce, Robin squawked, "What the?!!" She stopped and stomped her foot in annoyance. "It's supposed to be partly cloudy and warm. ALL DAY!"

"Don't worry, we got this!" Bryce replied encouragingly.

Soon the clouds were descending on them, and simple rock hopping became dangerous. Mindful of each and every footstep, they slowed their pace but continued on.

Making their way to Indian Falls, which was a little more than halfway to the summit, they reloaded their water bottles using the filter pump Robin unzipped from the base section of her pack. She also pulled out a few rocks.

"Are you purposely trying to make hiking more difficult? Bryce asked.

She laughed and answered, "Take a look around. You won't find one, loose, fist sized rock."

Like an owl, Bryce peered from side to side and then threw an inquisitive look back at Robin.

"You'll see at the top," she began, "people place rocks at the edge of the alpine vegetation to protect it from the wind. It provides a barrier and it's very helpful. It also prevents people from walking on it."

"Funny how you light up when you talk about this stuff," Bryce said, marveling at her. Though Robin knew better; it was he who made her glow.

* * *

Everything about the trail was sodden now. Out of the murky distance, a few figures appeared heading toward them. As they passed through, one of them called out, "Pretty tough coming down in this. You might not want to head up. The bedrock at the top is really slick."

Robin stood on a boulder off to the side allowing them to pass. "Thanks for saying," she said as they hurried by.

Then she began to slip. Not able to grab any footing, frantically she looked side to side for a branch or something to hold on to. Immediately Bryce crossed the path and caught her mid-fall.

Once swept up and into his arms, she looked intently at him and said, "I think we need to reconsider the plan."

He gave her a playful kiss and set her back down on her feet. "I'm sure most of the climbing is still ahead of us. I know we are past the halfway point, but we need to be smart."

Robin blushed, "Yes, yes we do."

She tightened her waist belt and made an about-face. "How about this?" she suggested as she marched on. "I noticed a yellow disk tent marker on the way up just before the Phelps trail cut-off. That's a designated spot and probably a good place to wait for this fog to move out... 'Cause it totally could!"

Following along, Bryce was about to agree, but she continued.

"On a sunny day, it's as quick as five hours up and a little less to come down. I checked." She insisted, "We can still make it."

Bryce was mindlessly trotting along and listening, when suddenly she stopped short and spun around to face him. "Oh, and thanks for the save."

He almost plowed right into her! Instead, he picked her up and threw her over his shoulder. "Anytime!" he said.

This was another save and the second time she found herself up in his arms. *He's quick on his feet,* she thought. *Prudent and attentive. I like that!*

Proceeding down the trail with Robin in his arms, over a challenging section of dewy rocks. "Anytime," he repeated.

They were already four hours in, and there was no way of knowing if the weather would clear up or not. By the time they made it to the yellow marker past the Phelps cut off, another hour had passed. The fog became even more dense.

"Assuming your tent is a one-man, I think we should set up my two-man to give us some kind of shelter if it gets any worse," Bryce suggested. "We'll take a break and let some time pass."

"Agreed. And yes, mine's just a one-man."

In no time, Bryce's tent was set up and they crawled inside. Zipping themselves in they stuffed the rocks, their damp jackets, and muddy hiking boots into the corners. Robin began to empty the contents of her pack. Sitting across from each other it became a game of sorts. She fixed her eyes on Bryce as she reached into her pack.

First, she pulled out a sweatshirt. He pulled out a fleece-lined flannel. She then pulled out a zip-lock bag with trail mix, cocoa powder, and two PB&J sandwiches. He pulled out a bear sack containing peanut butter and granola clusters, beef jerky and a couple of Clif Bars. Robin grabbed his flannel and threw it over her shoulders.

"Are you cold?" he asked in sudden concern.

"No, it just looks comfy... AND..." she snickered, "I can't believe you have a bear sack!"

"Borrowed it from Stu," he admitted.

Looking into her pack and then back up at him, Robin muttered, "Besides this,"—she exhibited a silvery square which she began to unfold— "the rest is pretty much just emergency and work stuff." She continued to unfold the shiny sheet. "My mom got this at the finish of the New York City Marathon back in the 90s. It's a heat-saving foil throw."

"Marathon? Your mom sounds pretty cool," he replied.

Now digging deeper into his pack, Bryce covertly looked across to Robin. In a final winning checkmate maneuver, from the bottom of his pack, he proceeded to pull out another sack. Once he opened that, a blue monster began to expand before their eyes. He unfurled it more and gave it a few shakes.

"I love this thing," he began. "This blanket can be cinched up like a sleeping bag or it can attach to the sleeping pad."

Robin sat in amazement watching the blanket grow in size.

"One pound, four ounces," he bragged.

Then he turned his pack inside out and zipped off the back-support lining. Looking to Robin for approval, he unfolded it, exposing a blow nozzle.

"Now this pack I special-ordered a year ago, but haven't had a chance to use it... Until now, that is." He blew up the sleeping pad and they resituated themselves comfortably on top.

As foggy as it was, the temperature never got below sixty-five degrees, but the weather did turn.

"Good God, is that rain?" Robin asked.

"It is," Bryce said as he leaned back and flipped open the window panel.

Robin took the foil wrap and threw it over her head. Half hiding, she whimpered, "Weather people suck. Only job I know where you get paid and are constantly wrong."

"Isn't *that* the truth," he agreed.

Defeated by the weather, Robin sighed. "Could certainly be worse though."

And with those simple words, she realized that she was completely alone in the middle of the Adirondacks with Bryce. *Couldn't possibly be any better!* she thought.

Trying not to get too caught up in her thoughts because that would just make her nervous and fidgety, she looked at her watch.

"Wow, It's almost 2:00 already, no wonder I'm so hungry."

She placed a couple of paper towels between them and put a PB&J sandwich in front of Bryce.

"Thanks!" he laughed. The game picked back up as he placed a granola cluster in front of her.

"Wait, no fair, you are so going to beat me at this too!" She reached over and pushed hard at his shoulder, attempting to knock him over. Keeping his balance, he grabbed her arm and pulled her into him. He kissed her and then backed off saying, "I am definitely winning."

They demolished the sandwiches and granola clusters, then he watched her as she fished out and ate just the blue M&Ms—one by one—from the trail mix. Bryce said nothing and watched her. When Robin realized she was being watched, she laughed in embarrassment. "What?"

"Nothing," he said, but he continued to stare.

A rush of heat overcame her; she could feel herself blush. The second she glanced back up at him, he rocked forward onto his knees so that he was now kneeling right in front of her. Taking her head with both his hands, he slid them through her hair. Holding her steady he looked at her intently. He pulled her in and kissed her deeply.

Tossing the bag of trail mix to the side, Robin willed him to throw her down right there and take her. But instead, like a gentleman, he gently released her and settled back into his seated position.

"Tell me the top five rarest alpine plants," he asked.

"You can't be serious?" she demanded. Flabbergasted and lustful, but still able to call up the alpine data. "Really?" she questioned again.

"Really. We're trapped here together, and I don't want to take advantage of that."

Fervently she then spit out: "*Boott's Rattlesnake Root, Dwarf Willow, Fernald's Bluegrass, Alpine Azalea,* and *Lapland Rosebay.*"

"Sounds like ingredients for a Harry Potter potion," he teased. Then he laid down on his side and leaned up on one arm to look at her.

Promptly, Robin added, "There's a total of twenty-seven imperiled or highly imperiled plant species… And I'm really OK being trapped with you."

He pulled the flannel shirt from her shoulders, rolled it up like a pillow and placed it down next to him, stretching out and gesturing for her to join him. Resting her head on the shirt, she laid down flat on her back. He pulled her in closer.

"What is your favorite alpine plant?" he asked next.

"Edelweiss!" she said with excitement. "But it's only found in Europe. Folklore says it's the ultimate love charm of the mountains."

"Why?"

"Apparently, love-struck young men would collect it from crags and ledges impossible to access, many would die from their falls. But if one were to collect enough to offer a bouquet, it proved they were brave and able-bodied and their intentions were then recognized."

He stroked her hair with his fingers as he listened to her every word.

She continued, "Sadly, with global warming, even edelweiss is at the risk of becoming extinct."

In the next moment, everything fell completely silent.

"I think the rain stopped," Robin announced.

Sitting up, Bryce looked at his watch and unzipped the tent, observing how he no longer could see the split-log bench that was only ten feet away. "How do you feel about spending the night here? The fog is even worse."

Robin sat up, glanced at her watch in surprise and replied, "It is pretty late now. Even if it cleared up, it'd be dark in a few hours. I didn't think to pack headlamps. You?"

He closed up the tent and grabbed his pack. He unzipped the small side pocket. "I've got a mini flashlight, a compass, this box of matches, and some lip stuff."

Realizing the desperate scene unfolding, Robin shrugged her shoulders. "I don't think we have much of a choice," she said.

"Beef jerky and Clif Bars for dinner," he optimistically offered. Putting his hand on her leg, he looked at her earnestly. "Are you warm enough?"

"I'm good," she said. "You?"

He knelt back up and looked to Robin for approval as he took off his shirt.

Robin's heart pounded.

Bryce towered over her as she sat in silence admiring his torso. A tuft of curls from his thick mane of hair had un-tucked from behind one of his ears, slightly hiding his gaze. Robin found comfort in this, assuming the look of desire was quite obvious on her face.

She then knelt up to face him; almost eye level. Longingly, she looked at him and touched his chest. Alternating her eyes from his eyes to her hands and back, she slowly pet him with anticipation.

He began to unbutton her shirt. Once undone, she slithered out of it and tossed it aside.

Then with a backhanded flick and a twist of her shoulders, Robin undid her bra and allowed it to fall to her side.

Bryce cradled Robin in his arms as he laid down with her, simultaneously tossing the big blue blanket up and over them. It floated down on top of them, sealing in the warm air they were lustfully generating.

"If we ever get out of here, I'll show you my alpine plant

rock garden where I'm growing edelweiss in a temperature-controlled terrarium," she announced nervously.

"If we ever get out of here, I'll make you a beef jerky free, home cooked-dinner," he promised.

Robin closed her eyes as he pressed his warm body against hers. He kissed her passionately, supporting her head with one hand as he caressed her with the other. He worked his way down, kissing her breasts and moving to her belly. Pausing, he said, "You sure you're warm enough?"

"You've made me quite hot now," she answered.

Squirming under the tightness of his torso, she pondered his actions.

Continuing to work his way down, he paused again when he reached her waist. He popped the snap of her pants open, "You sure?"

"Positive," she breathed.

He gently pulled off her pants and underwear together while making sure the blanket maintained their haven of warmth. He nuzzled his face between her legs and she moaned out, "God, I love camping!"

19

Déjà Vu

Robin emerged from the tent into thick diffused gray light with absolutely no idea of the time. It had to be somewhere around 6:00 a.m., but instead of morning's first warm glow, their camp seemed to be blanketed by low-lying clouds. The quietude that surrounded her was nothing shy of eerie. No birds, no wind, just stillness. Afraid to make any noise, she delicately removed her backpack from the foot of the tent. Digging to the bottom of it, she pulled out a small orange box, a canister of butane, and a small pot. A few feet from the tent by the split log bench, she cleared a level area thinking, *I knew one day this thing would come in handy*. She set up the ultra-light stove she had bought on a whim during her last year in college

Robin struck a match and lit the mini stove. Emptying her water bottle into the pot, she thought, *Voilà, now I can make hot chocolate*.

Just as the water began to boil, she heard a zip. Slowly, he rose from the tent, running his hands through that awesome hair. She felt her heart thump, and suddenly she had butterflies in her stomach, remembering how intimate last night was. He pleasured her for what seemed like hours. She thought, *I can't wait to tell Tommy about Bryce*.

He stretched as he walked toward her. "I promise you I usually don't sleep with someone so early in a relationship," he said.

She zeroed in on the word *relationship*. She was excited he chose such and felt herself blush.

"You call that sleep?" she asked. "How are we supposed to hike with so few hours of sleep?"

"Hike?" he questioned back. "We can't go anywhere yet."

With an extended arm, he fanned the area and pointed toward the trail. The campsite should have offered a wide view through the trees and to the valley and brook below, but the fog obscured everything. "If this weather doesn't clear, we'd be wise to sleep in."

With that, he stepped up so close to her she could feel the heat from his just woken skin. He gently cupped her chin and tilted her head to the side. She felt him breathe her in as he kissed her neck. Speaking softly, he continued, "I'm serious... if it doesn't clear up, I know what we can do for breakfast."

20

In A Pinch

At 10:00 a.m., in the same foggy conditions, over a second cup of hot chocolate, Robin and Bryce ate the jerky, the Clif Bars, and two flattened granola clusters.

"This weather..." she said, shaking her head, "Really is a crime."

"Typical for June. One day hot, the next day not," Bryce replied matter-of-factly.

"Yeah, but today they actually called for perfect weather!" Robin huffed.

Bryce then handed Robin the little orange box that contained her mini stove, stating, "Any day that starts with hot chocolate and you, is pretty perfect to me."

Snatching the box from his hands, desperate for a comeback, she came up with nothing. Bewildered and amused—butterflies and all—she just peered at him.

Together, they packed up the supplies and the tent in silence. Glaring at one another, only their eyes spoke, like they were having a complete conversation about last night's rendezvous. Robin finally giggled.

"What?" he asked.

"Nothing," she replied, but she did ask herself, *How can I possibly be this lucky?*

Bryce clipped the tent to the bottom of his pack and threw it up onto one shoulder. "Besides a date and a romp in the woods with me, I know you're actually working. I understand the mission and know you really need to make it to the top. How about a rain check?"

Then he lifted Robin's backpack, allowing her to put her arms in like a coat. One at a time, she slid her arms through. He secured her straps nice and tight on both shoulders and spun her around so she faced him. Looking anxious, he zipped up her jacket and tugged on the harness of the pack. "All snug," he said.

Robin looked up at Bryce adoringly. "Definite a rain check." She yanked him in and gave him an affectionate kiss.

Most of the way down the trail, Robin couldn't keep her mind straight. She thought back to when she had hiked Algonquin alone and Bryce had just given her his number. Even then it seemed her feet didn't touch the ground. Now she didn't know what to make of it! She couldn't focus; he was consuming her thoughts. *Shit, from a distance, I see him and I get butterflies. I get next to him and chills run down my spine. I look into his eyes and my insides feel like they are going to explode! Good God this is so not me. I'm not used to this.*

Then she thought about how she had just spent the night lying naked next to him. She retraced in her mind how he traced her whole body with his hands.

Stumbling on a root, Robin chuckled to herself, remembering how sweet and apologetic he was because in the still of the night, and the heat of the moment, Bryce had rummaged through every pocket and zip section of his backpack. "I swore I had a condom in here somewhere!" he cried out. Then he rolled over in dismay and leaned up on one arm and looked dauntingly at Robin. Placing his hand between her legs he caressed and prodded her, eager to please. "Tell me how this feels."

"Hey, let's fill up!" Bryce announced out of nowhere. His voice broke the erotic rampage swirling in Robin's mind, and she snapped back to earth. Bryce had stepped off the trail towards Phelps Brook.

Robin drifted up next to him and pulled out her filter pump. Pumping water into their bottles, she shouldered up against him, almost afraid to look directly at him. She might erupt right there.

Back at Marcy Dam, the fog was starting to thin out.

"It's probably going to be clear by the time we get back to the parking lot, you know," Bryce said.

"I know!" Robin huffed out.

But she wasn't really bothered. She realized how infatuated she was and how she wouldn't have changed one damned thing.

"You OK?" he asked. "You seem a little quiet."

"Are you kidding? I couldn't be better. That mountain isn't going anywhere, and I'm already looking forward to that rain check." (That rain check had a completely different meaning to Robin than it did Bryce.)

They continued along the trail, heading out of the woods, passing many who were just heading in. Bryce was still concerned by Robin's silence, so he began to question her again about vegetation.

"Look at those mushrooms!" he called out, pointing to a bright yellow patch emerging out from a pile of wet leaves.

"I think those are yellow waxcaps," she replied quickly. "But I really don't know much about mycology. It's overwhelming actually. There are about 80,000 species of fungi identified, and they say that *that* is only about one-eighth of what is actually out there."

"Overwhelming indeed," Bryce agreed.

Just ten feet further ahead, Robin stopped in her tracks and pointed to something that looked like a broken piece of wood that had been painted a bright blue.

"That there is also a type of fungi. Chlorociboria."

"Chloro-say-what?" he laughed.

"It's such a brilliant blue-green color, people think it's rotting wood, previously painted. But what we are seeing is the production of the pigment Xylindein during the decaying process. The wood itself, known as 'green oak', was once a commodity, and it was collected for intricate, inlaid designs in wood furnishings. But the really awesome thing, and why I ultimately know about this stuff, is because Xylindein can inhibit plant germination, essentially becoming an algaecide. It makes wood less appealing to infestations and it's been studied for its cancer-fighting properties.

"There you are!" Bryce pleasantly announced.

He grabbed her hand and they continued down the trail, fastened together.

I can't believe he actually listens to my rambling, she thought. Then she shouldered into him, realizing he was at fault for causing another impromptu nature lesson.

It was 1:00 in the afternoon when they reached the trailhead kiosk near the end. They signed out, noting they had camped overnight because of the poor conditions. And yes, it was now sunny, warm, and beautiful.

At the cars, Bryce removed his pack and helped Robin out of hers, setting it on the ground. Abruptly, he pushed his body up against hers, ambushing her on the side of the car. Seeing no one around, he took her hands and placed one on his waist and one on his shoulder.

She thought, *I like this dance…*

Then he widened his stance allowing his height to meet hers. He touched his nose lightly against hers, and quietly asked.

"We made it out alive… I owe you dinner, right?"

Breathlessly, Robin muttered, "Yes."

He kissed her and slowly stood back up.

"I can't wait. How 'bout tonight?"

"Tonight would be great."

"It's crazy for you to head back to the hostel just to shower. I can set you up with whatever you need back at my place," he offered.

Robin couldn't resist. While the hostel had become comfortable—in a transient kind of way—she was excited and quite curious to see if Bryce's cabin was what she'd imagined. And an opportunity to spend another full day with him completely intrigued her.

Together, they decided it would be best if Robin followed him, in her car, to Fish Creek Pond. First, they stopped at the grocery store in Placid to pick up dinner items.

Strolling through the aisles of the grocery store together, they polished off a bag of grapes and an 'All Day Gourmet' tuna and arugula sandwich. "It's good... but my mom makes the best tuna salad," Robin muttered, wiping her mouth."

"A marathoner that makes great tuna salad? Now I *have* to meet her," Bryce asserted.

Robin wondered (and hoped) if that simple act would one day come to be. She began to daydream of where, when, and how she'd introduce him to June. Then Tommy popped into her head, and she anxiously thought, *Oh my God, Tommy has to like him.... I don't know what I'd do if he didn't.*

Interrupting her distressing thoughts, Bryce placed a package of filet mignons into the cart.

"You eat red meat, right?"

"I do."

"Phew," he said out loud.

"Mmmmm. Now I'm really looking forward to dinner," she replied.

* * *

On the way to Fish Creek Pond, Robin phoned up her mom, then Tommy, then Daisy, but got no answer from any of them. *Where the hell is everyone?* she wondered, and left the same message for all three:

"Hey, it's me. I've accomplished a lot up here already, and everything is going GREAT! I hope it is for you. I'll try you back in another day or two."

The road opened up to two lanes, and she sped up next to Bryce's car, but seeing that he was on his phone, she ducked back not wanting to distract him.

Robin knew she was in his home stretch when she saw lakes pop up on either side of the road. She grew excited. *This whole area is laced with bodies of water,* she thought. *Once I settle in up here, I might have to get myself a kayak.*

Turning onto a narrow dirt driveway, they pulled past his cabin and parked at the end of the property. Completely contained by a split rail fence, she could see that just beyond it, the land dropped off and made its way down towards the water. Through a thick mix of pine and birch, she could catch shimmering bits of Upper Saranac Lake. It was almost 4:00 in the afternoon, and the bright sun had now completely warmed the day.

Robin tried to help Bryce carry a few packages, but he stopped her.

"No way. I'll bring in all this stuff. You just take a look around." He pointed to the corner of the property. "There's a stone pathway that will take you down to the lake. Maybe we can catch the sunset there later. Or swim!" He hoisted up his pack and two full shopping bags. One of which contained Robin's most anticipated dinner, EVER!

Robin made her way down the stone stairs to a tiny dock wedged between a few boulders and an outcropping of wild iris. Looking back up towards the cabin, she spotted a dirt path that meandered off to the right along the edge of the water. It ended with a few more stone stairs leading up to a grassy ledge, where two red Adirondack chairs were perfectly placed.

She knew exactly where the sun would set. *Pinch me now,* she thought. She knelt down and ran her hand back and forth in the water.

Bryce startled her when he jumped onto the dock. "Nice spot, right?" He reached down to help her up.

She nodded, shook the water from her hand, and grabbed his arm, wrapping it around behind her. They stood on the dock, wordlessly surveying the beauty.

"Want to swim?" he asked.

"I don't have a bathing suit."

He peered down at Robin. "It's not like you need one."

Not two seconds later, a beautiful antique Hacker-Craft luxury boat sped by.

"Oh really?" she laughed.

"Can't blame a man for trying!"

He motioned her back towards the stairs, anxious to get her to the cabin. There was a certain spring in his step.

It was an old log cabin like Bryce had described. She could

tell by the porch roof which seemed to sag a little between each post that held it up. It was dark brown with red trim, and the chinking between each log was a clean shade of replacement white. The entire front of the cabin had a long narrow porch, only three steps up so there were no railings, just a boot brush and a porch swing that hung to the left of the door.

Robin entered and she could instantly smell the fireplace. Thinking to herself, *No cabin would feel legitimate without it.*

It was modern but rustic, beautiful and simple. An open layout with the majority of the kitchen against the back wall. The big stone fireplace and living room took up the entire left-hand side of the room.

Bryce motioned her to pass on through, but a welcome table stopped her. On the table was a beautiful flower arrangement with local flora, including wild iris—like those down by the lake. There was a cheese platter and a fruit platter, and a huge antique silver cup trophy loaded with ice, chilling a bottle of white wine. Behind that stood two more bottles of wine: a pink and a red. Off to the right, on the kitchen counter, sat a sparkling pitcher of lemon water and a series of wine glasses.

Just then Bryce's phone rang. *Da, na, na, na na.* "Sorry," he said, as he turned his back to hush his conversation.

"It's great.... No, I promise we're perfectly fine.... No, you can meet her some other time." He hung up the phone looking at Robin, again he said, "Sorry."

"Sorry? For what?" she asked. "This is amazing. How did…?"

He interrupted her line of questions, "Stu is working today, and I asked him to set us up with a snack and some wine. You do like wine, right?"

"Hell yeah!" Robin gleefully announced. She wanted to twirl right there as her dream happened before her very eyes.

"Stu went a little crazy, but I'm glad. Should we start with white?" he asked.

She nodded, feeling completely smug… and excited.

Bryce handed Robin a glass full of wine and led her down the hall, showing her where the bathroom and bedroom are.

"Will you be OK if I jump in the shower first? Then when you are in, I can start dinner."

"Absolutely."

Bryce looked to the foot of his bed and laughed. There was a pile of fresh white towels, a bathrobe, a small pair of matching slippers, and a box of mints with *ROBIN* written on it. Robin picked up the robe and held the soft of it to her face,

"Stu?"

"Stu."

"I love Stu," she said.

Bryce then sidestepped into the bathroom. Closing the door behind him, he beckoned, "Make yourself at home."

Robin did twirl. She sampled some cheese, ate a gigantic strawberry, and topped off her glass. Then she twirled some more. Dancing and swaying her way through the living room, she slowed to notice his collection of books. Based on what he'd explained to her, about Urban Studies, she rationalized. *I guess these books make sense. Your Money or Your Life. Mastering the Inner Game of Wealth. Landscape; The Outdoor Living Room. Love or Money, Pick One. Resort Management; Simple = Happy. Greek Mythology and the Dominant Gods. Humm, except that.* She laughed, to herself.

Then she glanced around, noticing his photos. Some were

with college buddies, some family shots, and then some curious antique photos.

Bryce came down the hallway with a wet mane of hair, an unbuttoned flannel, a pair of draw-string sweat shorts, and chunky scrunched down woolen socks.

Dreamy! again she thought, standing there holding an old black and white photo of a man and a very large weasel.

"That's my grandfather with a record mink!"

"Oh my God, I thought it was a badger or something. It's huge!" She placed the photo back on a shelf and met up with him in the hall.

"Besides what Stu set out, I *can* offer you clean underwear, but I bet they won't fit," he joked. "I pulled out a few smaller shirts and shorts like these, if you don't mind baggy. I can also launder whatever you want."

"You know…" Robin began as she walked herself backward down the hall, leading him into the bedroom, "you really know how to spoil a girl."

She grabbed the fresh white pile from his bed and then brushed up against him, making her way past and into the bathroom. Then she threw him a lascivious smile and gently closed the bathroom door.

She too came out with locks of wet hair. Sporting her own—*Thank God I packed a spare* —form-fitting Patagonia tank top, a very baggy pair of his shorts, and a new pair of bright white terry cloth slippers.

Bunching up all her hair, she clipped it into a loose pile on the top of her head and she claimed, "I'm not really dressed for dinner." Pointing at herself from head to toe and back.

"Never mind that!" he blurted out, hurrying over to Robin

he grabbed her hand—as well as the cheese platter—and scurried her out the front door. "We've got a sunset to catch!"

It was only 6:00 p.m.

"That sun is not going to set for another two plus hours," she said, descending the stone stairs.

They turned onto the small dirt path. Robin noticed that Bryce had previously brought down the fruit platter and the—now in trophy—chilled bottle of pink wine. Spinning the bottle in the ice he said, "I'm hoping the wine matches the sunset."

Then he positioned the red Adirondack chairs to perfectly face the right spot, and gestured for her to have a seat.

She did.

"Tomorrow is the summer solstice," he stated. "We'll probably have at least two and a *half* hours before the sun sets tonight. Lots of time to get to know you more."

Robin felt herself blush. *Good God here I go again!* she thought, but he continued.

"I can't think of a better way to usher in the summer, than to sit here, drink wine of a sunset color, *and* have you here to enjoy it with me."

OK that's it! Robin thought. *There is no way in hell I'm not dreaming. I mean come on! This hot guy, this perfect setting.... How can this be?*

He broke her thoughts by grabbing her hand.

"Don't you agree?"

Speechless, flustered, and in complete awe, Robin squeezed his hand and looked at him ardently. "Pinch me," she said. "Oh my God, did I just say that out loud?"

21

The Rain Check

The sky did in fact become pink. Behind a veil of pine trees and mountains in the near distance, dabs of orange and purple surrounded the simmering sun. The lowest band of color along the horizon was a pale yellow, but it reflected brilliant streaks of gold on the water. Out on the edge of the sky where blue meets the night, laid a soft pink blanket trimmed in satin.

"During the winter equinox, it takes the sun two and three-quarter minutes to set," Bryce mentioned, catching Robin in a moment of pure wonderment. "But during the summer solstice, it takes about three and one-quarter minutes. That's a whole thirty seconds more!"

He raised his glass and she followed suit. "Here's to long sunsets," he said.

"And pink! My new favorite color," Robin gushed.

Once every fleck of gold had melted away, they grabbed the trays and glasses and clambered up the stone steps together.

Earlier, Robin had told Bryce about Peter and Astri moving to Norway. In her scamper she continued, "Right now in Norway, they have what's called the Midnight Sun, which means twenty-four hours of light."

"One day, I'd like to experience that," Bryce said.

"I can hardly imagine, but even crazier, they tell me, is the total darkness in winter. Brrrrrrr," Robin said, shivering.

"Speaking of brrrr," Bryce added, "It's going to drop about

twenty degrees in the next hour." Balancing trays and bottles, and holding the door open for Robin with his foot, he enthusiastically ordered, "I'll start a fire and you can start the salad."

Once in the kitchen, Robin became more relaxed, chopping up lettuce and rummaging through his fridge. The salad was almost done, and a fire was crackling. He came up behind her, kissed the back of her neck, and unclipped her hair so it cascaded down. The chills he sent down her spine were noticeable.

"Your little tank shirt; you must be cold. Go in my closet and grab one of my flannels. Until we're in front of the fire, I don't want you to catch a chill. I'll finish up."

"Well, all righty," she said, and padded her way down the hall thinking, *I really love how he is always so concerned for me.*

Robin was not used to this type of treatment. It seemed for her entire life, she was always the one concerned with everyone and everything. Her whole being was structured around discipline. Making sure her grades were perfect, working at the café to make ends meet, making sure her mom never had anything to worry about. Basically, making sure every aspect of her life was in order and going as planned. Robin thought she had complete control of everything. Except for Tommy of course. She had resigned to the fact that she couldn't count on him until he figured out his own stuff.

"Not the closet on the right! The one on the left!" Bryce yelled out, just before she entered his bedroom.

Humm? Now she was curious about the closet on the right.

He placed the small table from the kitchen on an angle so that once Robin sat, the heat from the fire behind, completely warmed her. Facing the kitchen, she watched Bryce move about, serving her like a dignified waiter. He uncorked a bottle of red wine, with a fancy label—*Grand Vin* something or other. Robin knew nothing about good wine. Other than that pink was now her new favorite.

"May I?" he asked before he began to pour.

"But of course," she answered, peeling off the flannel and tossing it on the couch off to her right. The lambent light from the fire cast a soft amber glow that licked her bare shoulders. It practically stopped Bryce in his tracks.

From the oven he pulled out an au gratin vegetable casserole that Robin figured must have been another Stu-ism. Then she watched him carefully turn the filets onto plates, pouring on a magical sauce.

"Smells delish!" she announced, remembering Margo's gourmet dinners back in the old afterschool days with Tommy.

"Medium-rare?"

"Perfect."

Across from Robin, sliding his chair in under the table, his bare knees rubbed against hers sending chills—once again—down her spine. With the fire blazing at her back, it was he that aroused her skin; she was the *furthest* thing from chilly. Her mind began to drift to last night's rendezvous. *His warm body, tight against mine.* She knew just where this night was going.... She knew before long she'd have her legs wrapped around him.

She realized her heart was wildly pounding, and her face was probably an interesting shade of red. She fought to contain her vivid imagination before she lost it completely and dove across the table right on top of him.

"You OK?" he asked.

She sliced deep into her filet and looked up at him. "You know," she began, "you always ask me about me. Tell me more about you!"

"Hmmmm?" he asked, "What's your favorite book?"

"Wait!" she laughed. "That's about me!"

He concurred and told Robin about how his parents had recently retired to Manhattan, and his sister, Whitney, is studying philosophy at Oxford. Then he back peddled, "No really, what's your favorite book?"

"Fine," she said. "My favorite book is Wild by Cheryl Strayed."

"Great book!" he said. "I think the movie's about to come out."

"Yours?"

"Well if you can believe, *Into the Wild* by Jon Krakauer. It's one of my all-time favorites."

"Oh, I loved that movie! But I didn't read the book. I'm sure the book was much better; they always are."

"Both are true stories.... Can you imagine?"

"I'll take hers any day over his." Robin shuddered. "The jury is still out on exactly how he died, but ultimately, it was from a plant called Eskimo potato also known as alpine sweetvetch. Its roots are edible, but the seeds contain toxins.

"Of course, you'd know the name of the plant!" Bryce gazed adoringly at her before adding, "But that poor guy."

He poured more wine into their glasses. Pensively, he lifted his, and changed the subject.

"My dad taught me about wine... well a little anyway. Mostly about Bordeaux." He held the glass higher and swirled it. "See these lines coming down inside the glass?"

"Uh-huh." She nodded.

"Well, they're called legs. You can tell a lot about the body of wine because of the legs."

"Stop! You're just making that up now," she said, looking incredulously at him.

"No, I swear," he laughed. "Now put your nose all the way into the glass." He stuffed his nose in his and she followed along.

"Now take a deep, but slow, sniff. Not a snort, not a whiff, but a nice slow analyzing kind of sniff. Inhale the aroma and lift your head."

She did.

"Now what do you sense?"

"Licorice."

"Good God, you're a natural!" he shouted with excitement.

She didn't know whether to take him seriously or not, but she was completely elated watching the excitement on his face.

He added some more wine to their glasses and slid back from the table.

"Finished?" he asked, though he already knew, as her plate was empty.

Elbowing up on the table, Robin plopped her head in her hand and in a dreamlike state, watched Bryce clear the dishes away.

"That was amazing," she said earnestly.

"Yeah, but I didn't consider dessert," he said solemnly.

"Please, don't even give it a second thought," she said, as she pushed back and got up, intending to help with the dishes.

"Absolutely not," he reprimanded her. Then looking even more sternly at her he placed the dishes in the sink and said, "They can wait."

He spun around and came right up to her. With the back of his hand, he stroked the side of her face and then scooped her up off her feet. He started down the hall with her clutched in his arms. Stopping at the end of the hall, he set her back down on her feet directly in front of the *"closet on the right."* Robin stood nervous but excited, waiting for his next move.

"Go ahead. Open the door," he insisted.

The door had a long vertical handle made out of an antler. Once she had it in her hand, she twisted back, looking apprehensively at him.

"Elk," he responded.

The door could only be opened with a robust tug. So, on the second try, she pulled even harder.

The heavy wooden door began to sweep across the floor with a hush. As it slowly opened, she realized just how thick and solid it really was. Then a blast of frigid air and the smell of cedar swarmed her. Standing like a deer in the headlights, the cold darkness swallowed her. Now the chills that ran down her spine were real. She felt Bryce's arm sweep past hers and he tapped on a light.

Right there before her very eyes, a huge collection of luxurious furs. Hanging on pegs, draped on large dowels, and piled onto shelves. She stepped in and immersed herself into the nearest one. Bryce stood back with his hands on his hips, watching Robin's awe unfold.

"Is this all mink?" she asked, lifting her arms and swooning in the extravagance.

"Pick one of the hanging ones on the left and we'll go sit by the fire," he chuckled.

She sidestepped into the plush layers and he lost sight of her until she emerged enswathed in a deep tawny cover. Robin then gathered the opulent mass up around herself and sauntered back down the hall.

Turning to sit on the couch in front of the fire, she stumbled. Looking down she asked, "Is that a real bear head?"

The large dark carpet—she hadn't noticed earlier—between the fireplace and the big leather couch, was of course, a bearskin rug.

"Yeech, I didn't realize they left the head on." She skirted around the head and dropped to the center of the couch.

Bryce laughed again at Robin. Taking a seat next to her, he handed her her glass, and poured in the last of the Bordeaux.

"I know it's a little weird to look at," he said. "And having the head protrude up like that is a hazard, but you were so engulfed in that fur you couldn't see it." He pulled at a corner of the giant mink blanket to cover some of his legs.

"Oh sorry, I'm hogging it," she laughed, fluffing it out, inviting him in.

Now partially covered, Bryce revealed, "Some of the furs in that closet are older than my grandfather. Pretty cool right?"

Robin pulled the fur down from her shoulders. "My God, this is an irreplaceable and priceless heirloom," she said, as she continued to writhe out from under it.

Bryce lifted it back around her shoulders and tucked it behind her, "Relax, there's a closet full if you didn't notice."

"A closet full of furs and a real bear rug...? Kind of sad really," Robin said.
Not wanting to offend Bryce, she continued, "Not that I'd protest and come back with red spray paint or anything, but these days it just isn't cool anymore. Ya know?"

"Oh, I know. I'm not a fan of real fur.... Well, *new* real fur that is. But every fur and skin I have is from so long ago that destroying any now would be a total waste. And way back then, it was a necessity. Plus, because of my heritage and my grandfather, they are treasures to me."

Robin held her glass and clinked his. "To *only* really old furs," she said.

He took the wine glass from her hand and set it on a side table. Looking at her intensely, he slid his body close underneath the fur and pulled hers even closer. Stroking her face, gazing into her eyes, with his fingers he began to trace her neckline. He kissed the top of her exposed shoulder. He then paused and fished the necklace out from under her shirt. With the sun charm resting in his fingertips, he said, "I meant to ask about this. It's appropriate for this time of year, I'd say."

Robin hesitated and placed her hand over his, essentially hiding the charm. "It's nothing, really. It's from a friend who thinks I have a sunny disposition."

"Well he was right," Bryce added.

Robin thought to herself, *How did he know he was a he?* But, wanting to distract him, she lowered his hand with hers and placed it in the middle of her chest.

"I can feel your heart beating," he whispered.

He pulled the neckline of her top down so it revealed the sun charm again. He kissed it. Then he swung it off to the side and kissed the skin in the center of her chest. He looked up to her for an invitation. Longingly, she gazed at him and she slid her body low and level to *his* gaze. She drew him in with a passionate kiss and slid down even more. Lifting her arms up, with his help, she squirmed out of her shirt and slid further down the leather couch, becoming horizontal underneath him.

Suddenly there was a loud knock at the door. Bryce peeled himself off Robin. With a demonic look in his eyes, he growled, "I bet that's Stu. He doesn't understand the concept of 'maybe later.'

Don't move!" he commanded, "I might have to walk him back, but I'm saving you all for myself tonight."

Robin stared up at Bryce and whispered, "I'll go nowhere." All the while thinking, *Are you kidding? This is the rain check I've been waiting for!*

As he turned for the front door, she slid completely flat and then slithered out of the baggy shorts. Tossing them out from underneath the mink blanket, she then buried herself in complete furgasim.

Bryce returned to the cabin miffed but anxious. Closing the door quietly behind him, he thought he'd sneak up on Robin and reintroduce a little excitement. Creeping up behind the couch, he peered down onto a sleeping beauty. He then thought about how he needed to establish some new ground rules for Stu.

Avoiding the bear head completely, he rounded wide to the front of the couch. Skillfully he uplifted and gently wrapped the fur blanket around her, levitating her from the living room to the bedroom. When he settled her on top of his bed, she let out a gratifying hum. She didn't flinch. He thought he could stand over her and stare for the remainder of the night. Instead, he tiptoed back to the kitchen to finish up the dishes.

* * *

The next morning Robin woke warm and content. Until she opened her eyes and realized where she was. Without moving, she lay there reviewing the entire evening in her head.

No, I specifically remember everything. I drank a lot of wine, but it was over the course of sunset, dinner, the fur vault, his kiss, and my pounding heart... Stu! Oh my God, I'm going to kill Stu, she concluded.

She knew it was still very early in the morning. She didn't

even chance rolling over—to look at Bryce—in fear of disturbing him. She could hear his deep breathing and wanted him to sleep well. Like she obviously did.

Lying there, she was content admiring his bedroom. Most of the bedding and accessories were different hues of brown. A polished rock cairn sat on a table with a few books next to an old leather chair and ottoman. *A perfect place to read,* she thought. The room was painted a light sage color. *I'd call this color, bliss,* she thought.

The sun was beginning to shine through a row of windows that sat high overhead lining the complete back wall of the room. Under the windows was a series of dressers and drawers that also ran the length of the room. There, Robin spotted a neat pile of her clothes and towels. *Shit, he even folded my stuff,* she thought.

In front of that wall, a few feet from the dressers and high up at the crook of the ceiling, a cable ran parallel from one end of the room to the other. A huge gather of curtains was pushed up against the end of the wall, where Bryce's clothes closet was; the one with his flannel shirts. Robin laughed at herself, initially curious about the *other* closet, *"the closet on the right."* Essentially, one could pull the curtain across the cable and completely seal off a portion of the room, creating a separate dressing area.

Genius! Robin thought. *I bet it blocks the light from the high windows; probably helps with glare on the TV too.* (Which hung on the wall across from the foot of the bed.)

The morning sun began to creep down from the ceiling, through the windows, and across the room. Then it dawned on Robin, *Today is the actual summer solstice! It will take the sun three and one-quarter minutes to rise.*

Now a solid golden rectangle was beaming into the room,

slowly moving toward the bed. *It's like a freaking gamma-ray. Who the hell could sleep through that?* she thought.

She tactfully rose from the bed and scurried over to the massive curtain.

Slowly pulling it across the cable, she snuffed out the light just before it met with the bed... and Bryce. The smooth beige fabric captured the light and illuminated the entire area behind it, leaving the bed and the majority of the room relatively dim.

Now partitioned off, standing naked on the sunny side of the room, she pulled Bryce's flannel from her pile. She held it to her face and inhaled his scent before she slipped it on, again thinking, *I could kill Stu!*

She clipped her hair back up in a mound and grabbed a towel. *I'll just tiptoe out and into the bathroom.*

Peeking her head out, she saw that Bryce was up on one elbow, watching her. Looking at him, she felt a warm flush completely fill her. He had a glow of his own and his watchful eyes sent her back behind the curtain, blushing.

"How long have you been watching me?" she asked.

"Only since you first drew the curtain," he answered smugly.

"It's amazing," he continued. "I haven't drawn that curtain in months. The backfill of light completely illuminates that part of the room so when you step near the curtain, it's a perfect silhouette of you."

Still flustered, she stood there silently.

"Put that towel back down and just stand there for me."

She did.

"Right now, your silhouette looks like Fred Flintstone with that big flannel shirt."

She giggled.

"Take it off," he demanded.

At first, she hesitated. Then she unbuttoned the shirt allowing it to fall to the floor. In complete silence, she continued to stand there.

"It's amazing. You're beautiful. I wish you could see your perfect lines."

"You're amazed that I'm beautiful?" she said as she nervously giggled again.

"Hell no! I mean, by how the sunlight does this. No one has ever been on that side of a drawn curtain, so I have never seen this effect."

Still not sure how to react, Robin nervously said, "Well now you just sound like Daisy." Then she heard the rustle of his sheets.

"No seriously," he continued. "Sway for me."

"Sway?"

"Yeah sway... or move slow... I like looking at you."

Now she was on display. She felt awkward. But the sunlight that filled that entire area, warmed her skin. She closed her eyes and swayed. She thought about the warmth, she thought about him, she moved gracefully.

She started thinking about last night and what she missed. She thought about how he began to kiss her. With her own fingertips, she delicately outlined her curves.

"You're killing me," he breathed from beyond the curtain.

She swayed more, thinking of how she felt under the mink next to him. She was careful to not move the curtain. If it billowed out, her silhouette would disperse. She moved her hands across her breasts, lightly caressing herself within her own movements.

Now hearing slight movements from the other side of the

curtain, in her excitement, she stopped and stood still again. She could sense Bryce was close. She sensed his body heat as if she was endowed with sonar; she knew he was just on the other side, immediately opposite of her. In a final sway, she whirled around, leaning her head back and brushing up against the curtain. She felt his hands deftly trace her over the curtain. She could feel his breath permeate through and onto her neck. She felt his mouth sensuously peck at her.

The silken material slithering between them was a complete tease, and when Bryce couldn't take it anymore, he threw the curtain open. He lifted Robin, walked her over, and laid her gently on the bed. His movements continued in the rhythmic pattern she developed with her solstice morning sun-dance. With his hands, he drew on her. He outlined her breasts and gathered them up in his hands, kissing them and licking her nipples. He moved sensitively from head to toe.

He flung open a drawer from the bedside table and slid on a condom without missing a beat. Robin ached for him, slithering along his side with her lustful movements. Then she felt his breath on her belly, between her legs, and then the warmth of his tongue slip inside of her. She thought she could die right there. She pulled him up and she lifted her legs, inviting him in.

Robin howled out as he entered her, and he moaned in succession. With Robin tight in his grips, he rocked up backward so she was now seated on top of him. Grinding, he continued to caress her breasts and curves. Pulling down on her hips with each of his thrusting movements, his pleasure was audible with carnal groans. Passionately glaring up at her, making sure she was satisfied, he looked for a sign. Robin threw her head back and let out a salacious cry. He rocked her back down and in a final thrust of his own, he too wailed out.

Melting down on top of her, he cradled her in his arms and rotated her back to rest on top of him. With both his hands, he held her head and looked lovingly into her eyes. "There you are," he whispered.

Not one word was spoken for the next ten minutes. Upon full reflection, Robin's mind had wildly gone where it never had before. She didn't know what to make of it lying there in a stupefied and wondrous state.

Their hearts settled to a calm, and the birdsong of the longest summer morning made them conscious.

Bryce kissed Robin's forehead. "I kind of feel like I need to thank Stu now," he said.

22

The Lasso

"Hi, this is Jan."

"Oh, hi! I'm Tommy. I got your number from your brother Bert. I promised him I'd call you. I'm looking for an apartment or studio in lower Manhattan."

Jan worked for Urban Realty Group. Her office was just across the street from Union Square Park, where she and Tommy decided to meet.

"There's a bunch of little green tables and chairs in the center of the park.... Will I be able to spot you in a crowd?" she asked.

"I've been told I look a lot like your brother."

"Wow, that's pretty funny. OK, how do you take your coffee?"

"Whole milk and Stevia."

"1:00?"

"Works for me!"

Tommy hung up the phone, excited. He wasn't quite sure if it was about apartment hunting or if it was about meeting Bert's sister. Already she seemed direct and efficient. *Like Bert,* he thought. Tommy had been seeing quite a bit of Bert since first meeting him at Bryant Park.

Hmmm, there's a theme here with parks, he laughed to himself, walking into Union Square Park. He decided to get there early and grab lunch from the pavilion at the north end, forcing himself to sit and relax before they met.

Relaxing for Tommy had become challenging over the past few weeks: Bert had been staying a few nights at Tommy's and in turn, Tommy stayed a few nights at Bert's place. The instant commitment was a little overwhelming for both of them, so collectively they decided to limit it to just three days a week. They thought their lust for each other would eventually fade but it didn't. Tommy was concerned that his fraction of a percent less than perfect performance—during any given show—might jeopardize his role. He performed six nights a week at the theatre and the curtain calls back home with Bert exhausted him. Thankfully, the understudy handled one roaming night as well as the matinees.

Most nights when they hooked up, Bert would come from the nightclub he managed, which usually meant it wasn't until the wee hours that Tommy would feel Bert's legs slip in next to his. Bert called it happy hour. Tommy was just happy to comply, feeling their connection was more than skin deep. To Tommy, cutting back a few days and slowing things down didn't mean anything other than a chance for him to focus more on his work. That was even more important now since *Significant Other* would end in August. Soon he would need a new role.

Tommy finished up his lunch and walked to the center of the park. Stopping in the middle of the group of green tables, he did a scouting 360-degree circumrotation. A beautiful woman with a white fedora and a long dark ponytail rose from a chair and approached him. The coffee in each hand was a dead giveaway.

Smiling and handing one off to Tommy, she followed up with a handshake saying, "Holy shit, you do look like my brother!"

Tommy followed her out of the park and began to explain what he was looking for in an apartment. Smirking at him, Jan gently cut him off. "Bert told me what you basically need. Apparently, you two have hit it off and spend a lot of time together!"

"Well, we recently put some limitations on it," Tommy

said, a tad embarrassed. "It's too soon to get serious. I mean shit, I'm only just moving out of my college dorm!"

"Good!" Jan replied. "The only thing you need to be serious about is finding a place. Bert mentioned you have to be out in a week, is that right?"

"Yeah, one week. Sorry 'bout that."

"I know, I know. You've been occupied," Jan moaned, taunting him with an arrogant grin and a tilt of her head.

They looked at two small places in the neighborhood and on their way to the third, Tommy clarified, "I need a big enough place that if my friend Pauly stays, it won't get weird. Bert doesn't know about Pauly...."

"What do you mean by weird?" Jan questioned with a look of uncertainty. (Her strict upbringing, together with her brother's lifestyle, always made her a little uncomfortable.)

"I mean weird because Pauly is straight, so I'd need enough room to be able to have a separate sleeping area for him. Not that I'd shack up with Bert when my friend is around or anything. Oh, hell no! He's a comedian and I don't want to be the complete brunt of his routine."

"Really?" Jan sarcastically questioned.

"Yeah, that's probably TMI, but I want you to know my feelings for Bert are sincere."

"Tell me whatever you want," she said, "but just please don't expose yourself too much."

"Expose myself?"

"Yeah like as in don't be vulnerable! Not expose, expose," she muffled shaking her head. "Crap, gay people are so sensitive."

Tommy realized at that moment, he was veritably confiding in Jan. It was probably for security reasons because he had thought,

OK, maybe I am a little concerned about where I stand with Bert.

He decided to say something more assuring. "Don't worry about me, I've been around the block. I got this." But even as he said that, he realized he really didn't and was quite unsure of this current predicament and Bert's true feelings.

It wasn't exactly a loft, but it was an open aired apartment, on the third floor above a Foot Locker on 14th Street—and it was perfect. Three flights up a boxed set of stairs in the middle of the building led to a hallway that only three other apartments worked off of. Once inside the apartment, a full wall of windows on the street-side of the apartment offered a ton of natural light. The only matter of concern Tommy had was the old radiators.

"Do they hiss a lot?"

"Not today!" Jan said, fanning herself with her clipboard.

It was now almost 4:00 in the afternoon. The sun was blaring through the highest part of the windows directly onto the kitchen island where Tommy was shuffling papers, getting ready to sign a lease agreement.

"Tomorrow you can swing by my office with the security deposit and the first month's rent. You can officially move in on the first."

Tommy made his way back down towards the Village to his NYU dorm on Third Avenue. Becoming melancholy as he walked next to Washington Square Park, he made a right turn and veered in. He sat on the long circular cement bench in the hot and humid late day sun, reflecting on his whole college experience and how quickly the past four years had gone by.

An impromptu choral performance of a Beatles medley popped up in front of the center fountain of the park. He listened to six students sing as he watched their—not quite professional yet—dance moves. Suddenly he became overwhelmed with emotion. A fusion of sad and happy swirled in his head. He was thrilled about how his career was taking off. He was excited about his new apartment. And he was elated to be in a relationship with Bert. But everything suddenly seemed so definitive. *Is this truly what I want?* he thought. He walked over to the fountain and dunked his head right into the pool of water.

Opening the door to his dorm room, he now thought about trite things like: *This will be one of the last times I put my key in the lock.* Then upon passing the closet, he thought, *I'll never hang my scarf on that hook again.*

Once he fully entered the room, he heard Bert in the shower. Needing to change his focus completely, he stripped, dropping all his clothes right there and stepped into the shower with Bert. He planted his forehead on Bert's wet chest and let the hot water beat down on his back. Bert grabbed a handful of body soap and began to wash away his cares.

Once Tommy returned to a conscious and cheerful state, he told Bert how awesome the apartment was.

"There's enough room for a guest…. The kitchen and bathroom are completely updated…. There's a big wooden step ladder that slides over a storage closet, giving access to a loft bedroom, up in the top half of the entire apartment!"

Handing a towel to Tommy, Bert stood quietly watching and listening, appreciating his excitement. He snapped his towel at Tommy asking, "And Jan?"

"Like you…" Tommy began, as he lassoed Bert with *his* towel and pulled him in close.

"…Your sister is beautiful too."

Together, they got dressed and ready for work. Their demanding nights were about to begin.

* * *

Even at night, the heat of the summer blasted them as soon as they stepped onto the sidewalk. Walking hand-in-hand, nine blocks north to the subway hub at Union Square, they decided they would invite Tommy's folks over for dinner the first week he was in his new place. Bert offered, "I'll make a special dinner."

Besides this being his first apartment, this would be the first time Tommy has ever introduced his parents to a lover. "Wow. Now I'm kind of nervous," Tommy admitted.

"Oh, relax! They're going to love me," Bert quipped.

"I'll stock up on wine. Margo loves her wine," Tommy added.

Bert stopped and looked earnestly at Tommy. "It really sounds like a perfect place." He kissed Tommy's cheek and dropped down the set of stairs into the subway.

Tommy shouted after him, "Jan's getting me an extra entry card and key for you!"

* * *

Tommy was startled at first by the odd buzzing noise. Then it dawned on him. *Ah, this is the first time anyone ever buzzed my intercom.*

A deliveryman announced himself and Tommy buzzed him up. The loud knock at his door turned into a huge bouquet of flowers. Tommy closed the door and fished out the card.

Congrats on your new place! ~ Jan

Expecting them to have come from Bert, they caught him off guard. *I'm not going to overthink this,* he rationalized. *Bert was sweet enough to take the night off so he could make a nice dinner. I will NOT overthink this."*

He texted Bert: *Please stop and buy a vase somewhere on your way here.*

He did.

* * *

Four hours later, the second buzz came, followed by the second loud knock that introduced Margo and Frank to Bert as he opened the door for them. Tommy—just around the corner—had been pacing in the kitchen.

"Mom! Dad!" Tommy shouted, rounding into the hall to greet them.

Taller than his dad for years, Tommy still felt like a little boy engulfed in his huge wingspan. Margo stepped in next and grabbed Tommy's face, kissing both sides. Then she stepped back to inspect him.

"Ya look good," she said.

Then she glanced back at Bert, who was icing the wine Margo had handed off.

"He's pretty cute too," Margo added.

Over dinner, the four of them dined, drank, and laughed. Margo asked Bert more questions than Tommy would have ever imagined. In fact, she seemed more interested in him than her own son!

"Mom, really? Let him come up for some air."

Bert laughed it off. "It's fine. You never told me your mom loved to cook. Now I totally have to up my game."

Before they left, Margo paced through the living room. "I'm sending you a Metro Living catalog. You pick out a nice L-shaped couch for this area, and a fun coffee table. Consider it a housewarming gift from us."

Bert saw Margo and Frank down to the street and walked with them towards the parking garage. "Really, it's no big deal. I need to shoot over to my club to check on things," he said. Back at the apartment, Tommy poured the last of Margo's Pinot Gris into his glass, dropped into his—soon to be replaced—black pleather dorm couch, and he pulled out his phone.

"Call Robin," he commanded.

23

Just the Right Place

"TOMMY! Oh my God, oh my God, I have so much to tell you! I MISS YOU! How are you?"

"Wow! You sound excited."

"I am! But really... how are you?"

"I'm great. Really, really great!"

"Mean it?"

"I mean it!"

Tommy told Robin all about the apartment and how great things were going with Bert.

"It's weird though, how people think we look alike. I don't see it. I just think he's so hot," Tommy laughed. "Man, my mom couldn't get enough of him, and Frank was his typical quiet, burly self. I'm pretty sure he's ok with my lifestyle now. It's too late for me to be a jock." Tommy laughed again. "Poor Frank... I know he'd rather have gone to college football games than theater shows."

Robin was compelled to inquire, "So you're ok with you? I mean I know how you've been struggling with your identity, and by that, I mean, I know how stressed and confused you were."

Suddenly Robin was concerned she might be offending Tommy. She was babbling. "I mean, well I don't know Tommy... I was really worried about you. Even the last time we spoke, I wasn't sure I could take you seriously when you said that Bert makes you feel the way you want to feel. He better be good to you! That's all I can say Tommy, you better be happy."

"Robin. Stop worrying. It's good. Really good."

There was a long pause. Then Robin demanded, "Well then I need to meet him. You can meet Bryce and I can meet Bert!"

"Bryce? You mean the one you recently met and had dinner with?"

"Yup. I don't know where to start Tommy. My heart skips when I think of him."

"Shit. Have you seen a doctor?" he laughed.

"Ha ha," she snipped.

Then Robin gave serious thought to pressing the issue of them all meeting up. *Tommy will be overprotective of me. But we all have to meet sooner or later.*

"Listen," she said. "Fall is around the corner and it's stunning up here then. Bring Bert up. We can do a hike. He can hike, right?" Wanting to retract her sarcastic statement, she quickly segued, "Seriously, I'm looking at a few apartments this weekend and should have my own place soon. Let's figure out a date. OK?"

"OK."

She hung up the phone, a little miffed. *I don't like this Bert,* she thought. She sensed that Tommy wouldn't trust Bryce either. *How is any judgment even possible at this stage?* Then she questioned her own thoughts. *Was it a competition? Who had the better guy? Who was happier? Now I'm just being ridiculous,* she rationalized. *Nah, I'm just PMS-ing.*

Robin planned to look at a few places over the weekend with Bryce, but her dad William and his fiancé Amanda came up for an unexpected visit. The message on her phone said, "We're staying at the Lake Placid Lodge for the weekend. Thought we'd check out your hood. Got any plans?"

Robin met them for lunch Saturday afternoon on her way to

look at a place right on the edge of town in Lake Placid.

"Our afternoon is open after lunch," her dad indicated. "If you don't mind us tagging along, I'd love to see what you're looking at and take in more of the area."

"Fine. You drive, Dad. I'll be the tour guide."

Not that Robin knew all that much about the area; mostly she knew how to get to the trails, and how to make her way around the mountains. And *now* she knew how to get to the Lake Placid Lodge. But if she was going to live here, it was time to learn.

The first apartment they looked at was walking distance to everything, affordable rent, and recently refurbished. It was one, in a series of studio units, with a street level entrance and parking right out front. The owner opened the door and let them in.

"Originally a motel, it was a big deal up here during the 1980 Olympics," he said.

The three of them walked in and sized it up. Robin noticed Amanda poking William's side, whispering. "Just tell her."

Robin stopped in her tracks and put her hands on her hips, signaling she wanted to know.

"Bin?" her dad questioned.

Cripes he hasn't called me that since I was little, must be important, she thought.

"Amanda is moving in with me and she has a ton of left-over furniture you can have if you'd like."

All the while, Amanda stood off to his side with a gleaming smile nodding her head. It reminded Robin of the Hillary Clinton bobble-head Daisy had in her car.

"Sure, Dad, I told Daisy she could keep most of the stuff we had accumulated, so I could probably use some. Moving in huh? That's cool."

Still just a wide nodding grin came from Miss bobble-head.

Robin was happy for her dad. Amanda wasn't that bad. She actually got him to take up bike riding, so she was good for his health. Now, Robin just hoped she had good taste in furniture.

Amanda finally piped in, "Let's see where you settle. Your dad and I can pack up a U-Haul and send it north. Most of my stuff is neutral; I'm sure you can make it work."

"Well thanks in advance," Robin said.

The owner of the apartment closed the door behind them and handed Robin his card. "If you're serious, you can move in as soon as next week. Take a look around back and check out the neighborhood, but I gotta run."

He hopped in his car and as he pulled away, he rolled down the window. "I hope to hear from you!"

No sooner had he left, a Harley motorcycle rider pulled quickly into the spot the owner pulled out of. A large leather-clad man rushed past them. He began to pound on the door—one door over from where they just exited.

Robin, Amanda, and William stood there astonished, watching a domestic dispute unfold right in front of them.

"Get the fuck out here!" the man yelled as he pounded.

A half-dressed woman swung the door open and stood there. She had to be 350 plus pounds, wearing a dirty white t-shirt and flip-flops.

Robin, Amanda, and William about faced and slowly walked back to the car, hearing:

"Mom! Why the fuck did you sell my rifle?"

"Why the fuck did you sleep with— " But the door slammed shut behind him, muffling out the rest of their screaming match.

As they pulled away, startled and laughing, they took turns finishing his sentence. "Why the fuck did you sleep with..."

"That whore?" suggested Amanda.

"How about... my sister?" suggested William.

"No, I got it... your sister," roared Robin.

Simultaneously they all howled, "Eeeewwwwwwww!"

William finished up with, "Yep! I don't think you want to live next to that!"

Their next stop was a tiny gray, modified saltbox house in the town of Keene, about fifteen minutes northwest of the hostel where she'd been staying. Robin drove past it every time she went to the High Peaks Information Center or to see Bryce. It was situated right on the main road. Not something favorable, but since she passed it so often it was obviously convenient.

The three of them stood on a large slab of cement that could be considered a front porch. Robin reached up and felt the key on the top of the window frame to the right of the door.

"Owner said it's cool. He rents it out seasonally but he's tired of dealing with vacationers so he emptied it out and plans to paint," Robin said.

Then she pointed to a mini camera tucked up behind them off the corner of the porch roof.

"He's probably watching us now. He said there's one around back too, but that's it."

"I don't know if that is a good thing or a bad thing," William grumbled.

It was tiny. Standing just inside the front door you could see the whole spread. A potbelly stove on the left with the kitchen just past that. A Dutch door in the kitchen led to a small wooden deck out back. The staircase was essentially the middle of the house, and a small bathroom was tucked behind that. The rest of the main floor wrapped around to the right of the staircase. It was a decent size for a living room, or *'parlor,'* Robin imagined, and then she stated, "This must have been some kind of road house back in the day."

Off the kitchen up the creaky set of stairs, a long, dark and narrow attic bedroom took up the entire floor. With only one small window at each end peak, Robin thought, *I wonder if Amanda's stuff will include lamps.*

Back through the living room and down the even creakier stairs, the basement was cold and damp. Two sets of sliding doors on the back wall offered the only light into the dingy room. The late afternoon sun lit up a back corner where Robin spotted a washer/dryer combo unit. The opposite corner had a pile of mountain climbing gear and cross-country skis veiled in cobwebs.

"Definitely needs a clean and bright coat of paint down here, I'd say," Robin announced.

"Agreed! Absolutely!" William and Amanda chimed in.

Through the sliders, stepping onto a stone patio outside, the backyard sloped down and opened up to a beautiful mountainous view. An old rope hammock, that stretched between two deck posts, swung in the summer breeze.

"This place has potential," Robin said.

"Let's discuss it over dinner. Join us at the lodge? And ask what's-his-name to come too, if he can."

"Bryce, Dad. It's Bryce."

Not willing to admit how head over heels she was for Bryce, she told them very little about him over the course of the day. She purposely wanted to keep them in the dark. Though her dad had been spending more and more time with her as an adult, being so absent in her teens—her formidable years—she wondered if she would ever completely forgive him.

* * *

The three of them, engrossed in conversation about the little house, barely noticed the waiter circling the table tactfully, pouring wine in each of their glasses. Robin looked up to thank him.
"What the heck?" She jumped up and out of her seat, and threw her arms around him. "Dad, Amanda, this is Bryce!"

He set the bottle of wine down, "I was able to cut out early, thought I'd surprise you."

He firmly shook William's hand. Then he took Amanda's and kissed it. "Pleasure to meet you both," he said.

"Wow, a real gentleman," William said. "Are you able to join us?" He reached over and pulled out the chair next to him. He then looked to Robin, "Or does he work here?"

"Nope, he works and lives a couple of towns from here at a high-end resort, or camp. I never know what to call it."

"Great Camp," Bryce specified. "It dates back to the Gilded Age, and that's what they all called it."

Bryce sat down and with a nod, he signaled the waiter over to the table. "Thank you for allowing me to do that," he said. "Now if you could just please bring *me* a glass."

Robin was finding it difficult to keep her composure with all the excitement of Bryce being there *and* having just found a perfect place. She had been smug all day (and during the walk-through), but once she saw the basement of the house, she knew it was a done deal. She couldn't wait to tell Bryce all about the little gray saltbox in Keene.

After a brief description, she excitedly leaned into Bryce and said, "I can conceivably turn the basement into a growing lab,

231

and I bet I could get my company to pay for it!"

Over dinner, Bryce and William discussed everything from the early mink trade business to urban renewal in the Adirondacks. Amanda and Robin reviewed the contents of what would be packed into the U-Haul.

"Yes, I'll make sure to include a few lamps." Amanda promised.

24

A Lot of Stuff

Friday, August 1st, Robin went to New Paltz to pack up her stuff. Her place in Keene was ready. Aron had a pickup truck. Daisy and he planned to follow Robin up with the bulk of the items; most of which seemed to be plant containers and terrariums that she had collected over the past four years.

Robin checked the ropes that held her mattress to the roof of her car and solemnly looked back at the second-floor apartment. "Many good times up there. I'm not gonna lie," she said, "I'll miss that place."

Aron rounded the car and double-checked her knots. "Come to visit whenever you want, just bring beer," he said with a snorting laugh.

* * *

Bryce was parked in front of the little gray saltbox when they pulled in. After appropriate hugs, handshakes, and introductions all around, the four of them proceeded to scurry back and forth until everything was inside the house. Including a full supply of beer and wine. "Well in case we get thirsty," Bryce said, kissing Robin's sweaty forehead. "Mmmm, salty. Got any lime and tequila?"

With an ardent smirk, Robin lightly punched him and said, "You're sick."

Daisy and Aron stood off to the side amused, rolling their eyes.

"Hey Robin?" Bryce questioned, while she unpacked a box of linens. "You know that mountain out back is called 'Owls Head' right? I've hiked it and I think Stu has rock climbed it; I bet there's a trail out back."

"That would explain the climbing gear in the basement," she said. "And what? Stu climbs?"

"Yeah. That boy never ceases to amaze me."

"Me either!" she answered, peering at Bryce. "Whom, I might add, I still need to meet."

"Yes, yes you do."

All four collectively decided to take a quick break. The house was positively torrid being so close to the road with no near-by trees to shade it. They grabbed a cold drink and made their way to the edge of the woods to look for a trail.

But with a sudden rumble up at the road, and per Amanda's earlier text, the U-Haul showed up and the drivers promptly began to unload, placing everything onto the cement slab; one could call a porch. Aron and Bryce insisted the girls just point and direct where things should be placed.

"Those two lamps can definitely go upstairs," Robin advised as she and Daisy continued to empty boxes.

An hour later the last thing to move was the monster couch. Aron hulked it by himself to the threshold of the front door.

"Yup, that's my Viking!" Daisy announced zealously.

They all stood and pondered how it was going to fit inside. They screwed off its feet, crossed their fingers, and scratched the hell out of the newly painted door frame trying to get it in.

"This thing weighs a ton," Bryce huffed out helping Aron.

Aron said nothing, just pursed his lip and blew out hard breaths. As soon as it cleared through, they situated it in the Robin-determined spot and Aron plopped down on top of it. "You know it's so heavy cause it's a pullout couch, right?" he said.

"Fabulous!" Robin exclaimed. "Now you can *definitely* spend the night!"

Except for Robin's plant management supplies and containers stacked in the corner of the living room, everything was surprisingly orderly.

Daisy and Robin were now relaxing outside on the kitchen deck. "Of course we picked the hottest day of summer to do this," Daisy said, cracking another beer. "I'm exhausted!"

"That makes two of us," said Robin.

Bryce had ordered, and since gone out for food. Aron insisted that he be the first one to test out the shower.

"You don't want to smell that," Daisy joked. Now filling her lungs with the pine-scented mountain air, Daisy asked, "Hey how's Tommy... and your mom and all? Even though Dad says fine."

"Mom's coming up next week and we're shopping for things I still need."

"Uh... Starting with bigger towels!" Aron suggested, as he walked out of the bathroom onto the deck, with a fist clenched to the one barely around his waist.

"You don't want to see that," Daisy joked again.

In walked Bryce, and Daisy promptly helped to empty the shopping bags he plopped on the—desperately needed to be sanded—picnic table on the deck.

"Wait!" Robin called out and returned with a bed sheet to use as a makeshift tablecloth. "OK, so I need more stuff," she laughed. "I'll start a list."

Bryce pulled a bottle of champagne from the fridge (pink of course), calling out, "Did any glasses make it out of a box?"

Getting no response, he walked back out onto the deck,

pouring champagne into coffee mugs.

"OK, OK I need a LOT of stuff!" Robin added.

They all hoisted their mugs. "To your new place!"

"WAIT! I have something for you," Bryce said. He ran through the house and to his car, coming back to the deck with a wrapped gift.

Anxiously, Robin ripped away the paper revealing a rustic sign made from birch bark and twigs. The twigs spelled out "Robin's Nest."

"I thought it'd look nice over the front door," Bryce suggested.

Robin hugged it to her chest and thanked him with a big kiss. Gushing she said, "Now I need to buy a hammer too."

Sitting beside Robin, Daisy elbowed her and spoke in jest, "Robin, where'd ya get this guy?"

Robin just smugly smiled. Then she pointed towards the setting sun, which was off to the far left and out of any true line of sight. "So much for sun sets," she announced. But in her next thought, she nudged Bryce and continued, "I guess that means that the sunrise will come from that direction"—she pointed opposite—"which will probably stream right into my bedroom window."

Bryce stood and circled around behind her. Pushing her hair off her neck, he began to nuzzle and kiss behind her ear, "Nothing like the sunrise in *my* bedroom I bet."

Daisy and Aron—off to the side—again, rolled their eyes. "I don't even want to know," Daisy laughed.

It was a perfect night to just sit around and BS. The lightning bugs began to emerge, which now gave Aron center stage.

"They're actually beetles you know," he began. "Two thousand species of fireflies out there, but they all don't light up. Like, people don't get to see this in California. Some varieties synchronize their flashes to find a mate. Randy little buggers they are!" He laughed.

Daisy stood, came up behind Aron, and started rubbing his shoulders. "If you haven't guessed, he's an entomologist," she directed to Bryce. "Hey," she continued, lightly smacking Aron on his head, "tell them about your new job! I have to egg him on. He doesn't like to boast, but it's the best thing to happen for us."

She smacked him on the head again. "Tell 'em!"

"Speaking of eggs..." he began, laughing with his deep goofy chortle. "I'm the official bug guy, working with a collaboration of aspiring agricultural entrepreneurs and sustainable farms. A business incubator if you will. My immediate operation is called Lily's Farm, and we produce eggs, culinary herbs, and edible flowers.

"Hence the egg comment," Daisy interrupted.

But this time, she kissed the top of his head and Aron reached behind and flipped her right over his shoulder, so she ended up on his lap. She looked tiny sitting there, like a kid sitting on Santa.

"For now, four other companies have teamed up to share resources," he continued. "We farm beef, lamb, mushrooms, even hi-quality compost. The growth potential is tremendous! Pun intended. It's an 850-acre parcel of land, acquired by the Mohonk Preserve and it's on the eastern escarpment of the Shawangunk Ridge, just outside of New Paltz.

"Right in our hood!" Daisy excitedly beamed in.

POP! Bryce uncorked another bottle of champagne.

Hoisting their mugs, one at a time they cheered.

"To Aron and his awesome job," Bryce called out.

"To the Mohonk Preserve," cheered Daisy. "Well they

made it happen so...."

"To new beginnings," Robin added.

"Skål," said Aron. He finished the conversation mentioning that if some day marijuana were legal to grow in Upstate New York, he'd probably acquire some land, develop, and cultivate a weed business.

Daisy turned in his lap and smacked the side of his head again.

"Just cause you did your thesis on spider-mites and their impact on cannabis, doesn't mean you can grow weed, you ass."

Aron flipped her in his lap and began to playfully spank her. "Whatd'ya say about ass?"

Playfulness emanated from Daisy and Aron 24/7. While Daisy certainly liked her weed, she was actually more fun-loving when she was straight than stoned.

Robin looked over to Bryce and said, "My face actually hurts from laughing so much when I'm with these two. Consider that a warning!"

"And if you need good shit, we can totally hook you up," Aron added.

Aron got up to get a beer, and right there, on the wooden siding next to the door, crawled a walking stick. He stood completely still, allowing it to crawl up onto the back of his hand. "I love these guys! A Phasmatodea."

Suddenly Bryce piped in, "You know walking sticks shed their entire skin in order to grow and they can regenerate legs, if necessary."

"Hey Robin, where'd ya get this guy?" Aron said also in jest.

* * *

The hot August night cooled down just enough to convince Robin she didn't have to block one of her windows with an air conditioner.

Daisy, Robin, and Bryce cleared the picnic table as snores echoed out from the living room. Aron had gone in for another beer and never made it back out.

"Tomorrow, he's in charge of breakfast!" demanded Daisy.

It was only 10:00 p.m., but between the heat of the day, their level of exhaustion, the amount of drinking, *and* the guy sawing wood in the living room, Robin insisted they call it a night. She grabbed Bryce's hand and they tiptoed past the snoring machine. She led Bryce towards the staircase and then threw Daisy a quizzical look. Daisy answered Robin's look saying, "You don't want to sleep near that."

Giggling, Robin and Bryce padded up the stairs. Once in the long dark bedroom, Robin clicked on each lamp. "Check it out," she said, nodding to a small terrarium that was placed under the window on the far side of the room. "For about three years I've been able to maintain the proper sun exposure, and with the attached cooling device I can adjust the temperature creating the proper alpine climate for it to exist."

Bryce made his way towards the window. He peered down inside the container. There—surrounded by green felt-like leaves and nestled between a half dozen rocks—were velvety white star-shaped blooms. They seemed to peer back up at Bryce like a tiny ensemble of celestial beings. Each flower had a cluster of fuzzy white bumps circling around a single yellow one. Bryce felt the cool air rise out of the terrarium and he backed off in amazement.

"Blossom of snow... Oh my God Robin, you have edelweiss!"

"I do," she gloated.

Robin walked over to Bryce and rested her head on his shoulder. For a moment, they stood quietly in the cold air emanating upwards.

Now intoxicated by a combination of exhaustion and champagne, Robin began to babble.

"The natural compounds found in edelweiss have the ability to neutralize free radicals which help prevent the amplification of oxides involved in the aging process. So, they are now making edelweiss and goats milk soaps." Switching her footing to maintain her balance, she added, "Another thing for my list... soap."

Bryce then faced her, tucking a strand of her hair behind her ear. Intently he urged, "Go on, you know I love when you talk like this."

Robin clicked the lamp behind her off and continued. "Because of its UV light absorbing substances..."

Bryce began to unbutton her shirt as she stood.

"...they are also adding edelweiss extract to sunblock products."

He kneeled down to help her out of her shorts, which she stepped out of one leg at a time balancing herself on the bend of his back.

"... They're even finding uses for it in treating vascular problems."

Bryce stood up and reached around behind Robin snapping off her bra.

"It's my absolute favorite Alpine plant you know..."

In a swoop, he lifted Robin and carried her to bed. He pulled back the covers and set her down gently.

"Edelweiss... it's like my treasure," she murmured.

He slipped out of his clothes and slid under the covers next to her. Pulling her close, spooning her, he buried his nose into her hair he whispered, "And you're my treasure."

25

Promises, Promises

Robin, did in fact, get an OK from her company, and redoing the basement was acceptable with the owner of the little gray salt-box... or, "Robin's Nest."

Over the next few weeks, with Bryce's help, she painted the walls, tiled the floor, and prepared the basement, setting up an optimal growing environment for the alpine species she collected. Equipped with UV lighting, a temperature control system, and a drainage system, she could monitor, propagate and conduct extensive research without having to run to Albany on a regular basis. Operating between the mountaintops and her own basement was practical, effective, and working out perfectly. Not to mention the fact that she and Bryce were perfect too. So perfect in fact, she worried.

* * *

The colors of late September were magnificent. Bryce had planned a day trip with Robin to explore the northern half of Upper Saranac Lake by canoe.

The steady rain of Saturday cooled the water, so by Sunday morning there was an extraordinary mist that hovered over the surface. They stood patiently on Bryce's dock.

It was difficult to see through the mist, but gradually appearing from the left, coming around the point, Robin could make out one canoe followed by another. As it got closer, she could tell it was one lone paddler towing an empty canoe behind.

"Stu?" Robin asked.

"Stu," Bryce answered.

Stepping up onto the dock, Stu didn't make eye contact until he had Robin's hand in his.

"Say hello to Robin, Stu," Bryce directed.

He took her hand, flashed a look into her eyes, and immediately looked back down at his feet. "Nice to meet you," he said softly. He forced himself to look back up again and smile, then let go of her hand before Robin could speak.

"Really nice to meet you, Stu," she blurted earnestly.

Stu then scurried off to the side with Bryce, muttering some information. Robin pretended to be busy refolding the picnic blanket.

Bryce then gestured to Stu, forcing him to hand Robin the line that was tied to their canoe. "I picked this canoe out for you. It's a good one," he said.

"Thank you, Stu!" Robin obliged, taking the line.

Then, in one single fluid movement, like a professional ice skater, Stu stepped one foot into *his* canoe and pushed off the dock with the other. Standing motionless in the middle of the canoe, he drifted back out into the mist and out of sight.

"Thanks, buddy!" Bryce bellowed out. It was obvious Stu knew his way around boats. "Don't try that at home," Bryce quipped to Robin.

Bryce sat first and steadied the canoe for Robin to get in. Noticing how tippy it truly was, she said, "Now, I'm really impressed. How'd he do that?"

"Stu is fascinating; that boy can do anything."

"Awe, he's so shy though."

"Oh, believe me, he was checking you out the whole paddle

here. He may seem shy, but once he's comfortable, well, it's like you've gained a brother…or a puppy."

"Aaawww," Robin sang.

They paddled up and around the first point, passing by the Great Camp where Bryce and Stu worked.

"Look there he is," Bryce pointed.

On the long dock that angled off the boathouse, Stu was running back and forth, setting up a table.

"Ah, Sunday brunch at water's edge," Bryce indicated. "A perfect morning for that!"

Being in a canoe—so low on the water—she couldn't get the scope of the entire resort, but Robin knew that staying there was *bucket list* worthy.

"One day I promise, I'll sneak you in for a tour," Bryce said.

The mist had fully dissipated by the time they rounded Butternut Point. The morning was dappled in sunshine and crisp balsam air. The rich autumn colors surrounding the lake revealed the true glory of the season. With unbelievable clarity, the early light that began to warm their faces now reflected the picturesque shoreline onto the surface of the water. They tucked around the point where the lake was like a sheet of glass. Calmly drifting into its stillness, Robin whispered, "Don't paddle. You'll disturb the surface."

"Why are you whispering?"

"Shhhhhhhh."

They continued to drift and suddenly—ten feet off the bow—a loon popped up onto the surface. Robin held her breath, fearing even that would startle it. Ten seconds later, it dove out of sight.

"That was freaking awesome!" she cheered. "I didn't know they had red eyes. A loon, right?"

"Yup! You've heard their calls at night, right?" Bryce asked.

"You mean those swirly sounds? I thought those were owls."

"Nope, loons."

"So cool!" she exclaimed breathlessly.

Robin dipped her paddle back in and Bryce followed suit. She couldn't remember the last time—or if ever—when nature actually had that asthmatic effect on her. She stopped again placing the paddle on her lap and she twisted around—enough to be able to look sincerely into Bryce's eyes. "Thank you for this," she said. She didn't know what more she could say. It was all breathtaking.

They continued paddling, passing Moss Rock Point and through the gauntlet between Green Island and Markham Point. At many significant locations, Bryce had a tale to tell, either of his youth or the olden days when Great Camps and huge hotels dotted the shoreline.

By noon they made it past Dry Island and to a much smaller island where Bryce thought they'd picnic. Pulling the bow of the canoe up onto its slope, he said, "This island is called *Tommy's Rock.*"

"That's ironic!" Robin responded.

"How so?"

"Well, this weekend is when Tommy and Bert were supposed to come up. He had some lame excuse why he couldn't. I'm dying for him to meet you."

"Likewise," Bryce said.

"And I want to see what this Bert is all about too. Tommy is completely infatuated with him."

Robin spread out the black and red checked woolen blanket that had covered her legs for the majority of the morning. Happy she had shorts on now, she plopped down and began to peel off her layers.

Bryce wrestled the large wicker picnic basket up out of the canoe and dragged it to their spot. Then he stood hovering over her... watching her. She pulled her sweatshirt up and over her head and looked up to Bryce.

"What?"

"Keep going!" he requested.

Up for the dare, she did! Tossing the sweatshirt aside, she continued and pulled her T-shirt up and over her head and tossed that to the side.

"Go on," he pressed.

Robin swiped her glance side-to-side, snickering. She unhooked her bra and shimmied it off. Bryce dropped to his knees and then flattened Robin out on top of the blanket, under his weight. Taking her breasts to his face, he burrowed into her.

Suddenly he jumped up, "Shit!" He walked up and over the crest of the island just behind where they'd set up. Coming back, he picked up and tossed the T-shirt back at her.

"We're not alone."

"Damn it!" Robin snickered again.

Bryce flipped open the lid of the basket. "I'm pretty sure everything we could possibly ever need is in here," he announced.

"I love Stu," Robin announced back.

* * *

Stu was there to welcome them back. "Did you like Tommy's Rock?" he asked Robin.

"Oh Stu, I really did! And thank you for packing us a superb lunch."

He blushed and turned away, retrieving the paddles, preparing to bring the canoes back.

"Thanks Buddy!" Bryce bellowed out as Stu pushed off onto the water again. They watched Stu drift away, standing, but this time he gave a little wave.

Robin threw her arms around Bryce as he waved back. "What a day!" she exclaimed.

Climbing the stone steps back up to Bryce's cabin Robin thought, *Tommy's Rock.... That idiot really missed out on a spectacular fall day. I'm not going to give it one more second of thought.*

And she didn't.

* * *

Tommy truly had made plans to head north for a visit. He was excited to meet Bryce *and* to show off Bert. He covered his Saturday's performance with the understudy and lined everything up. But Bert's schedule imploded.

"You've got to be fucking kidding me?" Tommy shrieked.

"I'm sorry, I'm sorry! Our head bartender quit, there's a big 30th birthday party in the private room, and my boss is freaking out. I just can't take off."

"Really Bert? One night… one fucking night. I covered my ass to take off so we could finally get up there."

"I know, I know. I'll make it up to you, I promise!"

The following weekend, Bert tried to make it up to Tommy. He took his sister Jan to see Tommy's show, but he planned a nice dinner for just him and Tommy later on.

After the curtain call, Bert went backstage to give Tommy a bouquet of orange roses. He lightly knocked on the dressing room door and entered with Jan following close behind. He walked through the room to where Tommy was seated in front of a huge lit up mirror. Tommy spun around in the chair.

Just then in the mirror's reflection, Bert saw another man seated across the room. Promptly this man got up and extended out his hand.

"Hey I'm Pauly. You must be Bert."

Surprised, Bert shook his hand saying, "Ahhh the famous Pauly." He stepped to the side to expose his sister. "And this is my sister, Jan."

Jan just stood there, nodding and smiling.

"Well, not famous yet," Pauly joked. Then making a play for the roses, "Are these for me?"

Bert snatched them from his reach and backhanded them to Tommy.

Tommy stood and kissed Bert's cheek. "Thanks! They're great."

"No Tommy, you're great. That was an awesome performance."

Suddenly feeling awkward, Pauly blurted out, "Hey, what's better than roses on a piano?"

Rolling his eyes, Tommy asked, "What?"

"Tulips on an organ!"

Jan finally piped in, "Oh Pauly... Tommy's college friend, the comedian."

Pauly bowed at Jan. "At your service."

Jan rolled her eyes, not sure if this guy was a complete ass or just a funny guy. *A cute funny guy,* Jan thought.

The autumn night was pleasant. Bert and Tommy walked, bouncing off one another's shoulders for the dozen blocks it took them to get to the Tick Tock Diner. Jan and Pauly lingered twenty feet behind them, chatting it up.

"I think they're smoking back there," Bert said.

"Probably," Tommy answered. "Pauly likes his weed."

As Bert held the diner door open, Jan whispered to him as she passed through. "He's pretty funny."

They all squeezed into a windowed booth.

"Pretty much every time I went home from the city." Tommy said to Bert, "Pauly and I would hit the Tick Tock Diner on Route 3 in New Jersey.

"EAT HEAVY!" Pauly blurted out.

Shedding light on Pauly's outburst, Tommy explained, "Eat Heavy is on the neon sign in New Jersey, but no one ever notices it."

"What's it mean?" asked Bert.

Tommy and Pauly looked quizzically at each other and together they shrugged their shoulders. Jan sat there cracking up, watching the nonsensical scene. Now Bert was the one rolling his eyes.

Afterward, they stood curbside trying to hail a cab. They'd need two. Pauly and Tommy were headed south to Union Square, and Bert and Jan were heading due east to Murray Hill.

Opening the taxi door for Tommy, Bert inquired to him about Pauly and Jan, "Did they just exchange numbers?"

"God, I hope not," Tommy laughed. He quickly kissed Bert and climbed into the cab. Then he motioned Pauly over. "Get in!" he shouted.

Tommy felt bad waving as they pulled away. He knew Bert really wanted to make it up to him, and he was looking forward to some one-on-one time. But tonight, was not the night. Pauly had planned to spend another night at Tommy's. Which seemed to be happening more often than not. Pauly promised to kick in on the rent if it became a regular thing.

On the ride home, Tommy reflected on his earlier conversation with Bert:

"I know you don't love the situation, but I got that place specifically to have enough room for Pauly if he needed to crash," Tommy had said. "Besides, I can always spend the night at your place, right?"

Bert ignored Tommy's question pretending not to hear him.

"You still owe me," Tommy reminded Bert.

"I'm interviewing another bartender tomorrow. Soon I'll have more time, I PROMISE," Bert pressed.

Now at home, Tommy made himself a strong vodka and tonic and handed Pauly a beer. "Spill on the new couch and I'll kill you," he warned.

Tommy noticed his answering machine blinking. Walking towards it, Pauly ridiculed, "I can't believe you still have that dinosaur answering machine."

"Hey, if you had talent scouts calling you all the time, you'd have one too."

"Yeah right! Your mom calls you all the time."

"Shut up!" Tommy laughed thinking it probably was his mom, regardless.

He pushed the speaker button.

"Tommmmmmy! I didn't want to bother you, so I called your machine. OK... I'm not mad anymore. You *promised* you'd come up in fall but SHIT! It's almost winter." The way she sang the word 'promised,' insinuated guilt. "It fricking snowed here already! Brrrrr! I miss you. I want to meet Bert... and you've got to meet Bryce! Listen, we've always talked about skating at Rockefeller Center. How about we make a firm plan for that? Get back to me with a few dates, OK? Oh, and we wanna see *Significant Other* too. Love ya bye."

"Robin?" Pauly asked.

"Robin."

"She's good?"

"She's good."

Tommy meandered around the living room, thinking, while Pauly futzed with the remote, clicking through channels.

I'm tired of promises, Tommy thought. *And I'm just pretty fucking tired too.* He slid the ladder that led up to the loft bedroom, over. He climbed up with his drink in his hand.

"Good night Pauly."

"Night honey," Pauly snickered.

26

It's a Long Story

Coming inside Robin's front door, Bryce stomped his feet harder than usual as he shook the snow from his jacket. "This really sucks!" he said sharply.

"What?"

"Every time a plow goes by, our cars get buried all over again. I'm going to make a few calls and see if the road department will oblige."

Robin was grateful for everything he did. The first storm of December was snowing them in. She had two cords of wood delivered earlier that day, and the two of them stacked it on the slab of concrete one could call a porch.

Bryce's responsibilities were minimal at the Great Camp in December so he was able to spend more time with Robin.

"I'm so glad you're here. My first big storm in Robin's Nest," she said.

He loaded up the potbelly stove while Robin made some final plans on the phone with Tommy. "OK, cocktails with your folks first and then a quick hit with mine." After a pause, she put Tommy on speaker so Bryce could hear the discussion. She continued and asked Tommy, "Wait, say that again."

Tommy repeated himself. "I can only get you guys tickets to my show on New Year's Eve. Is that OK?"

Bryce nodded his head, simultaneously striking a match for the fire.

"That's fine. I really can't wait Tommy," Robin answered.

* * *

The second big snowstorm of the season was not in the forecast, or part of their plan.

Stu had previously set up a fire pit down by Bryce's dock. He, Bri, Bryce, and Robin, planned to have a simple fire, drink hot chocolate, roast some marshmallows, and just hang out. It was supposed to be a great star gazing kind of night.

"Who's Bri?" Robin asked.

"That's the friend he works with at the senior center."

"The one who patched him up on Cascade Mountain?"

"Exactly."

Robin and Bryce carried wood down to the fire pit.

"You know how Stu always over does it, right?"

"Right," Robin agreed.

"Today I mentioned having a simple fire. Instead, he lugs over a cast iron frame and lined it with flagstone blocks. I figure the least we could do was bring more wood."

"Indeed!" Robin agreed again.

Carrying the wood down, Robin noticed a big open space where a huge tree had been cut down and removed. A tall section of its trunk remained, standing oddly alone in the woods. She inquired, "What the heck happened there?"

"Ah, that's what is left of the huge Norway spruce. We cut it down in November and donated it to a town for their Christmas tree lighting. I'm going to have that huge stump carved up like a statue of Pan."

"Pan?"

"Yeah. In Greek mythology, Pan is the god of the wild. The personification of wilderness and nature."

"Really?" Robin thought it was odd but figured, *Wilderness and nature, why not?*

"Yeah, for years Greek statues have been a *thing* in my family. Hey speaking of my family," he said, changing the subject while poking and blowing at the almost started fire, "we're still on for New Year's Day with my parents, right? I'm anxious for them to meet you."

"Definitely! I really can't wait to meet them too," Robin said.

Which was true, but it was Bryce whom she was anxious about. Over Christmas, he was traveling to Europe with his folks to visit his sister, Whitney. Robin wouldn't see him until they all were in Manhattan on New Year's Eve, when they had plans to meet up with Tommy and Bert.

Bri and Stu scampered over from the main lodge of the Great Camp hand in hand. As soon as they came into sight, they dropped their hold.

Robin squeezed Bryce's hand signaling excitement for Stu. Then Stu spoke.

"Robin this is my girl Bri."

Bri's sweet face was surrounded by a big fur hood. Her dark brown eyes glistened in the dim light. She looked like a little kid all bundled up. Robin remembered she was a nurse's aide, so a kid she was not.

Hesitant to shake hands, Robin smiled and lifted her hand with a little wave. "Great to meet you!" she said.

Bryce poured and handed out cups of hot chocolate. Robin ripped open the bag of marshmallows, and Bri volunteered, "I'll go find some sticks."

With sticks in hand, on an infinitely clear night, the four of them stood roasting marshmallows and gazing up at the stars.

"Once your eyes adjust to the darkness, you can see the true radiance of the entire Milky Way," Stu said, out of nowhere.

Robin squeezed Bryce's hand with excitement, again.

The ice on the lake was *just* beginning to form. The slight-est movements on the water made tingling and pinging noises like mini wind chimes and distant breaking glass. It was both eerie and beautiful.

Dodging the smoke because the wind kept shifting, the four of them looked like they were doing a tribal dance. Stu insisted everyone needed blankets so he and Bri ran back over to the lodge to grab some.

Robin topped off her and Bryce's cup and in earnest, she said, "Bryce, I need you to do me a favor."

"Sure, what ya need?"

"Please don't drink hot chocolate with me, when we're with Tommy."

"Wait what? Why?"

"I never told you... And it's why I've hesitated before. It's going to sound weird...."

"Why already!?" he anxiously cut in.

"Well, it's always been like a ritual for me and him. I think he needs to keep a special connection with me. When we see him, just please don't say anything, He's super sensitive. OK?"

"Special connection? Well it's not like you slept with him, right?"

Robin looked up at the stars, but they offered no answer. "Ummmmm, it's a long story," she said.

Bri and Stu came bounding out of the woods with their arms full of blankets. Robin emptied what was left in the thermos into their cups. The crackles from the fire and the pinging noise from the ice seemed extra loud to Robin now. Now that Bryce had completely quieted.

Stu burned every marshmallow that Bri put on his stick. "They're good like that!" he insisted.

Then from out of nowhere, the winds kicked up and wildly carried in a snow-squall. With the blankets, they individually tented themselves.

"Yeeooow! You want to come inside with us?" Bryce asked loudly through the blast.

"I need to get Bri back!" Stu resounded. He grabbed her hand and they ran off faster than the squall.

Bryce's words chased them. "We'll have a do over next week!"

Out of sight, Bri's voice reverberated from the woods, "S o u n d s g o o d."

Robin and Bryce rushed their way up the snow-dusted steps, saying nothing.

Once inside, Robin didn't know what to do with herself. She watched Bryce's every move. He hung up his coat and she followed. He kicked off his boots and shook out the blanket. She did the same. Then he came up to her. He didn't make eye contact, but he stood right in front of her. He fished out her necklace and let the sun charm lay in his fingertips.

"Is this from Tommy?"

"It is," she answered.

He stepped back away from her.

"Is this why I haven't met him yet? Is there still something there?"

"Oh my God no!" Robin yelled. "I told you he's gay. He gave me this sun when I was a freshman in college because... well... He said because he'd know I will always be there for him—

you know, like the sun?"

Robin felt herself getting angry now having to defend herself *and* Tommy. She continued, "In fact, he has the same necklace but it's the moon, because I'd know he was always there, but at times concealed, like I wouldn't be able to see him. He's had a really difficult time with his sexuality and...."

Completely agitated, she paced back and forth in the hall. Then she grabbed her head. "SHIT! I never realized the significance with this... until now! SHIT! I think he was trying to tell me then, when he gave me this, that he was gay. He's the fucking moon. He'd been hiding!"

Robin threw herself down on a chair in the kitchen. "Oh my God I wasn't even there for him. And all those years back, he was trying to tell me." She held and shook her head in shock, in disgust, on the verge of tears.

Bryce never left his spot by the front door. Melting snow from the coats and blankets hanging on the hooks seemed to cry onto the wooden floor. A tiny stream of water rolled toward his feet. He stood there deep in thought.

And Robin sat, indignantly holding her head.

Snow and now sleet pelted the front windows. Bryce moved toward them, looking out. With an audible breath, he announced, "OK, I'm good."

"Wait what? Good?" Robin asked. She looked up, bewildered.

"Yeah, I had to give it some thought, and I did, so I'm good."

"Just like that?"

"Listen Robin, I have a past too. You've never asked, and you were upfront and honest with me just now. Completely up

258

front! Your past is part of you and it's what has made you, you. So how could I possibly have a problem... how could I have the audacity to judge? I love who you are now, not before."

Robin sniffed back her looming tears. Silently she thought, swiftly reviewing his words. *Love? Did he say love?* The word swirled in her head. *He didn't say I love you directly but he did use the word.*

Her head swelled in thought and she felt herself diffuse. She didn't dare ask about his past now, based on what he just said, the same should hold true for her. His past has made him, him, and she definitely loves who he is.

He broke her churning thoughts, asking, "I know you said Tommy was gay, but I never realized just how close you were, or are. You have a special thing and I would never change that."

Robin breathed a huge sigh of relief and slid back her chair. Apprehensively, she then stood and walked toward him. Bryce met her halfway and they embraced. She was compelled to explain and offer full disclosure.

"Bryce, Tommy was never with a woman, he never had sex. He wasn't sure if he was gay or not—that's another long story—but I offered to have sex with him. You know, *friends with benefits?* But that was it, just that one time. I thought I could convert him. At the time he really didn't know what to think. I'm still not one hundred percent sure that he does now either, so I'm very curious about this Bert and their relationship."

Bryce held Robin's face and with his thumb, he wiped away the lone runaway tear; the one that snuck out, reminding him that they both had things inside that would eventually have to come out.

"I'm curious about Bert and Tommy now too," he said.

"Two weeks, right?"

"Yeah, New Year's Eve. Two weeks and we'll all finally meet."

The storm outside continued, but the air inside seemed to clear. Bryce lightly toyed with her now.

"Here's a question," he said.

"I'm listening."

"How about you go pick out a mink and we get naked in front of a fire?"

"Is that a question or suggestion?" she asked.

"Your question, questions my question," he teased, while un-tucking her shirt. "Let me rephrase that. I'll start the fire, you go pick out a mink."

"Oh, the fire has already started," she admitted.

* * *

Just before Bryce left for Europe, he stood in Robin's kitchen and held her. Robin felt organic in his arms, like her whole being was derived from his. Standing there like that, she realized her recent existence was now completely entwined in his. Suddenly she felt foolish and childish, thinking, *Get a freaking grip already*. Playfully, she pushed away and ushered him towards the door.

"Seven days will fly. I'll catch up on work. Now you go have fun," she said.

He careened around and gave her a spirited kiss. "We'll meet at Rockefeller Center, in front of the Atlas statue like we planned. Across from St. Pat's on 5th Ave."

Robin leaned against her front door after closing it behind him. She listened as he started the car and then she hurried to the window. She wiped the moisture off the glass with the sleeve of a jacket hanging on the coat stand. Peering out the window and through the rear window of his car, her heart sank. She knew his absence would weigh heavy on her.

Glancing into the reaview mirror as he pulled out, Bryce focused on the wiped off spot and threw Robin a reassuring wave.

Robin moseyed into the kitchen and decided to do something different. She put on a pot of tea. She needed something to help her relax, something to ease her mind and regain some self-confidence. It had been only six months that she'd been seeing Bryce, but now she felt empty.

She sat back with her tea and wondered what happened to the independent, self-assured, always in control Robin. *Fuck that!* she thought. *I miss him already.*

* * *

Robin, Tommy and Bert leaned against the base of the giant Atlas statue where Bryce had planned to meet them. The taxi dropped them there, having come from Tommy's apartment.

"I really do love your place, Tommy. Don't forget to tell your mom I LOVE the couch too," Robin sang.

Robin—for some strange reason—had been nervous to meet Bert, and was a chatterbox since Tommy first opened up his apartment door and introduced them an hour earlier. But now she was a tad more comfortable and realized Bert hadn't gotten a word in edgewise. "Bert, remind me where you live," she asked.

"Murray Hill. Eleven blocks south, three blocks east," he quickly spit out as he pointed due east. Then he looked at his watch and changed the subject. "What time did he say?"

Robin pressed, "We're early. He'll be here at 4:00.

"It's 4:00," Bert snapped.

At 4:03, a taxi stopped directly across from them. Robin couldn't contain herself and she ran towards it. She threw her arms around Bryce as he stood, fumbling with money to hand the cab driver. Then she stepped back saying, "Whoa, look at you all dressed up!" She threw herself on him again and gave him a huge kiss.

Bryce looked dashing. He had on a camel hair double-breasted trench coat and a Burberry scarf. Robin was used to his mountain-man attire only. But she was thrilled as he looked even more handsome now.

"Come and meet Tommy and Bert!" She practically skipped her way to them, towing him along.

They all shook hands and it was truly genuine. Robin stood off to the side, excitedly nodding her head like a proud mom watching her child's first recital. She could tell by Tommy's smile he was pleased too.

After the quick and polite introduction, they made their way around the corner and down the stairs to the Rink at Rockefeller Center. Standing in line to get skates, Bryce pulled four tickets from his pocket. "These are vouchers for skates and skating."

"Awesome. Thanks!" Bert was the first to say.

Robin kissed his cheek. "You're the best."

"Yeah thanks!" Tommy added.

Looking at the voucher, Tommy announced, "My show is at 7:30. I need to be there at 6:30. That gives us almost two hours to skate."

"We're going to need it," Bert piped in, as he pointed to the Zamboni that was making rounds. The rink was temporarily shut down.

Tommy grabbed Robin's hand and looked to Bryce. "Can I steal her for a moment? We'll come back with some hot chocolates."

Bryce winked at Robin (without Tommy seeing, of course). "Go for it. I'll get all our skates in the meantime. What size?"

"Get me a size 12, please."

"I'm an 8!" Robin said.

Tommy pulled Robin away and they dashed into the crowd. Heading around the backside of the rink, they stopped for a second near the famous Rockefeller Center Tree. With childlike wonder, they both compulsively looked up.

"Tommy?" Robin asked. "Remember the last time we were here together?"

"You mean the famous day after? When we fessed up and bared our souls— among other things—to each other? No, I don't remember."

Like old times, Robin knocked into him. "God, I miss you. Please tell me you're OK and Bert is good to you."

"Robin, he is. And I'm really falling for him so please don't worry."

* * *

Sitting next to each other on the bench, strapping on their skates, Bert glanced over at Bryce with a funny look and said, "You look familiar to me. Where'd ya go to college?"

"Well, I finished my degree here at Columbia. Urban Studies."

"Maybe that's it. I started at Columbia, Pre-Med. Didn't finish."

"Humm, maybe we shared a class. Biological Sciences?"

"Possibly. I still plan to go back and finish one day," Bert added. Then he dropped the subject, noticing Tommy and Robin making their way back with their hands full.

Bryce helped Robin get her skates on. Bert had to go back for a second pair. He tugged too hard on a lace and it broke in his hand.

"Don't wait for us, we'll see ya out there," Tommy said, motioning them away.

The waist high rink gate, automatically unlocked with a loud click, and Bryce and Robin stepped through. They were the first on the ice. Bryce started skating slowly backward, taking Robin's hands and leading her out.

"I'm pretty good at skating. You?" he asked.

"Terrible. Let go of me and I'll kill you."

The elevator music that was piped into the rink was abruptly cut off. Robin was completely focused on not falling and noticed nothing until the new music filled the air.

It started with a lone sweet violin. Gradually, melodious string instruments swirled through and a harp floated by. This prelude seemed to create a grand entrance that welcomed a full-blown orchestra.

The last cold breath of December was now infused with beautiful music; the enchanting song of the Alps.

"Oh my God…. It's *Edelweiss*," Robin breathed.

Robin suddenly became overwhelmed, her eyes welled up. Trying to not get emotional, she concentrated. She steadied her feet with the firmest stance she could without looking down. If she did, her tears would surely let go.

Holding Bryce's hands, she eased her grip just enough, allowing him to direct and glide her across the ice. She slipped a fraction and Bryce lifted her high off her feet and spun her around. She gazed down at Bryce and a tear rolled down her cheek. He kissed her tear away and gently set her back down.

"Could this be any more perfect?" she whimpered.

It could. It started to snow. Big fluffy snowflakes floated down and swirled around them. Robin didn't notice that they were still the only ones on the ice.

Bert and Tommy watched them, questioning how they got

out there yet no one else did.

"The lock must have given way for a split second," Bert said, banging his thighs against the gate.

"But look how sweet they are," Tommy said.

He grabbed Bert's hand and held it up against his chest. Moments later they heard a click. Still hand in hand, he and Bert skimmed to the middle of the freshly shaved ice. They were far from graceful. Tommy led, towing Bert behind with his hands glued to Tommy's shoulders.

After skating, they walked back towards Atlas where it would be easier to hail a cab. Bryce made urban study small talk, initiating a conversation about the rink at Rockefeller Center itself. He stated, "The water feature and the gilded statue, Prometheus..."

Then Tommy cut in with, "Who brings fire to all mankind."

"Hey, you know about Greek mythology?" Bryce asked.

"Not really, just knew about that one," Tommy laughed.

"Athena is over at Columbia University," Bryce now looked at Bert. "Do you remember seeing her?"

"I'd be lying if I said I did. I really don't remember too much from that time in my life."

"Too much studying?" Robin asked Bert.

"I wish. It's a long story, but the short is, my dad died when I was a sophomore at Columbia."

"Oh crap, my bad. I'm so sorry," Robin said solemnly.

Tommy put his arm around Bert as they all stepped up onto the sidewalk lining 5th Avenue. Then he threw an arm out to signal and a cab promptly pulled up. He kissed Bert's cheek and whispered something in his ear.

Bert kissed Tommy's cheek back and said, "Break a leg!"

With the taxi door still half open, the driver began to pull away. Tommy blurted out, "See you at the show!" and slammed it shut.

At the theater, Robin sat snugly between Bryce and Bert. She realized that it wasn't often (or ever) that she traipsed through the city with three extremely good-looking men. Satisfied, she adjusted her posture thinking, "How lucky am I?"

Bert narrated the entire first half of the show, but Robin didn't mind. It proved to her that he was sincere, *and* proud of Tommy.

During the intermission, Bryce reviewed a plan with Bert for dinner, assuming it would be OK for all of them.

"It's New Year's Eve so I thought we'd do something special," he said. "Eight blocks south, not sure if you've heard of it, it's called the Skylark.

"Ah, the swanky place over in Times Square South?"

"Yes sir," Bryce said respectably.

"Works for me!" Bert said.

* * *

Tommy flung opened the backstage door after hearing the light knock. "What, no flowers?" he joked.

Robin jumped and threw her arms around him. "Tommy, that was incredible!"

"It really was Tommy. You're very talented," Bryce said.

"Obliged," Tommy said, bowing in front of him.

"It's definitely time to celebrate," Bryce suggested. "And I appreciate your hospitality with the tickets to the show, so the rest of the night is on me."

Bert came up around behind Tommy. Proudly pawing at him he said, "Seems he's got a nice night planned for us."

Tommy grabbed his coat from behind the door. "Lead

the way!"

On the cab ride there, Bert told the story of how he had met Pauly and thought Tommy was cheating on him.

"Pauly?" Bryce asked.

"Tommy's obnoxious comedian friend," Bert mumbled.

"Oh, so you don't like him either?" Robin catechized.

Tommy shut them all down, "Stop! One day he'll be famous and you'll all be sorry."

Thirty stories up, The Skylark offered fantastic panoramic views of the city and the Hudson River. The rooftop terrace was closed due to the flurries and the major cold blasts that rip through on winter nights.

Bryce had reserved a spot in the classically styled cocktail lounge. A huge L-shaped, silver plush velvet couch lined the corner of the room. The Empire State building stood majestically just outside the full wall of windows while the adjacent wall of windows glistened with all the buildings and spires of midtown.

Bryce helped Robin out of her coat as she walked through the room in a trance toward the windows. She was in complete awe, "I've never seen the Empire State Building lit up like that."

Tommy and Bert were equally astonished. Tommy asked, "Is it lit like that specifically for New Year's?"

"No, I called it in," Bryce sarcastically said.

Bert shot Bryce a scrutinizing look.

"I'm kidding of course," Bryce laughed. "Yes, it's for New Year's!"

Robin backed up to Bryce's side not taking her eyes off the building. She slid her hand into his. "This is absolutely magical."

It truly was. The top three layers of the building that are typically lit up, now glowed with brilliant jewel tones. Rich blues met with magentas, making spectacular purples. Neon green vertical shots of color blinked in and out. Pinks and reds crossed with yellow, making brilliant lines of orange. It twinkled and glistened, motioning upward to the needle on top. Ribbons of color streamed up and then faded into different hues. Then all at once, the streams of colored lights all turned gold. It flickered like a smoldering fire, fading then glowing. It was vivid and scintillating. "Did I say how magical it *really* is?" Robin again said aghast.

The service at the Skylark was impeccable and the food was ideal. They decided to share a variety of small plate offerings that were accompanied by signature cocktails or paired with wines. The crowd of people was attractive and eclectic, like anyone would expect for a place of such swank.

Robin gained confidence watching Tommy and Bert interact with Bryce. They joked how ironic it was that they were about to watch the ball drop on the TVs at the bar, when the actual ball was only about five blocks away... and twenty stories down.

The night finished up without a hitch, and by 1:00 a.m., the crowd had calmed. Collectively, they decided to call it a night.

"Aren't we a bunch of old farts!" Robin laughed.

Tommy had a performance the next day. Bryce had only just flown in that afternoon and was dealing with jet lag. Bert complained of having to stop in at his club, and Tommy insisted on joining him. "Otherwise it'd be daylight before you resurface," he insisted.

In the elevator heading down, Tommy brought up his idea of their next possible outing together. "Now before you all say ANYTHING, I'll get back to you with dates and information."

He took a deep breath and rushed out, "Pauly is appearing at a few places in the area. I think we should go."

Robin and Bert both rolled their eyes but Bryce announced, "I'm game!"

"I knew I liked him!" Tommy said, nudging into Robin.

They said their goodbyes in the lobby. Robin and Bryce watched Bert and Tommy walk away hand in hand. Robin leaned her head on Bryce's shoulder asking, "Think they're happy?"

"No, I think they're gay."

Robin pushed him hard and he stumbled backward, laughing. "What?!!"

They crossed the lobby to the other side and as luck would have it, they were able to quickly hail a cab again. Robin realized in the whirlwind of the day, she never asked Bryce where he had planned for them to spend the night.

"Where to?" the cabby asked.

"Waldorf Astoria."

"Really?" Robin suddenly perked up. The night was starting to catch up with her too. "Wow, what a way to end the day... I mean, start the year."

She leaned in close to Bryce and kissed him lovingly. The cab driver adjusted his rear-view mirror, trying to catch a glimpse at what might ensue. Bryce hindered his attempt by retreating and then clearing his throat. "The Waldorf has an impressive brunch and my folks plan to meet us there at 10:00."

"You think they'll like me?" Robin asked.

"Like? I think they'll love you."

There's that word again. It swirled in Robin's head for the rest of the night. *Especially* when she made love to him later that night. (Morning actually.)

They approached the table hand in hand. Bryce's dad stood and his mom beamed at their approach. Bryce hugged his dad first since he was standing. He circled around the table and pulled his mom up and out of her chair, giving her an even bigger hug. He stood smiling in between them with a hand on each of their shoulders. Then he announced, "This is my friend, my companion, and the one that makes my heart soar. I'm pleased to finally introduce, Robin."

Robin *never* imagined she'd be displayed like that. Standing across from all of them. It wasn't a problem; it was more like an honor. She felt herself blush. She held out her hand and Bryce's dad firmly shook it.

"A complete pleasure. Please call me David," he said.

Then his mom held out her hand. It was dainty in Robin's, small and warm. She gave one hard shake and said, "So nice to finally meet you, I've heard so much. Please, call me Avery."

Bryce circled back around and held Robin's chair out for her as she sat.

So formal, she thought. *I like this.* She slid in and looked upward at Bryce. "That was quite an introduction."

"Well you are quite a lady."

Good God who are you and what have you done with my mountain man? she thought. She was enamored and she enjoyed every second of his exploit of class and elegance. (Though the man of the mountains wasn't too bad either.)

Sitting there, watching Bryce speak and carry on with his parents, showed their pure endearment for each other. It also allowed Robin to realize she really didn't know that much about Bryce's past besides his mink trading ancestors. Now was hardly the time to ask, or even sidetrack her thinking. It was a delightful morning and she couldn't be happier about the way things were going.

Avery talked about the different places she had lived in the city over the years. She was charming.

Bryce and his dad talked mostly about real estate.

"If it sells, it will probably be the most expensive hotel ever sold," David mentioned, leaning towards Bryce.

Robin was compelled to inquire, "You mean this hotel? The Waldorf?"

"Yes," David began, "I've heard there's a Chinese investment group that's interested. The sale and transaction won't actually happen for another two years."

"David, do you work with an investment company?" Robin politely asked.

"No not at all," he laughed. "Let's just say I invest an interest in all things Manhattan. But that's a long story."

27

Something's Fishy

Tommy sat at the bar, waiting for Bert. It was just after 1:00 a.m. when they walked into Tanked, the club where Bert worked. The crowd was thick. Bert had immediately walked over to the area where the midnight buffet was set up to inspect it. He stormed into the kitchen seconds later. Tommy heard loud voices transmit out from the kitchen through the swinging doors.

Tanked was trendy gay club in the Lower East Side. The decor of the club made patrons feel like they were underwater in a giant fish tank. Sitting at street level, the complete wall of windows out front allowed any passerby to look right inside. The windows were double-paned glass, filled with water and air bubbles. At night when it transitioned from restaurant to dance club, the amount of the bubbles increased, so passersby couldn't see inside. Similar to the windows, and placed throughout the entire room, were floor-to-ceiling thick transparent cylinders of water and bubbles. Colored lights inside them synced up with the sound system. Turquoise leather couches and low cocktail tables surrounded the dance floor in the middle of the room, which at night, took up most of the floor space. In the back of the room, the full length of the wall behind the bar was giant fish tank. Exotic fish swam back and forth in a tiny Lower Manhattan cityscape. It implied that you are the one underwater and the fish are the city dwellers. Just to the left of the bar was the set of swinging doors that Bert had disappeared behind. Each door had a small porthole window. The club's whole motif was aquarium-worthy and whimsically entertaining.

Tommy was almost lulled to sleep watching the fish take long, lethargic glides down mini Broadway. He looked over to the swinging doors and saw somebody peering out at him through the porthole. He could only see the top of someone's head and a pair of eyes. The person ducked out of view each time he looked toward the doors.

Bert finally came back out and walked behind the bar and over towards Tommy. Following directly behind him was a short Latino man. Bert introduced him to Tommy, rolling his eyes while doing so.

"Tommy, this is Pepé. Pepé, this is Tommy."

"Feliz año nuevo!" he said

"Happy New Year to you," Tommy replied back.

Pepé immediately scurried back behind the doors. Bert apologized to Tommy, "I know he was staring at you. He thinks you look like me."

After a gratuitous laugh, Tommy pointed and moaned, "I don't know if I feel sorry for those fish or happy for them."

Bert pointed out one in particular. "We saved that one from a sushi restaurant so consider him lucky."

"Really?"

"Actually no… I'm kidding. But can I get you a drink or something? I really shouldn't be much longer."

"Just a Diet Coke, and yeah, please hurry up, I'm falling asleep here."

The kitchen door opened up again, but no one walked out. Suddenly a giant Maine Coon cat jumped up onto the bar.

"What the!?" Tommy gasped.

The cat sauntered over and banged its head up against Bert's arm as he leaned against the edge of the bar, filling a glass for Tommy.

"This is "Pussy," the owner's cat.""

"You're kidding."

"Nope, not this time!"

Bert then smiled at Tommy and ducked back into the kitchen. Pussy followed.

Tommy spun around on the barstool, a little bewildered thinking, *A cat in a fish tank? Strange... Maybe I am sleeping.*

Then he realized he wasn't, when an older man rushed past him so fast, he could feel his wind. The man marched toward the exit, threw the door open, and slammed it shut behind him, startling a few people on the dance floor. The colored lights weren't pulsating anymore; instead, they were slowly fading in and out to go along with the slower music, lulling them toward sleep.

Tommy watched the slow dancing crowd and realized there were quite a few good-looking men there lightly grinding on each other. He wanted to be included. Nothing was familiar about the music they were swaying to; it was sultry and sexy, and he wanted to be in someone's arms. He got lost in his thoughts imagining himself pressed up against a warm body swaying in a darkened room with soft red lights and erotic music. He thought he would insist Bert dance with him when he came back out.

Bert came quickly out of the kitchen and walked directly over to Tommy.

"Let's go!"

"Wait! How about a dance?"

"At home," Bert demanded.

He grabbed Tommy's hands and pulled him outside. They practically ran towards 3rd Avenue where it'd be a straight shot back to Bert's place.

Bert dented the sheetrock, pushing the door to his apartment open so fast. He was fiendish and frenzied.

Tommy stood up against the entry wall, motionless. Right there, Bert undressed, and then he savagely undressed Tommy, who stood firm, allowing him. Bert didn't speak one word. Tommy, not knowing what to make of it, went right along in silence. He knew where this would end and he got hard just thinking about it.

* * *

Ever since that first night of the year, Tommy felt a little disconnected from Bert. They saw each other on a regular basis, but something wasn't right and Tommy couldn't put his finger on it. Bert didn't look deep into Tommy's eyes like he used to. There was a time when he would and he'd say things like, "I can see your thoughts, I can sense your will and desire." It was always in earnest and it was always a turn on for Tommy. But that look went missing. He wanted it back. Tommy thought, *He's just completely stressed at work.*

Bert explained to Tommy how their new chef, *Chef Pierre*, turned out to be HIV positive.

"It's discrimination to fire him for that, but word got out and business was dropping. Out of the goodness of his heart, he quit. He completely changed industries and became an advocate for fighting AIDS with nutrition. There is actually an organization out there called FAWN which stands for just that. So, Chef Pierre flew off to Africa, and Tanked decided to donate to it monthly."

Tommy understood Bert's stress and took it on as a challenge. He had something up his sleeve and he was waiting for the right day to spring it on Bert. *I'll surprise him with a romantic getaway. Robin's been all over me to get up there during the warmer months,* he thought.

Robin had sent him a few brochures of charming and romantic places in the Adirondacks. It was kind of a trade off. "You come up and visit with us for a couple of days and I promise we'll come down and see Pauly's show with you guys."

In spring, Pauly started a regular routine at a few comedy clubs in Connecticut and he also patched things up with his parents so he wasn't on Tommy's couch as much.

"Dude, it's cool to be able to crash in my old room at my parents, and your couch is pretty sweet, but a man's gotta get some snatch and the chicks in Connecticut are banging!"

"Really Pauly? Banging? I hope you're at least nice to them, and buy them dinner and like... DATE them!"

"Dude, they come up to me! It's fucking beautiful man. Yeah, I'll buy them a drink or something, but shit! It's not like I even have to. Come on man, you get it. Don't you gay guys just want to fuck all the time?"

"Fuck you Pauly, you're so fucking shallow! I honestly LIKE an emotional commitment, but YOU don't even know what that is?"

"Yo! Take it easy buddy. You know I love you!"

Pauly did get it though, that was all part of his act. He didn't settle for any one girl because he thought it was helpful for his act—to constantly move on and get new material. He purposely stayed single.

His heart did want different, though. It was Bert's sister, Jan, who put a dent in Pauly's heart. Which was something he'd never confess to anyone. They'd gone out a few times, but she dumped him.

"Yo Tommy," he had said, "I think she liked me just for my weed. Chick's pretty screwed up, man. Once we were all wasted and she was like telling me about how her dad died and it was really fucking sad. She said it screwed up Bert too dude, so just giving ya a thumbs up there."

"You mean heads up."

"Whatever."

Tommy knew Pauly was stoned during that conversation so he didn't take it too seriously.

Pauly also landed a gig as one of the opening acts for the headliners at Mohegan Sun. It was a real career starter, it paid well, AND he stayed for free on the nights he performed.

"Yo Tommy, you should come and gamble. Bring your boy."

"Oh, I'm already gambling with Bert now."

"Uh ha ha, I get it, like you play *poker* with him, right?"

"Oh my God Pauly, you are such a pig!"

Tommy was in a much better mood than the last time he spoke to Pauly so he didn't take offense to the comment. After all, it was Tommy who always said, "Pauly hangs around me for gay material." Which was true, but they were friends first. Tommy coming out was just a bonus for Pauly.

"Maybe we'll come see one of your gigs next month. I'm planning a trip to the Adirondacks with Bert, first," Tommy said.

"Yo, tell Robin I miss her?"

"Really?" Tommy laughed. "You miss her?"

"Yeah I miss looking at her tight ass!"

"You're the ass Pauly. You really are," Tommy laughed again. "I'll just tell her you say hi."

With Tommy's plan beginning to take shape, on his night off, he popped into Tanked. He knew Bert wouldn't be working because of that morning's statement:

"I need me some sister-time, so I'm hitting up Jan for dinner tonight. Let's meet back at your place like 11:00," Bert suggested.

Tommy planned to speak with the owner or the boss—he didn't know just whom he'd inquire with—but he planned to ask about dates they could cover for Bert so he could whisk him away on a desperately needed rendezvous. He thought, *How could they say no? Bert's been working like a dog and they just hired a new chef, who according to Bert, is 'spectacular!'*

Prime dinnertime at Tanked was around 7:30 p.m., and Tommy figured someone with the proper authority would be there to help. He decided to stop in, figuring that once they saw him, they'd give even more consideration since he looked so much like Bert.

The main entrance to Tanked was down a narrow alley on the side of the building. Since it was early enough, Tommy could see through the air bubbles in the windows. He walked quickly past them but caught a glimpse of someone who looked like Bert, seated at the bar. He stopped right at the edge where the window and bubbles began and peered inside.

"Shit, it is Bert!" he grumbled to himself. At first, he backed away, but then realized he was out of direct view. He nosed up again for another look. "Who the fuck is that?"

Some older guy was standing next to Bert, rubbing his back. Then Bert half spun on the bar stool to face the guy. Splitting the guy's legs with his knee, he angled in even closer into him. It was very conspicuous. *Very fucking conspicuous!* Tommy thought. Then the guy standing over Bert put his hand on his shoulder. He was caressing it and they were talking close. *Too fucking close,* he thought. Looking sincerely at each other one minute, then laughing the next, they carried on. Tommy felt like he'd been standing there for hours…watching…seething. "This is more than just fucking flirting," he concluded. He felt sick to his stomach.

He backed away from the window and slammed against the alley wall.

Think, think, think… now what the fuck do I do? He leaned in to peek again. The bar stool was empty. He saw Bert and the old guy step in through the swinging doors. Then seconds later they emerged back out with their jackets in hand. *Shit, they're heading this way.*

Tommy shot one store over and hid behind a spinning postcard rack that stood at the entrance. He watched them walk by. He backed into the cheesy souvenir shop and grabbed an "I LOVE NY" knit hat. He threw a $20 at the man behind the counter. "Keep the change."

With the knit hat pulled to his brow, he trailed them from three to four stores away. *Of course, they won't look back,* he thought. *That shit just happens in the movies.*

They were heading north. Bert's place was north. *They better not be fucking going there!* he thought.

As he followed along, he thought about how he and Bert would bounce off one another, walking together holding hands. He started to get sad but brushed it off. Instead, he got mad at himself, thinking, *I could just be overreacting here. It's not like we genuinely committed to each other.*

Yet in Tommy's mind, he did commit and now he was selling himself short. No vows were ever said, but one intimate night, Tommy had confessed to Bert that he was falling for him and had pledged to be faithful. That now infamous night of passionate sex, even Bert confessed to Tommy by saying, "I enjoy having you around and want you all to myself."

What the fuck? Lies! Am I nothing but his little sex toy? he thought.

Now three-quarters of the way there—if in fact, they were heading to Bert's—they stopped and went inside a liquor store. Tommy ducked into another entrance, a food market this time.

In Tommy's head, he started to call the older guy *Geezer*. Minutes later, some *other* geezer walked out with them and handed off a bottle of wine. The three of them stood outside the store chit-chatting. Tommy peered through the market window astonished. *WTF? Looks like the Geezer and Bert know the owner?*

Completely bewildered (and out of sight), Tommy followed them a few more blocks. He stopped to watch them cross the street. As they approached Bert's building, he saw the Geezer reach into his pocket. He pulled out a set of keys and opened the side door for Bert. He slapped Bert's ass as he stepped in.

"What the fuck!?" Tommy shrieked. He wanted to run across the street, but the traffic prevented him. His head felt like it would explode. His heart was pounding and he was short of breath. *They were fucking going there, and now they're going to be fucking, there!* he thought.

Completely distraught with having no idea of what to do next, he pulled out his phone and scrolled for Jan's number.

She answered and everything she said was not what he wanted to hear.

"No, he wasn't here tonight ... No, I haven't seen him ... What's going on?... Shit Tommy, I'm sorry, I didn't even know you two were still together!"

Tommy paused in shock for a moment, but then Jan continued. Her tone was now defensive.

"Hey, I tried to warn you. I told you almost a year ago, I remember saying, '*Don't expose yourself.*' Remember? I *specifically* remember telling you that. You were confiding in me and I warned you, I said don't be vulnerable."

Tommy then asked about the Geezer.

"Old? I don't know, he's probably a father figure. Tommy, I don't know what to tell you..."

Still in shock, Tommy ended the call. He thought about calling Robin, but he couldn't, he was too enraged. He needed to calm down and think.

He had walked deliriously west, passing Bryant Park, where he first met Bert. He started to think back to where and when it got weird with Bert. *How did the disconnect start?* he wondered. Then it dawned on him: the night he waited for Bert at Tanked. On New Year's Eve, before they went home, some old guy had stormed out of the place. *THAT'S HIM!* he recalled. *Jesus Christ, how long have they been seeing each other?*

Tommy now had an even longer walk to get home. He decided to make it longer still by heading to the hardware store on the other side of town. He bought a new deadbolt.

The whole time installing it, the word 'deadbolt' echoed in his head. *Why is it even called that?* he wondered. *But how fucking ironic, since Bert is dead to me now.*

Something had happened back on the night of New Year's Eve. Something Tommy would probably never figure out. It hurt to think about.

28

Fuck That

Bert pounded on Tommy's door at 11:00 p.m. that night.

"I know you're there. Listen, I can explain. I talked to Jan. She's got it all wrong."

Tommy dug out a set of noise-canceling headphones, poured himself another very strong vodka and diet tonic and basically drank himself to sleep.

* * *

He woke up the next morning on the L-shaped couch his mother bought him.

He thought, *Yeah, I'll call mom.* Then on second thought. *No, I don't want to make her sad. She really liked him too. I'll call Robin.... No. I'm not ready, she'll try to convince me to come visit regardless, and that will make me sadder since I had the whole damned trip planned for both of us. That prick!* He took a huge forlorn breath, rolled up onto his feet, and made his way to the kitchen. He opened the fridge. He stood in despair, looking at the two porcelain ramekins of Créme Brûlée.

Yesterday afternoon, Tommy Googled the recipe and made them. It was Bert's favorite dessert. Bert promised to have dessert with Tommy after he had dinner with Jan.

Standing there he thought, *He fucked that guy then planned dessert with me?* "Fuck that!" he screamed out loud.

He pulled them out, set them on the counter, sprinkled sugar on each and fired up the mini butane torch. He caramelized the sugar.

In the few minutes it took him to do so, he pictured burning down Bert's apartment. *No wait... I'll torch Tanked! That fucking Geezer probably owns the fucking place.*

Then Tommy realized, *He probably owns the apartment too—like why the fuck does he have keys?*

He slid out one of the stools from the kitchen counter and sat. Deviously thinking, he demolished both Créme Brûlées. *This is crazy, I'm going mad. But that's better than sad; sad just hurts. I feel like I've been mauled.*

His cell phone rang. It read B E R T. He switched it to silent mode.

Next, his house phone rang. He unplugged the old answering machine and turned the ringer off. He pulled the chain on the vertical shades and darkened the apartment as much as he could. He sat down on the couch and stared at his phone. For the first time in a complete year, he called in sick.

"No, I'm sure I'll be fine for tomorrow's performance. It's just my throat."

He held his hand tight against his neck to alter his voice. "Really I should be fine by then. Again, I'm sorry. Thanks."

He flopped down and pulled a blanket over his head thinking, *I need time.*

The next afternoon, the sad was beginning to recede, but Tommy was still very angry. Sad hurt too much. Instead he became vindictive. He thought about ways he could get back at Bert. He convinced himself these crazy thoughts were heart-strengthening therapy. *Therapy that prevents my heart from dislodging within my chest, sinking deep into my bowels, and being shit right out.*

He called Robin. She was a great listener. He completely spewed.

After hearing the whole story, "Tommy," she replied sincerely, "If it helps any, I'm actually relieved. I didn't get good vibes from him—AT ALL! I know it sounds mean, but I'm glad."

"Thanks Robin. Do you know where I can buy arsenic?" he joked.

At this point, Tommy was too agitated to tell Robin how he had gotten similar vibes from Bryce; how he didn't really trust him and felt that something was off. But he also realized that he was a shit judge of character now, as he had felt something was brewing with Bert. But he never expected this!

Robin didn't know what she could do for Tommy. In the past, she mentioned seeking professional help, maybe a psychiatrist or someone who could help him understand his feelings. But this time was different. Tommy felt burned and it wasn't his own doing. He had been trying to figure out his own sexuality and find love within it. Then wham!

"Robin, I really thought he was the one. Am I naive? Am I a pushover?"

"Tommy, he's the one who's really fucked in the head. Stop beating yourself up! You'll get through this," she consoled.

Even Robin thought Tommy was better off being mad than sad. Then she tried to lighten the subject by telling him about her latest Alpine plant restoration project.

"… And next week I'm working with SUNY and the Adirondack Botanical Society on Whiteface Mountain. We're assessing the condition of the vegetation on Veteran's Memorial Highway's effected area. Alpine Goldenrod and Bearberry are both threatened species, and Snowline Wintergreen is an endangered species. Thankfully, seeds are being propagated in SUNY's greenhouse."

Then Professor Evan Gains unexpectedly flashed into Robin's head. She remembered their steamy night near the greenhouse at SUNY.

Tommy made an exaggerated loud snoring noise into the phone.

"Ok, Ok, I'm boring you," Robin quipped.

She wondered if she should bring up Evan as a reminder, so Tommy would realize there are plenty of fish in the sea, but he started to grumble again.

"Robin, I think I'm an endangered species?"

Robin wouldn't allow him to wallow anymore. She cut him off by trying to convince him to visit. "Just get your ass up here. The fresh air will do you good."

"Robin, I literally have to get my act together. Maybe in a few weeks."

* * *

Summer was around the corner, and now one of Tommy's major concerns was his show. *Significant Other* would end its Off-Broadway run in August. It was set to hit Broadway, real Broadway, in February, but shows notoriously never meet production schedules. He wasn't sure he could sustain his rent and lifestyle—as of late—if he didn't have an ongoing role.

While the play's off-Broadway version continued, his role was now divided fifty-fifty between him and the understudy. The director was going to have to decide who would take the lead when it hit Broadway. Tommy's split with Bert not only affected him, it affected his performance. Often during an emotional scene in the play, Tommy got over emotional. The director warned him, "Damn it, Tommy! It's supposed to be sad but we really don't want the whole audience leaving in tears!"

With his extra time, he hit the pavement. Casting calls for upcoming new shows and readings for existing ones filled up his days. It was his nights that were now much more open.

Being extremely good-looking, working in the theatre, and living in Manhattan gave him boundless opportunities. In the recent past, one such opportunity literally popped up for Tommy.

He had done a reading with a film production company. Afterward, the producer led him off to the soundstage. The door closed behind them. Instantly, the producer took off his own shirt and moved right in on Tommy. Then just seconds later, when the producer's pants were around his ankles, Tommy was able to move around him and escape.

Tommy had always considered himself monogamous. And even though he was now ready to throw that notion way out into left field, he did maintain his ethics: never mix business with pleasure. That was NOT how he wanted to land a part! Tommy was very talented and never would he stoop that low for a part. Again, literally!

But Tommy was now on a furor: soul searching, exploration, self-discovery, and even character building. He tried to convince himself it was one of those. He immersed himself deep into the open and active gay scene. He decided he was going to have at it. However, he wasn't quite sure about his approach. This was all completely new territory for him.

Ten clubs came up on his first search: "Best Gay Bars in NYC." He'd already been to The Stonewall Inn, which was number eight on the list. He knew that place was a tourist attraction, so he had no real faith in the Googled list. Regardless, he decided to just give number one on the list a shot: Atlas Social Club. He perused the website thinking, *I'm pretty sure this is the place Ander-*

son Cooper owns. The bartender looks hot.

He pregamed, having a few drinks at home, while he was on the phone with Pauly. Pauly himself was getting ready for his stand-up routine at Joker's Wild in New Haven.

"Pauly, one of the clubs on the list is called, "Flaming Saddles Saloon.""

"Get the fuck out!"

"I swear. I can't make this shit up!"

"Dude, you gotta tell me everything! Well not *everything,* everything. But everything!"

"Come with me!" Tommy urged.

"Sure!" Pauly said. "It's at the corner of Fat and Chance, right?"

"You're such an ass! Call me tomorrow if you want."

"Can't wait. Bye honey! Love you!"

Tommy put the phone down. It was Friday night, and at Atlas Social Club, it's "DTF Fridays." There was an underwear party. He decided to leave his phone home. *Like where am I going to keep it?* he laughed to himself.

He decided, *I'll go with my short style black briefs, with the white shoelace closure.* He was embarrassed just thinking about what he was about to do. But then he got mad, thinking about Bert. *Fuck that! I'm going to have a good time.*

He walked three blocks west, took the A train north, then west two more blocks. Walking the final block on 50th, he thought to himself, *Welcome to Hell's Kitchen, please don't let that be an indicator.*

Tommy walked in and made a beeline for the bar. The bartender was definitely hot. He ambled his way towards Tommy, stopping directly in front of him. With only a bar towel flung over a shoulder, his hairless chest was tan and broad. His abs were defined so perfectly it reminded Tommy of his grandmother's old-style ice tray. The bartender, now straddling his arms wide on the bar, leaned halfway across it and grazed Tommy with his eyes. "You're new," he said.

Tommy realized he was staring at his nipples and quickly slid into the only open bar chair. "Well yes, I guess I am," he answered.

The bartender said nothing, pulled the towel from his shoulder, picked up a glass, and began to twirl it in the towel. Tommy felt a flutter deep in his gut.

"Can I get a Tito's and tonic?" Tommy asked, "You have diet tonic I hope."

"It's a gay club, of course we do."

The bartender handed Tommy his drink and pointed to a door across the room. "You can check your pants there." Then he pointed to the crowd on the dance floor. "The party started."

Tommy didn't know if that was hospitable information or if the bartender was hitting on him. The way he eyed him up made the flutter in his gut stronger. But Tommy was game, at this point, he was up for almost anything.

He sucked down the entire drink with one sip. He glanced at the bartender who was now mid-bar, spinning a bottle of Tito's. He nodded at Tommy. Tommy nodded back, got up, and headed over to the pants check.

Standing in just his underwear and a pair of leather flip-flops, he took a deep breath and surrendered his pile of clothes to the guy behind a counter. Then making his way back towards the bar, he sidestepped around the edge of the crowded dance floor. Lights were flashing, music was pulsating, and the dance floor suddenly swallowed him in. Engulfed in a throng of buff and young go-go boys, his sought-after escapism was about to be met.

* * *

A call from Pauly woke him. Not quite sure where he was, he reached for his phone and answered, "Let me call you back in a half."

He sat up, relieved to see he was alone in his bed. His head felt like a cinder block. He climbed down from his loft and made his way to the bathroom. He splashed cold water on his face and visions of last night splashed up with it. He looked down and thought, *Shit, I liked that pair of underwear. I wonder where they are.*

As promised, he called Pauly a half hour later. He answered on the first ring, "DUDE! How was it?"

Tommy slurped his coffee. "Not a hundred percent sure. I drank too much."

"Does anything hurt?"

"Just my head, don't be vile."

"Dude, I'm just messing with you," Pauly laughed. "I don't want details, but I do want to know, what the hell does DTF stand for? Diet Tonic Farts?"

Tommy slurped again, "I don't know where you come up with this shit Pauly," he laughed. "But if you must know, it stands for Down To Fuck."

"Man dude, really?"

"Really."

"Well did ya get lucky then?"

"I don't think that was his name."

* * *

The last performance of *Significant Other* was Aug 16th. The summer was moving way too fast. On his nights off, Tommy continued with risqué outings. During the daylight hours he'd have readings and interviews but the callbacks didn't come. He even tried out for a part in *A Bronx Tale,* which was opening at a regional theater in Millburn, New Jersey. So, while in Jersey, he met up with Robin. She and Daisy were home for the weekend to celebrate Little Robbie's birthday.

"He's officially a teenager now," Robin said. "Braces, zits, and middle school."

"Worst time of my life," Tommy apologetically offered.

"Well that's actually good to hear. You had me all worried again."

"Robin, you have to stop worrying about me."

"Sorry Tommy, that's never gonna happen."

Tommy thought if he got the part in A Bronx Tale, he'd consider spending a little more time at home with his parents. *Maybe it would be good to lay low for a while.* Then on second thought, *Fuck that!* He Googled "Bath Houses."

Two clubs immediately came up with his search. East Side Club and West Side Club. West Side Club was only six and a half blocks from his apartment. Instead of lying low, he went extreme. Tommy practically dropped out of sight.

Robin did, in fact, worry. She left messages for Tommy everywhere but he returned not one. Finally, she dictated a note and insisted they leave it for him in his dressing room.

If I don't hear from you within the next two days, I will come for you! ~ Robin

She convinced the stagehand that took the call and wrote the note, that it was just a joke. She didn't want to jeopardize his job and introduce concern. The stagehand was curious who this woman "Robin" was, and considered not leaving the note just to see. Because now-a-days, the only people that Tommy left his dressing room with were men.

Tommy called her. He had to. He was furious with Robin,

"Really Robin? You'll fucking come for me?"

"Hey, I told you I'm never going to stop worrying about you. Where the hell have you been?"

Tommy lied and told her he'd been bartending on his off nights. He didn't want to have to explain himself to her. He always did confide in her, but he just couldn't anymore. She'd never understand. She never really did! How could she? Who does? Tommy knew this was his problem and no one could fix it. He knew he could fuck his way through the city, but that wouldn't fix it either.

Then without warning, shame consumed him. He remembered only feeling like this once before. Once, way back when...

He stood in the Monsignor's kitchen, guzzling what was left of his now warm orange fizz. He spat in the sink. He heard the door creak open behind him. He looked over his shoulder at MS who said, "Now be a good boy and tell no one. I'll see that you make confirmation and go on the summer church trip."

"Robin, I'm not feeling well. I think I'm going to puke. Call me next week. I promise I'll be around."

29

Setting the Stage

Robin called Tommy. He answered a simple, "Hey."

"Wow, I wasn't expecting an answer… and on the second ring! How are you?"

"Not very good. I'm sad, I'm lonely, and I'm still looking for a part."

"What happened to mad? Aren't you better off mad?"

"Trust me, you don't want me mad."

"What that's supposed to mean?"

"I'll explain another time."

"Fine." Robin paused, wondering what to say next. She was concerned, she wanted to be there for him, but she knew there was really nothing she could do.

"Well then, speaking of another time... we're planning a reunion."

"Who's we're?" Tommy asked.

"Me, Bryce, Daisy, Aron, Peter, and Astri. You know, my friends that moved to Norway?"

"Peter… as in Peter your college pal from SUNY?"

"Yup! He and Astri will be in Manhattan and there's a concert in Central Park that Daisy is setting up. You should come! Plus, your birthday is soon, so you HAVE to come!"

"Concert? Who, what, and when? You said the where."

"Phil Lesh & Friends, part of Central Park's Summer Stage series. Wednesday, September 16th. Supposedly an old friend of Daisy's is the lead guitarist."

"Who's Phil Lesh?"

"Original member of the Grateful Dead."

"Ohhhh this has Daisy and Aron written all over it. I can smell the weed already," Tommy laughed.

Wow, Tommy laughed, Robin thought. She ran with that and the slight possibility he'd try to join them. She continued, "I won't give any more details now, but let's just say Daisy is working a VIP angle, so please consider it. AND in the meantime, Daisy and I plan to rendezvous at home and go through my mom and Robert's old albums to gear up for it. Maybe you and I can meet up back at home too?"

"Maybe."

"Maybe?"

"Maybe."

* * *

They decided to meet up at their old luncheonette spot.

"Shit! It's been like five years since we last sat here," Tommy said looking around. "Still the same though."

"I'm thinking four years, can't be five. Can it?" Robin questioned.

A waitress walked up. Robin and Tommy looked at each other, then up at the waitress. Simultaneously they said, "Two hot chocolates."

They bust out in laughter. Then Robin sat back and took a deep breath ready to speak, but Tommy beat her to it.

"I'm sorry Robin. I know I haven't been myself. I've been prowling around, dissing you and avoiding all contact."

The waitress set two hot chocolates in front of them. Tommy wrapped his hands around his mug. Robin reached out and wrapped her hands around his.

"Well you *are* my moon," she offered.

He tried to smile but he couldn't. "Robin, if I don't land a part by the end of September, I won't be able to afford my apartment. I may have Pauly take over my lease and I could stay with him. But how much would that suck?"

Then Tommy looked up at Robin and his eyes started to well up. Without too much detail, he told Robin how he 'dated' a few people and how it was like a revenge act on behalf of Bert.

"Shit Robin, the way I've been carrying on… it's not right. It's not me. I know you can't really understand."

He didn't want to make himself or Robin any more upset, and he certainly didn't want her pity. He was just being honest. He felt terrible for being dishonest with her. He even told her how he made up the bartending job.

Before the conversation got any more somber, he changed the subject.

"How's Daisy?" he asked.

"She's home again, this time she's taking Robbie clothes shopping for a school dance." Robin pondered for a moment then continued, "Tommy, Remember our prom?"

"Seriously Robin? I'll never forget it."

Then intently she added, "I wanted you to kiss me so bad that night."

She let go of his hands and took a loud slurp from her mug. She sat back and scowled at him. Then in a defensive tone she snapped, "Don't tell me I don't understand how you feel. You feel lost and alone right?"

He sat back silent and astonished.

"You feel like there is something wrong with you right?" she continued. "Like what you want you'll never get. You don't

understand why you feel the way you do, and you can't do anything to fix it. Right? RIGHT?"

"Oh my God Robin, I'm so sorry," he answered.

"All I wanted was for you to kiss me! Yeah, I get it now,
why you didn't. But all those years... I was the one who doubt-
ed myself. Are you fucking kidding me? I questioned myself; I
thought there was something wrong with me!"

They sat there in silence.

When the waitress came back to take their order, Tommy
looked up at her like a lost soul and said, "I have no idea."

She backed away and Tommy looked to Robin who
wouldn't even make eye contact with him. He grabbed for her
hands but she pulled away.

"Shit Robin, I really hurt you. And I still do by saying you
don't understand... but I guess maybe you do." He lowered his
head and mumbling, he continued, "All those years ago. I'm a
fucking idiot."

Robin looked across the table to him and shuddered in
place as if to shake it off. "Damn it Tommy, I didn't plan to yell at
you, I'm sorry," she said.

"No, I'm sorry. Really sorry!"

She shifted in her seat again and took another deep breath.
"That was a long time ago and it's the past. I know you're having a
really tough time right now, but I know you, and I know you'll be
fine. I'll never fully understand what you're going through. How
can I? I'm not a fucking gay guy!"

"Ohhhhh Robin. I've been quite a fucking gay guy lately."

They looked at each other eye to eye. No words. They
shook their heads and snickered. They were good.

"Ok, now that that's out of the way, Bryce has someone he

wants you to meet."

"Ohhhh shit," he breathed.

"Chill! It's a friend of his from... well he says a long time ago. If you come to the concert, I'll see if Bryce can set something up."

"Do we know anything about him?" Tommy asked.

"His name is Parker, he's some kind of producer or promoter. I think he's a little older than us."

"How much is a little?"

"Not sure."

The waitress came back over and they ordered. Again, Tommy wanted to touch on the fact that he didn't get good vibes or trust Bryce. But after the blowout he and Robin just had, now was definitely not the time.

* * *

Fall was an extremely busy time for both Robin and Bryce. She needed to hike and collect as many samples as she could. Snow was just around the corner. And for Bryce, September at the Great Camp was even busier with more weddings than any June had ever seen. Adirondack autumn weddings were the latest trend.

Bryce told Robin, "I can't really complain, but I miss spending down time with you."

On busy weekends, he would have to send Stu off to work at one of his other jobs. "It's just too hectic for him, so he gets frazzled. But I'll be able to get away midweek, and I'll catch up with you guys at the concert. Parker said he'd be able to meet up with us too."

* * *

Robin picked up a Cat Stevens album. "Teaser and the Firecat," she called out. Then she read the lyrics silently for *Morning Has Broken*. It made her content and grateful, and the words made her yearn for Bryce. She passed the album off to Aron. "Here, play this."

Robin and Daisy had been sitting on the living room floor of their old apartment in New Paltz, (now Daisy's and Aron's place). June and Robert's albums were spread out all over. Aron was the DJ, patiently standing in the corner, near the borrowed turntable, and waiting for their curious selections with rowdy hand offs.

Some of the album covers were simple sleeves of protection, and some were like books that opened up to reveal photos, weird artwork, or lyrics to the songs.

Daisy opened the Frampton Comes Alive album. Pot seeds and remnants lay in its crease. "NO WAY!" she howled. "So busted! Is this June's or my dad's album?"

She tactfully stood up and walked the album and weed shrapnel over to show Robin and Aron.

Aron piped in, "Think they're still viable? Shit if anyone can grow this, it's you Robin!" He eagerly looked to her for a response.

"No way! I'm out. Save them until it's legal!" Robin argued.

Aron was excitedly looking for something to put the seeds in. He grabbed an old film canister from Daisy's office (Robin's old bedroom).

"Perfect," he shouted, sliding them delicately into the container.

Robin and Daisy weren't able to bring the complete album collection up with them. There were just too many. Robert had advised them when he loaded the old-style turntable into Daisy's car, "They scratch, so pleeeeease be careful!"

298

"Thanks dad, I will."

Daisy sat contently sifting through the fifty or so that they did take. She announced many:

"Crosby, Stills, Nash & Young... Zepplin... Marshall Tucker... LOTS of Beatles... Alabama... I bet these are my dad's. Humm, some of these bands I've never heard of: Seals & Croft... REO Speedwagon... ELO... WTF?"

"WTF? That's a band?" Aron asked.

Daisy rolled her eyes answering, "No ya knucklehead." Then she added, "LOL."

Flipping through most of them, Aron grabbed the book style ones, hoping he could find more seeds.

Daisy again called out: "Ramones... Depeche Mode... Surf Punks... Go-Go's. Robin, I think your mom had a new wave and punk phase!" Then with a puzzled look she shrieked, "Dead Kennedy's? Who the hell names a band that? Here Aron, play that next!"

"Look at this weird one," Robin announced, holding it over her head.

Its cover art was a blue sky with clouds and birds. The sky had black diamond-shaped cutouts, and people's faces were inside them.

She pulled out her phone and snapped a picture of it. She added a caption and sent it to Tommy, while she announced, TOMMY, The Who.

"Who's that?" Aron asked.

"The Who," she answered.

"Who?"

"Yup."

"Oh my God, this is ridiculous!" Daisy mocked. "Aron, can

you please go get us a few beers?"

He obliged. Daisy saved the assortment of Grateful Dead records and jam bands for last.

"How's this for an oxymoron? Live Dead!" she scoffed.

"This is going to be *a crazy* concert!" Aron laughed.

"Tommy better freaking come!" Robin grumbled.

They spent the rest of the night drinking and dancing.

Well Robin drank. Daisy and Aron rolled one up. They used the Peter Frampton album and debated who they thought owned it for sure.

* * *

Bryce texted Robin: *I'm in the park near the stage at the Will Call stand, where are you guys?*

Robin texted back: *Stay right there!!!!!*

It was 5:30 in the evening and the crowd was beginning to funnel through Central Park. The pathways were like arteries bustling with people who marched along with purpose. Those that casually meandered were undoubtedly in route to the Summer Stage, as they were colorful and carefree. Closer to the stage there was a complete sense of calm in the air—most likely due to all the smoke that also lingered in it.

Robin was the contrary. She dashed off in the opposite direction and didn't slow until she was lifted tall into Bryce's arms.

Still grinning at each other, they stepped hand in hand up onto the VIP side-stage. It was a huge elevated platform with linen tables, a custom Hendricks Gin cocktail bar, and a vegetarian snack buffet. Giant individual pita chips hung from hooks. The delectable triangles pointed downward to an assortment of veggies, hummus, and ganoushes.

Daisy came over to intercept and welcome Robin and

Bryce. "Pretty sweet eh?" she bragged.

Bryce smiled at Daisy, giving her a head to toe once over. She flared out the sides of her long multi-colored skirt as she spun in front of him. With a purple tank top and a tie-dyed scarf, she topped things off with a simple ring of daisies on her head.

Bryce was amused and inquisitive. "You look great, all hippy-like!" he said. "And who do you know that got all of us into this sweet VIP set up?"

Daisy pointed to the lead guitarist tuning his guitar and setting up on the stage. "There, that's Neal," she said. "A good friend of the family. Killer guitarist. He plays with Phil Lesh pretty often. I'll introduce you later if he can break away." Daisy then tugged at Bryce and Robin. "Come on, we're over here. I grabbed the best spot!"

She certainly did. Positioned in a corner, at one glance you could see the whole stage, and with a counter glance, you could look out over the entire audience. Aron stood up from the table and in typical Aron fashion, he scooped Daisy up off her feet into his arms. Dangling her on his shoulder, he held out his hand to shake Bryce's.

"My girl did good!" he gloated.

"She certainly did… and with that outfit she has certainly set the tone too."

Aron placed Daisy down and she bowed, again holding out her long skirt.

"When in Rome!" she chuckled.

Robin interrupted the little pageant to introduce Peter and Astri who sat in awe at the whole bohemian scene unfolding in front of them. Bryce shook Peter's hand and took an immediate interest in him and Astri by asking them all about all things Norway.

Aron, still vicariously living through Peter since his move there, joined in when the topic changed to careers. They began discussing the future collaborative effort on Pollen Beetle Reintroduction.

Daisy rolled her eyes and stole away with Astri and Robin announcing, "While they sit and talk about PBR, let's go and get some cocktails of our own!"

Before Robin walked away, she mentioned to Bryce, "Please keep a look out for Tommy."

"Oh crap, I forgot to say... Parker called me an hour ago. He apologized but something came up. He asked if we could set something up for next week. Preferably on the 24th."

"Fine by me!" Robin said. "I'll put money on it that Tommy's a no show."

While they waited for their drinks, Robin stepped off to the side and dialed up Tommy. He answered.

"I'm sorry, I'm sorry, I'm not coming. I'm just not into it, Robin. I think I need to spend some QT here with my parents. I drove out this morning."

"You suck Tommy! Seriously suck! What should I tell Bryce when Parker comes?"

"Shit Robin, pick a day next week. Any day... I'll swear to it."

"All right, you SUCK. I'll get back to you with a *FIRM* date."

Robin had decided she would mislead Tommy and make him think Parker would be there. She wanted him to feel bad about blowing them all off. This way he wouldn't dare blow them off again. As in the past, when he didn't stick to his word, he usually made good on plan B. So now she knew that the 24th would be a lock. And it just so happened to be Tommy's birthday. She thought the four of them might be able do something fun together.

For the encore song, Neal and Phil Lesh & Friends, finished up
the night with a rendition of the Grateful Dead's, "Sugaree." The
audience had turned into a congregation of singing and swaying
Dead Heads. Every age and walk of life became enthralled with the
smoke laden display. Every spectator was on their feet, bellowing
out lyrics along with the band. Though, of their little circle, only
Daisy knew the words. The others did a good job of faking it.

Robin decided to firm things up by calling Tommy when
they walked out of the park and down 5th Avenue. Sternly she said,
"Next week, Thursday, the 24th. It's good for Parker and it's OK
for us. We'll make it fun too, since it's your birthday…. But listen
Tommy, Bryce is sticking his neck out for this. He's got to get back
the next day so it's a lock, right?"

"It's a lock. I've got a reading the next day, so I'll be back
in the city with a new perspective. And what do you mean by sticking out his neck?"

"It's crunch time up at the Great Camp and his schedule is
tight. I just don't want you to make light of this."

"I won't!"

Tommy sounded defensive. Then he asked Robin how everyone else was and apologized again for blowing them off. Thinking he could soften the situation, he then offered, "You guys can
spend the night at my place if you need to tonight."

"Thanks, but we're cool. Peter and Astri already split for a
full week of family shit and Bryce got the rest of us rooms at *The
Plaza*."

"You're talking like a hippy… And ooooh The Plaza,"
Tommy sang sarcastically.

"Shut up, but yeah, he's got a connection. He took a few

etiquette classes there a few years back. Ya know?" Robin's tone took a turn towards sarcastic as well. "For the kind of business he's in?"

"Of course he did," Tommy snapped.

"What's with the sarcasm?" she asked.

He sang in a high-pitched voice, distancing himself, "Nothing!"

Robin was in no mood; she decided to go for the final stab. "Jesus Tommy, pull up your fucking panties and figure your shit out OK?" She hung up.

She felt bad, but she was fed up with his drama. He didn't show up for the concert, regardless of the pending meeting with Parker. This BS was getting to her, but she was not going to let it ruin the rest of the night.

Bryce caught wind of her frustration and offered, "How about we hit the Todd English Food Hall on the lower level first. Plenty to eat, drink, or just look at."

Robin grabbed his arm and snuggled into him as they picked up the pace. With Daisy and Aron following just behind, they knew they'd be in for serious entertainment during what was left of the night. A very stoned Aron was singing a Dead tune while walking down 5th Avenue. He had no idea what the real words were, and his ad lib wording was hysterical!

Tommy, on the other hand, hung up the phone with a growing realization that his angst was getting the best of him. Besides his solace, his feelings about Bryce besieged him, and now he figured Robin was catching his drift.

Tommy, in his latest state, thought it would do him some good to lay low at home with his folks. A mental breakcation, if you will. No show, no readings, no responsibilities, and no clue what to do. Hanging home for a week should help heal his mind and his heart. Nothing would even remotely remind him of Bert while there.

Margo and Frank knew something was wrong. In the recent past, he never visited for longer than two days, so a week seemed extreme. He was up in his old room playing video games. His dad went in and sat on his bed.

"Son, tell me what's bothering you."

Frank was a man of few words. If he spoke, it was always direct and to the point. Tommy took that same direction and blurted out, "Dad, it's tough to be gay. My heart hurts. I just want to be somewhere where I can safely lick my wounds. That's why I'm here."

Frank bent over and took the video controls out from Tommy's hands. Then he pulled him to his feet and gave him a huge bear hug. He finished off with a firm (but loving) punch to his shoulder. "Hearts mend stronger after a break. Suck it up, buttercup! Your mom is making a nice dinner. Be down at 7:00."

Tommy thought, *Amazing, what his few words can do*. He was glad to be home.

After dinner, Margo set out a homemade lemon meringue pie.

"Mom, the way *TO* a man's heart is through his stomach. That's the old adage. Not, you can fix a man's broken heart, through his stomach."

"Oh, one piece won't kill you," she said.

"Fine! But please DO NOT get me a birthday cake or anything else for that matter. I have a reading next Friday and I need to be slim."

Regardless of his request, Margo fed and spoiled him rotten. Five pounds heavier, Tommy was ready to go back into the city and face reality... And the gym.

It also helped that his folks sent him off with a big fat

birthday check. Now he could keep his apartment for a couple more months, at least.

30

Traffic

Sliding a plate in front of Bryce, Robin said, "I worked with a mycologist last week when I was in Albany, so yesterday on my hike up Skylight, I found Chanterelle mushrooms, and voilà! One mushroom and upstate cheddar omelet."

"I've never hiked Skylight. Any rare alpine plants up there?" Bryce asked.

"Alpine azalea. In fact, it's the only population in all of New York State! On the way back down, I spotted the Chanterelles."

Before she took her seat, Bryce pulled Robin down over his plate. "Lucky for me!" he said, giving her an eggie smooch.

Over breakfast, Robin tried to explain to Bryce about Tommy's foul disposition as of late. "He really needs to snap out of it!" she moaned.

"That's why I'm eager to get him and Parker together. I think it could prove to be a great thing for both of them," said a very smug Bryce.

They were out the door and on the road at noon sharp. It would take almost five hours to get to midtown Manhattan. There shouldn't be any traffic heading south on a Thursday afternoon.

Robin called Tommy about an hour outside of the city. "Happy birthday to you!" she sang, then asked, "How's your day so far?"

"Thank you. So far, so good. What's your ETA?" Tommy asked back.

"5:00 is still looking good for us. We thought we could meet at our hotel for a drink first, and if all goes well, you pick the place for dinner."

"What hotel ya stayin' at *this* time?" Tommy squawked.

"The Roger Smith Hotel on Lex. You got a problem with that?"

"No, that's fine. Parker?"

"He's waiting to hear from us first. So listen, at the hotel there are two bars. Go to the outside one, it's called Henry's Rooftop Bar. OK?"

"Sounds good. See you 'round 5:00."

Tommy stood in front of the full-length mirror in his hallway. He pulled up his shirt and flexed in his abs. It wasn't bad but he was not happy. He thought, *I'm gonna kill Mom.* Then with a dose of shame he conceded it was *his* fault, not Margo's. *Shit, she didn't force all that food down my throat.*

He made himself a Tito's and diet tonic. He needed to neutralize his mood. Deducing the fact that Bryce and Robin were going out of their way to introduce Parker—and since he already kind of snapped at Robin—he made a conscious effort to be upbeat. He began a new little mantra: *Happy comes from me. Happy comes from me.*

He went back in front of the mirror and pulled up his shirt again. It's not that his jeans were tight—he just didn't see the definition in his abs like he did a month ago. He tucked in his indigo linen band collar shirt and slid on his brown wingtip Andrew boots. He unevenly cuffed his jeans, purposely going for the "not so concerned" look. He inspected himself and ran his hand through his hair. One turn to one side, one turn to the other. He un-tucked his shirt and out loud declared, "Parker should be so lucky!'"

It was 5:10 and there was just one open seat at the bar. Tommy grabbed it.

Henry's Rooftop Bar was small, casual, and comfortable. It was an open corner spot, almost like a chunk was taken off the building's exterior to expose the people within. There was not one pretentious thing about it. *Good,* he thought, *I'm in no mood for stuffy a-holes.*

Tommy relaxed in the bar chair, ordered a drink, and leaned back against the huge brick wall behind him. Coming up through the lobby he realized this was a boutique/art gallery type of hotel, and not quite what he expected from Bryce.

Before any other doubtful or negative thoughts surfaced, he began his mantra again while taking in the eclectic people, and trying to guess what they were drinking to pass the time.

He looked at his watch just as his phone rang. It was 5:30 and it was Robin.

"Hey! Did you know the Pope was in town today?" Robin asked.

"Shit, that's today? You guys stuck in traffic?"

"Yes, and we're having a hard time crossing town."

"New ETA?"

"Figure like 6:30."

"That bad?"

"Really bad, we're at a standstill right now."

"Parker?"

"We plan to call him when we get closer to the hotel."

Tommy didn't want to sit there for an hour to wait. He sucked down his drink and then hit the street to kill some more time.

Strolling three blocks north and one block east, he spotted

another boutique hotel: The Kimberly Hotel, also with a rooftop lounge. *Why not?* he thought. So, thirty floors up he went. To the "Upstairs" bar.

The sun was beginning to set and the skies were transitioning to a darker blue. String-lights that draped overhead cut through the view where the Chrysler Building and its beaming white lights began to steal the show. The ambiance was classy and elegant with a variety of furnishings. Black tufted leather chairs circled low tables. Long fabric couches and ottomans dotted the outside edge where glass half-walls kept the evening breezes to a lull. Around the corner, the atmosphere softened with green topiaries crawling up walls and boxy red cushions that simplified the vibe. The main bar stretched long across the inside wall, cornered with more topiaries.

Tommy spotted a good place to stand; the place was jam-packed. A just-wed bride and her entourage monopolized the primary corner of the balcony where Tommy thought the view itself was more beautiful than the bride. He snickered to himself but then realized he was being a dick. *Happy comes from me. Happy comes from me.*

At the bar, he spied a couple with empty glasses hoping he could swoop in for one of their seats. Standing there he sipped his drink and took in the snobby, hipster, but definitely interesting crowd. He hovered even closer as the couple paid their bill. The woman slid out her seat offering it to him with a nod.

"Why thank you," he said.

Simultaneously another guy seized the other seat. Pulling it out, the anxious patron elbowed Tommy. "My bad, I'm sorry," he apologized.

"No problem," Tommy said in return.

They both sat neatly settling at the bar, but his elbow met

Tommy's once more.

"Sorry again!"

"All good."

The guy then called out to the bartender, "Makers Mark rocks, please."

Tommy thought to himself, *Yeluchhk, I hate bourbon.*

Just then, an open hand rotated towards him, announcing, "Chadwick W. Travers the Third."

Tommy therefore extended his hand, announcing, "Thomas W. Mayfield the First."

A zealous handshake, a pause, and then with curiosity, Tommy inquired, "What's your W for?"

"Warren. Yours?"

"Wade… if you can believe. It's Native American for dancing girl. But I don't tell that to too many people," Tommy admitted.

"So why tell me?"

Tommy looked directly into his eyes and said, "Not sure, just a fun fact, *and* it's hilarious."

Then, somewhere in the middle of Tommy's chest, low in his lungs and back behind his heart, he felt his pilot light flicker back on.

"At least you have a story for yours. Mine's just a dead uncle."

Tommy laughed into his drink, and some of it splashed up onto his face. A cocktail napkin appeared. "Please, call me Chad."

Tommy grabbed the napkin. "Thanks, Chad."

Chad watched as Tommy wiped his face. Then he caught Tommy glance at his watch. "Meeting someone?" he politely asked.

"I'm supposed to meet a few friends, but they can't seem to

cross town because of the Pope."

Tommy pulled out his phone and coyly texted Robin a simple question mark.

Robin responded back, "*OMG, we haven't fucking moved! Figure more like 7:30. I'll keep you updated.*"

Tommy texted back a smiley face and, "*No worries!*" Then he swung around in his bar seat, facing out, to take in the view.

Chad mimicked his spin and expanded on the conversation. "Before I came here, a local radio station announced major delays across the city." He then looked at *his* watch, stating, "At 6:45, the Pope is scheduled to be at St Pat's. I was just on Park Ave and you can't even make a left to head west. The city's a mess. They said he's here in the U.S. for a six-day visit."

Chad re-spun around in his seat and signaled the bartender for another drink. He glanced sideways at Tommy and continued. "He's asking for us to do more to fight climate change, and global poverty, and he's praising the bishops for their"—he rolled his eyes and sarcastically motioning air quotes— "'courage' in handling the sex abuse crisis within the church. Critics say he should have focused more on the victims and *their* suffering."

Tommy made a growling noise as he spun to also face the bar again.

When the bartender came with Chad's drink, Chad looked to Tommy, his hand grazed the top of his, and he asked, "Can I get you one?"

Tommy looked up at the bartender. "Tito's and diet tonic?"

"Sorry, no diet."

"Then regular will do."

Chad pushed back away from the bar and glanced up and then down at Tommy. "Diet?"

"I just spent a week at my parents. My mother loves to cook."

Chad raised his glass when the bartender handed Tommy his. "To Mom's!" he announced.

Chadwick W. Travers III was a little older. Tommy figured twentynine-ish. He was about an inch shorter than Tommy (who happened to notice before they even sat). He was impeccably dressed. *He must be some kind of white-collar professional, or a model fresh off a fashion shoot—he definitely qualified*, Tommy thought. Broad shoulders filled his jacket. Two days of trimmed scruff lined his strong jawline, dark hair, and low eyebrows, accented a piercing set of amber eyes.

Not wanting to revisit the crisis within the church, Tommy decided to snuff out the subject and said, "I'm against all things Catholic.... Oh shit, you're not Catholic, are you?"

"Hell no!" he laughed.

Then Tommy's phone buzzed with another text. He was almost afraid to look. He didn't want to leave.

Still trying to get there. Unfuckingbelievable! Parker is out. He's having traffic issues too. I'm sorry! I'm so pissed... I need a drink.. What's your cutoff?

Tommy texted back: *We can always make another plan. I have a reading in the morning. Need to rehearse tonight before it gets too late. I'll give it until 9:30.*

"Friends coming?" Chad asked.

"It's looking less and less likely."

"Well, I'm planning to grab a bite. They have a great tuna tartar, and a roasted butternut squash salad that I'd practically kill for. Care to join me?"

Tommy's pilot light ignited all four burners at once. "How

could I say no to that!"

Chad queried the bartender who came out from behind the bar and sat them in a set of black leather tufted chairs at a low cocktail table.

The sky was now pitch-dark, the Chrysler Building was erect, lit, and fabulous.

And Tommy was too.

* * *

Tommy flipped the business card with Chad's number on it between his fingers on the subway ride home. Then he tucked it into his wallet. *So what if it was almost midnight.* His reading was at 9:45 am and there was still adequate time to rehearse the script.

Just before his head hit his pillow, he sent a closing text to Robin.

I hope you were able to salvage the night with a nice dinner somewhere. Your hotel looks inviting and romantic. I met a nice guy tonight—long story. Pope sucks. I feel so bad you came all this way. Thank you, thank you, thank you!

Robin texted back.

If you say stuff like the Pope sucks, you'll get struck by lightning. LOL. Our night didn't start until 10:00 — Can you believe!?! Still at dinner now. Dying for your long story. I'm sorry about Parker, we'll try for a new date. A G A I N ! We're here until noon tomorrow. I hope your birthday somehow turned out OK.

Tommy completely forgot about his birthday. Instead of feeling sorry for himself, fate interrupted. Maybe it was his mantra.

He texted back, *It did!*

* * *

9:45 a.m., Tommy stood in a room full of clones. They all had on white shirts and black ties with black pants. Just like the role. Tommy was no different. It was too late to go back and make himself stand out by wearing something colorful. Dressing the part wasn't expected but hell, everyone owns a white shirt and black pants, how could you not?

"Thomas W. Mayfield!" His name trumpeted through the room. He followed a guy with a clipboard who was hurried and fanning himself with the head shot Tommy had sent in when the casting call was put out a few weeks earlier. He led him along the length of a huge black curtain and abruptly stopped. He turned around and held his finger up signaling *one second*. Then he handed the head shot off around to the other side of the curtain and moved close to Tommy whispering,

"Wait for your name, then walk in and look for the mark on the floor."

After a few seconds, his name beckoned out again.

Tommy flung the curtain to the side making a more dramatic entrance than simply stepping around it. A short diagonal walk, past a piano, and to the X on the floor, he spun on his heels, smiled, and nodded at the four people sitting across from him in big swivel chairs. They passed along his photo taking turns looking down at it, then up at him, flipping it over to read his stats. When the photo made it to the last person in the row, this man looked up and asked:

"So, Thomas W. Mayfield, have you performed in a Broadway show before?"

"Just off Broadway, sir. Please, call me Tommy."

Then the man cut to the chase and simply requested, "Please begin the dialog first."

The dialog was a three-minute segment. There were a few short pauses where the woman of the four read the supporting part. It was odd since that part was also a male's role. *They do that to throw you,* Tommy thought. But it didn't. Not one bit.

He finished.

"Thank you," said the man on the end.

They immediately followed with a request to perform just half of the specified song. Tommy had the whole song nailed down, which his mom was able to witness the week before. His biggest fan obviously, she would sit and clap like an excited kid when he would finish.

The piano began with a single note dictating the key for the song to be sung.

Halfway through the song at a natural pause, again the man said, "Thank you."

Though dance experience was not listed in the casting call requirements, Tommy was fully aware of the necessity for this role. The man on the end flipped over Tommy's headshot and said, "Says here you haven't performed any professional dance, yet there's a simple yes that you can. Is that correct Tommy?"

"Sir, yes, it is."

"While it's not imperative that you are a *fabulous* tap dancer—this is not 42nd Street—but there is a requirement."

"That I understand sir, and I can assure you I'd be solid."

"Well, thank you again, Tommy!"

All four of them stood, then smiled, and nodded at Tommy. The man on the end held out his hand as Tommy passed.

With a firm grip, Tommy took his saying, "Much obliged."

The man looked over his shoulder back at the three others. "Now's a good time to break." They were all on Tommy's heels as he went to leave the room.

The man opened the door for Tommy and they all walked out into a hallway. This door was different than the one Tommy had entered coming from the room full of clones. When he sat waiting to be called earlier, he wondered how many actors had actually come for the part thinking, *not that many.* Now he gingerly padded down the hall with four casting people following close behind. He thought, *Well, that explains it. I bet there were many others.*

Then suddenly, "Excuse me, Tommy?" Came from behind. Tommy turned around and stopped. The man also stopped allowing the others to pass. Placing both of his hands on his hips he stood curiously looking at Tommy. Tilting his head to the side, he asked, "You wouldn't happen to know Bryce Hamilton, would you?

"As a matter of fact, I do?"

"Well then!" he held out his hand once again. "Pleasure to finally meet you. I'm Parker!"

* * *

Tommy sat indignant on a bench in the subway, waiting… and thinking.

"I don't want any set-ups or handouts from Bryce. What the fuck was that? How is that Parker?"

The MTA had changed schedules adding a few more trains to specific lines causing other trains to run behind. Seemed even at the subterranean level the Pope had caused all kinds of traffic problems.

31

So Gay it's OK

Robin and Bryce were on their way back up to the Adirondacks. Her phone buzzed. "It's Tommy," she began. "He says in his text that he's not sure about how well his reading went, but I should ask you? Then it says, 'Call me later.' What the heck is he talking about?"

Bryce glanced over at Robin. "I have no idea. You sure he typed that right?"

"Strange. I'll call him when I'm home."

Five hours later, they were back at Robin's Nest. Bryce tugged at Robin as she leaned into his car to give him a kiss good-bye. He reminded her, "Let me know about Sunday." Then he continued straight on to the Great Camp.

The last weekend in September was forecast to be an Indian summer. A family had rented out the whole resort for a wedding. The rehearsal dinner that night was to be followed by a sunset boat cruise around Upper Saranac. Bryce needed to hurry. Thankfully it would be a less hectic weekend because the family had planned to make it small and intimate. The actual headcount was only about thirty. Stu was back on hand, and Bryce hoped he could get Robin up on Sunday to enjoy a little down time; possibly another picnic on Tommy's Rock. It had been almost a whole year since their first canoe venture there.

Driving there, Bryce thought, *How is it even possible that a whole year has passed?*

Over the summer, he finally toured Robin around the Great

Camp, but he was never able to do an overnight with her in the famous boathouse like she had hoped. The previous year in *Condé Nast Traveler*, the camp was listed in the Top 100 Hotels and Resorts in the World, so every night that Robin was available, the boathouse was not.

Now, suddenly aware of how much time passed, created a dilemma for Bryce. He was afraid of what might happen—what the consequences could be. Dismally he thought, *I have to tell her. I just don't know how or when. It's not fair to continue like this... all the deceit.* It ripped at his heart. The only way to tell her was to ask her.

At home, Robin settled in and texted Tommy. *Good time to call?*

Her phone rang seconds later. Tommy blasted her.

In response, every word out of Robin's mouth seemed defensive:

"Wait? What? Calm down! No, we NEVER said it was a date—or a blind date.... What, no! I know I mentioned weeks ago that he was some kind of promoter or producer. Christ, Tommy, calm down. Yes, yesterday when we were all supposed to meet up. I'm sorry about the traffic. You can take that up with the Pope! It's simple: Bryce thought he'd get you two together because Parker has experience working with actors and playwrights for philanthropic and scholarship efforts. I thought it was a great idea because maybe it would humble you. You've been so fucking scorned and sour, you *DO* realize? I thought giving back, or something like that on the side would offer a different perspective for you! No, I didn't know he was a talent agent or an actual Broadway producer. And how the hell would we know that he'd be there for your reading? We don't even know what you did a reading for! Shit Tommy, cut me a fucking break!"

There was an awkwardly long period of silence. Tommy obviously needed to mull everything through his head. Robin broke the silence.

"I don't know how Bryce knows Parker. That wasn't important. Would you like me to ask him?"

"Yes!" Tommy insisted. "Please do! Listen, Robin, I don't trust Bryce. I've never said before, but I'm concerned for you. Something's not right."

Robin knew how pissed Tommy was, and now having just flown off the handle, he wasn't thinking straight. *How could he not trust Bryce?* she thought. *We just spent the last thirty-six hours trying to do something nice for him.*

"I'm a big girl now, Tommy. Don't worry about me."

"Oh, but it's OK for you to worry about me all the time?"

"OK fine. Worry about me if you want, but I love Bryce and I completely trust him. I'll see him this Sunday. I'll ask him and I'll call you next week."

"Fine."

"Fine!"

She hung up. She couldn't stand thinking about how Tommy felt about Bryce. She needed to get to the bottom of it. And now that she unexpectedly fessed her love for Bryce to Tommy, she thought, *I guess I should probably tell Bryce too.*

Tommy did consider the facts. Yes, he was scorned and soured, but he was also unemployed which made him delicate and defensive. He did realize Robin and Bryce just did an insane trip to the city and back to make something happen for him, but he was still disturbed. Something didn't smell right. There was just something about Bryce. But it was now Friday night, the weather was incredible, and he had a date.

Tommy dressed in front of his full-length mirror, anxiously trying on a variety of clothes. Staring up at Chad's hand-written cell number (the card was tucked into the frame), he thought about trying a *calming* mantra....

He couldn't, he was way too excited, and he just couldn't. Instead, he danced around in his boxers, a crisp white shirt, and tweed vest. Pulling out a brown tie that matched his belt and his shoes, he decided to finish his look with brand new jeans. He laughed to himself, thinking about the last time he excitedly dressed in front of the mirror. That was supposed to be for the infamous Parker, yet it ended up being for Chad anyway. *Where will this all lead?* he pondered.

A gold nameplate hung on a fabric-covered wall to the right of the door at the end of the hall. Tommy walked toward it in a trance. Chad had asked him to meet him there, at his office. *Chadwick W. Travers III, Psychological Counseling, Behavior Modification, and Education*, was engraved into it. Tommy read it a second time thinking, *He said counselor, but I didn't expect this.*

Trepidatiously, he knocked. Chad abruptly swung the door open and stood there for a moment beaming at Tommy. Tommy blushed. "You going to invite me in?" he asked awkwardly.

"If I do, I'll have to charge you," Chad joked.

Chad grabbed his jacket from behind the door and quickly closed it. Motioning to walk back down the hall, he said, "I didn't tell you what kind of counselor I was because it freaks people out."

"Yet you asked to meet here?" Tommy questioned.

"You are here aren't you? If I told you straight up, you might not have come. Would you have?"

"Probably not."

"Do you have any psychological problems? Chad asked laughing.

"Don't we all?"

They stepped into the elevator. Tommy became quiet. The door closed and Chad said, "Please don't think of me as rude. It's a way to show you what I do professionally. I gave you this address for a date, NOT for business."

Tommy let out an audible sigh of relief and Chad then stepped directly in front of him. He folded his arms, looked directly into his eyes, and jokingly asked, "How screwed up are you?"

"How long ya got?" Tommy snickered back.

It was early in the evening. They walked over to 5th Ave and decided to stroll into Central Park. Chad assured Tommy there would be no cross-examinations. "People are instantly afraid of me once they find out what I do. Honestly, I don't want you to keep anything from me because you'll worry about what I might think. That would be a bad way to start things off. Right?" He looked to Tommy for assurance.

"Well, what if I tell you something thought provoking, or personal? Won't you feel like I'm using you for your professional advice?" Tommy asked.

"This is a date, right?"

"Right," he agreed.

"Do you actually think you'd tell me something that you wouldn't tell someone else, simply because I do what I do?"

"Probably not. But I guess I'd be afraid I'd let something slip out."

"Think about this," Chad suggested, "if I was a medical doctor and you stood here bleeding, shouldn't I assist you?"

"That's different," Tommy pressed.

"OK. If I was an artist and I wanted to use you as one of my subjects, would you let me?"

"I like the way *that* sounds…. But still…"

"But still nothing!" Chad laughed. "You're impossible!"

They made their way just a few more steps and Chad announced, "OK fine, let's get it over with!"

They stepped off the pathway and sat at a bench. A full view of the Gapstow Bridge and pond was in front of them. The tree to its right was turning orange and with the autumn sun setting low in the sky, the light streamed under the bridge and danced across the water. The foreground was illuminated in gold, and shadows stretched long across the park.

Tommy adjusted his position to properly face Chad, but the beautiful scenery distracted him. "It looks like a painting!" he exclaimed. Then he laughed, suddenly aware of how goofy he sounded. "That's soooo not something I'd typically say. It must be because of your artist remark." He inquisitively peered at Chad.

Chad responded matter-of-factly, "See, already you see things in a different light." He adjusted his position so *he* could face Tommy directly. He cleared his throat but waited for Tommy to speak.

Tommy realized Chad was already toying with him. He liked that. Casually, Tommy threw his arm around behind Chad resting it on the back of the bench. "So, tell me then, *what* exactly are we supposed to get over with?" he asked.

"Two things!" Chad held up two fingers. "First, tell me something about your life that you don't like. Something you can't change. Second, tell me something that is bothering you. Something you think you *can* change."

Tommy, a little unsettled, pulled his arm from around the

back of Chad and leaned forward on the bench, resting his elbows on his knees and his chin onto his fists. Deep in thought he considered his options.

"Second one, first," he requested. Then he stood up and held out his hand, suggesting they continue their walk.

"OK, second one first," Chad agreed.

Tommy began, "So a recent concern that I think I can change, is the way I've been treating my best friend."

They wandered along as he explained all about his concern for Robin and his mistrust in Bryce. "I don't get a good vibe from him. I don't know how else to explain it. Robin is very important to me, and I think now since I don't see her as often… well, I worry. Maybe I make these things up in my own head. Maybe I'm the actual problem?"

Tommy confessed even more by telling Chad how he recently broke up with Bert, and how the whole trust thing was a major issue for him.

Chad listened intently. And before he advised, again he reminded Tommy, "See, you'd tell these things to anyone right? It's just regular stuff you want to get off your chest."

Tommy agreed and added, "Yes but except for Robin, because I fear telling her too much about how I feel about Bryce. That would make her REALLY mad. And I think that's the line I just crossed."

Chad considered everything and earnestly spoke, "You are genuinely concerned for Robin. You don't want her to get hurt like you did. Your defenses are up because of your recent break up, like you are in a protection mode, and it's spilling out to her. Emotions are reactionary, like reflexes. You are angry with her, simply because she is angry with you."

"You make all this stuff seem normal," Tommy sincerely stated.

"It is normal," Chad advised.

"Then what do you think? Like what can I do?"

"I think you need to spend more time with the two of them to figure it out. Tell me, when did you see them last?"

"It was supposed to be yesterday, they were the friends I had plans with."

"Well, lucky for me they never showed!" Chad threw a provocative smile at Tommy.

Tommy blushed and continued, "But I did see Robin just a few weeks ago. And Bryce? Wow, I guess it's been a while. Like since January."

"Definitely make plans to get together with them," Chad pressed.

"I will."

Tommy felt satisfied and content about how the evening was transpiring. But then the next dreaded question.

Chad broke Tommy's thoughts. "OK, first one second? You want to talk about the thing you can't fix?"

"Hold on! It's only fair if *you* tell me something you can or can't fix."

"Over dinner then," Chad insisted.

Then he playfully stepped behind Tommy and placed his hands on his shoulders as if to lead him forward. Tommy laughed as he was marched out of the park and down 5th. He reached his hands up to his own shoulders securing Chad's underneath his. Full out flirting was now underway.

"I like the view from back here," Chad mumbled.

* * *

"The Monkey Bar" must be in a bunch of movies, it looks familiar. Tommy thought as soon as they entered. He was not very familiar with the Midtown east section of the city, aside from having just been there the night before to meet Robin, Bryce, and Parker. Apparently, Chad was, and he chose this place for a reason.

They were seated in the curve of a huge bright red leather banquette. Tommy slid in first and Chad followed. Before the waiter had a chance to hand them menus, Chad had Tommy's hand in his. The corner spot tucked them in so they were diagonal from each other. Dramatic red lighting matched the seating and mirrored pillars reflected the colorful jazz inspired mural that covered the inside walls. There was something special about the place; it oozed romance.

Chad ordered a bottle of Cabernet Sauvignon and recommended they split a chopped salad. Based on the previous night's menu suggestions at Upstairs at the Kimberly, Tommy sat back only to request that Chad complete their order by picking entrees they could share.

He did.

Tommy tilted his glass to clink on Chad's and said, "Here's to firsts and seconds in dates and lessons."

"Well said," Chad uttered with an enticing smile.

At the side of their table, the waiter mixed and then split the chopped salad between them. He topped off their wine and then rolled away with the salad cart.

"OK," Chad began. "The first one first. The one I *can't* fix."

Taking a huge sip from his glass, he sat tall in his seat and took a deep breath. "My dad can't get over the fact that I'm gay. He's a *manly man* and it kills him I'm not. Well he thinks I'm not. Like what the hell is a manly man anyway? The whole situation is pretty much why I went into the psychology field."

Tommy grabbed for Chad's hand this time and he firmly held it in his. Sliding in even closer he lowered their hands to rest on his lap. Tommy looked down at their cupped hands and opened up Chad's. He looked down and stroked the inside of his palm. "What's he want, a lumberjack?"

Chad laughed. "Yeah, no calluses on *my* hands, right?"

"Maybe over time your dad will come around," Tommy suggested.

"I can only hope."

"But that totally sucks," Tommy continued, "My folks are great. Like, I can't even imagine…"

Chad was now vulnerable *and* adorable. Tommy was planning to shelve the conversation about his 'first thing, second.' His, 'something he can't change.' But the time suddenly seemed right and the wine started talking too. He blurted out, "So here's what I can't fix. A priest molested me when I was twelve."

Completely astounded, Chad muttered, "What the fuck?"

The waiter's eyes almost popped out of his head as he cleared the salad plates. Tommy looked up and asked, "Can we please get another bottle of cab?"

Tommy looked to Chad for his approval.

Chad, still in shock, nodded saying, "Yes, definitely more wine."

Tommy had never given anyone the quick of it like he did for Chad right then and there. It took the waiter all of thirty seconds to uncork the next bottle, deliver the entrees, fill the water glasses, top off their wine, and ask if they'd like more bread. Obviously overhearing too much, he couldn't remove himself fast enough!

With every sentence Tommy spoke, and every minute that passed, he felt lighter and lighter. The rusted-on dead weight that he carried around for so many years was beginning to erode.

"Here's the thing," Tommy admitted. "I question my homosexuality because of this priest."

Chad contemplated the issue and then questioned Tommy. "So, you wonder whether or not he brought your homosexuality on?"

"Correct."

"OK," Chad continued. "This is going to sound outlandish, and it's very personal so don't answer if you don't want to. Did you enjoy it? With the... what did you call him?"

"MS"

"Yeah, did you enjoy it with MS? Do you remember?"

"I remember I was really scared and I felt pressured. But to be honest, I didn't exactly hate it. I didn't really know right from wrong. Do you think maybe I hold that particular moment in time responsible for my sexual preference?"

"No, but you certainly suppressed it. And like all of us you were afraid of it. He made it easy for you to have something to blame it on. I think you were gay, you are gay, and you'll always be gay. MS probably saw that little spark in your eye."

Chad couldn't help but giggle when he said that, given that he's the lucky one currently enjoying that spark. Then he sat back and turned serious.

"But damn him for acting on it. He's a fucking criminal! You were just a child, for God's sake, and there is nothing you can do now but make peace with it. Peace in your own head. If you can, find and take something positive from it. Did he hurt you?"

"No."

"So while the bastard should be behind bars, let go of the

blame. You're gay. That's OK! Don't let it tarnish your thoughts and make you afraid to reflect on your own childhood."

Tommy felt relieved, rejuvenated, and rebooted. "How have I managed all this time without you?" he asked Chad.

Now Chad was the one who blushed. Then *he* slid closer to Tommy. Placing his hand on the back of his neck, he fiddled with his collar. Wanting to convince Tommy it was never his fault, he continued.

"This problem goes so far back. For centuries, men of the cloth stifle their sexuality by choosing celibacy. It's a punishment of sorts, for their unsacred thoughts. They bury their desires deep in their cloaks. Sadly, now we find at some point the truth prevails, especially if you throw alcohol in the mix. Ironic, how the Pope just addressed this yesterday."

Tommy's face relaxed and his eyes softened. The boy hidden inside was sneaking back out. There was now almost an aura about him and Chad had the pleasure of witnessing it.   Tommy placed his hand over Chad's—still on the back of his neck—and he leaned in and kissed him. "Thank you."

The waiter removed their dinner plates and handed them dessert menus.

Chad didn't bother to open it, instead he looked to Tommy and suggested, "Two cappuccinos?"

Tommy returned with his own suggestion, "How about two hot chocolates?"

Chad grabbed Tommy's hand and gave it a squeeze. "You are really just a sweet little boy, aren't you?"

Tommy blushed, tilted his head, and marveled at Chad. Completely gratified and notably relaxed, Tommy asked him, "Tell me, was all that the clinical psychologist in you?"

"No, that came from someone who really likes you and wants you to be OK…. Kind of like Robin."

32

The L Word

When Robin woke, she noticed a text from Tommy, from Sunday at 2:00 a.m.: *I just had one of the best dates of my life with Chadwick!* It was followed by a vibrating pink heart emoji.

She was still angry with him; this was not an apology. Not that she'd get one, she knew Tommy and she knew he was sniffing around—out of guilt—to make nice. She still planned to call him in a few days, after she talked to Bryce.

"Bryce, how do you know Parker?" Robin asked.

"I thought I mentioned before. He's a friend of the family. Why?"

"Tommy was all bent out of shape when we talked. If you can believe, he met Parker at his reading yesterday. He thinks maybe you were trying to hook them up, to get him a part in a show."

"Parker was there? Hmmm, well he is a producer. I guess it's not all that surprising. But do you mean hook up, hook up? Like Tommy thought I'd pimp him out?"

"Well he was really agitated when we spoke, so I didn't exactly understand. But I suspect he thought it was supposed to be like a blind date, so *maybe* he thought that."

"First of all, Parker is straight. And you agreed that introducing them might be a good thing."

"I know!"

"What a fucking brat!"

"Yeah he is," Robin agreed. "But please don't hate him. He's just being oversensitive, again!"

"Robin, I hate no one. Tell you what, let's all do something together. Something fun like last New Year's. We all haven't spent much time together." Again, Bryce was thinking of how much time had passed. "Make a plan so we can all hang out. He's being unreasonable. He needs to realize I'm a friend and not a foe."

"Good idea. He kind of owes us now anyway," Robin claimed.

Bryce tugged at Robin's hand to make their way down the hall to the mink closet. What was supposed to be a beautiful Indian summer weekend, by late Sunday morning, it had turned cold, wet, and miserable. Robin pulled into Bryce's cabin early that morning prepped for a canoe outing, but due to the weather, they decided to spend the day lounging around watching movies.

Leaning against the thick door frame of the closet, Bryce spoke in earnest, "Robin…" but she dove into the furry layers.

Before she became completely enthralled—deciding which one to choose—he continued to speak, "Listen. You know my dad is *all things Manhattan,* right? So, for years my family has donated to a variety of arts foundations. Parker is our main contact for that. He helps distribute funds via scholarships to theatre alliances and performing arts schools. Didn't we decide something like this could interest Tommy while he continues to look for a role?"

"We did!" she bellowed from the cold air. "But I think when he unexpectedly saw Parker, he put two and two together and came up with his own warped scenario."

"Well his two and two don't add up properly," Bryce voiced back.

Now looking to change the subject and definitely the tone, Robin called out, "Bryce!" Alluringly, she appeared from the back of the closet wrapped in a gigantic silver fox/mink combo comforter. "Say no more! I'll call him in a few days and figure it out. I'll set him straight."

Bryce laughed. "Well I doubt you will actually set him straight."

Bryce hunched down and kneeled in front of Robin, slipping his arms around her waist burying himself completely into the fur with her. He lifted her shirt and kissed her middle. Completely covered up by the fur, he blindly boosted her up as she straddled him. With only her head popping out at the top, she directed him carefully out of the closet, across the hall, and into the bedroom. He purposely bounced like a pinball off the walls, laughing and pretending it was all her fault. Once in the bedroom, she guided him to tilt her enough that she was able to grab the remote control. When she had it in her grasp, she clicked on the huge flat screen TV and directed him slowly to the edge of the bed, where he could safely plop her down. He did. Flat on her back surrounded by fur, he slid in next to her.

"I pick the first movie," she demanded.

A wrestling match for the remote ensued. They wrestled and rolled around, toying with each other. She had no choice but to surrender when he pinned her on her back and held both arms up over her head.

"I give!" she screamed.

She let go of the remote. He sat back keeping her pinned at the waist, but he freed her arms. He clicked the TV off and threw the remote across the room. He lifted her shirt again and started kissing her middle where he left off.

Robin's concerns diminished with each one of his kisses, thinking now of how deeply she loved Bryce. She loved every second they were together, and she yearned for him every second they weren't. She never loved someone like this; it was all new territory for her. Never imagined it could be so grand. Just thinking about it drummed up her passion, but it also drummed up her fear.

What they had—or what she assumed they had—was so deep, so profound, that she was afraid. Now with blurred thinking muddled in passion and fear, she thought, *If I say anything, if I tell him I love him, I could scare him off. If I say nothing, nothing will change.*

They were both completely naked by the time she convinced herself to keep quiet.

Things were about to get loud.

* * *

The weather that next day was nothing shy of a monsoon. It wasn't a problem for Bryce—Mondays were leisure clean up days over at the Great Camp. Robin spent the night there knowing her day of hiking would be shot. Also, not a problem because the alpine plants germinating in her basement were in no hurry to be transplanted.

The smell of bacon wafted through the cabin and lured Robin into the kitchen. Practically in a hypnotic state, she came up behind Bryce and wrapped her arms tightly around him.

"I love..." she caught herself from letting the words slip, "...the smell of bacon!"

He spun in her arms to face her and fed her a crispy sliver. Then he enthusiastically said, "Check it out!"

He pointed to his laptop which sat open on the desk portion of the kitchen counter. Robin slid out the chair, sat down, and began to read the email that filled the screen.

Bryce mentioned over her shoulder, "From Parker. He sent it last night."

Hi Bryce,

I met your friend Tommy Mayfield. So ironic since only Friday night we were all supposed to meet! Sorry again about that; I was coming from New Jersey and it sounds like we were all stuck in the same Pope traffic.

Anyway, I just thought I'd let you know I no longer have an interest in discussing the arts foundation opportunities with him. To be completely honest, I was a little shocked meeting him because it was during a reading just this morning. He was unbelievable. I thought you'd be interested in knowing:

Actors possess the ability to transport an audience. With a set and costumes in a theatre, it is expected. When readings are done, there is no stage and no props. In fact, most times the actor stands and holds a script with nothing but a light shining on them. It's comparable to an interrogation. A few rare times, those lucky enough to sit in at a reading (like myself) can actually cease seeing an actor flip through the pages of a script; one will actually stop noticing the music stands and the dirty coffee table in the background. It's uncanny but all is immediately forgotten once an actor, like Tommy, who is fully committing to a script, can pull you in. His focus was intense; he was encumbered by nothing except sheer talent. This by far was one of those rare times and one of the best readings I've seen. Not to mention, he has quite a set of lungs and hit a home run in the song portion.

You said he was a struggling actor? How fortunate that is for me. So, with that, I thank you. The reason being is this: I was there for the reading exclusively because I was in the city for our foiled meeting the night before—otherwise I wouldn't have been there in the first place. (I sit in on so few readings these days, leaving it up to the co-producers.) It's crazy to think that our meeting was supposed to be for a completely different opportunity for your friend.

We need to finish out the interview process, but he's a shoe-in for a part and I have no doubt that the one small part we currently need to fill (way too small a part for him I might add) will eventually turn into a lead role.

P.S. Had dinner with your folks last month. They said things are going great with you and they love your girlfriend. Let's all try for another date when you are back in the city. Now I really need to meet her!

Robin wasn't sure what element to be excited about first. The fact that his parents "LOVE" her, or the fact that Tommy would no longer be unemployed. But based on her apprehension about using the L word, she chose the latter.

She slid back her chair and jumped into Bryce's arms. "OH MY GOD! OH MY GOD! OH MY GOD! I can't wait to tell Tommy!"

"Wait," Bryce interrupted her. "Scroll down and look at the PPS."

She scrolled.

P.P.S. Please don't tell your friend that you know any of this. I meet with the review board in two weeks and the decision has to come from the majority. Hands down I'm sure, but better to wait for the official casting notification.

Thanks again.

Parker

"Shit!" Robin excitingly shouted. "Now we all *have* to get together. I promise to keep quiet. This alone calls for a celebration!"

"Then let's," Bryce agreed.

He looked at his watch. *Almost noon,* he thought. So he suggested, "A bottle of Champagne for mimosas? Shall I have Stu bring some over?"

"Champagne, definitely Champagne!" Robin shouted.

The heavy rainstorm continued to pelt the windows. Snuggling up against Bryce, Robin daydreamed while he read the headlines from the digital version of the New York Times out loud. This, plus the comfort of the cabin and the roaring fire, was all Robin could ask for. Now she really contemplated declaring her love for him.

With a loud knock at the door, Stu carefully entered juggling an umbrella, a canvas tote, and a large covered tray. He was dripping, "What's that saying...?" he asked Bryce. "The one about when it rains really, really, hard?"

Bryce chuckled offering, "You mean it's raining cats and dogs?"

"Yeah, that's it. I still don't understand. But it's raining cats and dogs."

Robin hurried over and took the tray and the tote from Stu's hands. Bryce helped him out of his raincoat.

"Wedding weekend extras. Finger sandwiches and Champagne!" Stu shouted into the room.

Robin set everything down and then went back to hug him. Shyly he stood allowing her to do so.

Stu insisted on making the mimosas. It was a solid workday for him next door; he made just two. Bryce smiled, watching him struggle with the wire cage twisted on the top of the bottle. To Robin he whispered, "Watch his face. He loves to uncork the bottle."

POP!

Stu stayed for a little while, listening to Bryce and Robin scheme and discuss ways to prompt Tommy to head north for a visit.

"Get him to stay next door. It's off season and there will be plenty of room," Stu suggested.

Bryce looked bright eyed, nodding at Stu then to Robin. "Ya think?" he shrugged to Robin.

"Well it seems he's mad crazy about this new guy Chadwick. I wonder if he's financially able. Maybe they'd be willing to book a night or two."

"Financially able?" Bryce laughed, questioning her.

Robin leaned in to Bryce and whispered, "I don't want to say *loaded.* You know who might take it the wrong way."

Bryce whispered back, "You're worried about the word loaded? How about the words, 'he's mad crazy' about this new guy Chadwick?"

Then from the kitchen Stu bellowed out, "Hey my cousin is gay. Robin, I didn't know you had a gay friend."

Bryce leaned in and whispered again, "I don't know why we bother to whisper."

Robin grabbed Bryce's head from both sides, pulled him in, and gave him a huge kiss. Stu caught sight of that and decided it was time to get back to work.

* * *

Once back home on Monday night, Robin decided to answer Tommy's Sunday text from 2:00 a.m. She texted:

Bryce and his family know Parker because he manages fundraising efforts for arts foundations to which they contribute. I cannot convince you what a great guy Bryce is. Please consider coming up, maybe for a weekend, you can see for yourself.

She read it back realizing it was short and it sounded harsh. "Screw it, I'm still pissed." She hit send. Seconds later a simple response.

OK.

Shocked, she called him.

Together she and Tommy decided mid-October could probably work.

"You think Chad would come up with you?" Robin questioned.

"I'm seeing him again this Friday. I'll ask and keep my fingers crossed. Not sure how he schedules his business."

"Would you consider staying at the Great Camp? It's an awesome place, but expensive."

"Let me run it by Wicky."

"Wicky?"

"Like in Chad…wick?" Tommy sarcastically snapped.

"Good God Tommy, that's so gay! That's not going to stick is it?"

"Stick?" Tommy pondered. "Hmmm…. Sticky Wicky!" he laughed.

"Oh my God no! Absolutely not!" Robin demanded, laughing along with him.

It was good to laugh with him. They continued to catch up. Robin was relieved to hear Tommy joke with her about being gay. She couldn't remember him *ever* doing that. She thought, *Something good is happening for him.* Then she remembered how something *great* was going to happen for him. She needed to quickly change the subject.

"So, where's this Chadwick W. Travers the third, from?"

"Boston. He graduated from Harvard with a degree in Psychology and he's brilliant Robin! I can't even tell you!"

"That's impressive! How old is he?"

"28 and catch this: I told him absolutely everything about my childhood!"

"SHUT UP!"

"I did!"

"I don't even know what to say about that Tommy. I assume it's all good, especially because he must understand it all?"

"He does Robin. He soooooooo gets it. I'm so relieved and happy, you have no idea. Now I just need to get a job."

Again, Robin needed to quickly change the subject. She didn't dare bring up Parker or ask about future readings, so from out of left field she asked, "What's up with Pauly?"

"I think he's got a few gigs coming up at the Pit."

"The Pit?"

"The People's Improve Theatre, Gramercy Park area, like ten blocks from me. Wanna go?"

"Let's get you up here first."

"K! I'll call you in a few days, once I've had a chance to speak to Wicky!"

"YOU MEAN CHAD!"

"Wicky!"

He hung up quickly before she could say another word!

She hung up excited that Tommy was finally coming to the north woods, hopefully with CHAD!

33

Thank You for That

It was Friday afternoon and Tommy casually trotted up and down the great steps of the Metropolitan Museum of Art. Earlier, Chad had insisted they begin their date there, since Tommy admitted he hadn't been there since a fifth grade class trip.

"For shame," Chad had sarcastically uttered. "You live in the greatest city in the world. You should absorb everything it has to offer."

Tommy remembered the same saucy look on his face then, as he did now, watching Chad slowly climb the museum steps toward him. Again, Chad was impeccably dressed. This time, in a steel blue Burberry suit.

Tommy stood there less refined in his gray suit. His shirt was casually unbuttoned and his necktie undone, loosely draped under his collar.

Tommy began to button up when Chad lunged to the step right in front of where he stood. Chad quickly pushed Tommy's hands away. "Relax, it's a museum, stay loose," he urged.

Then Chad lunged up two more steps, sliding in a quick hello kiss to Tommy's cheek as he passed. He reached the top step with a final light-footed jump and spun around to survey Tommy.

"You sure I look OK?" Tommy asked.

"Are you kidding? You look like you're about to undress. One of my favorite looks!"

Tommy smirked and jumped up to his side, wondering once again, *Where will this all lead?*

Chad loosened *his* tie as they passed through the huge stone neoclassic entrance doors.

Map in hand, they sauntered through the Egyptian Art section first, admiring, discussing, and questioning many items and works of art. Shortly thereafter, Tommy realized Chad had an abundance of art knowledge.

"Art History minor?" Tommy asked.

"Am I boring you?" Chad questioned back.

"Not in the least," Tommy assured.

Chad disregarded Tommy's question, purposely creating intrigue.

Once they made their way to the American Wing, Chad was even more knowledgeable. They stood for a few minutes in front of the famous and larger than life painting of George Washington Crossing the Delaware. More than twelve feet high and twenty feet long, the painting allowed the viewer to step right into the small wooden boat alongside George Washington.

Chad stopped three feet from the front of it. Standing with his arms folded, a tilt of his head introduced the onset of a few random facts and bits of information.

"Note some of the historical inaccuracies," he began and stepped sideways close to Tommy. Putting one hand on his shoulder, he nimbly swirled the other hand as he continued. "For example, this was painted in Germany forty years after the actual river crossing. Due to the time-lapse, the flag that is depicted here was not designed until *after* this particular battle. Also, they did not cross in this type of boat. And George? Look at how gray and old the artist made him. He was only 44 at that time."

"So, what kind of boat should they have been on?" Tommy prodded, seeking to get a valid answer to a question.

"A much bigger one!" Chad laughed. "For God's sake, look at him standing there. They'd capsize if those were the true proportions."

Chad then pulled at Tommy's arm to continue through the room.

A few galleries later they approached a bronze sculpture, where Chad dodged another question when Tommy asked.

"Are you as familiar with sculptures as much as you are paintings?"

"I know that that Remington is called *The Bronco Buster*," he muttered, quickly passing the stand on which it stood.

So again, he avoided answering Tommy's question.

They hurried through a few other galleries after Chad indicated there was just too much to see within the amount of time they had. Scurrying along, they stopped at a painting on a singular wall that was precariously placed in the middle of a particular room.

"I want you to take note of this special painting," he began. "Completed in 1931 by Grant Wood. You are probably more familiar with his 1930 painting, *American Gothic*. You know the one. It's an old farm couple and the man is standing holding a pitchfork?"

"Ah. I do know that one!" Tommy was elated to admit.

"OK, so really examine this," Chad commanded. "Take in all that you can. I want to talk about it later."

Completely intrigued, Tommy stood quietly trying to take it all in. It was perplexing and downright difficult since he was truly more intrigued by Chad's request than the painting itself.

So, there he stood, "taking it in," and thinking:

The steeple on the church seems ridiculously long. The mountains in the background look like nuclear silos more than

*mountains. The forest is a scattering of strangely rounded bumps.
It's a bird's eye view of a quaint colonial town with a river ... and
a road, which both ribbon through. The lights that come from the
windows of the houses reflect an odd yellow out onto the ground.
Every house has a chimney but none have smoke. Ah ha! This must
be a spring or summer night. Besides a few people standing outside and in a doorway, there is but one lone horseman, galloping
through the town.*

Tommy stepped back and looked at Chad, feeling strange,
like there would be a test later. He snidely asked, "Is this some
kind of psychological test?"

"Oh crap, not at all. I'm sorry. I don't want you to think
that. I'm just having fun with you. Really, I mean it, don't worry.
You'll see."

Chad grabbed Tommy's hand and gave it a reassuring
squeeze.

"Phew!" Tommy said out loud. "OK, where to next?"

"Just one more painting," Chad said, "But we must head
to the other side of the museum. Then we'll go grab some dinner,
OK?"

Tommy enthusiastically agreed, "OK!" Still completely
intrigued, Tommy was hungry for answers more than food.

They dashed back past the front entrance, completely
across the building, and then diagonally to the southern end of the
second floor.

Making their way over to the 19th and early 20th Century
European Paintings galleries, Chad stopped just before entering
gallery number 827. "This gallery is considered 'Salon Painting,'"
he said intensely.

Chad was impressive and intelligent, sophisticated and

handsome; he was the whole package.

Tommy enjoyed watching Chad explain as they slowly entered and continued into the room. He drifted along with his words, watching him in lust-filled awe.

"The Paris Salon," he continued, "was a juried exhibition of the Académie des Beaux-Arts."

Kill me now, Tommy thought. *He speaks French too?*

"A high-profile venue for contemporary art, one successful submission could make a career. Cosmopolitan elitists would snatch up the paintings by both French and international artists. Collectors and enthusiasts from that time were the benefactors of the treasures that hang here today."

Chad and Tommy approached a viewing bench and with a wave of Chad's hand, Tommy was directed to sit. He did.

Chad slowly walked around to the other side of the bench compelling Tommy to slowly spin around to face in the other direction. He did.

Now standing just a foot in front of Tommy, Chad raised his hand to cover his mouth. Tommy could see he was getting emotional.

He then took one step to the side, revealing the huge painting behind him. With a deep controlling breath and another step to the side, Chad gained composure and announced, *"The Storm."*

After a few seconds, he added, "My absolute favorite painting."

Tommy gazed at the gigantic oil on canvas. Signed and dated Pierre-Auguste Cot, 1880, in an elaborate gilded frame, the eight-foot by five-foot masterpiece instantly struck him.

Out of a dark forest, a couple runs from the rain, leaping through an isolated patch of sun that magnificently shines on them. They attempt to cover themselves with a large piece of fabric—which must be the girl's cloak—as she now wears only a transparent white sheath, revealing her youth, her beauty, and their complete innocence. The way the golden fabric billows and dances, hovering just over their heads, romanticizes their forest frolic as the handsome young man holds it high overhead to protect her. His gaze at her shows adoration. Her gaze is one of concern.

"Because of the storm..." Tommy said, suddenly understanding. He then pondered how perfectly it was named.

Its sister painting, *Spring*, that hung only three feet to the left, was equally impressive, but to Chad, less captivating.

"This painting speaks profoundly to me, but it has a much deeper meaning than you could ever imagine," Chad expressed.

He moved closer to it with his hand cupped again to his mouth. Then he resigned, stepped back, and took a seat on the bench next to Tommy.

"You must think something is wrong with me," Chad whispered.

Tommy grabbed his hand saying, "Not in the least."

"I'll explain later," Chad promised.

Now Tommy's intrigue was monumental.

Together they nonchalantly moved through the museum as Chad explained the history of the painting to Tommy. How its portrayal of a young couple comes out of a scene from a French novel and that they had fallen in love. He told of how it was commissioned by Catharine Lorillard Wolfe, an American philanthropist, and her largest bequeath was of which contained this painting.

"It was her most significant philanthropic endeavor. Her complete art collection now lives here at the Metropolitan Museum," Chad cited.

Exuberantly Tommy added, "Whoa! And I thank her for that."

Then with a purposeful wide and final step, they both exited the museum.

* * *

Climbing out of the cab, Tommy was complacent being back in Greenwich Village. He thought he might surprise Chad with obscure knowledge of the area, possibly stop at an old favorite spot, thinking there might be a way to equally develop some intrigue on his own behalf.

"NYU. Love this area. This is your old hood, right?" Chad asked.

"It certainly is," Tommy said, laughing to himself. *Damn, there goes that notion,* he thought.

Coming off 7th Avenue, they turned onto Barrow Street. Tommy indicated, "I'm remiss to admit, I've never been here though," as they made their way to the entrance of One If By Land, Two If By Sea.

Cited as one of New York City's most romantic restaurants, and once owned by Aaron Burr, the historic carriage house was also rumored to be haunted. The candlelit tables, the massive and numerous chandeliers, the fireplaces, and baby grand piano, confirmed that romantic citation.

Once inside, Chad stepped silently up to Tommy and buttoned his shirt and tied his tie. Tommy said nothing standing there. He just wondered, *Can he feel my heart pounding out of my chest?*

Chad gave the Maître 'D his name and they followed him in alongside the bar to a set of large leather chairs and a table in front of a fireplace. Chad scurried by Tommy to grab a specific seat. (Enabling the proper view from the seat Tommy would therefore take.)

A bit confused, sliding his chair out and about to sit, Tommy glanced to his right and lowered himself in slow motion and awe. The look on his face was perfect; just what Chad sought after. Then, dropping into the comfort of the chair Tommy roared, "Oh my God! You *are* having fun with me!"

"I am!" admitted Chad. "Let's order some wine and I'll explain."

Tommy now stared at—and realized—that a huge mural of the Grant Wood painting, that Chad had asked Tommy to take note of, covered the entire wall behind the bar they just passed and now sat directly across from.

The wine was poured, the fire was crackling, the night was young, and Tommy was completely elated.

Like back at the museum, Chad once again, began to explain. "The original painting is called *The Midnight Ride of Paul Revere*. It was inspired by a poem written by Henry Wadsworth Longfellow. The poem was written in 1860 when America was on the verge of the Civil War."

Chad reached into his jacket pocket and pulled out his phone. Tommy sat with his elbow on the arm of the chair, balancing his head in his hand, gazing at Chad in amazement. Chad searched for the poem.

"Wait, you're going to read poetry to me now?"

"You got a problem with that?" Chad laughed, trying to sound like a tough guy.

"I DO NOT have a problem with that!" Tommy laughed back. "In fact, you...Chadwick W. Travers the third, never cease to amaze me!"

Chad scrolled to the beginning of the poem. He smiled at

Tommy and said, "Here it is. Take in all that you can."

Tommy repositioned himself, angling to the right to obtain a full view of the mural behind the bar.

Chad began:

"Listen my children and you shall hear
Of the midnight ride of Paul Revere,
On the eighteenth of April, in Seventy-five;
Hardly a man is now alive
Who remembers that famous day and year.
He said to his friend, "If the British march
By land or sea from the town to-night,
Hang a lantern aloft in the belfry arch
Of the North Church tower as a signal light,
One if by Land, and two if by sea; (He emphasized.)
And I on the opposite shore will be,
Ready to ride and spread the alarm
Through every Middlesex village and farm,
For the country folk to be up and to arm."
Then he said "Good-night!" and with muffled oar
Silently rowed to the Charlestown shore,
Just as the moon rose over the bay,
Where swinging wide at her moorings lay
The Somerset, British man-of-war;
A phantom ship, with each mast and spar
Across the moon like a prison bar,
And a huge black hulk, that was magnified
By its own reflection in the tide..."

Chad paused there to take in Tommy's guileless expression.

He soaked it in. It made his heart full.

Tommy then looked affectionately at him and said, "One if by land and two if by sea." He held up his glass. "To my new favorite place."

They clinked their glasses and Chad added, "There are about ten more paragraphs but the waiter is watching us like a hawk. This place is famous for their Beef Wellington. Shall we order?"

"Let's."

Chad mentioned a few more facts about the restaurant, the poem, and art in general over dinner. When Tommy noticed people coming in with umbrellas, he found the perfect segue.

"Can we talk about *The Storm*?" he asked.

Chad acquiesced with an audible sigh, then sat straight and began to explain how he was studying that particular painting when he decided to "come out."

"So, my first year at Harvard, I was enrolled in the History of Art and Architecture program. *The Storm* was my favorite paint-ing. We were assigned to do a complete presentation on a piece of art. Of course, I chose that. Somewhere in the thralls of compre-hending the virtuous love depicted in the painting, I realized that I would only find true love if I came out. So, I did."

Tommy, now speechless, topped off their wine glasses and breathed out his own audible sigh. Chad continued, "Go figure! A 19th-Century painting of a straight couple, made me come out.... But their true love spoke to me; I had to."

"Thank you for that!" Tommy cheered, nodding and grin-ning at Chad.

"It's poignant because that's also the time I told my parents. My dad flipped out; he just can't stomach that I'm gay. And now the rest is history."

Tommy coyly added, "So art history was history and you changed fields?"

"Exactly," Chad said. "I needed to understand—and I needed my dad to understand—so I decided to minor in that, and major in psychology instead. Sadly, my dad still doesn't get it."

In that somber moment, Tommy felt exceptionally close to Chad, realizing how deeply it affected him. Yet there was nothing he could do to help with the situation.

"Well maybe he'll like me!" he blurted out unconsciously.

Chad beamed up at Tommy. His tension broke. He grabbed Tommy's hand across the table and said, "How could he not?"

* * *

On the way out, Chad promised the Maître D they'd return the borrowed umbrella with another visit in the near future. "This is his new favorite place," Chad added. "We promise to be back soon."

It wasn't raining just then, but the threat was still there and it was a valid excuse for Chad to get nice and close to Tommy—underneath the umbrella—for the walk up to Tommy's place. Previously, during dessert, they had decided a brisk walk, in the cold night air would do them well.

"Two desserts? How decadent were we?" Tommy speculated en route. "My mother would absolutely *love* that place."

Continuing twelve or so blocks, Tommy spoke a little more about his parents. Chad was envious. Chad mentioned his mom was basically OK with the state of things. Tommy assured him his dad would come around.

"I can only hope," Chad concurred.

Turning out of sight, and into the street-level alley entrance of Tommy's building, Chad seemed hesitant.

"You'll come up right?" Tommy asked.

"I shouldn't, it's late."

"But you walked all this way with me? A cup of coffee…. Anything?"

Chad closed the umbrella and leaned it on the brick wall that Tommy was backing up to. He straddled his arms on either side of Tommy, essentially trapping him in, forcing him against the wall. He looked zealously at Tommy and inched in close, finally kissing him. Tommy lifted his arms to embrace Chad and his kiss, but Chad pinned him at the elbows and firmed his stance as he passionately continued to kiss Tommy. Then slowly he let up and remained just an inch from Tommy's face. "Coffee is not going to do it for me," he said. "If I go up, I'll be all over you."

"Works for me," Tommy breathed.

Chad trapped Tommy again, but this time he allowed and accepted Tommy's embrace. After a very fervent round, when they both let up, Chad uttered, "I want to take it slow. I want to savor every second."

Tommy thought he would explode right there just listening to him. Dumbfounded, he said nothing.

Chad pushed hard against the wall with his hands, ejecting himself backward away from Tommy. "Oh, how I want to take you now. But I will wait."

Tommy closed his eyes and threw his head back. He felt for the umbrella at his side. Once it was in his hand, he blindly held it out, offering it to Chad.

Chad grabbed the umbrella and pressed back into Tommy with his lips up against his ear. He whispered, "Next time." And then with a final fleeting kiss, he vanished.

Tommy made it up the three flights to his apartment, completely spellbound. He closed his apartment door behind him and leaned against it, salaciously glazed over. With his heart pounding out of his chest, he pulled out his phone and texted Chad:

Come away with me next weekend.

Seconds later Chad responded:

Next weekend can't come soon enough.

The next day when the spell subsided and Tommy could think straight, in a series of texts, he and Chad decided they would drive up to the Adirondacks early the following Friday morning.

Tommy would borrow Pauly's car (which thankfully he owned because of his out of town gigs).

"Dude, it's a used Beemer, but I love it and I'll kill you if you wreck it!"

"Pauly, I really owe you man. I promise to come back with a definite plan for a group of us to come and see one of your shows."

"You freaking better man, you freaking better!"

The following Thursday night, Tommy alternated his pacing back and forth with packing, while deliriously thinking about what the next few nights could entail. Friday morning was only hours away. Tommy couldn't remember ever being this excited. His phone buzzed in his pocket and he pulled it out. It was from Chad. He anxiously read:

You home?

His simple text back:

Yes.

Standing in the middle of his living room, Tommy grew confused as there was no response back. Instead, there was a low rap at his door. Tommy walked to the door and squinted through the peephole. Astonished, he threw the door open.

Chad entered, rolling a bag in behind him. Tommy—completely tongue-tied—flattened against the wall in the hallway, allowing him to pass. As he did, Chad frankly stated, "A neighbor let me up. Friday wasn't coming soon enough."

Chad rolled his bag into the living room, stood it upright against a chair and then rushed back to Tommy, still standing motionless against the wall in the hallway. He pressed up against Tommy, devouring him with a kiss. He could feel his own heartbeat against Tommy's as he pressed hard into him. He couldn't get to skin fast enough. He needed to be slithering along Tommy's bare chest.

"Where were we?" Chad breathed into Tommy's ear, kicking the front door shut.

Tommy felt Chad's lips lightly skim along his neck and down his shoulder as his shirt was being unbuttoned and pulled off. Tommy continued to stand there completely silent with his eyes closed. He didn't want to open them and chance being woke from his arousing dream. He was now the one to savor every second.... He became breathless and hard. Chad rubbed up against him and with his eyes still closed Tommy felt for Chad. Piece by piece their clothing fell to the floor.

The silence and the passion continued until they woke at some point, in the black of the night and in the white of the sheets.

Tommy reached to Chad and pulled him in close. Finally, he spoke.

"Thank you for that."

34

I will

Pauly helped Tommy and Chad with their bags as they loaded them into the trunk. Handing the keys off to Tommy, Pauly said, "Dude, now you totally owe me! Come see me at the PIT. I'll be there Thanksgiving eve."

"I know, I know, I do owe you. I'll try and lock everyone in, I promise."

Tommy held out his hand for a handshake, but Pauly spread his arms, forcing a hug instead. Mid-hug, Tommy looked over to Chad and rolled his eyes because he expected a sarcastic comment from Pauly any second. He wasn't disappointed.

"You know I love you man!" Pauly delivered. Then Pauly laughed and lowered his hug and gave Tommy's ass a squeeze.

Tommy shook his head and gave Pauly a friendly push away, saying, "You know Pauly, if *you* were gay, you would never do that, right?"

Then Pauly stated, "You know if I was gay, I'd be putting more than suitcases in your trunk."

Chad couldn't help but laugh.

Tommy snapped at Chad, "Don't egg him on!"

Pauly then held his hand out to Chad. "Please never take offense to anything I say. It was a pleasure to meet you."

Chad returned with a firm handshake back. "No offense taken. I look forward to the real show."

"Drive safe, honey," Pauly said, smacking Tommy's ass on his final pass.

"I will."

On the drive up to the Adirondacks, they had about five hours to discuss, deliberate, and divulge. Tommy decided to spill some beans.

"I must confess… I'm a bit superstitious," he began.

"You mean like you just saw a black cat cross our path and now we'll die in a fiery car crash?" asked Chad.

"Not that bad," Tommy laughed. "More like coincidences, and karma, or fate and destiny."

"How so?"

"Well it's dumb really. Like, say if I was throwing out a piece of paper. I'd crumble it up and toss it across the room and see if I can make the shot into the garbage. If I do, I'd think, 'Good! That means I'll get the part.' If I don't make the shot, I won't. Does that make sense?"

"It does actually. Everybody does some form of that. It's positive reinforcement. You do it knowing you can probably make the shot, so you set yourself up with a greater percentage for positive results. If you don't make the shot, and therefore you don't get the part, then you have luck to blame. It's easier to blame it on luck than yourself, and afterward, you probably tell yourself how dumb it was to do that in the first place, right?"

"Right!"

"Think of it this way: it's usually because you are concerned about something. It's a protective measure, or a way to keep from feeling hurt. You're actually making it easy on yourself in the event it doesn't go the way you really want."

"I guess that makes sense," Tommy admitted. "Then good!"

"Why, something bothering you?" Chad asked.

"You'll think I'm crazy if I tell you."

"Well now you have to tell me!"

Chad repositioned himself, angling sideways in the passenger seat to look directly at Tommy. He reached over to his shoulder and began to lightly caress it.

Tommy stared straight ahead with the steering wheel firm in his hands. "Yes, now with more thought," he said, "I realize how stupid it really is."

"Shut up and tell me already!"

"OK... Well... when I met Bert,"—Chad knew of Bert but only that he was an ex— "I was in Bryant Park and I met him over a napkin and then we ended up going to a museum."

"What the hell are you talking about?" Chad laughed.

"I told you it was stupid. But... I was sitting in Bryant Park eating a sandwich and a chunk of avocado fell out. Out from behind me appeared a hand with a napkin. Bert was on the other end of the napkin. We started to talk, sparks flew, and then we ended up going to a museum in his neighborhood. The rest is history. That was basically our first date. And you know I dated him for quite a while."

"I do. So, what's the concern or coincidence?" Chad asked.

"Well, when I met *you*... we were at the rooftop bar and *you* handed me a napkin."

"Yes, I did! You laughed into your drink and you had vodka on your nose. I remember it well." Chad nodded and smiled at Tommy, enjoying the recollection.

"So, there's that." Tommy continued, "And then there's the fact that you and I went to a museum!"

Chad let go of Tommy's shoulder, folded his arms and slid down into his seat. He tilted his head back on the headrest and closed his eyes stating, "Give me a minute."

He slid back up and grabbed Tommy's shoulder again. He gave it a squeeze at the start of every fact that he was about to state:

"First off, we had a complete conversation about our names before I even handed you the napkin. We didn't initially meet over the napkin, per se. I said something that made you laugh into your drink, hence the napkin. Secondly, our date at the Met Museum was a full week later, and more like a second date. So, it's a completely different thing! Besides, me taking you there was a confession on my part if you recall. You're thinking like it's a jinx, or superstition. You're setting yourself up for hurt."

Chad leaned across the console and kissed Tommy's shoulder. He continued, "I'm not going to hurt you Tommy. Negative thoughts are a complete waste of time. Don't set yourself up for failure. Go back to throwing things in the trash and making the shot! Please tell me you will stop drumming up negative ideas and looking for crazy comparisons as nodules of fate."

"I will."

* * *

Staying at the Great Camp and being next door to Bryce's cabin was convenient *and* doable thanks to Stu's suggestion of booking two nights during the off-season, and the fact that Chad did very well for himself. The GPS had indicated an accident on route 87, north of Lake George, so they turned off and rerouted northwest onto route 28. The trip just got a little longer, so it went from spilling some beans, to Tommy opening up a can of worms.

"So, you know we're heading up to visit Robin and Bryce, but also, I can rethink things and cut him a break, right?" Tommy asked.

"Right."

"Well, check this out..."

Tommy reached for his briefcase behind Chad's seat. He slid his hand into its front pocket and pulled out the Playbill that he grabbed from his last reading. He handed it to Chad and continued.

"Check out on the first page, in the really small print. Find 'special projects.'"

"Wait," Chad demanded, "this Playbill? You did a reading for a part in *Book of Mormon*? That's incredible!"

"Well it could be... but go ahead and look at what I'm talking about."

Chad opened to the first page. "Wow that is small type. OK here... Special projects: Bryce R. Hamilton? Is that Robin's Bryce, or is it a coincidence?"

"I don't know. But go a few more pages in, and look for the page that lists the theatre, the show, and all the production information. Look at the directed by."

Chad read a few bits on what he thought was the right page. "Eugene O'Neill Theatre.... Presents.... Casting."

"Yeah that page, down further, on the bottom of the page. I think it's the last thing listed."

"Ah here. Parker? Is that the guy you met and told me about?"

"Not 100% sure on that either. Robin said Bryce knows Parker through fundraising efforts and earlier she mentioned he was some kind of producer. But director?"

"I sense your concern, but I can't imagine this being a problem. Do you have one?"

"Maybe.... I don't know.... I guess I do. I just worry about Robin. If this is him, and they are they, then what is Bryce keeping from her? He's supposed to be a simple, backwoods caretaker that comes from a line of Adirondack mink traders. Something is not right. Just look at the way they gallivant all over the city. It's just suspicious. Right?"

Tommy looked over to Chad for some kind of reassurance.

"Isn't this one of the reasons we're going up in the first place?" Chad asked. "So you can rethink Bryce and figure it out?"

"It is."

"Then relax! If that Bryce is Bryce, and that Parker is Parker, I still don't sense foul play. No pun intended." Chad slid low into the seat again, rolled his head to the side and looked up at Tommy, "…Though you do look charming with that concerned look on your face."

"Charming?"

"Yeah, like how much longer until we check in?"

Tommy smiled back at Chad and stepped a little harder on the gas.

* * *

"OK that's the fourth time we've crossed the Hudson River. I don't understand. Are we even close yet?" Chad asked.

"Robin says you can trace the Hudson River all the way up to Lake Tear of the Clouds on Mount Marcy, the highest peak in the Adirondacks. She knows a lot about the mountains up here. GPS says, thirty six minutes."

"Beautiful area. Can't wait to meet Robin. *AND* Bryce!" Chad sternly added.

Tommy glanced over at Chad still low and comfortable in the seat. He raised his eyebrows with a questioning look, but said nothing.

Twenty minutes later, Tommy handed Chad his phone. "Please text Robin. Tell her I think we're close."

Per GPS info, he texted: *We're coming up on Fish Creek Ponds. I think we're close.*

* * *

Robin snuck up behind Bryce and held her phone and its message in front of him. He was standing at the kitchen counter slicing apples to add to the cheese platter Stu brought over earlier. It had just started to rain. The wind that often whipped through the area was beginning to wreak havoc.

"Wow, they made good time. That's way earlier than I expected," Bryce said. "Are they checking in or coming here first?"

"Not sure; does it matter?"

"Not one bit."

Bryce put the knife down, spun around, and wrapped his arms around Robin. He delicately asked, "Do you think Tommy left his drama at home and brought only Chadwick?"

"I certainly hope so!"

Robin laid her head against Bryce's chest. She closed her eyes and took a deep breath. She was excited about the next few days and how they all would spend some quality time together. The weather was supposed to be lousy, but it was a perfect way to enjoy each other's company; sitting by a warm fire, sipping wine, and just relaxing.

Listening to the classical music that Bryce queued up, Robin stayed in his arms, breathing deeply. Bryce stood equally relaxed, stroking her hair, tucking it behind her ears, kissing the top of her head. Robin then looked tenderly up at Bryce. He held her face and looked deep into her eyes.

If love could speak for itself, it would have screamed out in that moment. It was evident and unmistakable. It was on the tips of their tongues and riding on the edge of their breath. The anticipation was daunting. But suddenly, there was a tremendous crack of thunder and lightning, and the lights went out. They quickly broke their embrace.

"That was weird," Bryce announced.

The music and all the white noise from the appliances stopped. Everything went quiet except the crackle of the fire and the whistle of the wind outside.

"This should be fun!" Robin cheered. "It's not like we need electricity. We've got all the essentials."

"We certainly do, and yup! It will be fun," Bryce admitted.

He loaded up the fire and brought more wood in from outside.

* * *

Around by the front side of the cabin, out at the end of Bryce's driveway, a huge tree had fallen blocking the road and the entrance to the Great Camp. Tommy and Chad had pulled down onto that road, witnessing the lightning strike that downed the tree.

Another car had just come out of the Great Camp entrance, barely escaping a hit from the falling tree. Both cars came to a halt facing each other in the road. A huge limb from the tree was leaning on some high wires. (It was most certainly the culprit of the power loss.)

Mystified by the bolt of lightning just seconds before, with concern for the welfare of everyone, Tommy jumped out of his car, as did the other driver. Tommy was the first to speak. "Are you guys OK?"

"We are. Are you?"

"We are. That was crazy! You saw that lightning bolt, right?"

"Brightest and scariest flash of my life!"

With a quick assessment, the imminent danger disappeared

and once everyone realized just that, Tommy and the other driver nervously laughed in relief.

Tommy then said, pointing to the downed tree and limb behind the man, "You just made it out. That was so close!"

"And now *you* can't get in," he replied.

"Not a problem. We can stop here first; my friend lives right here." Tommy pointed to Bryce's cabin visible through the pines at the other end of the driveway.

"Hey you know Bryce? He's my son!"

Tommy then approached the man, offering his hand.

"John," he said first, "pleased to meet you. My wife, Bryce's mom, Avery." He pointed to her inside the car. She leaned to see out and waved at Tommy.

Chad then leaned towards Tommy's open door with a wave to John and also to Avery.

"That's Chadwick, I'm Tommy. Pleasure is mine." Then he added, "Should we call this in and get someone out here?"

"I'll call it in," John offered. "But please tell Bryce what's happened. I need to go and change my pants," he joked.

Tommy joined him in laughter. Shaking his head, he confirmed, "That sure was crazy. Won't you come inside Bryce's cabin?"

"No, we're running late and can't. But please do me a favor and also mention to Bryce that I left a package for him over at the camp?"

"I will."

They shook hands one more time. Tommy hopped back into the car and turned into Bryce's driveway. John drove out of sight.

"That bolt scared the shit out of me too!" Chad admitted when they parked.

Thumping up onto the porch, Tommy was about to knock but Robin swung the door open and jumped into his arms.

"I'm so excited you're here!" she yelled.

She looked beyond Tommy at Chadwick who stood off to the side, in the drizzle. Immediately she noticed his piercing amber eyes. She let go of Tommy and waved Chad up the few steps. "Tommy's told me so much about you! Come in, come in!"

Robin realized she probably sounded like a fool because Tommy really hadn't told her all that much. She was enchanted by Chad's good looks and started babbling.

"Put your jackets here." She pointed to the hooks on the right. "Where are your bags? How was the ride up?" Then she called out for Bryce, who came down the hallway and appeared in front of them.

Tommy hastily interjected a roundabout introduction cutting her babble short, "Chad, Bryce; Bryce, Chad. Robin, Chad; Chad, Robin."

As they moved in toward the living room, Bryce announced, "Power went out about four minutes ago. We'll hang by the fireplace." Then he asked, "Red, white, or something stronger?"

Robin followed Bryce into the kitchen area while Chad and Tommy both stood for a moment in front of the fire to warm up.

"Red is great by us!" Tommy bellowed out. Then he launched into the lightning bolt story. "So, we're heading towards the entrance to the Great Camp, right? Then BOOM! Right before our eyes, a phantasmagorical flash! This huge tree goes down near the end of your driveway. It's probably the reason for the power outage. One of its limbs is lying on some wires. It blocked us from heading directly to the Great Camp to check in. I hope we're not too early."

Bryce looked quizzically at Robin. "That very loud crack of lighting? We must have heard it hit the tree." Then he looked to Tommy and Chad. "How bad is it?"

"Your dad is calling it in. He's sooooo lucky! The tree fell just behind him! I guess he was on his way out."

Then Chad piped in, looking at Tommy, "Which means we were pretty lucky too. We were just on our way in!"

Chad then looked at Robin and Bryce, and continued telling the story. "We all saw the bolt strike! It hit the tree in front of us. Your parents passed by it and then *WHAM*! The tree fell right behind them! It was awesome. I felt it in my chest!" He held out his arms and looked at them. "The electricity was in the air... I think my hair is *still* standing on end!"

Bryce looked ruefully at Robin and back to Chad and Tommy, who were settling in on the couch by the fire. "Wow, a close call for everyone," he said. "Sounds pretty effin' scary if you ask me! I knew it was close when we heard the crack, but shit, you all were right there! Glad you're all OK. That's what matters."

He shuddered and spun around reaching high to grab wine glasses from the cabinet. Robin stood leaning against the kitchen counter. Her arms were folded and she looked confused. Snidely she questioned Bryce, "Your parents were here?"

Bryce poured and then walked two glasses of red over to Tommy and Chad.

Taking it from his hand, Tommy continued, "Oh, and he asked me to tell you that he left a package for you over at the camp. They seem nice. He made us laugh when he said that after the bolt hit, he needed to change his pants."

"Yeah my dad can be pretty funny." Bryce looked at Robin, knowing he hadn't answered her question.

"Why didn't you tell me they were here?" she asked again.

"It was a quick hit. I didn't want to make a production of it. I knew they had to rush back to the city."

"Rush back? Bryce that makes no sense! No one just makes a *quick hit* here, not if they drive all the way up from the city?"

Robin looked over to Tommy and Chad, now sitting silent on the couch trying to busy themselves flipping through magazines.

"Tommy....what'd it take you, five, six hours?" she asked sarcastically. "A quick ride, right?" Now she sneered at Bryce. "How long were they here?"

"Just one night. I didn't make any plans with them and us... I didn't know your schedule."

Robin had never seen Bryce try to defend himself like that before, especially with utter nonsense. She was at a loss. She was confused and couldn't understand why Bryce was being so vague. Bryce handed her a glass of wine and she waved it off.

"Something's not right," she said.

Tommy and Chad could sense the brewing conflict and were afraid to even look towards the kitchen. Tommy leaned into Chad and with his teeniest voice whispered, "That's what I always said; something's not right."

Chad, looking to break the tension and steer Tommy away from the drama, stood up and said, "So the road is blocked and we still need to check in. Bryce, what do you suggest?"

Happy to evade another series of questions from Robin, he offered, "How about I help with your bags and you can check in at the camp by way of the path around back?" Bryce practically ran to open the door for Chad to lead him out.

The door shut and Tommy looked over at Robin who stood

incensed, still with her arms folded, leaning against the counter.

"What the hell was that about?" he asked.

"I don't know Tommy. I'm really, *really* confused. Supposedly his parents really like me, so why would he hide them from me like that?"

"Shit Robin. Is he hiding anything else?"

"What? What do you mean? No! Shit I hope not!"

Tommy got up and walked to the window and watched Bryce and Chad trail off onto the path toward the Great Camp.

"Wait here a sec," he said.

"Oh, I'm not going any-fucking-where," Robin mumbled.

Tommy went out to the car and grabbed the Playbill that Chad had tucked up into the visor. He ran back inside with it and quickly flipped to the page that showed the special projects.

"What do you make of this?"

Robin's eyes widened as she read his name. Out loud she said, "Bryce R. Hamilton. Special Projects? What the F is that supposed to mean?"

Then Tommy flipped a few pages further and pointed to Parker's name. "And what the fuck is this supposed to mean? Director?"

Robin stood, bewildered. Tommy handed her the glass of wine that Bryce had poured for her. She took a huge sip and stared off into space.

"Tommy, I don't know what to think. It must be Bryce! I mean with his connection to Parker and all. I don't know…. But why would he… what is he keeping from me?" She looked at Tommy and her face hardened.

Tommy bumped up against her, threw his arm around her, and pulled her in for a hug. "Don't worry. When they get back, we'll get to the bottom of it. I mean like how bad could it be? It's just his name in a Playbill, right? Well at least we think it's him, right?"

"But why would he hide his parents from me?" she questioned. "That makes no sense. Oh my God, is he embarrassed by me? Is there someone else? He does spend a lot of time in the city... shit... shit... SHIT!"

Her mind was scrambling. She was trying to collect her thoughts. Nothing came up as a valid reason for anything.

Tommy was now even more suspicious than he was before. He was pissed too. He didn't want to see Robin upset. And now that he knew Robin had no clue, it was obvious that Bryce *was* hiding something.

Robin heard laughter coming out of the woods, off the path, and towards the cabin. She thought, *Laughing? How the hell are they laughing?*

The door opened. Chad walked in first. Bryce closed the door behind him and lingered near the coat hooks like he didn't know what to do with himself.

Tommy grabbed the Playbill from Robin's hand and held it up high in the air. Looking at Bryce, he abruptly asked, "Isn't there something you need to tell her?"

Bryce's eyes bugged out as he sent a look of shock to Robin. He questioned her, "You didn't tell him, did you?"

Robin glanced up at the Playbill and it dawned on her. *Fuck!* she thought. She realized just then, that the Playbill was from The Book of Mormon and Tommy's reading. Only she and Bryce knew about the role that Tommy was going to get.

"No, I didn't tell him!" she snapped at Bryce.

Tommy looked to Robin, then to Bryce. "Tell me what?"

Together Bryce and Robin, at the exact same time barked, "Nothing!"

Chad poured more wine in his glass, walked over in front of the fire and asked, "Would someone like to tell me?"

They all ignored him.

Tommy became angry. *Nothing? What are they keeping from me?* he thought. He was confused and didn't know who or what to question next. He stepped over towards Chad and with a short huff—just as he was about to blurt out—Chad walked to the middle of the room.

Chad centered himself between all of them. He stood for a moment holding his finger up and said, "Just wait." He considered words that would calm Tommy, but then with second thought, he made an about-face and walked back to the fireplace, deciding maybe it was best to let him get things off his chest. He knew with the pause that he had just created, there was sufficient time for everyone to gather their thoughts; like counting to ten before speaking in anger. Chad then simply held his wine glass up and said, "Honesty is the best policy."

It was the perfect segue for Tommy to speak. So, he did.

"Bryce, I don't think you're being honest with Robin, or me for that matter! Like what was all that Parker shit? You're hiding something and I worry about Robin. Something's not right."

Bryce paced from the living room to the kitchen and back. "Shit, you guys have no idea what's at stake here!" he said sharply.

"At stake?" Robin pondered. Bryce was confusing and agonizing to watch. Now she was truly worried. She had never seen him so agitated.

He continued to pace. He stopped at the kitchen counter near Robin and threw open a drawer. He pulled out a roll of aluminum foil and tore off a small section. He put the roll back and began to twist up a small piece. He continued to pace. "You guys have no idea what I've been trying to do," he said nervously.

He fiddled with the piece of foil as the others watched him pace anxiously.

Robin remained in her position, arms folded leaning against the counter, waiting for answers. But with growing concern, she thought, *He's losing it. Is this a nervous thing; playing with foil?* Her anger morphed to uncertainty.

Robin's concern for Bryce made her glare at Tommy like it was now his fault. She broke into the desperate situation by shouting, "Please someone tell me what the hell is going on!"

Bryce stopped in front of Robin with his back turned to the others. He continued to fiddle with the piece of foil. Robin dropped her arms and threw her head back and looked up at the ceiling.

"What?" she demanded.

Bryce lowered to his knee. His face softened and he began to spin a round, band of twisted foil on his finger. "Robin. This was not the way I planned."

He took a deep breath and grabbed both of Robin's hands.

"Robin, I can't even begin to tell you… how much I love you. I'm sorry it's taken me so long to say. You're independent and smart, with the world completely in your hands… I was afraid I'd scare you off. I'm an idiot."

He bowed down in shame, looking at her feet.

Robin lowered her head and looked down at him. She thought her legs would give out right there. Her heart stopped and she was sucked into a space where everything around her became blurry and indistinct.

He continued, "You are wonderful and beautiful, why

would you settle for me? I don't know what I'd do without you. It's hard for me to breathe when you leave. It's even harder for me to breathe when you're gone. I need you with me all the time so I *can* breathe."

She listened to his words as they soaked in and penetrated deep into her soul. His gaze now alternated from her hands to her face.

"Since the first time I saw you, and then our first date and first kiss, I knew I wanted you to be mine. I needed you to be mine. My complete fear of telling you then, remained all along. Please forgive me for never saying."

Robin dropped to her knees. She looked eye to eye with Bryce. Catching her breath, she professed, "Bryce, oh my God. I have loved you for so long, I was afraid to scare *you* off! Countless times I thought I'd find the nerve to tell you, but my fear of losing you was far worse than the truth. The truth was always with me, and as long as you remained with me, I knew I'd be fine. I love you Bryce! My God... I—love—you—Bryce.

Her eyes welled up and they stared at each other incessantly.

He breathed deep and continued. "I need to know if your love for me is as true as mine is for you. Please understand that right now, the only way I will know, is to ask you. I can only tell you everything, if I ask you."

He spun the ring of foil off his finger and held it against the back of her hand. "I need you to stand back up."

"I don't know if I can," she said, stumbling for proper footing.

"Robin...?" He looked up at her and his eyes welled up. His lips were quivering. And if it weren't for the gasps he heard coming from over by the fireplace, that zoned him momentarily back, front, and center, he would have totally lost it.

He cleared his throat and took a final deep breath, "Robin, will you marry me?"

"I will. Oh Bryce, I will, I will……………….. I will!"

35

Yup, That's Right

Dumbfounded in front of the fireplace, Tommy and Chad held their breath and stood there completely motionless. What felt like hours, were mere seconds. Witnessing the most tender moment anyone could possibly ever imagine, they too were transported into the blurry and blissful world that Robin had spun into.

But Tommy was quickly pulled back to reality when he felt his phone buzz in his pocket. Chad heard it too and elbowed him.

Tommy delicately pulled out his phone to take a peek. It was a text from Gardiner Casting.

Congratulations! You got the part. Please call Monday for details.

He held the message in front of Chad who out of excitement elbowed him even harder. Tommy winced and whispered, "I don't know what to make of it!"

Robin, embracing Bryce across the room, looked over to Tommy and Chad. With sheer excitement, she trumpeted, "I'll tell you what to make of it! The love of my life just proposed!"

She held out her hand as she and Bryce moved forward arm in arm towards them. Showing off her ring of foil, she laughed and looking at Bryce said, "I'm still confused though."

"That was amazing. Congratulations!" Chad cheered.

"Aluminum foil?" Tommy howled in question.

Baffled, they all exchanged hugs and Bryce motioned Robin to sit on the couch. He nodded to Chad and Tommy. "Please, everyone, have a seat. I've got some serious explaining to do."

Tommy wasn't quite ready to sit. He called up his latest text and then held it in front of Bryce.

With a quick glimpse, Bryce responded with a defiant glance to Robin. Then he motioned to Tommy, saying, "I think you need to sit here."

He walked over and pulled out the chair at the desk end of the kitchen counter. He opened up his laptop and waved Tommy over. He booted up and retrieved the e-mail from Parker.

Tommy sat. His eyes slowly crossed over each line while Robin anxiously and excitedly bobbed along the length of the couch. Without taking his eyes off the screen, Tommy threw his hand behind and quickly waved Chad over. "Chadwick!" he beckoned urgently. Chad scurried up behind Tommy and began to gloss over the page with him.

Bryce leaned over the couch and nuzzled into Robin. He kissed her ear and whispered, "Please be patient with me. Let's let him get through that first."

Robin grabbed Bryce's hand and with a huge sweeping motion, she forced him around the couch and down next to her. She grabbed his face and rooted her gaze deep into his.

"I love you Bryce. I'm not going anywhere."

It was exuberant and liberating for Robin to finally be able to say that.

Tommy finished up moments later. He slid the chair back and spun around to face them. Robin's grin was a mile wide, and the look on Bryce's face said nothing shy of, "I told you so!"

Now aware of the email's content, Chad hovered adoringly over Tommy and pointed to the screen as he proudly quoted out loud from it:

"His focus was intense; he was encumbered by nothing

except sheer talent…"

"To think our meeting was supposed to be for a completely different opportunity…"

Then Chad finished up loudly declaring, "AND DOT, DOT, DOT, *'will eventually turn into a lead role!'"*

Chad pulled Tommy up and out of the chair and gave him a huge kiss and hug. Tommy flopped around in his arms, smiling deliriously, thrilled to know he got the part but even more thrilled that the actual director of the play had such high regard for his acting abilities.

Then Tommy straightened up and became quite serious. He walked over to the couch and stood, holding his hand out in front of Bryce. Bryce then stood, took Tommy's hand, and shook it firmly.

"Bryce, I owe you an apology. First, I thought you were pimping me out to Parker so I could get a part. Then when I saw your name in the Playbill… well I just questioned your connections. I really didn't want a handout; I don't want to be obligated to anyone. I hope you understand why I'm so defensive. I'm concerned about Robin"—he threw a loving look to her still smiling on the couch—"and I always will be. Oh, that's an FYI! If you're going to be her husband, you better get used to me," he laughed. "But I'm not done yet…. I'm still a little concerned and confused."

Bryce then interrupted, "First, there is no if! She said yes!" Now *Bryce* gave Robin a loving look. He tossed another log on the fire and gestured for all to—once again—sit. "Please sit. I mean it! I will explain everything. But right this second, with all this sensational stuff happening, we need champagne!"

Chad and Tommy dropped into the wing-backed chairs to the left of the fireplace. An overjoyed Robin had bounced her way across the long leather couch towards the end where she now held her head on a bent arm, gazing up at the ceiling mystified. Bryce pulled his phone from his pocket and texted the champagne request to Stu.

When Robin resurfaced, she jumped up to clear the magazines from the table. She brought over the cheese platter that Stu had delivered earlier. (Which after all that just transpired, felt like a week ago!) She realized she needed to quickly describe Stu to Tommy and Chad before he got there.

"He's honest and sweet …. He's Bryce's right-hand man. Please don't say any clichés or something that is figuratively confusing. He takes things literally."

Bryce brought over champagne glasses and sat next to Robin. He grabbed her hand and looked distressed as he began to explain. "When he comes in with the Champagne, DO NOT let him know it's because I proposed. Please let's leave it as celebration for Tommy's Broadway debut ONLY. He knows how and when I was supposed to propose, and he's expecting that to happen, so you can't say anything. I totally wasn't planning to ask you like that, Robin."

"Obviously!" Tommy laughed then coughed, "Tinfoil."

"Why did you then?" Robin questioned.

"Like I said before. I could only tell you if I asked you. And now that I've asked you, and you said yes, I am prepared to tell you everything."

"OMG you're killing me, I'm so confused!" Robin balked.

Bryce let go of Robin's hand and stood up. This time he paced in front of the fireplace. Certainly not as anxious as before, but he did bellow out, "GOD I can't believe I have to tell you all this right now!"

Robin, Tommy, and Chad all sat straight up in their respective spots, patiently glaring at one another, waiting....

Bryce began, "OK, with you guys running into my folks... well that was a complete mishap. The package they brought up is the real ring. I had this weekend all planned out." He looked unnervingly at Robin. "I couldn't explain why they were here—that was all part of the surprise. I promise I wasn't keeping them from you, or you from them."

Bryce then looked purposefully at Tommy. "Questioning my connections because of the Playbill? Well the only way I can explain that was to first have Robin say yes to marrying me."

Chad threw a hand up like a kid in a classroom and said, "Still confused!"

Bryce sat back down next to Robin. "My proposal was supposed to be a surprise that we could later share and celebrate by having your best friend here. My folks will be back later. They know what's going on.... Well, kind of."

"Still don't!" Tommy said, throwing *his* hand up. "But that's really nice of you Bryce," he added.

Bryce laughed and then looked sincerely at Robin. "OK so I didn't know I'd be up against the wall like that; it forced me to hastily propose to you right then and there. Not having the ring... which is next door... I needed something symbolic so you'd take me seriously."

"Tinfoil?" Tommy blurted out.

"You got a better idea when you have to make a split-second decision?"

"OK, I'll shut up."

Chad grabbed Tommy's shoulder and squeezed it saying, "Maybe we shouldn't even be here right now. I'm pretty sure he wasn't planning to pop the question with us here. And now if he has to explain things…" Chad looked over at Bryce and asked, "Should we leave?"

"No stay, it will make sense soon enough."

Robin sneered at Tommy, "Wait. Did Tommy's suspicions and running into your folks, cheat me out of a real proposal?"

"Pretty much," Bryce answered.

Tommy slid down into his chair and covered his face with a throw pillow.

"Tommy?" Robin angrily (but sarcastically) questioned.

"Like I knew?" came his muffled voice from behind the pillow.

Robin threw another pillow at him and continued, "Wait? So you were going to propose to me this weekend?"

"Yes."

"Can we still do it the way you planned?"

"Yes."

Just then there was a knock at the door. Bryce got up saying, "That's Stu, we must stick to the plan… please, say nothing!"

Bryce introduced them all and explained to Stu that Tommy was just cast in his first Broadway show, and how they needed to celebrate.

Stu, knowing that the big secret proposal was to unfold the next night, didn't want to chance a slip on his part. He quickly uncorked two bottles and pretended to be busy. With haste, "Congratulations!" he said. "Now I need to get back to work." He handed off the bottles and looked indirectly at Chad and Tommy on his way towards the door. "If you two need anything during your stay, just let me know. I work right next door."

"Don't go bananas, I'm sure we'll be fine!" Tommy called

back out.

Chad, not close enough to elbow him this time, leaned forward in his seat and swatted at Tommy.

"Really? Bananas?"

"Shit." Tommy laughed. "My bad!"

Everyone resumed their positions and Bryce filled the champagne glasses. He handed the first to Robin stating, "I'm going to cut to the chase here."

"Good God please do!" Tommy mumbled.

Chad swatted at Tommy again.

Bryce looked at his glass, took a cleansing breath, sipped his champagne and started, "This particular vintage…"

Robin shouted out, "I will kill you!"

Bryce looked at her and laughed. "Seriously…" he held up his glass. "Cheers! Congratulations Tommy, and congratulations to us! Not the way I planned but here goes…"

They clinked their glasses.

"The Great Camp next door, originally called Camp Wonundra is owned by my family. We've owned it since the 1930s. It was a summer home for my great great grandparents. William Avery…" Bryce stopped dead in his tracks. He looked directly at Robin. "If you take my name Robin, I guess you should know mine. It's Bryce R. Hamilton. The R is for Rockefeller. My full name is Bryce Rockefeller Hamilton."

Tommy sat forward and asked loudly, "You mean Rockefeller, Rockefeller? The industrial, political, and banking family that made the world's largest fortunes in the oil business, Rockefeller?

"Yup, that's right."

Tommy threw himself back against the chair, breathing out a long winded, "Fuuuucck!"

Bryce then looked earnestly at Robin. "I'm sure you have a ton of questions, but let me explain a bit more. Over the years, and mostly during college, it seemed once people found out who I was, they came out of the woodwork to know me, or befriend me. It made dating very difficult. I was convinced everyone gravitated to me because of my family's wealth. And there was plenty of proof mind you. Lots of people took advantage."

Bryce then threw his look to Tommy. "Tommy, you remember how Bert thought I looked familiar?" he asked.

"I do, actually. Bert tried to convince me that you weren't who you said you were. Shit... I guess he was right!" Tommy laughed. "I think that's when my suspicions about you first started in fact. Did you know him?"

"Not really. But at one point, he knew I was a Rockefeller because back in med school at Columbia, one particular professor had the audacity to announce me when I walked in to the class for being ten seconds late. A class that I believe Bert and I shared. If he remembered me from then, I could have been called out. But the next year I switched to Urban Studies. I think that was about the time Bert dropped out because his dad had just died. He was a wreck and so was his sister, Jan. She also dropped out and supposedly went into real estate. I dated her *VERY* briefly, but she tried to get her hooks into me!"

"No shit?" Tommy exclaimed. "She got me my apartment! *AND* she dated Pauly for a while. Apparently broke his heart."

"She's got the last laugh now!" Robin caustically added.

"Staaaaap," Tommy sang out. "I don't know what you have against Pauly. That's his car out there and we all have to go see one of his shows. I promised him you know."

Robin sat there, rolled her eyes, and then lurched up making a puking gesture with a finger down her throat.

"Oh please. That was a long time ago!" Tommy then swept his look to Chad. "You met him… he's a freaking riot! Don't let her taint your thoughts."

Not knowing what to make of *any* of this, Chad shook his head. "This is all unbelievable *AND* entertaining. I mean, what a small world!"

Robin pat the couch, insisting Bryce and *his* puzzled look take a seat next to her. "I'll explain that whole puke gesture later. Can I ask some questions now?"

"Fire away."

"Your name in the Playbill? Special projects?"

"OK. My family and I donate to arts foundations. Parker knows the inside track and consults us on funding. He really is a friend of the family. I had absolutely no idea Tommy was doing a reading for *Book of Mormon* or that Parker would be there for it. Total coincidence there, I swear!"

"OK, next. So, I assume you didn't want me to know who you are because of what has happened in your past?" Robin asked.

"Right," Bryce admitted.

"You want me to love you for you and not your past… or your money."

"Correct."

"And if I recall, last winter when you found out I slept with Tommy, you were adamant about the past making me, me. And you were totally cool with it. No judgment what-so-ever."

"Exactly."

Chad then peered at Tommy with such a surprised look, one might think his eyes would pop out of his head and roll across the floor. "Oh please, do tell!"

Tommy once again slid down into the chair and covered his face with the pillow. "Robin, really? I can't believe you told him," he muffled out.

Chad piped in again, holding his glass high and laughing. "I'll say it again, honesty is the best policy!"

Bryce topped off all their glasses and clinked on Chad's saying, "Agreed."

Robin sat forward and looked at Bryce. "Yet all this time, you've been keeping the truth from me. That's cause for concern isn't it?"

"Robin, I didn't expect to fall madly in love with you the *second* after we met. And I certainly didn't expect this much time to pass without telling you everything. The longer I waited, the more difficult it became because I wouldn't know what to do if you left me. I couldn't imagine any existence without you. I just couldn't."

Robin withdrew against the back of the couch, leaned her head back, and closed her eyes, absorbing his words. Realizing his poignant honesty, she opened her eyes back up and blurted out, "Mink traders?"

"All true! Those photos"—he pointed to the shelves next to the fireplace—"all real. The furs in the closet? All real. Some original, and some I've purchased at estate sales so they don't make it out into the public and get ruined by activists."

Chad and Tommy now gawked at each other with inquisitive looks. When they both raised just one eyebrow at the same time, they burst out laughing.

"Closet? Furs and Minks?" Tommy questioned.

"Later," Robin hastily insisted. "We'll show you later."

Then she grabbed Bryce's hand and angled more to face

him. She continued with her line of questions.

"Rockefeller Center? When we went ice skating?"

"Yeah, I wanted it to be really special. When you guys went for hot chocolate, I pulled a few strings so just you and I could be the only ones on the ice."

"I KNEW IT!" Tommy screamed.

"Shusssssch!" Robin ordered, then continued. "That was such a magical moment… Edelweiss… Bryce…. Oh my God this is *ALL* so astonishing." She leaned back and closed her eyes again, remembering. A tear rolled down her cheek. Bryce slid off the couch and kneeled in front of Robin and laid his head in her lap.

"Thank God I didn't lose you. Robin, I'm so sorry. I was so scared. I really am an idiot!"

"No, you are not. You are my fiancée!"

Tommy leaned over to Chad, whispering, "Maybe we really should leave."

They finished off the champagne and decided that it was best to regroup and meet up for dinner a few hours later. The storm that wreaked more havoc than anyone could ever imagine, had cleared and the electricity hummed back to life. Buzzing from the chainsaws out front signaled that the road would still be blocked for a while, so Bryce and Robin walked Tommy and Chad over to the Great Camp via the wooded path.

* * *

The early chill of autumn was descending on the evening now. Moisture rose up from the rain-soaked forest floor, creating a mist that accentuated the sunlight slicing between the tall pines that lined the path. Mid-way, they stopped at the large stump that had been carved out and completed during the summer months. Bryce announced, "I guess I can explain this now too."

Robin threw her hands on her hips and tilted her head. "I thought this was a little weird. Of course, there's a story behind it!"

Robin wrapped her arms around Bryce before he began. She looked respectfully up at him and started the story herself. "This is Pan. In Greek mythology, he is the personification of wilderness and nature. He is the God of the wild."

Bryce adoringly looked at Robin and said, "I can't wait to propose to you again."

They stood in the misty golden blades of sunlight, gazing at each other, until Tommy hurried things along with a loud, "AAAH-HEM!"

"Oh sorry." Bryce explained, "So the tree that once stood here was a 110-foot Norway Spruce. We left the bottom ten feet for this sculpted wooden statue. The other hundred feet were this past year's Christmas tree at Rockefeller Center.

"The very one we skated under?" Robin asked.

"Yup, that's right."

Bryce looked up at the intricately carved face of Pan and said, "One can tell from the sporadic installations around Manhattan, we Rockefellers truly admire Greek Gods."

Turning outward onto the path to continue their jaunt through the woods, Tommy grabbed Chad's hand and said, "Don't we all?"

* * *

In the main lodge, four of them sat at an elegant candle-lit table, tucked into a quiet corner. Two massive fireplaces faced each other across the spacious room. A roaring fire in each warmed the atmosphere and matched the amber glow from various lamps and candles placed against the logs and wooden beams throughout. Hunting trophies and zebra skins draped over seating, provided a small glimpse of the lifestyle and history of the bygone era the Rockefellers had once experienced.

Robin first sat in awe, looking up into the rafters of the rustic and colossal room, until she landed her eyes on the hunter-plaid couches surrounding the fireplace across the way. Giving Bryce's hand an excited squeeze, she requested, "We have to sit there at some point tonight. This room is magnificent!"

Bryce squeezed hers back. Noticing (and rather embarrassed by) the tin-foil ring, he started to pull it from her finger.

"Wait! Don't... I love this!" She pulled her hand away. "Unless, of course, Stu is here and I have to."

"Fine, you can leave it, but it really is awful."

"I'll say!" Tommy laughed, reaching for the bread.

During dinner, Tommy joked with Bryce, boasting about how he knew all along that something was awry. "I just knew with the lavish places you went with Robin. I mean SHIT? That New Year's Eve at the Skylark? I Googled it afterward—you know you gotta know someone to book that, or even get in that place, right?"

Robin, who didn't let go of Bryce's hand since she sat, gave it another excited squeeze. She slid her chair as close as she could to Bryce and leaned up against him. "I didn't care what we did or where we were, as long as I was with him, I was fine," she announced boldly.

Tommy held off from making his next statement, waiting for the white-gloved waiter to finish removing the golden charger plates. He then lowered his voice, though he laughed as he said, "Don't think the thought of you being some big time Adirondack drug lord didn't cross my mind either."

Bryce confessed to Tommy that he had gotten weird vibes from him too. And why it concerned him. "I mean, every time

Robin mentioned you, it prompted me to tell her everything, but I always chickened out. I think there was even one point when I was actually jealous of you. Gay and all, I was still jealous. But next thing you'd know, she'd be off and busy in the mountains so when we were finally able to spend time together, I didn't want to spoil it."

The waiter poured a taste of the 1982 Château Magnan, St-Emilion Grand Cru, into Bryce's glass. Getting an approving nod, the waiter continued and poured for the others while Bryce continued.

"Tommy, you are an unbelievably good friend to Robin and I guess I should appreciate the fact that you are overprotective of her."

"Overprotective?"

All at once, Bryce, Chad, *AND* Robin agreed announcing, "Overprotective."

In Tommy's own defense, he challenged, "Really Robin?"

"Yup, that's right," she admitted.

"Well it's purely because Robin is my soulmate," Tommy countered.

He fished his necklace and moon charm out from under his shirt and dangled it for all to see. It became his shield of proof.

Robin concurred and fished her sun necklace out from under hers and smiled endearingly at Tommy.

Chad, never having inquired about Tommy's moon, now asked, "Well if she's your soulmate and your sun, what am I?"

"Chadwick, you are a kindred spirit, my heart's desire… my shining star."

Chad looked affectionately at Tommy and held up his glass.

Then Robin looked affectionately at Bryce, held up her glass and said, "And Bryce is the love of my life, the salt of my Earth. My world."

Bryce completed the ceremony, "To our little galaxy, CHEERS!"

Wining and dining on top of an extraordinarily mega-emotional day, Robin yawned in utter exhaustion. She leaned her head against Bryce who summoned the waiter and requested dessert at the fireside couches across the room.

Sitting beside a platter of bite-sized melt in your mouth morsels—chocolates and cakes and buttery tarts—they finished with decorative cups, filled with homemade Di Saronno ice cream, accompanied by four steaming mugs of hot chocolate. Robin and Bryce listened in while Tommy told Chad stories.

"Ever since grade school, our lives have revolved around each other, hence the sun and the moon." Tommy said. "Hot chocolate had become our celebratory drink of choice and it's what we would always find comfort in."

His recollections included: where, and when, and what the specific occasion was. Maybe it was because he's an actor, but his focus on the humility of it all was utterly endearing. The details he reminisced about amazed Robin. Tommy's storytelling emphasized the true relationship he and Robin have had over all those years.

"In my darkest hours, she was always there to warm me. Even the few times when I chose to shine, she was there to complete my day."

He finished his stories, then got up and sat next to Robin. He took her hands into his own and rested them in his lap.

"Robin, I couldn't have wished or even dreamed anything this great for you. I'm completely overjoyed and thrilled for you and your future with Bryce."

Robin threw her arms around Tommy and cried.

* * *

In a hexagon shaped log entrance foyer, with white tail deer, ante-lope, elk, and gigantic moose antlers surrounding them, they all bid each other a good night.

"Besides *your* big secret plan for tomorrow, do *we* have a plan for tomorrow?" Tommy asked Bryce.

"We do! Meet us at the dock 11:00 a.m. sharp, dressed for a boat ride.

"A boat ride?"

"Yup that's right!"

36

Literally

With a soft knock from the steward, Chad accepted and placed their breakfast tray on the small table for two by the windows. He put the copy of The New York Times on top of the tufted leather ottoman that sat between its matching chairs in front of the fireplace. He planned to burn it. The paper reminded him of his regular daily routine, which was something he sought to completely avoid for the remainder of the weekend.

It was just after 7:00 a.m. and Chad was sure it was the call of a loon that woke him. He glanced over at Tommy, buried in the lush bedding of the extra tall bed in the room appropriately named *Morningside*. With the sun just now making its appearance, the light stretched and yawned its way across the tranquil waters of Upper Saranac Lake, only steps from their room. The light slowly rose up through the windows, and glistened on the frost that curved in the corner of each pane of glass.

He poked at the coals from last night's fire and delicately placed some kindling and logs on the grate. Tommy rolled over and watched Chad ball up and stuff a few pages from the Times into the fireplace. In a poof, the fire came back to life.

"Just save the crossword if we have any downtime," Tommy rumbled in his morning voice. Then he sat up, piled some pillows, and leaned against the headboard with his arms behind his head. Admiring the room with a deep audible inhale he said, "Love the smell of a fireplace, don't you?"

"I most certainly do!"

Chad continued to ball up and add a few more pages, assuring a crackling fire would be enjoyed with breakfast. Tearing away at sections he questioned, "I wonder how they get the Times delivered way up here so early?"

"Midnight Ride of Paul Revere," Tommy snickered.

Chad looked at Tommy and reverently said, "You and I have really had some exceptional nights together, haven't we?"

Then from the breakfast tray, Chad poured two glasses of orange juice, while Tommy, overwhelmed with appreciation and affection, divulged, "Last night was probably the best night of my life Chadwick."

Chad walked the juice over, handed one to Tommy, and took a seat on the edge of the bed. He held out his glass and, in what was now becoming a regular thing for them, they clinked and they both said at the exact same time, "To many more."

Over breakfast, they discussed going into the town of Lake Placid for dinner.

"…And shopping!" Tommy eagerly suggested.

Neither of them had realized, or were appropriately advised of—by Robin, whose sole job it was—that on Wednesday and Saturday evenings, the Great Camp maintains the tradition of its ancestors, with formal black tie dining only.

Chad had apologetically intimated, "I can't believe I over-looked that? I'm so sorry, totally my bad."

"No problem, It's on Robin. Besides, it will get us into town earlier, which I hear is like a postcard. But damn! I bet you look unbelievable in a tux!" Tommy said lustfully.

They both speculated how Robin and Bryce would be busily engaged in something. "LITERALLY!" Tommy shouted. "I'm so excited for her, you know?"

"Oh, I do know!" Chad agreed, laughing at Tommy's excitement. "Bryce said we'll be able to join them later on, after the formal dining."

* * *

Bryce came through the front door of his cabin with fruit and bagels, and his own hard copy of the New York Times.

"I just spoke to Stu and he's going to meet us at the dock with a boat, gassed up and ready to go at 10:00. It dropped below freezing last night so we need to dress warm. Can you text the boys and tell them?"

Robin was kneeling in front of the fireplace poking away and heard not a word.

"Robin?"

He dumped the items on the counter and noticed most of the coffee was already gone. He walked over and sat next to Robin on the hearth. He took the poker out of her hand and placed it back in the stand. He recognized the look of panic on her face.... Remembering the very first time they met. It was the same look as when she realized Pauly had just walked into the class at the High Peaks Information Center. Then another time when the fog hampered their path and she slipped, nearly falling off the side of a cliff. Even the time when he inquired about her sleeping with Tommy. This look of dismay, was unforgettable.

He lifted her up and hugged her. He gently tilted her head back and stared into her eyes.

"Relax. We're going to have a perfectly beautiful regular day, I promise."

"I'll try," she whimpered.

She grabbed the paper still tucked under his arm and looked at the duck clock in the kitchen that used to quack every hour.

(Bryce had turned it to quiet mode because it always made her jump.)

"I'll kill the next two hours and catch up on some news," she said.

Robin was nervous, fidgety, and hardly able to sit still.

Bryce toasted a bagel, cut up some fruit and sat a plate down in front of her. She ate like a ravenous animal. Bryce couldn't help but laugh, realizing that the second pot of coffee she started on, didn't help matters. He texted Stu:

Please see that there is extra champagne and OJ for mimosas on the boat. Thanks pal!

He didn't want Robin to get hammered or anything, but he knew a few drinks would help to calm her.

Suddenly Robin jumped up with the newspaper in hand and ran out the front door. "I'll be right back!" she screamed out.

She was halfway down the path, on the way to the *Morningside* room, when she stopped dead in her tracks, realizing how Tommy had been, literally, sickened because he and Bert never got away for their romantic Adirondack weekend. *I can't say anything and chance ruining this one,* she thought. The second thing she realized was, "It's as cold as the freaking Antarctic out here!"

And that's precisely what she said, slamming the door closed behind her as she re-entered Bryce's cabin.

"What the heck was *that* about?" Bryce asked.

"I'm sorry, I'm not at liberty to say. But I promise you I will be able to tell you everything later."

"No way, you're just making that up to mess with me."

"Oh, Bryce, I wish I was. But I truly am not. Just trust me and know this will all work out."

Bryce was not convinced that Robin wasn't messing with

him. But she did suddenly seem less nervous. Having something in her control was like a sedative and positive thing for her, but Bryce was extremely curious now.

* * *

11:00 a.m., the four of them carefully walked down the stone stairway to Bryce's dock. The steps were slick with last night's frozen dew, but now with the promise of day, they were just beginning to melt.

"The Adirondacks always seem to have a jump on winter. I promise it will warm up soon," Bryce announced apologetically.

Long orange pine needles and mini pinecones, the size of jelly beans, bobbed in the water stuck between the dock and the outcropping of rocks. Like the fast approaching winter, there was no escape. The last of the red leaves from the sugar maples lay on the dock in small gathers. Chad picked up one solitary leaf. The frost outlined its intricate edge appearing like soft white velvet. A set of mallards landed a few feet off the dock right in front of them, and the morning light danced on the ripples they set in motion.

"Good God, can it get any more beautiful up here?" Chad asked, spinning the leaf in his fingers.

"I think it can," Tommy said, stepping up next to him pointing outward.

They heard it before they saw it. Stu rounded the point in a beautiful 1933 replica Hacker Craft Mahogany speedboat. It was loud, it was long; it was a shiny antique dreamboat. Impossible not to marvel at in its approach.

"Oooof, that thing is sexy as hell!" Chad exclaimed.

With excitement, Robin stood in front of Bryce and popped up onto her tippy toes to give him a quick kiss. Bryce scooped her up and off her feet. She remained draped across his arms until the boat pulled up and then he placed her gently down in the front section of the triple cockpit wooden beauty.

Stu tied up and stepped out to review a few things with Bryce.

Robin watched Stu's head bob and nod. It was obvious he and Bryce had plenty to discuss.

"I really, *really* like your friends," Chad excitedly said, stepping into the second section of the boat, lending a sturdy hand to Tommy.

A giant wicker picnic basket sat in the third section of the boat, and per usual, it was filled with many items one would consider delightful for lunch.

Now ready for a leisurely day of sightseeing, Bryce called out, "Blankets are in the front, and Tommy, you can be in charge of the mimosas, The champagne and OJ, is in your section."

"I really, *really* like my friends too," Tommy announced.

Stu ducked into the wooded path and was swiftly out of sight. Bryce untied and hopped in behind the wheel taking immediate control.

They cruised north and curved along the first point that the Great Camp encompassed. Bryce announced, "Whitney Point!"

Tommy reached forward handing Robin two mimosas.

"Hey, wait a minute…" Robin challenged, looking at Bryce.

He leaned into her with a guilty look, realizing there was still much to learn. Taking one mimosa from her hand, he then admitted, "Yes my sister Whitney. I can't wait for her to meet you! She'll be home during the holidays."

Robin sat back with a smug look and raised her glass high up into the air. They all followed suit and the sun magically lit up all their skyward mimosas. With that simple move, they realized the sun was literally around the corner. Bryce sped up and raced towards the light. They curved into the shoreline and around another point until the sun cast completely down on top of them.

"Aaaahhhhh!" Robin sang out, still holding her glass up high.

With the speed of the boat, Robin's hair whipped behind her and Tommy and Chad tightened their grip on the blankets. Their cheers and laughter echoed across the water, and the morning couldn't be any more glorious.

It was 3:00 in the afternoon by the time they pulled into the middle bay of the Great Camp boathouse. Tommy was going on and on about how he thought it would be necessary to one day, camp on *Tommy's Island.*

"Come on Wicky!" he pressed. "We'll pitch a tent, build a fire..."

"Wicky?" Chad questioned. "Is that the mimosas talking?"

Tommy suddenly looked uneasy. "My bad. That kinda slipped out."

Chad shouldered into him. "No worries, I kinda like it."

Robin rolled her eyes and just then it dawned on her. There was something she needed to do. Something important, before her extraordinary night commenced.

"Bryce! Are we having dinner here tonight?" she asked.

"Absolutely!"

"I need to run into town and get something extra special to wear then."

"Want me to come?"

"NO! I'll be fine. I mean... I'm sure I can find something. I won't be long. What time do you need me back?"

"Back by 6:00ish to be ready by 7:00. Is that doable?"

"Totally."

No sooner, Robin darted off into the wooded path.

Bryce motioned to Chad and Tommy to follow him up and out of the boathouse. "Let's hit the lean-to cocktail bar for one," he suggested. "The bartender there makes distinctive Adirondack Maple, Old Fashions. Plus, I'd like to bounce my plan off you guys."

* * *

Robin stopped at the Starbucks in town and sat at the window counter constructing a note. It wasn't easy for her to get the words right, but when it was finally complete, she stuffed the note and a page clipped from the newspaper into an envelope. She buried it in her purse.

She slurped the rest of her latte and dashed down the street to the high-end women's clothing store called Ruthie's Run. *Gotta be an omen since I really have to run. Literally*, she thought.

Once in the store, she anxiously approached a woman behind the register.

"Formal attire?" Robin asked.

"Back left-hand corner, past the jewelry case."

"Thank you."

Robin slid the hangers, one by one, across the high rack. She was impressed by the variety, but nothing was hitting her. She paused at a black tea length dress, with Swarovski crystal rhinestones, rimming a box cut neckline. *Nah, I need something unique*.

She made it completely through the rack, discouraged.

The woman from the front matter-of-factly approached Robin. She stopped and looked completely up and then down at her. With her finger curling inward, she ordered, "Come here."

Robin followed along as Mrs. Bossy Pants spoke, "Here

is a sampling from a new designer we'd like to carry. This is what she has bestowed upon us for the season."

Still covered in plastic, there were only three dresses to consider.

"They all are size six," the woman indicated. "Small for most of the athletic types that shop here, but you look like a six... a good six." She looked up and down at Robin, again. "Am I correct?"

"You are."

"Fine, I'll leave you be."

Robin didn't know what to make of the woman, bitch or brilliant. The fabric that peeked out from the bottom of the plastic offered three colors. Green... "Yuck!" Black... "Typical." And an off white... "Maybe," Robin wondered....

The dress was a knit material and far from anything she'd consider for a formal evening. She pulled off the plastic on her way into the dressing room. She hung it on a hook and stared at it as she undressed. It started to speak to her.

The dress was a cashmere blend. A floor-length gown that lightly flared out past the knees with a slit up the right side to mid-thigh. It had extra-long sleeves, and at the end of each was a fluffy collar of brown fur. It was extremely low cut. *No bra tonight,* she anticipated. She rotated the hanger to check out the backside, revealing a fur-lined hood that delicately draped from shoulder to shoulder. *Hmmm...?* She slipped the dress over her head. It fell smoothly on her, reminiscent of a scene from Cinderella getting dressed by the magic mice, *or was it birds?* she thought.

The crème color and the knit fabric softened the entire look and feel. Robin smoothed it along her hips and twisted in front of the mirror to see the hood. It was so low, it exposed much of her back, but the fur-lined drape of the hood was unique and *fan-fucking-tastick!* she thought. She twisted around to the other side and back again. She stood staring at it, petting herself. The bunched-up fabric along the length of her arms was both casual *and* elegant.

"This is amazing," she said out loud. Then she thought. *If this is real fur, I don't even give a damn!*

Now thrilled, she twisted to the left and right one more time and then spun around in the tiny space of the changing room. Suddenly she stopped. *Oh my God what can I do with my hair?* Looking at her watch she thought, *I'll never have time to get something done.* She quickly got dressed and ran to the counter.

"Special occasion?" the brilliant lady at the counter asked.

"An engagement."

"Wow fancy. Must be a dear friend."

"Actually, it's my own…." Robin blushed with excitement. But just as suddenly, she was racked with panic. "Shit! Oh shit, I'm sorry. Pardon my tongue. I need shoes!"

"What size? And congratulations!" The lady laughed this time.

"Eight."

The woman left the counter and in thirty seconds came back with a size eight.

"They're called Rome, originally $200 now just $80."

She placed them on the floor in front of Robin. Robin kicked off her shoes, pulled off her socks and slipped into them. Twisting her feet side to side, mesmerized, she now had visions of Cinderella, again!

"Miss… Missss……… MISS?"

"Oh sorry…. They're perfect."

A mid heel golden shoe, with several golden leather straps

meeting in the middle at a rectangular patch adorned with gold and silver chunks of glass. Still rocking her foot side to side, Robin looked up at the woman, "I absolutely adore you and I love your store. I can't thank you enough."

The woman smiled and nodded at Robin, stuffing the credit card receipt into the garment bag with the shoes. "Pleasure is all mine."

Robin didn't even realize how much she'd spent until she unzipped the bag and hung the gown in the bathroom. When the receipt fell out, she gasped. She then took a few deep breaths to calm herself, thinking, *There's probably going to be other fancy galas in my future.*

She was having a hard time processing everything that had happened within the last twenty-four hours, and still considered it all to be a dream.... Until she looked at her own reflection and reality came crashing back. *What the hell can I do with my hair?*

She stepped out of the shower and heard Bryce on the other side of the door in the bedroom. Wrapped in towels, she quietly opened the bathroom door to peek out. Watching him across the room, she remembered being completely taken by him at the nature class at the HPIC (well over a year ago) when she spied on him through the steam of her hot chocolate. Now she leaned against the door jam and lost herself watching him futz with his tie. He looked amazing.

In front of the full-length mirror, he stood in an espresso brown tuxedo with an off-white shirt, dark brown shiny wingtips, a textured fawn-brown vest, and a matching striped two-tone tie.

Robin never had to imagine how handsome he could look. She always loved the way he did, regardless. Never *ever* wanting anything more, she was completely happy with everything about him. But watching him now was like winning the lottery. His hair was a fresh cut and slicked back neat. The few streaks of summer color were still long enough to tuck behind his ear—something Robin loved. Her heart began to pound thinking about how, so often, when she would stare into his eyes—she'd reach up and tuck that stray strand of sun-bleached hair away from his face.

"Whatdya think?" he called out, catching her spying him.

"I think I'm dreaming."

Bryce walked up to Robin and leaned one arm up and over her against the door jam. He leaned into her and gently kissed her, saying, "While you are currently wearing one of my favorite outfits, I hope you were able to find something a little fancier?"

"Oh, I did!" she answered.

She pulled his arm down and began to direct him out of the room. "Scoot!" she demanded.

He snapped her back into his arms and began to unravel her towel. She unraveled right out of it and spun into the bathroom. Peeking her head around the corner she again yelled, "Scoot!"

"7:00 sharp," he beckoned back. "I'll be next door in front of the fireplace in the main dining room."

Robin dried her hair and piled it up on the top of her head to do her makeup. Glancing at the clock often, she didn't have a concept of how long makeup actually takes. Makeup was not a regular thing for her. She had to add water to the mascara tube to get the dried-up muck to the proper consistency. The only lipstick she had was a sample she had thrown in her overnight bag years ago. It was cherry red and LOUD. The bright lights of the all-white bathroom didn't help. *I look like a hooker!* she thought. She toned it down with a topcoat of Bert's Bees frosty lip balm.

She slipped the sweater gown over her head and it instantly made her twist from side to side. Going braless made it even sexier and because of her perpetual hiking up and down mountains, the gown accentuated the firmness of her body… and her curves. Curves she never paid attention to because she lived in hiking pants and loose tops. She stared at her reflection and suddenly felt glamorous.

Her phone buzzed. A text from Bryce:

Stu will be there in fifteen minutes to golf-cart you over. Good?

Good.

Then she noticed there on the bed, a note and a small black velvet box. She opened the note. In Bryce's simple scribble it said, *You, are beautiful.*

Of course, he hasn't even seen her yet. *How can I possibly be so lucky?* she thought. Then she thought she might cry. She even thought of dropping to her knees and thanking God for him right then and there, but the clock was ticking.

She opened up the little velvet box, revealing a pair of sparkly diamond studs. Robin didn't know carats. These were the size of pencil erasers. In diamonds language that was *huge*! She scurried to the bathroom mirror and put them in. Containing her excitement—and her tears—was becoming more and more difficult. Again, the clock was ticking. The diamonds answered her question…

She gathered up all her hair and twisted it to a bun. She plopped it on top of her head and jabbed a few mini combs and bobby pins into it. It sat elegantly stabilized, but loose enough to allow a few tendrils to fall to either side of her face. *No one will notice anything other than these sparklers!* she thought. She slipped into the shoes and made her way to the front door.

Robin saw the top of Stu's head rocking back and forth in the small window of the door. She opened the door and he stood still just looking at his watch.

"How long have you been here Stu?"

"Four minutes." He started to rock back and forth again and when he finally looked up, he said, "You look extra pretty tonight."

She hugged him and choked back tears. He handed her a mink throw. "Bryce said to use this if you're chilly." But by now, in all the excitement, Robin was practically numb.

On the golf-cart ride over, she thought how she'd better get a grip, being on the verge of tears and all. She took deep, focused breaths.

When they curved onto the road towards the Morningside, feeling bad she'd forgot to mention formal dining, she wondered what Tommy and Chad had planned for the night.

"Wait!" she suddenly screamed.

Stu slowed to a safe stop and just looked at Robin.

"I'm so sorry, I forgot something."

Robin had no choice but to ask for Stu's help. It was two minutes to 7:00 and this night, of all nights of her entire life, she was not going to be late. She never was and now was not the time to start. She thought of the most direct way to ask.

"Stu," she seriously began. "There is a white envelope in my purse, on the table, in the living room. Please get that envelope to Tommy tonight. OK?"

"No problem."

With much consideration, Robin had decided, if Chad and Tommy were meant for each other, the envelope and the information in it, shouldn't make one bit of difference.

Stu stopped at the hexagon shaped log entrance, under the

gigantic moose antlers.

"Let me help you out," he offered.

Robin allowed him to come around to her side of the cart. He bent down, gathered the bottom of her dress and held it as she walked up the few steps. It was awkward and it was charming.

"Do you know how much I appreciate you Stu?" she asked.

He dropped the dress from his hands, pet it flat, and looked up only to smile.

"More than you can imagine," she added.

He opened the door for her and when she passed through, she kissed Stu's cheek. He blushed and looked down and then disappeared behind the slow closing door. She heard the golf-cart spin out on the gravel as she stepped through the entrance foyer.

Now standing at the edge of the main dining room. Bryce spotted her just as she spotted him. He rushed to greet her. He kissed her cheek and nuzzled into her ear whispering. "My God, you are truly beautiful, and that dress is spectacular!"

She pulled away to look at him. Lifting one hand up she cupped behind her ear, "No, these are truly beautiful… absolutely stunning! I don't know what to say."

"Say nothing," he said softly, still awed by her radiance.

Before he allowed her into the room, he handed her a golden-feathered mask. For himself, he put on a simple black velvet one. "Tonight's a masquerade party!" he exclaimed.

Bewildered, Robin snapped hers on. *At least it matches my shoes,* she thought. She found it utterly strange and wonderful, never expecting anything of the sort.

He took her hand and led her to the fireplace. A waiter walked by with a tray of champagne glasses.

"How fun is this!" she gleefully declared.

They each took a glass and sat on the extra-large, extra comfy, hunter plaid couch. "I thought we'd have appetizers here, and dinner in the room," Bryce suggested.

"Room?"

"I've booked the *Boathouse* for the night."

Robin took a deep breath and gazed at Bryce. It was hard to demonstrate sheer appreciation and affection using your eyes, when there are feathers on your forehead. She held out her arm. "Pinch me," she said, remembering the very first time she was at his cabin, when they watched the sunset and drank pink wine.

They enjoyed the clamor of the formally dressed and masked dining crowd, sipping champagne and nibbling savory bite-sized appetizers. Stuffed melt in your mouth figs and squash blossoms. Beef Wellington tots and smoked trout, fresh from the waters of Upper Saranac. The parade of silver trays seemed to never end.

"I don't know if there is room in this dress for anymore!" she said.

Bryce stood taking Robin's hand pulling her up, "There better be!" he laughed. "We can walk to the Boathouse if you'd like. Or should I summon Stu?"

"A walk in the night air would be nice… and necessary," she admitted.

On the way out, Bryce took off his jacket and set it over Robin's shoulders.

As they were about to exit, once again Robin yelled, "Wait!" She looked down at her hands realizing she had nothing with her, no purse, no phone… She asked Bryce, "Can you get a picture of us in front of the fireplace? I promised Daisy I'd send her one." Robin handed his jacket back and Bryce handed his phone to a waiter.

On the walk over to the Boathouse, they sent Daisy two photos: One with, and one without the masks.

Daisy responded: *You guys look fucking awesome! What's with the masks?*

"Wow, reception here is great!" Robin said. "That was a quick response." She sent back only a kissy face emoji with two champagne glasses.

* * *

Bryce pushed the door to the private room in the boathouse open. As Robin entered, he lifted his jacket from her shoulders. As she walked, she seemed to levitate right out of it and into the room.

There in the middle of the room sat a four-post bed, engulfed in white billowy tulle fabric. Draping all around it from the highest point in the ceiling down to the floor, the tulle lay gathered in tufts. Tiny white lights were layered in its folds bathing the entire room in warm white light. Slowly making her way around the bed, every table, ledge, and surface of the entire room had small white votive candles flickering in silence. The sailing flags that hung in the rafters and the bold colors of the plush fabric couches gave the whole room a refined yet nautical ambiance. Robin meandered through. She stopped at a perfect table set for two that was placed between the bed and the wide windowed view of nothing but the complete starry darkness outside. All the windows and doors reflected back what seemed to be a million flickering white lights. It was magical.

Bryce walked up to the table, and from the tall silver sailing trophy vase, he removed the gather of flowers. It was a perfectly tied bouquet of edelweiss. He handed it to Robin and motioned her around to the other side of the bed, stopping between the fireplace and a couch.

She was speechless.

The fireplace was glowing, with not a fire, but a congregation of white candles. It felt sacred. From the mantle he grabbed another black velvet box.

"I was going to wait until after dinner... but I know you aren't really hungry yet... and... well I just can't wait any longer."

He took the bouquet from her hands and placed it on the mantle. He dropped to one knee and opened the box.

Two sparkling pencil erasers sat on either side of a larger, dazzling pink, Kunzite. It was the same pink as their first sunset—the one with the matching pink wine. It was breathtaking.

Robin gasped.

He waited for her to exhale and then took her hand. He began to speak as he slowly slipped it up her finger.

"Robin, yesterday I actually felt the world stop spinning. That moment when I thought I might lose you, everything just stopped. My insides began to drain like sand in an hourglass and in mere seconds, I thought I'd wither and become dust on the floor... Dust where someone would open the door and I'd blow away in the wind."

With the ring now completely on her finger, he grabbed both her hands and held them to his face. He kissed her hands and caught his breath. The back of her hands glistened with his tears. He was shaking. He continued.

"Yesterday, when you looked down at me and didn't resist when I grabbed your hands, the wave of relief was like a tsunami. Robin, I've never loved like this, and never knew love could be even remotely close to this. You give me purpose, you give me joy, and now I officially ask if you'll give me your hand."

He sniffed back tears and he looked up at Robin. Then he chuckled. "Yeah, I know I have your hands now… and yeah, I know I asked before, but this is what I *want* you to remember."

He cleared his voice and looked intently at her.

"Robin, will you be my wife? Marry me and care for me, and promise me your love?"

Robin let go of his hands and hiked up her dress. She lowered to her knees and re-grabbed his hands.

With the abundance of candles in the fireplace, their shadow cast behind them across the floor and up onto the couch, flickering, like two dancing elves.

Robin looked deeply into his eyes. Never more positive of anything in her entire life, she answered.

"I'm completely in love with you Bryce. I was so scared yesterday. My world hadn't stopped it had turned upside-down. Those few moments of despair were utter agony for me; I thought I might die right there. Bryce, my whole life I've focused on making sure everything was orderly and everyone around me was OK. But when I'm with you… there is absolutely nothing to worry about. I can simply throw my arms into the air and let go. I'm free. As if I don't have to work for happiness anymore, because when I'm with you it's guaranteed. With you, I'm carefree and content and completely fulfilled. Bryce, you slay me. You've had my heart for quite a while now and you can most certainly have my hand."

She chuckled, squeezing his hands in hers. She looked down at her ring and back to his eyes. "I will love you, and care for you… and I will *soooo* be your wife."

Their professions of love were indeed vows. In the silence and the flickering lights, they completely focused on each other. She sensed his breath and became his air. It was authentic, beautiful, and peaceful. There on the floor, on their knees, their universe imploded into a solid core.

A light knock on the door forced them to their feet. Robin sat on the couch wiggling her hand, watching stars shoot out from her ring finger.

A waiter rolled a cart inside and around to the table. He bowed and nodded as he backed out, closing the door behind him.

Bryce looked at his watch. "I wonder where Stu is. That was supposed to be him. He set all this up: The candles, the lights… but I was the one that scaled the mountains for the edelweiss mind you," he joked.

"Well *that* I know is false, but I can just imagine what you had to do to get them!" She lifted the bouquet from the mantle and smiled. "They are magnificent!"

He sat down next to her. "Robin, I would… I would climb any mountain for you."

"I realize that now Bryce. But actually, I want you to climb them *with* me!" she laughed. Then she breathed a sigh of relief.

They stood, embraced, and made their way to the table. "Wait!" Robin urged once again. "I asked Stu to do me a favor. I asked him to get something to Tommy tonight."

"Uh oh," Bryce said. "Tell me exactly how you asked. You know he takes everything literally."

"Oh my God, I don't remember Bryce. I was in a daze."

Bryce texted Stu: *You OK buddy?*

* * *

Tommy was shocked to see Stu walk through the dining room of the Lake Placid Lodge and directly up to him. "Stu? Is everything OK?" he asked.

"Yes, everything is OK. Our concierge told me you were

dining here." He stood at the table looking confused, wondering why Tommy seemed worried. "Robin asked that I get this to you." He handed off the envelope.

"So, everything is going well with her and Bryce?" Tommy asked.

Stu looked at his watch. It was 8:30 and he knew that Bryce—if he hadn't already—was about to propose. "Everything is perfect."

Tommy had never seen a genuine smile from Stu quite like that very moment. It was reassuring and admirable.

Stu reached out and shook both Tommy and Chad's hands. "I need to get back. Please enjoy your dinner." Like a soldier he spun on one foot and marched away.

Tommy shook his head in a stupor as he opened up the envelope.

* * *

Robin placed the edelweiss back in the vase. Bryce removed the giant silver dome from the dinner cart, popped the cork, and poured some champagne. He looked at his watch; it was just 8:40. He hid his concern for Stu.

"Roasted Sea Bass filets with Chanterelles," he announced. "Now those I actually *did* pick myself, thanks to you for teaching me how to identify them!" He then grabbed a remote control from the mantle and clicked on the *Music and Sounds of Nature*. "If you hear a loon," he chuckled, "it's embedded in the music. I thought it'd be perfect for this room, and tonight."

Robin sat smugly and marveled at everything. Twisting her fork in a side dish of julienne squash, she questioned, "What if I said no?"

"Are you kidding?" Bryce chuckled again. "Aside from the

momentary lapse of ill fate yesterday… Robin, like I said before, I knew you'd be mine since the moment I laid eyes on you. We're unbelievably good together. Call it kismet, but I have always felt—deep down— that you felt the same way. No was not even an option."

Robin nodded her head in agreement about feeling the same way. Yet still pondering, she asked, "Well you were forced to spill the beans yesterday so, what was your real plan? Like how were you going to tell me about your family and your legacy, and the point of it all?

"Well, of course after you said yes…" he began, "and after a passionate night of carnal lovemaking," he lustfully smirked, "I was going to explain everything to you and your family at brunch tomorrow."

"My family?"

"Your mom and Robert, little Robbie, Daisy and Aron, your dad and Amanda. Well… they are all here tonight for our engagement brunch tomorrow.

"Wait, *what?*"

"They were all in the main dining room… ogling at you I'm sure. Hence the masquerade!"

"*Oh my God*! They're all here?"

"As we speak!"

Robin stood up and paced. Her head was spinning. "This is all so unbelievable Bryce!" She threw herself into his arms and he spun her.

Suddenly his phone beeped. He grabbed it from his pocket. "Thank God. It's Stu." He read the text out loud.

Sorry, I was driving, just got back. I ran into town for Robin. Plan is still on.

Robin sat back down and shook her head, "I asked him to get an envelope to Tommy tonight. I'm an idiot! I never said how or when, I just said tonight. He must have gone into town to find him. Oh Bryce, can you please get him here so I can apologize?"

Bryce looked at his watch. "I will, but not just yet."

From the mantle, Bryce grabbed another small remote. With a click here, and a click there—except for the abundance in the fireplace—every candle in the entire room went out. He rushed around the room, stating, "Real fire is allowed in the fireplaces only. This place is too old, historic, and beloved, to mess around with real candles."

He topped off their champagne glasses and ushered Robin to the giant glass doors that led to the outside deck. He opened them and walked her to the porch swing off to the right. Of course, there were mink throws waiting. They sat and gently swayed with the extravagant fur up and around them. The night was crisp and cold, dark and wondrous. He looked at his watch one final time and clinked against her glass. "To a spectacular life, with my future wife."

In the chilly October air, in the middle of the Adirondacks, on a quaint porch swing at one of the most romantic rooms of a magnificent 19th century Great Camp, Robin and Bryce became one. They kissed as they watched dazzling fireworks pulsate in the sky and echo across the beautiful mountain waters of Upper Saranac.

* * *

Tommy waited to unfold the newspaper clipping that fell out of the envelope. He read the handwritten note first.

My Dearest Tommy, my Moon,
This clipped article is from today's newspaper. I don't know

if you and Chadwick have discussed this or not. I didn't want to tarnish your time with him while you were up here, but after much consideration, I believe it won't. Deep within my heart, I know what you two have together, is truly special.

For me, tonight is a night I'll never forget. Maybe it will be that way for you too. Like you are for me, right now I couldn't possibly be any happier for you!

I love you Tommy. Always and forever, your Sun.
Robin

Tommy set the note down and then flattened out the newspaper clipping. His eyes widened as they trudged across each word. The headline read:

Catholic Church in Mass. Priest indicted for sexual crimes.

Tommy gasped. Then he urged, "Chad, slide over and read this with me."

Chad thanked the waitress who had just placed two snifters of 43 and two hot chocolates down in front of them. He eagerly pulled his chair right up next to Tommy's and placed his arm broadly around him. Together they hunkered down and absorbed every printed word.

After a thorough investigation, Monsignor McCloonin, 54, (Lords of Mercy Church, Stonehem, Mass.) a.k.a. Monsignor Stoyer (Long Island, NY), has been indicted by the Grand Jury and sentenced to 22 years at the New York State Penitentiary, based on case findings after a string of child molestations. According to witnesses, who had come forth and stood on trial, indicated: (editor's warning: includes graphic details of a sexual nature.)

Findings: 2003-05, sexual molestation of 11-year old boy, asked child "What do you think God would do?" Victim reported to diocese who responded by hiring detectives to investigate victim, never taking matters to police; among those interviewed was Rev. Wollinsteel, also accused of child sexual abuse in this report. Findings: 2008, engaged in sexual abuse of a boy, 10-11 years old, reported to state police and placed on leave by Bishop and returned to active ministry a year later; accused of groping and raping another boy and then giving him gifts; sent to treatment. Findings: 2011, engaged in anal and oral sex with child at orphanage building, boy reported to another priest who told him, "Be a good monk and pray and think not of this again." Findings: 2014, close to a group of boys 9-12; would take boys to camps and were instructed to "sleep naked," the boys were sexually abused. One anonymous letter said, "I estimate being abused over 70 times." Other claims are still pending. Monsignor McCloonin pled guilty to 15 counts of child endangerment and 7 counts of aggravated sexual abuse. Grand Jury has sentenced him to concurrent terms of one year per count, imprisonment to begin immediately.

"*Holy shit!*" Chad exclaimed.

Tommy looked at Chad defiantly and said, "Literally."

About The Author

This is Willa's debut novel. She is a graphic designer by
profession, an environmentalist by her actions, and
she never planned to be a writer... That's a story in itself.
(See preface.) A mom of two boys and two cats.
A certified outdoor enthusiast and adventurist.
Married 28 years and living on the largest lake in New Jersey.

Photo: Taken at the rooftop bar at The Kimberly Hotel
in Manhattan. (See Chapter 30.)